UNNATURAL

A HOLLOWAY PACK NOVEL

BOOK 4

J.A. BELFIELD

UNNATURAL
A HOLLOWAY PACK NOVEL

Published by J.A. Belfield
www.jabelfield.com

Copyright © 2019 Julie Anne Belfield

Cover art by Aimee Laine.

First Printing: 2012
10 9 8 7 6 5 4

ALSO BY J.A. BELFIELD

UNNATURAL

For every person who has ever given me a reason to chase the rainbow

1

Warm breaths hit the side of Brook Nicholls' neck, the rise and fall of a chest pressed into her back like a heartbeat in slow motion, and the deadweight of the arm across her stomach told her he had fallen asleep.

With the heat of his body lulling her to join him, Brook's breathing slowed, her lids lowered, and the fingers of oblivion beckoned her weary and sated mind forth.

A beat kicked in somewhere below—*his*, she thought with a smile.

The drumming picked up, in volume as well as in tempo.

He probably ran in his sleep. Brook did, as feline, so it stood to reason that he would as her opposite.

"Brook!" More bangs, followed with thuds. "Brook! I know you're in there!"

Her eyes snapped open.

"Brook! If you don't open this door, I swear I'm gonna knock it down myself!"

Clive!

"Oh, no!" She spun around, fingers already reaching for her lover's arm. "Wake up," she whispered, shaking him. "Kyle, you have to wake up."

"Whah?" His lids fluttered, and he rapid-blinked. "Brook?"

"We are in big trouble. You have to get up." She thrust into a sitting position, grabbing his arm and dragging him with her. "Please, Kyle."

"What's going o—"

"*Brook*!" Clive roared again.

Kyle's eyes widened. "Shit!" He dove from the bed, fingers folding around his boxers on the floor where they'd fallen. As he bent to feed them over his feet, the door rattled beneath more blows.

"Dammit, Brook, open the door!"

"Quickly." Brook's attention flickered between Kyle and the relentless pounding. She knew Clive could enter any time he liked, knew only his respect for her father kept him from forcing the door from its hinges. "You have to hurry."

"What do you think I'm doing, River?"

"*Brook*," she hissed, though she couldn't control the smile that crept in and widened at Kyle's deep chuckle.

Rough denim slid over his hips, and he scooped up his shirt without bothering to secure any buttons on his jeans, leaving the trail of hair south of his navel exposed below his muscular, scarred torso. With his boots in his other hand, he strode back to the bed, the mattress dipping as he knelt before her.

Combing fingers into his wild red hair, Brook urged him closer, found his willing mouth with hers, and gave him a farewell that in no way compared to the one she had initially planned.

A deep crack signified the first splintering of wood, and she jerked backward. "Go!"

"*Brook*!"

Kyle turned toward the bedroom door with a growl rumbling deep in his chest. "And leave you with *that*?"

"Please." Brook's pulse thrummed at the implication of his words. "He'll not harm me—but he will hurt *you* if he finds you here."

Kyle's brow lifted. "A cat?"

She scowled.

He raised his palms in mock surrender. "Just kidding. I'm going." He backed away from the bed to the window, opening it and sticking out his head.

No shouts rang out, no cries of outrage.

His head reappeared, hazel eyes finding Brook's. "Call me when you can."

Before she could respond, he'd hooked a leg over the sill, followed by the other, and he thumped down below as the unmistakable smash of the front door seemed to shake the entire guesthouse.

With a gasp, she jumped from the bed and raced from the room, closing the door on the proof of her encounter.

"*Brook*!" Clive's yell bounced from wall to wall in its journey up the staircase.

She bolted for the bathroom, dark hair billowing, and pushed the door closed at her rear with as little noise as possible.

Footsteps thudded up the stairs. "Quit messing around, Brook! I'm sick of your games!"

She darted across the room, flicked the tap, and dove into the shower cubicle before the water had the chance to warm through. Her heart threatened to claw its way free of her ribcage, breaths taking her to the verge of hyperventilation, as Clive trampled the length of the landing with the elegance of an ogre.

Brook grabbed the shower gel, and after squirting a liberal glob onto a washcloth, she rubbed it over as much of her body as she could, to disguise any remnants of Kyle's scent.

The door to the bathroom burst open, sending a draught swirling into the shower.

Clive's six-foot-seven mass filled the empty frame.

She pressed the washcloth over her breasts, her free hand across her womanhood. "Do you mind?" She sent a glower across to him, as she tried to control the sounds of her body's anxiety.

His amber eyes made a track of the room from beneath white-blond hair that would have been erratic curls if he didn't keep it cut short.

"I put up with a lot from you because my father requested I be polite." Brook growled, and his eyes drew back toward her. "But I am certain he did not intend for me to tolerate this ... invasion of my privacy."

"I thought ..." Clive scratched at his head, *almost* appearing vulnerable.

She raised her eyebrows. "You thought *what*?"

"I dunno." He sighed. "I thought you were gonna lock yourself in for weeks and refuse to speak to me again."

"What an excellent idea. Thank you for suggesting it."

"You're still mad at me. I get that. And I'm sorry for ... what I did .... But, damn, Brook ..." His eyes made a slow tour of her body before returning to her face. "How long do you expect me to keep waiting?"

"I do not recall ever asking you to wait to begin." She spun away and resumed washing. "Close the door on your way out."

For seconds, nothing happened. Brook thought he would refuse, but after another murmured 'sorry', the click of the door told her he had gone.

She could not contain her sigh of relief, just as she couldn't suppress her tremor as the washcloth passed over the parts of her body still tender from Kyle's touch.

Her lips curved into a smile as she remembered each caress.

Under no circumstances would she be able to wait another week before she saw him again.

I chuckled to myself as I mounted the wall surrounding the Cheshire property belonging to Brook's father. One of the Toms had almost caught me as I'd hit the ground beneath the guesthouse window. I'd scarcely ducked around the corner in time—though, the crash of the door opening almost had me leaping back in there to teach that inconsiderate bastard a lesson. Instead, after pausing long enough to check Brook could hold her own, I'd raced for the perimeter.

A left scan showed the exterior to be clear, and a peer to the right assured me my Mitsubishi waited exactly where I'd left it farther up the road.

Shirt and boots still clutched in my hand, I broke into a jog toward the pickup.

Before I'd taken more than a handful of steps, Kings of Leon's *Closer* sounded out—from my mobile where I'd left it inside the glovebox.

Shit!

I surged forward, slammed against the driver's door, snapping at the catch to get it open, and dived across the seat to snatch up my phone. Pressing connect, I placed it to my ear. "Yo!"

"Where the hell are you?"

"Dad ... um ..." I glanced at the dashboard clock. Three twenty-three. *Fuck!* I'd been gone the entire afternoon.

"Straight there and back, you were supposed to go ..."

He meant straight to the brickyard to price up materials for the new construction project. Could I help it if Brook had worn me out?

"... this is the fourth time now you've volunteered for a run and taken hours over it. What the hell's taking so long?"

"I ... fell asleep?" My brows lifted as I waited for his response.

The silence on the end of the line told me, way more than any words could have, that he didn't believe me for a minute.

"Kyle, what's going on?" he asked.

I climbed into my seat and closed the door. "Nothing, Dad."

More silence.

I wouldn't have believed my lying arse, either.

Dad sighed. "Just get back here, okay? And if you don't want Nate gunning for you, you'd better make sure you've actually done what he sent you out for this time."

The disconnect tone hummed at me. I tossed my mobile down on the passenger seat and raked my fingers through my hair, closing my eyes as I leaned my head back.

I hated lying to my family.

I had no choice.

As a werewolf, the pack'd go apeshit if they found out I'd spent the last few months shagging a cat.

2

Brook smelled Clive as she descended the stairs. Past experience warned her he would be around the corner, standing propped against the other side of the wall, awaiting her covert antics that never happened, just so he could hop out and pretend to catch her doing nothing.

Sinking to the second step, she swept her still-wet hair over her shoulder and pressed her forehead to the divider. Her chest rose high with a sigh as she prepared to irk his less-than-clever mind once more. "I thought you would be gone," she said.

"You don't seem to understand, Brook. I'm not going anywhere."

Beneath an impressive eye roll, Brook's teeth ground out her frustration—though, did she have the right to blame a male whose life was as out of his control as hers had become? "You say that as though you do not have a choice."

"Everyone has a choice, Brook." A quiet pause followed, before he said, "They just don't always like their options."

She couldn't dispute his words. Brook had been given a choice—one of which her father approved.

Clive or Stefan.

Stefan's murmured threats—ones he only shared when no one but Brook could hear—had lost him her vote. And at constant rebukes and her refusal to acknowledge Stefan, Clive had assumed himself the winner.

Of Brook.

"Besides," Clive said, "I made my choice a long time ago." A quiet scrape travelled down the other side of the wall. "I Chose you."

"I was never an option."

He gave a low growl. "Your father says otherwise."

"My father does not own me."

He chuckled. "Your father believes otherwise."

"He has no right to dictate my life."

"That I'm standing here at his order tells me otherwise, Brook."

Her teeth ground again, as she realised he had been sent to summon her. "What does he want?"

"He wants to see you."

"You make that sound like an amicable request. Why don't you quit with the falsities and simply tell me I have been ordered to his office?"

"Dammit. You're difficult on purpose, I swear. Get yourself to the house 'cause your dad wants to see you—now!" His feet stomped on his way to the door.

At five-fifteen, I rolled off the road that ran through Derbyshire's Wild Woodington and pulled up onto the otherwise empty driveway outside home.

Dad, Josh and Danny would still be at the new site with the Holloway's—the other family in our pack. I knew going straight home would get my ear chewed again, especially once Nathan caught up with me. As pack Alpha and top partner in the construction business owned by the pack, he pretty much ruled us with a firm hand.

Again, though, I'd had no choice.

No way could I have turned back up to work stinking of sex. Not when the pack had already met Brook, thanks to an incident that drew us together like a freight train collision—and not when they all knew her scent and would recognise right away who my frolicking had been with.

None of them would understand. Not in a gazillion years. I didn't get to choose who I fell for, though. My inner wolf seemed to have taken that decision out of my hands.

With a groan, I climbed from the truck and let myself into the house. In the kitchen, I tugged my clothes off, bunging them straight in the washer, and set the details I'd grabbed for Nathan on the table. On my trek upstairs to the bathroom, I flicked on lights to brighten the dimness, like that could chase off the shadows walking away from Brook had left with me.

Water smacked the cubicle glass with a spin of the shower dial, and pummelled me once I'd stepped inside. I jerked forward with a wince when it lanced my lower back, and as my fingers grazed four parallel scores across my lumbar, the sizzling memory of the infliction blasted me in a wave of heat.

Shaking it off, I reached for the sponge and soap to set about de-Brooking myself—though it would take more than a shower to shift her from my mind. Damn feline had entered my life by happenstance and gotten wedged into a corner of my soul that wouldn't let her go.

The corner probably held shackles.

Ones that had slipped around Brook's wrists and denied escape.

My body hardened at the image of a very detained Brook, confirming the obsession I seemed to be harvesting. "Not helping matters," I muttered, my forehead pressed to the glass like the contact could ward off the sudden overheating of my flesh. To aid the cool-down along, I reached behind and knocked the temperature dial to the left, gritting my teeth when the initial shock of cold smacked me. Releasing a long blown-out breath, I stepped back beneath the chill spray, and began the torturous task of losing the scent I'd have been happy to drown in.

Fifteen minutes later, I stepped from the shower smelling only of me and subtle musk and snatched up a towel from the permanent pile on the hamper. My reflection rebounded off the window overlooking the back garden and surrounding forest, and I made a quick scan for damage that couldn't be hidden as I rubbed myself down. Finding none, I secured the towel around my waist and padded from the room to go in search of sustenance.

I hadn't even descended the stairs halfway, when the hairs bristled along my nape, and I froze. Inhaled.

Bollocks!

Where the hell had my head been in the shower? Not that the question warranted an answer, but at some point, Dad and my brothers had returned home.

They'd also brought Nathan with them.

Tipping my face toward the ceiling, I released a slow exhale before jogging down the rest of the steps and rounding the banister toward the kitchen.

Propped against the cabinets, arms the size of tree trunks folded over his chest, Nathan stared my way, eyes icy blue beneath his dark hair.

I leaned against the doorjamb and nodded to him, before the weight of being studied drew my attention left, to the rest of the inquisition in the form of Dad, Danny and Josh at the kitchen table.

Three sets of green eyes peered back at me, from amidst two heads of blond scraggy curls and one ginger mop I'd inherited. Despite the couple of year's age difference, my younger brothers could have been pegged as twins to any who didn't know them. The humour-dominated curiosity in their eyes held far more appeal than the questions in Dad's.

I turned back to Nathan. "'Sup?"

"Do you all mind if I speak with Kyle alone?" Nathan's gaze remained on me as he made the request.

No argument. Chairs scraped back.

I stepped aside to allow my three family members past, my lips curving as Josh, the youngest of us, bumped my shoulder with his own on his way out the room.

"Close the door, and sit down," Nathan said, the second they'd gone.

I spun and reached for the handle.

"You're injured," he said.

My shoulders stiffened as I realised I'd turned my back to him. "It's nothing," I muttered, ignoring Josh's raised brows, where he loitered near the living room entrance.

"How did it happen?" Nathan asked.

Peering at him over my shoulder, I smiled. "Wouldn't you like to know?" With all the false bravado I could summon, I closed the door on my nosy brother and sauntered across to take my seat at the table.

Nate didn't join me—at the table, or in my attempted humour. I'd have accused anyone else of trying to assert their superiority. Nathan didn't need the added height for that—he had it in spades even in his sleep.

Only the slight tilt of his head told me he tracked my movements. "You have something on your mind you want to talk to me about, Kyle?"

Shaking my head, I leaned back into my chair. "Nope."

"How about where you've been today."

I stared at him. If in doubt of how to answer, stay mute.

"What about the other times you've headed out—voluntarily, I add—for job related trips and gone incommunicado?"

Did England recognise the Fifth Amendment? Did werewolves?

"Your dad tells me you've snuck out a few times at night over the past couple of months, too." His sharp attention could have drilled a rig into the ocean.

I shrugged. Better than lying. I *had* met up with Brook of a night. Five times, if memory served. One of those nights had ended with us both falling asleep in a Cheshire park and being woken by a disgruntled badger. I smiled at the replay in my head—even more so at what'd occurred before we'd gone for a run.

"Do you find this funny, Kyle?"

Sobering fast beneath Nathan's glower, I shook my head.

He sighed before unfolding his arms and stepping across to the chair opposite mine. His gaze never once left me, and only intensified as he sat down and leaned forward over the table. "I know you had a difficult time with what happened last autumn ..."

Difficult? That was one word for being kidnapped by vampires who'd forced supernaturals to cage-fight against one another. My opponent had been a vampire who'd bitten me into what should have been an early grave.

"... I also know we're still not too sure of how being bitten has affected you ..."

Yeah. I hadn't quite figured that one out myself, either. Though, my head felt pretty fucked some days. Or confused. Probably both.

"... not to mention, Catherine is still on the loose somewhere ..."

His reference to the only vampire who we knew for certain held responsibility and had escaped punishment— translated: death—had my eye twitching.

"... and all this sneaking around. I've got to be honest with you, Kyle. It has me worried."

I frowned as it dawned on me. "I'm not a vampire, Nate."

"Yes, but—"

"I have no vampire tendencies. No urge to chow on people's blood." Just a shitload of other stuff I'd been noticing and trying to interpret since the whole fricking shoddy affair.

Just as I'd noticed how Ethan and I seemed to be on the hotlist of 'pack members to keep an eye on' since we'd gotten home. Because he, too, got questioned every time he left the house. All because he'd been quieter than usual for a few weeks.

What the hell did they expect? Didn't they get that some stuff took longer to bounce back from?

"I'm not a vampire," I mumbled, when Nathan continued to stare at me. "I can swear that on my mother's

20

grave." A low blow, and I almost cringed as I said it, but it was a vow I knew would never be questioned.

Nathan's barely-there frown lined his forehead for a split-second, but then he gave a slow nod. "Okay. I believe you."

"Good." I pushed back from the table.

"I'm not done," he said, halting my escape.

My eyebrow arched up, as he extended the silence. It seemed to be a favoured tactic of his—to stare us down with that steely glare, until we cracked and promised him our souls on a platter if he'd only spare us. I clamped my lips shut. I suspected he wanted me to ask what else he had on his mind, but in all honesty, I didn't want to know.

After almost two full minutes of optical penetration, however, I couldn't take any more and ended up compromising by drawing my chair back beneath the table and sitting up straight like he had my full attention.

"We still don't have any answers from you with regards to your disappearances," Nate said after a few beats.

I scratched my head, which didn't itch, to give me an excuse to avert my eyes and to grasp a moment to think up a plausible reason for my behaviour. In truth, I should have been better prepared. Should have known I'd only get away with crap for so long before the roasting arrived.

"Is it a female?" Nathan asked.

As my face lifted, the heat claiming my cheeks could have singed my lower lashes. *Damn having ginger hair.*

"Is it the same one each time?"

Attack! Attack! my mind screamed. I leaned back into my seat again, clasping my fiddling fingers on the table-top in front of me. "Nate, I'm thirty-five years old. Do I seriously have to have this conversation with you?"

"Do I need to remind you of pack rules regarding females?"

I didn't miss a beat. "No bringing them home without permission ..." Although the surrounding forest separated our home from the Holloway's, both were considered pack

21

property, both subject to pack rules. "No long term relationships without approval." I smirked. "But we can bonk as many ladies as we like so long as we're cautious and don't leave a stream of pups in our wake."

"You have a smart mouth on you today, Kyle." Despite the quietness of his tone, his lips twitched a little.

"Spending too many years hanging around Ethan will do that to a male." Ethan just happened to be his eldest son, as well as my best friend.

Thankfully, Nate chuckled and pushed to his feet. "I'd better be getting back before I get into trouble with Beth for being late to dinner."

I tamped down the huge sigh of relief I wanted to draw, when he headed for the back door.

"Tell your Dad I'll speak to him tomorrow. And, Kyle?" He paused, his fingers folded around the handle, and half-turned back toward me. "I'll be watching you."

The door swung in. He stepped out. The second it closed at his rear, my held breath gushed past my lips.

As Brook watched from the guest chair, her father stalked his study from one wall to the other, his eyes focused straight ahead as though she'd infuriated him too much for him to even look at her. Although considered quite short in the shifter world, Donald Nicholls' solid breadth gave him an imposing presence, which made him appear so much taller than his five-eleven height.

To Brook, at her five-foot-five, anyway.

"You are being unreasonable, Brook." He halted, and his amber stare—common amongst feline shifters—glowed golden as he turned it on his daughter. "Must I make my requests into orders before you will comply?"

Brook fidgeted in her seat. "I don't believe I've been unreasonable. You asked me to be polite, and I have."

"No. I said you owed it to yourself to get along with Clive. That it would be easier if you accepted your

22

future—which you cannot do without first learning to, at least, answer him with words, instead of the glares and tantrums you seem so insistent on sharing."

And what then? she wanted to ask. Who would he expect her to cosy up to next?

He sighed and paced to the window, shoulders high with tension. "You promised me you would try, Brook."

"That was before I realised that life exists beyond these four walls," she said before she could stop herself, "and whatever four walls you choose to deposit me in for the rest of my life."

Donald whirled, his growl deep as his fists clenched. "How dare you disrespect me in that tone, young lady!"

Brook stiffened her spine in a refusal to cringe. "I mean you no disrespect, Father. But I am an adult, and—"

"An adult with responsibilities."

"Responsibilities to *whom*?"

"To the *Coalition*." His finger shot from his fisted hand and poked at the air.

"Maybe I do not wish for this role into which I am being forced."

Donald roared, the sound vibrating the frames of the pictures hung about the paisley décor'd walls.

That time, she did cringe, her shoulders hunching over until she had no choice but to peer up at him through her draping hair.

"It is not entrapment, Brook," he said, his voice a gravelly tenor. "It is your birth right. And you *will* honour the Nicholls name."

"But, Daddy—"

"This discussion is over. Go to your room. And when Clive, or Stefan—or anyone else, for that matter—calls to show an interest, you *will* be polite. I shall not have you bring embarrassment upon my corner of the Coalition. Do you understand me, young lady?"

A singular tear broke past her lower lid, one of frustration, for her inability to fight against the cause her father seemed so bent on adhering to.

"Brook?" Donald asked, his tone stern.

"Yes, Father," she whispered. "I understand."

"Good girl." He crossed the room and pressed a kiss to her forehead with such tenderness, the past ten minutes might never have happened—except Brook knew they had. "You may go."

She couldn't quite bring herself to utter any thanks, instead dipping her face in acknowledgement of what he would consider to be his generosity. The instant he stepped back, she pushed up from the chair, taking great care to measure her steps so as not to run from the room. Her fingers shook as she reached for the handle and swung the door inward.

"Oh, and, Brook?"

She closed her eyes for a split second, before she opened them and turned back to him.

"If you lock yourself in the guesthouse again when you have visitors, I shall ground you."

Aaarrgh!

She spun and raced from the room before the scream could be vocalised. What sort of twenty-four-year-old woman ended up grounded by her parents?

Clive straightened from where he leaned against the hall wall like he'd been waiting for her. "Brook?"

Heedless of her father's demand spoken only moments before, she shoved past him, rounded the banister, and raced up the stairs.

"Go after her," her father said from below. "She'll be nice."

Like hell. Swinging around the top banister took her to the first door tucked into the left-hand corner of the landing. Beyond that, her bedroom. She barged in, slammed the door, and tossed herself down on a bed that resembled a giant doily.

Footsteps ascended the stairs.

She pressed her face into the white lace bedspread. Folds of the fabric gathered within her fisting hands as she forced back the Shift poking at the edges of her mind. No doubt, her inner animal sensed her distress and wanted escape. Brook had never been so trapped within her own life. Not even when she had been kidnapped and caged a few months before.

A double knock sounded through her door.

Go away! she wanted to scream, but knowing her father would be listening in, likely stood at the bottom of the stairs awaiting proof of her compliance, she lifted her face from the bedding and forced out a sweetly spoken, "Come in."

The handle twisted and the door opened.

She smelled Clive before he'd even entered the room. "Please shut the door behind you."

The click told her he had.

With her face still close enough to the bed to suck up dust-mites, she flopped her arm out to the side and extended a finger toward her vanity dresser. "Please, have a seat."

When the mattress depressed beside her, her head shot up.

Looking far too at-home with his back against her headboard, Clive gave a smile of satisfaction as he swung his legs up onto her bed.

Brook pushed to her knees, shoving at his feet. "Shoes off my bed."

"Feel free to remove them for me." He reached out and entwined his fingers in the ends of her hair trailing on the mattress. "Maybe if you prove you can be amicable, I could convince Don that a long-term mating might be a better option for you."

"Ha!" She knocked his hand aside. "In other words, kiss your behind, and you will put in a good word?"

"Would it kill you to try and get along?"

Kicking back, she landed on her rear and crossed her legs, the stubborn set of her jaw all but giving her answer.

"You've gotta realise I'm a better option than Andrew ... or Chris ... or Ray ..." He ducked toward her a little as he ran through some of the other male Coalition members. "Please tell me I'm a better choice than Stefan."

"Every choice offered to me stinks of petty politics I want no part of."

Pain flittered across his features like a passing shadow. "What happened between us that you started hating me so much?"

She had known Clive for a lifetime. Since the day she had left her mother's womb. "I do not hate you."

"You think you're the only one backed into a corner here?"

She knew she wasn't. Clive probably had as many bruises from the manipulative nudges as she did. "But I am not the only female in the Coalition, Clive." For decades, though, the male shifter population had outweighed the females by at least seven to one.

"I know that." His golden gaze settled on hers, something akin to yearning glossing the orbs. "But you're the only one I'm interested in."

Brook didn't need to ask him for what. The males in the Coalition chased the females for one reason only: the creation of successors.

"Well, maybe I ..."

He toyed with her hair once more until it curled around his forefinger, his warm gaze lifting to hers. "Maybe what, Brook?"

Maybe I want more, her mind said, though she couldn't bring herself to speak the words that would hurt him. She sighed.

"Maybe I do not want to speak about this anymore."

3

Winter sun always seemed to have two primary goals: to burn my eyeballs and freeze my bollocks off. Who the hell knew something so hot could create zero temps. At least it had chased the last of January's snow away the week before, unplugging the stoppage on our latest work schedule.

Unlike the last block of apartments we'd built, the Douglas Street plot held just enough land for a duet of semi-detached houses—which meant our usual contractor's wouldn't be needed to lend additional hands.

Gabriel Lewis, the youngest and newest male pack member, as well as son to Ethan's human mate, stood beside me, as I awaited the first delivery of bricks.

Untrained for any of the regular tasks that came with building a new property, thanks to only being offered the gofer job eleven weeks earlier, he pretty much got ordered to play tag-along—and I'd been chosen to be 'it'.

He toed the solid earth, sending clumps in an upward spray. "Nate kicked up a shit-storm yesterday."

I nodded. "So I heard."

Silence resettled between us, Gabe with his hands tucked deep in his pockets, shoulders bunched high beneath his thick hoodie, and me watching one vehicle spin past after another while tuned in for the deeper rumblings of a delivery truck.

"You, er ..." Gabe sniffed deep, like he needed to clear his thoughts. "Everything, you know ..." His startling blue eyes cut toward me, the turn of his head shifting the hard-hat atop his bright blond curls. "... everything been okay for you?"

I studied him a second, unsure if he asked out of concern for my wellbeing, or concern for his own.

Gabe, not even turned twenty, had been dragged into the fray of cage fighting, too. Ethan had left the ordeal with a bruised ego and damaged emotions. I'd come out the other side no longer fully understanding my body—sometimes my head, too. Gabe, though? He got well and truly fucked up six ways from Sunday and made the hands Ethan and I had been dealt look like a slap and tickle.

Somehow, though, the kid seemed to have pulled through it just fine—on the surface, anyway.

Wanting to keep it that way, I nodded. "I'm still walking, talking ... breathing." I shrugged. "You?"

He glanced away, his hands seeming to dig deeper than ever into his pockets, drawing his jeans along with them until they only barely clung to his hips.

Behind us, the grumble of the mixer rolled through the air, the scrape of tools, the thudding steps from the others' boots across the compacted soil, all of them emphasising the fact Gabe didn't answer.

For one paranoid moment, I imagined the pack's stares aimed our way, boring into our backs, as well as heard their mutters through my mind. *Gabe and Kyle together. What d'you think they're talking about? Better keep an eye on them.* As though they daren't take their eyes off the fractured few who went through the shit we did, like they couldn't trust any words that might pass between us each time we got allowed a moment unsupervised.

I rubbed at my face, lifting my protective helmet as my palm swept around my nape and up over my head, wishing I could erase my obsessive thoughts with one brush.

We both lifted our chins at the chugging engine of a flatbed truck, as it slowed to a stop at the outside kerb.

A guy wearing a fluorescent vest hopped from the cabin. He rounded the front of the vehicle toward us, a sheet of paper in his outstretched hand. "Delivery for Holloway?"

"Yeah." I took the invoice from the driver, pointed to the right. "Drop them just inside the fence."

For the next twenty minutes, we organised the brick delivery, waving at the driver each time he swung a new pallet over the fence, until the entire order sat stacked side by side.

After we'd signed for them and sent the driver on his way, I turned back to Gabe. "You going to answer me now?"

"About what?" he asked, though his darting eyes told me he knew exactly.

"About whether, or not, everything's been okay for you?"

His jaw twitched before his slanted half-smile matched his half-shrug. "You know, walking, talking ... breathing."

I studied him, but his expression never wavered. "If you ever need to talk. About stuff ..." Even as I said it, I wondered how much of me made the offer for selfish reasons. Wondered if I hoped he'd come forth and admit he'd been dealing with some crazy shit, just so I didn't have to be the only one with kooky after-effects of being bitten by a race venomous to us and pumped with an anti-venom filled with the same crap. I nodded, as if to reassure myself of my motives. "You can always come to me, Gabe."

"I know." Hands returned to his pockets, he pivoted on one leg back toward the site—halting before he even took a step.

I swung, too, stopping mid-turn as my gaze followed Gabe's.

Nathan and Dad both stood over by the last lot of footings. Hands on their hips, the pair of them stared our way from beneath their hard-hats.

"Ever get the impression you're being watched?" Gabe asked, his lips barely moving.

"Yeah," I muttered. "All the damn time."

Free time.

Brook seemed to be granted more and more of it.

Anyone else would likely have shown gratitude. Brook, though, knew the expanding hours she didn't have to work for would eventually come with a price—and said price would no doubt arrive in the form of a Tom.

That didn't mean she couldn't appreciate the moments of true solitude she managed to steal.

The evening before, Clive had lingered until well after midnight, like he believed she'd eventually cave and invite him to stay. Why couldn't they all understand that the very fact they gave her only choices they deemed suitable negated them from being true choices at all?

Everything in Brook's life, though, had to be approved by her parents—her mother, who agreed wholeheartedly with the Coalition way of life, and her father, who went to great lengths to uphold it. She doubted either of them would approve of the choice her heart seemed to be cheerleading.

At least being in the woodlands that filled almost every unbuilt-upon space in her father's property allowed her the illusion of escape. Away from her mother's disapproving stares that alternated with her father's expectant ones.

More so, away from the bickering of whichever Toms decided to show their faces.

Maybe their visits wouldn't seem so corrupt, if they didn't make regular rounds to every Coalition home housing an unclaimed female.

Letting out a hiss at the direction her thoughts had travelled, Brook slunk off in a quiet trot west, toward the corner of the woods that hid her childhood tree-house.

Her pads cushioned the steps she took across the earth. The breeze, gentle in force yet bitter in temperature, bristled every hair across her body. With her silken coat warding off the worst of the chill, she concentrated wholly on the ever-present scents she had always loved, the quiet scurrying and flapping and pitter-patters that helped bring the woods to life, and the beaten trails, fallen branches, and bushes that had grown alongside her own body for each of the years since she had found respite in her sanctuary.

All of them held so much familiarity, she barely had to pay attention to the route she trod, and as her tree-house came into view, her shoulders, which had slowly unknotted with each step along the journey, relaxed even further.

Which meant the crack of a twig at her rear barely registered.

Her head snapped up.

She inhaled.

Stefan.

Claws digging into dirt, Brook kicked off into a leap.

In the next breath, she hit the ground with a heavy thud, beneath a great weight along her spine, as teeth clamped over her nape.

The force around her neck strengthened, as her face rammed into the dirt a second time.

She spat out a hissed warning.

When his jaws released her, she thought he'd heeded—until he began urging his cheeks across the back of her head.

Oh, no. She bucked beneath him.

He whined out an objection, his paw slapping across her shoulders, pinning her down as he continued with his Marking.

Bastard.

The only thing worse than being Marked by a Tom was being Sprayed by a Tom. Although the Coalition had laws against that particular act, she didn't put it past Stefan to ignore them.

Muscles tensing, she pushed upward with her legs, but at almost double her body weight, Stefan was an uneasy force to move.

With a deep yowl, he locked onto the back of her head and forced her down again. As his tongue licked across the spot his teeth had grazed, his front leg held her in place, and his weight resettled.

Lip curling, teeth exposed, Brook kicked up a hind leg.

Stefan's deep screech rang out as her claws made contact.

Brook wriggled, her torso twisting, claws digging into soil for traction.

She'd scarcely gotten out from beneath him, when his jaws clamped over her rump. Her high pitched roar ruffled her lips, but he clambered back over her like he hadn't even noticed.

Closing her eyes, she willed her body to Shift, the sensation that accompanied the transformation no more than a tingle rolling across her flesh, like a tidal wave of tiny pinpricks.

By the time his hot breaths hit her shoulder, Brook resembled human, and with a spin of her body, she rammed her elbow into his ribcage. When that earned no more than a whine, she tucked her knee in close to her stomach and booted downward as hard as she could— straight toward Stefan's groin.

His howled screech blasted her ear, and, teeth gritted, she rammed her shoulder against his side. "Get off me!"

He rolled to the left with a thud, his body already partially altered from black fur to flesh, hands already reaching for his most prized possession, and his eyes screwed tight.

Before he could open them, Brook bolted for the tree-house.

With years of practiced ease, her soles hit every second rung on the sloped ladder.

A sideways glance showed Stefan still rolling on the floor, only his scrunched features exposing his pain with his diminished wails, as Brook flew into the elevated wooden cabin.

The musky scent of weathered pine smacked her senses as she shot for the far opening and burst out onto the rear suspended deck.

From there, she thrust off with her right leg. For a fraction of a second, only air supported her, her body curling in on itself, until her feet hit the high shelter of the sturdily-branched silver birch.

"You're gonna pay for this, Brook!"

She jerked at Stefan's shout, arm flinging out, but folded her fingers around a branch above before she could lose her balance.

As though mimicking a monkey, she wove through limbs as naked as herself, legs lifting and swinging, body twisting to fit through narrower gaps, until she'd found a decent perch with a view of Stefan's fallen spot and enough timber between them to offer some protection.

Only then did she notice the thud of her heart against her sternum as breaths panted from her, and the sheen of sweat coating her skin.

Below her, Stefan rolled to his knees and made an ungainly climb to his feet. His body swayed to the left a little, head tilting upward as his gaze swept the tree.

He grinned like the threat hadn't just left his lips. "You're touchy today."

"And you are presumptuous today."

He chuckled, hands coming to rest on his hips, as he took a couple lazy steps back. The colour of burnt Satsuma shone from his mesmerising eyes—inherited from his father, Rufus King—beneath flawlessly-tousled chestnut hair that always managed to flop just so. Every square inch of his perfectly toned six-six broad frame hosted nothing but sculpted muscles.

No matter that Stefan came wrapped in a ridiculously handsome package, Brook knew it to be no more than a mere vessel for the ugliness within—just as she knew not to trust his easy stance.

He waved an arm at her, beckoning her down. "Come back and play."

"Play?" Flicking her hair aside, she leaned over the branch afore her and spat at the ground. "Is that what you now call attacking females when their backs are turned?"

He laughed, though the sound reflected little humour. "You've always been a good storyteller. Shame nobody's ever interested in your crappy yarns."

"What do you *want*, Stefan?" she asked, ignoring his dig that nobody believed her accounts of his behaviour. "You should know better than to disturb me here."

"Why shouldn't I? It's not like you've never invited me into your hole before."

She hissed at him, the hairs prickling the entire length of her spine. The times Brook had allowed him to share her space had been long before his true colours had made an appearance—and those occasions certainly hadn't been on the personal level he implied.

As if her outburst hadn't even occurred, he shrugged. "What can I say? I got bored of listening to our dear old dads talk business. You were the better option."

The business he spoke of probably consisted of relations between enterprises. The entire Coalition owned companies mutually beneficial to one another. From her father's string of hotels, to restaurants and health spas, all the way to Rufus King's casinos, each of them had been set up to complement the others and ensure the Coalition had a steady stream of funds from all directions.

Brook had been earning herself a hands-on education in the hospitality industry, before her father had suddenly announced that her place was at home.

Her hackles rose even further as she thought of her father's idea of 'her place'—until her eyes refocused on the problem below her. "Well, this is my personal time, and you've no right disturbing it." Though she knew it wouldn't work, habit had her saying, "Wait until my father hears of this."

Stefan chuckled, before doing a three step sprint to his right and leaping up until his fingertips enfolded one of the higher rungs on the tree-house ladder. Muscle swelled across his shoulders as he swung himself up and over, and bunched in his thighs when he straightened and balanced his stance. "Who do you think told me where to find you, Princess?"

A low growl rumbled in her chest at the title he always insisted on calling her. "My name is *Brook*."

As he disappeared into the tree-house, Brook curved around the trunk and worked her way to the next branch, bringing him back into view, when he reappeared on the deck from which she had left.

He cupped his groin and jutted his hips forward. "As soon as I claim you, your name'll be whatever the hell I want it to be."

Brook rolled her eyes, a small laugh breathing from her. "That is *never* going to happen."

"Oh, yeah?" His flared nostrils exposed how much her words bothered him. "Try telling that to Daddy, Princess." With a scowl marring his features, he ducked back into the tree-house. "'Cause your days are running out."

She stretched forward, shivering for the first time as adrenaline ceased to fight off the cold, already looking toward where he'd emerge at the other end.

Seconds passed and no Stefan.

Instead, squeaks started up, a sound pattern of *e-ee, e-ee, e-ee*, each one vibrating through the moist timber. "This cot of yours still has a lot of spring in it, Princess."

She ground her teeth at his use of the pet name *again*.

"It's as good a place as any to do the deed." The pine surround hollowed his voice, as though acting as a buffer and absorbing some of the sneering intent. "Come to me by free will. Or come to me under command. Makes no odds to me."

Her hands folded into fists. "The only way I shall ever come to you is in your dreams."

She should have recognised the triple thud for what it represented before Stefan bulleted onto the overhang and dove for the tree where she sat.

The branch he landed on bounced beneath his bulk, despite his agility, and his hair skimmed the limbs he brushed past, as he slid through the obstacles with a fluidity his size belied.

It took all of Brook's willpower not to fling herself from the tree and run for home—all of her inner strength not to scramble away to a higher branch.

"You're an idiot, Brook."

Her heart stuttered as he came to a stop on a branch a foot or two below the one she balanced upon. His abdomen leaned against another no more than three feet away—the only barrier between them.

"No female is permitted to pass her twenty-fifth birthday without becoming a Queen." His smile held all the charm of a leech. "Daddy did you no favours sending you to that all girls' school. He'd have been better off sending you to the same schools as the rest of us. Then you might have paid more attention to what happens around you."

With one hand gripping an overhead branch for support, she dropped her face to his level. "Nobody can force me to do anything," she said through gritted teeth.

"You keep telling yourself that." His hand shot out, but Brook jerked back, and his fingers only managed to skim her arm. "Keep closing your eyes and refusing to see."

A growl left her throat. "My father would never—"

"No? Then, how come Don has just let me in on a big fat secret?" His arm whipped under the branch a second time, sending Brook back again and her spine smacking against the timber at her rear. "Seems he's already got his eyes on his favourite suitors, eh?"

She slammed a foot against his arm, as he made further grabs for her calf. With his wrist pinned beneath her sole against the trunk, she leaned in close to his face where his chin pressed against the bark beneath it. "What secret?"

His slow smile distorted beneath Brook's hold. "That your Season's due to fall in two weeks."

She rolled her eyes. "Is that it?" she asked, dropping her foot.

The second she'd released him, he pushed away. "Your birthday's in two weeks, too, Princess." One measured backward step took him to where the limbs began to thin out. "Just in time for you to become a Queen. Like I said, the clock's ticking." He wagged his finger side-to-side like an inverted pendulum, complete with sound effects. "If you haven't Chosen, the choice will be made for you. Guess who Don has just stuck first in line?"

With a sideways leap, he vacated the tree, his body arcing downward until he hit dirt with a thump.

Like he hadn't just made a twenty-foot plummet, he straightened and rolled out his shoulders. "I keep telling you, Brook ... I always get what I want." He sauntered off in the direction of the house. "I *always* win!"

Brook growled after his retreating back. "Not this time."

Though, as she drew her hair over her shoulder and his left-behind scent wrapped around her like a mocking cloak, she realised he already partially had.

4

Passing traffic, as well as the wails of kidlets in pushchairs that strolled by, had created a steady hum all morning, but lack of noise from the site equipment, after listening to it for hours, allowed the first quiet calm of the day.

All thanks to Jem.

Jem had given birth to a girl September gone, one that smelled suspiciously like she carried the dominant werewolf gene. Since then, panic slam-dunked her mate, Nate's younger son Sean, into uselessness pretty much every time she and the baby left the house.

I couldn't blame him. In his shoes, I'd have probably been the same.

The only time Sean didn't climb the walls was when they visited the site—and, primarily, him.

Unfortunately for Jem, her role as interior designer for the company wouldn't be needed until we had at least a couple shells for her to size up. Jem, being Jem, however, found a loophole for turning up every day. She'd made herself designated lunch provider.

Better all round for everybody concerned. It meant Nate's wife Beth didn't have to struggle with keeping a growly Jem cooped up all day and even tagged along for the ride, Jem and baby Lia got to see Sean and feed their needs before withdrawal kicked in, and Sean only had to spend half a day, instead of its entirety, sick with worry over whether, or not, they were all right.

Hence the quiet. Nate insisted all machinery be shut off the instant his granddaughter entered the site.

Beth had settled beside Nathan on a makeshift bench, the pair of them chomping on sandwiches. Sean and Jem sat perched on the bonnet of the pickup, Sean scoffing his porkpie, with Jem brushing away his sprayed crumbs the second they landed on Lia tucked in the crook of his arm.

Watching them all as I chewed, my chest tightened. Was it wrong that I felt a pang of envy that they saw each other every day?

No questions. No reprimand. No fucking guilt.

No matter that they'd see each other on the evening, anyway, *and* get to fall asleep in each other's arms.

I wanted that.

Over the past handful of weeks, I'd noticed that the more I tried to ignore it, the more the tightness twisted in my chest, as if punishing me for denying what, deep inside, I already suspected.

I wanted that *with Brook*.

As I shovelled the second half of my third sandwich into my mouth, Jem hopped down from the truck. After a few swipes of her palms across her butt, she trod dirt, and the second her gaze locked onto mine, I knew her destination.

Me.

Her leg swings widened, her arms doing exaggerated winging to match.

I chewed some more. *Here we go.*

She plopped down on the bucket-and-plank loveseat, her shoulder bumping mine as the bench shook beneath me. "Hey."

"Nothin' to see 'ere," I said in my best northern accent, mimicking something I'd seen on TV.

She gave a quiet laugh. "That's not what the grapevine's telling me."

"Maybe the grapevine should grow some fruit of its own instead of nicking mine."

"Cagey," she said, humour in her tone.

Brow arched, I twisted toward her dark blue eyes and the blonde hair that tumbled over the cream fleece covering her shoulders. "Didn't the pack agree that the word cage, and any variations of it, would never again be spoken?"

She matched my expression with a quirk of her own brow. "Don't you Larsen's know I can't be distracted with a change of subject?"

I snorted, but glanced away. Her eyes carried as much intensity as Nathan's when she headed into probe-mode, and I couldn't deal with it right then. I nodded toward the truck, where Sean had discarded his lunch in exchange for nuzzling on his tiny bundle, though his gaze stayed riveted to Jem. "How's Lia doing? Nate said she's been teething this week."

"She has, but she's okay. You men always think everything's a hundred times worse than it is when it comes to her." She poked my shoulder. "And you're changing the subject again."

"Maybe you should take the hint." The second I'd said it, I frowned. I'd never been rude to Jem, never had reason to—not even then.

She merely nodded. "Maybe I should." She pushed up from plank, though before she straightened, she leaned in close to my ear. "If you ever need to talk to someone," she whispered, "you can come to me. I don't give a monkey's uncle what you've got wrapped up in. I just want you to be okay."

"I am okay," I murmured, not even believing it myself.

"Kyle …" She swung her gaze back round to mine. "You haven't been okay for weeks. Please don't try and kid me otherwise."

Before I could respond, she spun away and made a slow trek back toward her spot.

Beyond her, Sean's eyes flicked up and down like something possessed. Each time his gaze dropped to his daughter, it just as fast shot back to his mate, down then up, back and forth—like he couldn't figure out who needed his attention more.

As I took a bite of my last sandwich, I couldn't help but wonder how it felt—to be that afraid to take your sights off those you loved.

My thoughts instantly flashed to Brook, and I shook my head hard enough to rattle, like that could chase out the crazy crap going on within. I jumped when a buzz vibrated through the pocket of my cargos.

Like some kind of attention magnet, the sound drew everyone's heads up.

Blanking them all, as well as trying to ignore the flutter that replaced the ache in my chest, I crammed the rest of my sandwich in my mouth as I stood and grabbed my mobile.

Just a quick glance at the screen brought a twitch to my lips. Without a word to any of them, I strode off toward the Port-a-cabin at the rear of the yard, my smile spreading the farther from them I got.

Thumb poised over the connect button, I tugged down the handle to the hut, nudged open the door … and halted.

Ethan paused in stirring a drink and peered over his shoulder.

When the hell had he gone inside?

He jerked his chin up. "You answering that?"

I was.

Until you *got in the way.*

Mug in hand, he turned. His gaze dropped straight to my phone before returning to me. "Won't *P* be peed, if you let it just keep ringing out?"

I stared down at the screen, where P blinked at me above the flashing 'Incoming Call' alert. *P for Puss.* The two of us had laughed about it when I'd entered it, just as we'd laughed over my number on hers. *D for Dog.*

Why the hell hadn't I hidden it from him? I wanted to kick myself in the butt and then some.

"Who is *P*, anyway?" He took a sip of his drink, but his focus never once wavered from my face. "Someone I know?"

The ringtone quit, its absence almost as obvious as its song, and I rammed the phone in my pocket.

"It's a female, isn't it?" Ethan took another sip and nodded as though answering himself. "Gotta be."

"What do you know?" I shoved the door closed and covered the few strides to the drinks counter like that had been my goal all along.

"Ah, but you forget. I've already been where you are now." He gave a self-satisfied smirk.

The buzzing kicked back in with a second attack of my pelvis.

Ethan pointed toward my pocket. "You know she'll be pissed, if you don't get that, don't you?"

I ignored the phone, as well as him, banging a mug onto the counter and reaching for the coffee canister. Fingers grabbed hold of my bicep and stilled me. "What the hell's going on with you?" Ethan's dark eyes held a shitload of concern from beneath hair the same colour as his dad's. "You don't hang anymore. You're sneaking around. Most days, you act like you lost your sense of humour, along with any trust you had in me. We don't have secrets from each other, remember?"

My lip curled before I could stop it. "Yeah, 'cause you were so forthcoming when it came to admitting you had something going on with Shelley. *Remember*?"

Hurt flickered in his eyes for a second as he loosened his hold. "So, it *is* a female?"

I grabbed up a teaspoon, averting myself from the clarity in his expression, and scooped out some coffee. "I never said that."

"You didn't have to. It's written all over your damn face." He pushed away from the counter, boots drumming the flimsy floor as he crossed the cabin. At the exit, he paused, drink in one hand, door handle in the other. "When you realise you need someone to talk to about it, you come find me. I'm here for you." He glanced back over his shoulder, his half-smile seeming out of synch with the seriousness in his eyes. "That'll never change, you hear?"

My nod arrived as a pathetic jerk alongside my quiet, "I hear you."

In the next beat, he turned away and strode out, the closing of the door like a barrier to more than the end of the conversation.

The teaspoon hit the side of the mug with a clink as I dropped it to rub at my face.

Ethan's words couldn't have rang truer.

Whenever I'd had a problem in the past, Ethan was close by, offering support.

In fights, he'd always been at my side.

In arguments, he'd always batted for my team.

No matter the circumstances, if I'd needed him, he'd been there—*always*—and I'd just smacked his hand-of-support aside.

A hand I'd always gladly accepted in the past.

I blew out a breath of frustration. "Way to go."

Still, though, like some kind of addict in reach of its next fix, I retrieved the re-buzzing mobile from my pocket and hit connect.

Brook hung up from her call with Kyle and frowned down at her phone.

Initially, she'd rang him in need of someone to reassure her that Stefan's words had been no more than his usual taunting. It had taken only his tensely-spoken greeting for her to hold back—for her to be reminded that the issues keeping them apart did not come from her end alone. One mention of Stefan's name would have sprung him into driving over to her, consequences be damned.

When, exactly, had they progressed to being so in tune with one another, to recognising what the other needed with so little to go on? When had each of their pain become shared?

"Brook!" Her mother's voice, deeper in tone than Brook's, yet far smoother than the gruffness of her father's, travelled from downstairs and snapped her from her musing.

Brook pushed up from her bed, tucking her mobile into the pocket of her jeans as she did so, and padded from the room. On reaching the head of the stairs, she found her mother's cool gaze already aimed her way from the hallway below. "Yes, Mother?"

Collette Nicholls narrowed her eyes. "Were you talking to someone up there?"

Brook kept her expression as impassive as possible, while making a mental note to no longer call Kyle from inside the main house. She couldn't think of a worse conversation upon which to be eavesdropped. "No, Mother."

Another few blinks passed, her mother seeming to study every inch of Brook's face, as though she need only see the slightest tic of muscle to detect the lie. She finally nodded. "You have chores downstairs."

Brook ground her teeth as her mother departed. Spine ramrod straight, shoulders back, chin held aloft, Collette carried herself as though she believed every nuance could be used as a potential lesson to her daughter. She even ate with dignity and poise and paused between every bite to send glances Brook's way, like she needed to check her example had been noted.

Taller than Brook, her mother's five-eight frame seemed to own the kitchen, as Brook trailed her into the spacious room—though Brook suspected her mother's attitude aided in that as much as her physical appearance. While her eyes held the oft-found hue of shifters, ash blonde waves spilling across her shoulders set Collette apart from her daughter and husband.

"The table needs laying," her mother said without looking up as she reached for a knife. "Please remember the napkins. Then you shall come and assist with preparing the salad."

Napkins and early table laying could only mean guests. "I thought the Kings went home?"

"They did." Another comment made without eye contact.

Brook opened her mouth to ask who, if not the Kings, would be joining them.

"You know better than to loiter when there are tasks to be done," her mother said before she had a chance.

The pattern had slowly increased in number over the past month, with Friday night guests, as well as on Monday, Tuesday, and Wednesday—four evenings of entertaining in one week. Stefan's warning tolled in her head. Only a fortnight until her birthday, only a fortnight until her Season—had there been more than taunting to his words, after all?

Ignoring the tremor of panic in her chest, Brook headed across to the cutlery drawer and slid it open.

"Tablecloth first!" Collette snapped. "Really, Brook, do you absorb anything, at all?"

Yes, actually. The perfect posture to lead into a roundhouse kick, the correct formation of a fist when throwing a punch ... Rather than vocalise her thoughts, Brook left the room to do her mother's bidding.

Many years before, she had learned life was simply easier that way.

5

Brad Campbell. Twenty-nine and a half years of age. In perfect health. Son to George and Veronica Campbell. Heir to Campbell's Carvery's. Manager of the head branch of Campbell's Carvery's in Chester.

Statistics.

Ones Brook could most likely recite, after her mother's very unsubtle, numerous mentions of them, and they hadn't even hit the main course.

"One day, Brad will be heading up my corner of the Coalition, too," George said, pride in his voice.

Must add that to the list, Brook thought as she poked at her prawn starter. As if the entire purpose for their dinner party hadn't already been obvious enough. *Eligible bachelor.*

"*Brook.*" Collette hissed, eyes practically glowering in Brook's direction.

Clearing her throat, Brook lowered her fork and turned to George. "What a great honour that shall be for him."

Although her voice had held no sincerity, George beamed at her and launched right back into his glowing report of his son.

Brook ordered herself to remain alert and at least give the impression of listening, noting that age hadn't been quite as kind to George as it could be to some shifters.

His hair greyed at the temples, while lines framed his eyes, and his features appeared permanently fatigued.

Brook couldn't help but wonder if those unflattering factors had anything to do with his son being so far un-obtained—because, at his side, Brad had all the health and youthful appeal of a Tom in his prime.

Almost black hair shorn close to his skull crowned a body for which any human male would have paid good money. Despite his exaggerated fidgets in his seat, as though to prove his discomfort over the situation, Brad stared her way far too often, the odd sea-green shade of his eyes made all the more startling by his tan skin.

His gaze connected with Brook's for around the twentieth time, and just like he had the previous umpteen, he flashed his teeth in a smile meant to impress.

Brook dipped her attention back to her starter, spearing a prawn to busy her mouth as an excuse not to return the expression. For some reason, Brad's oozing charm didn't appeal to her, and not for the first time, she found herself pondering over his lingering un-attachment.

"What about you, Brook?" Brad asked.

Surrounding conversation ceased, and Brook lifted her face to find all eyes focused her way. "What about ... me?"

"What aspirations do you have?"

For about the billionth time that day, her thoughts flashed to Kyle—to a relationship with an impossible future. Her brows knotted before she could stop them.

"Where do you see your future heading?" he asked, as if he thought her expression meant she hadn't understood.

"I ..." Dragging her thoughts back to the present took immense effort. "I *was* training to run one of Father's hotels."

"But not anymore?"

Brook gave a small headshake. "No, I'm no lon—" A warning glint in her mother's eyes stopped her version of the event leaving her lips. "I've recently retired."

"Pity." Brad grinned. "With your hospitality background, combined with my management skills, we could have made the perfect team."

Silence settled again. While everyone else seemed to be staring at Brook in expectancy, she couldn't find it within herself to return Brad's smile—not when she heavily suspected his words held intent left unsaid.

"What do you think?" Brad asked after the pause had stretched for a few seconds. His grin had yet to leave, as though painted in place, and his pale eyes remained focused on Brook. "Could I convince you to come out of retirement to play?"

Not with you, Brook thought, yet she daren't voice it with the anticipation humming through the air—almost as though the lives of all those present hung on the balance of Brook's response. Deciding to play the safest answer she could think of, she said, "It is an option."

The tension that had the others all poised in their seats seemed to filter away, as shoulders lowered, movement recommenced, and breaths sighed.

Her mother released her frown lines and actually smiled. "Such a considerate, boy," she said, as she began gathering cocktail glasses.

Brook couldn't bring herself to agree, as the intensity still claiming Brad's eyes continued to churn in her direction.

Once the dinner guests had left, Brook had escaped to her room. Her initial intent had been to duck off to the guesthouse, but her father had curtailed that, the second she'd moved for the door, with a shake of his head— which meant she'd spent the past twenty minutes whispering into her mobile so as not to be overheard.

Each time Kyle's deep voice rumbled along the line, her stomach tightened. Each time he chuckled, her toes curled against the rough covering of her bed. More than either of those, the promises he made, of pleasures to come, the commentary of his body's responses each time she answered with promises of her own, all left her chest rising high beneath hastened breaths.

Kyle's low groan hit her ear. "Jesus, this is killing me. I hate—" He blew out a breath.

"I know." Brook's hand tightened around the phone at the desperation in his tone.

"I hate all this sneaking around," he finished.

"Me, too."

"I hate having to hide." Emotion deepened his voice. "I hate not being with you right now."

Brook frowned up at her ceiling, its usual crisp whiteness muted to a shady grey, with the flashes of moon through her window as the only source of light, but she didn't interrupt. Most of their recent calls had devolved into Kyle spilling his frustration.

"I hate having to wait. I fucking hate the gap." Another groan arrived. "I mean, it's been, what? Two days?"

Not even that. Thirty-one and a half hours, according to Brook's estimation. Rather than sound obsessive, she said, "Almost, yes."

"Fuck five more days!" A growl chased his words.

"Then, meet me sooner," Brook whispered. "I'll get away ..." ... *somehow*.

"Tomorrow? No, not tomorrow. Shit! Can't do the weekend. Daren't. They're all bloody watching me like hawks. Be too conspicuous to get out tomorrow."

She smiled at his rambling, warmed, despite the irritation pumping from the earpiece, by his evident need to see her.

"Monday," he said. "Meet with me Monday."

Although Monday seemed an age away, it beat waiting until Thursday. Brook sighed. "Monday sounds good."

"Where?" he asked. "Or you need me to come to you again?"

Kyle sneaking onto her father's property had been the biggest risk they'd taken yet, but Brook couldn't deny it had been a risk well worth the effort. "We ca—"

Footsteps hit the stairs, accompanied by Donald's tenor. "It will be fine, Lettie."

"Brook?" Kyle murmured. "Everything okay?"

"I have to go." She shut off her phone and tucked it beneath her pillow.

"How?" her mother's low voice asked. "She hasn't shown an interest in a Tom yet."

"Not strictly correct," Donald said, a board creaking as they ascended.

"Fighting with Clive and throwing eye daggers at Stefan does not count."

"Yes, well, the attitude will improve."

Shadows cut across the strip of light showing beneath Brook's door.

"It hasn't improved yet," Collette said, the brush of feet over carpet travelling toward the room at the far end of the landing.

"It will," Donald said with more force. "Because it has to."

A door handle clicked, and Brook tracked their entrance into her mother's room.

"I blame it on the kidnapping," her mother said, as Brook listened to them moving about. "She's been intolerable since then. Her behaviour's unacceptable. What if the Toms see her as damaged? What shall we do then?"

"They won't. And anyone within the Coalition knows better than to even suggest it."

Brook gritted her teeth against the retort that wanted to fly from her. Not accepting a part in their manipulation, or a Tom who saw her as no more than a kitten breeder, did not make her damaged, and the urge to scream as such grated at her throat. Even the kidnapping had left her mentally unscathed—physically, too, except for a few scars.

Unlike Kyle, a voice whispered in the back of her mind.

Brook gave a low growl at herself. She had known Kyle only since the kidnapping, and it had been that version of him which had captured her interest.

"At least before the incident, she willingly spent time with Clive," her mother said.

"She'll come around."

"In two weeks? We should never have given her so much free range."

Free range? Working in her father's hotel could hardly have been considered that. The vampire who'd sweet-talked her away from her family had done a good job of posing as a charming guest—no more, no less.

"Then she would not have had opportunity to behave like a whore ..." Collette continued.

A whore? Book's hands balled into fists.

"... and get herself into trouble. The whole affair would never have happened."

Typical of her mother to turn Brook's entire kidnapping around to be her own fault.

"That may well as be, Lettie," Donald said. "But it has happened now, and we will have to deal with the outcome."

Her mother's bedroom door thudded shut, and Brook let out her breath on a huff.

Only her parents could discuss their daughter being kidnapped in such a detached way. Only they would place all responsibility for it having happened at all on her shoulders alone.

She rolled over, as the bedsprings kicked into action in her mother's room, burrowing her face into one pillow as her arm curled a second across her ear, to muffle the noise she loathed hearing.

Not that Brook found their sex distasteful. More that she equated the lack of sounds, other than those made by non-living objects, with lack of enjoyment. Like her parents still participated in the act merely because of expectations, or bodily requirements, rather than for a pleasurable experience.

Brook hated the very idea.

What she did with Kyle held so much more meaning than that. The two of them gave as much as they took—they connected— and the yearnings his absence created were born of more than lustful wanting. Brook craved not only his body but his soul.

Shuffling drifted out from her mother's room, before the door opened and footsteps hit the landing.

A moment later, the stretch of light beneath her door extinguished, and the door to her father's room opened and closed—the usual ending to a far-too-clinical need.

Yes, Brook wanted so much more than that.

6

Fifteen minutes after Brook hung up on me, I still held my mobile in a death grip, my mood at rock bottom from the call having ended with me mid-complaint.

Again.

All of our calls, lately, seemed to end that way, with my damn gripes and grumbles plummeting whatever tone we'd set.

Rubbing a hand across my face, I let out a low groan, pissed at myself for not having the chance to apologise, to tell Brook I missed her, that I—*that I what?*

I gave another groan.

I'd *had* the chance—I'd had plenty—and I'd blown it by whining instead.

"Way to go, Romeo." I tossed the phone up into the air and ducked my head aside before it could smack my temple on descent. It hit the pillow beneath me, bouncing off and landing on the floor with a quiet thud.

As I rolled to my side, hand reaching to grab it back, a rap sounded at my bedroom door.

"Kyle?" Dad's quiet voice sifted through the wood.

Almost unbalanced as I snatched up my mobile, I pushed up to sit, one leg on and one off the bed. "Yeah?"

The handle squeaked down, the door swung inward, and Dad stepped forward, filling the frame. "Hey." Shoulders high, he tucked his hands into his jeans pockets, eyes seeming to search my room, my body language, my face, all in a single sweeping glance. "Thought I heard you talking."

I gave a slow headshake, tucking my mobile behind me as his gaze darted toward it in my hand. He didn't move, his stare returning to my face and staying there, until warmth crept across my cheeks, and I found myself saying, "Just mumbling to myself."

Dad heaved out a sigh, removing his hands and raking fingers through his ginger mop that looked even more out of control than my own usually did.

I expected him to leave then. That had been how other similar conversations between us had concluded. Instead, he stepped into my room, closed the door at his rear, and grabbed up the chair from the corner, bringing it to my bedside. The position he took, facing me, leaning slightly forward with his elbows propped on his knees, brought his face level with mine.

I considered swinging up onto the bed, lying back to stare up at the ceiling, if only to escape the inquisition in his eyes, but the hand he clamped around the back of my neck, tugging me to within a few inches of his face, fast put a stop to that option.

"Talk to me." Though low, his voice weighed heavy with plea.

For a half second, I contemplated spilling the goods. I really did. The very idea of off-loading to my dad, just so I could have at least one person I didn't have to keep everything from, didn't have to hide from, almost sent my lips into action. Common sense won out, though, and I clamped them shut.

His sigh, even fuller than the last, breezed my cheek as he released his grip on me. He leaned back a little, elbows once more balancing atop his knees, and the intense stare-down recommenced. "Are you in some kind of trouble, Son?"

I shook my head, averting my eyes.

"Because, whatever it is, you know we can work it out. Talk to me, and I can help. If you're in a hole, we can dig you out. I'm not going to judge you."

"There's nothing to judge, Dad." My tone barely concealed the lie within the words.

"You could never do anything to make me ashamed of you. You know that, don't you?"

I wanted to nod, my head almost went to, but even I recognised the falsity of a declaration made without all the facts.

Seconds passed, my heart bumping in time to each ticked notch of the alarm clock on my bedside table, the silence between us seeming to grow in density the longer it stretched. Yet, as close as he sat to me, I couldn't bring myself to look at him, couldn't bring myself to meet his gaze. I knew he believed what he said, trusted in himself to be non-judgemental, but I doubted any guesses he made about my shadiness hit anywhere near the mark. Mine wouldn't have.

"You wouldn't understand," I ended up saying. How could I expect him to, when I barely understood myself?

"You'd be surprised," he said, pushing to his feet and rounding the bed.

Head tilted, I tracked his path to my window, turning fully when he came to a stop.

He faced away, his solid arms crossed, fingers folded around his biceps. Only the high set of his shoulders showed his tension, as lack of light in the room prevented any kind of clear reflection in the glass.

I waited to see if he'd turn, if the interrogation would kick back in, almost wondered why he still occupied my damn room when all he did was stand there ignoring me.

He cleared his throat. "I'm going to go out on a whim here and assume this has something to do with a female." He paused a moment as though to see if I would disagree with him before continuing. "You know, when I took interest in your mother I hadn't even had my first transformation."

I frowned but didn't interrupt.

"Nate started taking notice of Beth at pretty much the same time. For a while, I questioned the coincidence of us two chasing after two females who happened to be best friends. But I know as well as the next werewolf who's fallen that you don't get to choose who trips you. Once your soul recognises its other half, what follows is no longer within your control."

"That's pretty deep, Dad," I mumbled.

He nodded but didn't turn. "The biggest problem for us, though, wasn't who we'd fallen for. It was *what* we'd fallen for."

My eyebrows twitched as his words hit stupidly close to home.

"Rob ..." He sighed at his mention of Nate's dad, the then Alpha. "He made no secret of his dislike of humans. Ignorant bastard thought they were beneath us. There for reproductive purposes and very little else. Luckily, his shitty attitude didn't rub off on his son."

I'd heard all the rumours about the single-mindedness of Nate's father. Seemed weird hearing them in such context from Dad. I wondered what Rob's standing would have been on what Brook and I had going on.

Dad twisted toward me at last and lowered his butt down to the windowsill, his green eyes capturing me before I could look away. "If you think you can't tell us about her, you're wrong. If you think there's no hope, no future, you're wrong. Yes, your mother's end came sooner than I ever imagined I'd have to deal with ..." He heaved in a deep breath, yet I couldn't look away from the flash of pain in his eyes. "I've spent every day since regretting not being here that afternoon."

He meant the afternoon, eleven years before, when a rogue pack had turned up on our property in hopes of claiming territory and found Mum home alone.

"But Beth and Jem are living proof that it's workable," Dad said. "Humans and our kind can co-exist ..."

Humans, yes.

"... so, please, quit feeling as though you need to hide. Because you don't." Dad shoved up from the ledge and strode across the carpet, leaving the room without another word, as though to quell any protest on my behalf.

I wouldn't have argued, anyway. What would have been the point when the example he tossed my way had nothing to do with my own situation?

"Yeah, thanks for the talk, Dad." I tugged my shirt over my head and flung it aside. As I shucked the rest of my clothing and climbed beneath the duvet, I realised that—for all his efforts and intentions—his words solved nothing.

Nothing he had to say would.

Because nobody in the pack had ever fucked up like I had.

Probably no one else in the pack ever would.

As the hopelessness of the situation crashed into me like a frigging juiced-up juggernaut, crushing my skull with the ease of a viable force, until my brain seemed on the verge of implosion, I couldn't help but wonder how the hell everything had gotten so out of control.

The whole bloody ordeal with Brook had only ever meant to be something simple. Something fun. I hadn't anticipated the unexplainable need to cling to some remnant of the female I had no reason to stay in touch with—to *want* to stay in touch with. Maybe I should have questioned it harder. I mean ... a cat, for frick's sake.

For a second, I wanted to growl at myself, to shake off the words I'd refused to acknowledge until then. Brook's origins had never bothered me before. They'd never been an issue. I couldn't have given a shit what form she changed into. All I'd cared about was how being with her made me feel.

It was no longer just a bit of fun, though. No longer just about me. Or me and her. Not like when I'd first met up with her.

Even on reflection, I still didn't get why I'd called her to link up.

The very first time I'd laid eyes on Brook, while the vampires had us, she'd been confined in a cage like a storm trapped in a bottle, and I didn't think I'd ever been so captivated by a sight.

I'd fast tried to shove out the dodgy ideas my head had entertained each time I'd looked at her. And I thought I'd succeeded, until she'd seemed all pally with Ethan, and I got slapped with a bad case of possessiveness I'd never have imagined even if they included prep classes for it in school.

Even once we'd all escaped, I should have walked away, pretended I never met her. Maybe I would have, if she hadn't stuck around, lingering at Nate's house as though in no rush to go home, visiting the room I recovered in from morning 'til night and watching me, those golden eyes of hers sending out all kinds of signals that should have sent me running for the hills.

Instead, I'd run in the opposite direction.

Straight to her.

I'd continued to do so ever since.

"Jesus Christ," I breathed into the darkness.

The whole blasted affair had gone more than out of control. It had raved like a bull confronted by a red cloak. Fizzed and sparked like an unsecure Catherine wheel.

I thought I'd done a decent job of containing the situation. What kind of fricking idiot did that make me?

Sure, the pack'd find a way to accept my *human* female. What about a cat, though?

What about Brook?

We had no fucking chance. How hadn't I seen that sooner?

Or maybe I'd planned on screwing around behind everyone's backs for the rest of my life?

Or until I got bored.

Brook deserved better than that.

She deserved better than me.

As though on autopilot, I slid a hand beneath my pillow and drew out my mobile. The screen lit up my room the instant I clicked the menu and navigated through to my texts. No incomings from Brook remained. I deleted those as soon as I read them—which only worked to solidify how sordid our relationship seemed.

My thumb clicked to compose a new message and began dancing across the keys:

Brook you deserve better. What we're doing can't work.

Probably for the best if we just cut our loss—

"Fuck!" My thumb hovered. What the hell was I doing?

Text message had to be about the shittiest way out there for me to tell her I was calling it off. Brook, at the very least, deserved to be told in person.

I scrubbed a hand over my face.

I'd tell her next time I saw her.

Definitely, on Monday, everything would be set straight.

So, if it was for the best, why did my chest ache at the thought?

7

Hiding out in the guesthouse Sunday morning didn't work as well as Brook had hoped. After spending the entirety of Saturday in the house, and enduring one 'spontaneous' visit after another, she'd ignored her father's orders and slunk off the instant her parents turned their backs.

From breakfast until supper the day before, Toms had shown up, claiming to be in the area so they thought they'd 'just stop by'. Funny how every single one of them had spent their visit sending surreptitious glances Brook's way, and smiling any time they found her gazing at them.

By bedtime, she'd about had her fill of the blasted males.

Unfortunately, with the arrival of three visitors, all by ten a.m., Brook suspected Sunday would fare no better.

She'd managed to hide for only twenty minutes, before Clive rounded the rear deck and interrupted the mental recall of her last conversation with Kyle.

"Here you are," Clive said, climbing the singular step to the shaded decking. "Hiding out?"

Gaze lifting from the pale taupe's and browns of the woodlands, to the cool blue of the sky, Brook silently asked for strength to deal with him. Her patience had begun to wear dangerously thin at around Tom number three of the weekend.

Clive happened to be the ninth.

With each new one who called, Brook gave more and more credence to Stefan's words—however much she hated to. Only a fool would continue to argue the point when everything that had occurred led toward his imparted information being truth—even if her mind did rebel each time she mentally approached the subject.

Clive hooked a foot around one of the patio chairs and dragged it nearer to where Brook sat wrapped in a fleecy blanket. "At least you didn't lock yourself inside this time," he said, plonking himself down.

"Maybe I did not feel a yen to today," she said without looking at him.

He chuckled. "Or maybe your dad's been tossing more orders your way."

She heaved a deep sigh and rested her head back against the rear of her seat. "Do you never get bored of all of this, Clive?"

His chair creaked at her side. "Bored of what, exactly?"

"Of ..." She hesitated only because to openly voice it could bring punishment if shared with the wrong ears.

"When have you ever held back what's on your mind?" he asked.

Her hair brushed the woven wicker as she turned her head to face him, and she found his warm gaze fixated on her beneath his pale hair gently tousled by the breeze. "Of the Coalition way of life?" she said. "Of never being given a choice."

"I thought we already talked about this." He smiled. "Just 'cause you don't like the choices on offer, doesn't mean they aren't exactly that. Besides, you're stressing over nothing." He lounged back into his seat, fingers laced behind his head as he stared out toward the woodlands. "'Bout time you relaxed and let yourself accept that you have a destiny ..."

At my side ... Brook mouthed, rolling her eyes.

"... at my side ..."

She kicked at a lone pebble on the decking. *As my mate ...*

"... as my mate ..."

A sigh escaped.

"You know I can make you happy if you just give me the chance."

Here we go again.

"And if you weren't so damned stubborn, you'd understand you made your choice a long time ago—ever since you showed no interest in any other male member of the Coalition, ever since ..."

You gave me your heart.

"... you gave me your heart."

Brook shifted and stared back up at the porch overhang as she slow-released a breath. The discussion echoed numerous ones she and Clive had shared since she'd turned eighteen.

She'd spent the six years since trying to explain that, just because they had snuck off together as children to climb trees and swim in the stream, Brook did not consider Clive her soul mate. Six years of trying to drum into his obtuse skull that a plastic heart she'd dug from the stuffing inside her teddy, given behind the guesthouse one Sunday afternoon, had been the act of a child, not a teenager in love.

Yes, she loved Clive, in a weird, connected kind of way. How could she not when they had spent so many hours together?

In love with him, though? No, she had never been that—no matter how much he hinted at, or *needed*, it.

Maybe she should have felt sorry for him. In a way, she did. Especially after meeting Kyle and coming to comprehend how much it hurt to long for something she could never fully have. She would never show Clive, though—and he would never thank her for it—so Brook kept her opinions to herself, and murmured her usual end to the conversation of, "Yes, well, you always were easily impressed."

He chuckled, deep and low, and Brook couldn't help but smile.

In truth, if Brook had been pushed into making her choice months earlier, the decision would have been an easy one, because Clive was, without doubt, the most desirable tadpole of those in the option pond.

Thanks to the run of events in the autumn, though, everything had changed.

Not only had her kidnap, and being missing for weeks, panicked the entire Coalition over the potential loss of one of their females, it had also been the catalyst for her meeting Kyle.

Since then, life had pretty much rolled right on down complication hill with no bottom in sight. The longer she rolled, the faster she seemed to spin, hauling her thoughts and emotions along with the momentum.

"Been a while since I've seen you smile," Clive said.

The instant he dragged her back to the moment, her lips uncurved, a frown settling in.

"Come on, Brook." He reached for her chin and turned her toward him. "I didn't mean anything by it."

Only truth shone from the brightness of his eyes as she stared up at him, her bottom lip caught between her teeth as she worried it. "Stefan told me something yesterday."

"And it was something decipherable that didn't end in him trying to dry hump your leg? Shocking." Despite the lightness of his tone, his face held only seriousness.

"Tell me, Clive ... what have you heard about my birthday in two weeks?"

His eyes shifted too fast, his head following a split second later as he released her and rested his elbows on his knees.

Brook's pulse increased. "Clive?"

He glanced Brook's way before twisting away again. "Stefan's got a mouth as big as his fucking ego."

"So, it is true?"

Furrows cut deep lines across his forehead. "I hoped you wouldn't have to find out."

"And how, exactly, did you think you would achieve that, when I am going to be stuck on a stupid pedestal an—"

"I've been trying for weeks to bloody side-line you, Brook, so it wouldn't get to that." His hands clenched.

"But your stubborn head can't see when the only way out of a potential fricking disaster is being handed to you on a plate."

"And you're doing it for purely selfless purposes?" She couldn't quite keep the sarcasm from her voice.

"I was doing it because I happen to give a shit about you, Brook!"

The sound of tyres rolling across gravel had both their heads jerking up before she could retaliate.

Brook's shoulders stiffened at the crunch of the brakes and doors opening and slamming. "Whoever next?"

Clive stood, his chair giving a protesting groan, and he marched the length of the decking. He hadn't even reached the end, when a second set of wheels sent pebbles pinging, followed by a third.

As Brook thrust to her feet, the blanket slid from her shoulders and pooled around the backs of her knees.

Clive ducked his head around the corner. "Shit!" He gave a low growl. "Roland's here ..."

Roland King—Rufus's eldest son, whose arrogance made Stefan's fade into the background. A tremble visited Brook's knees as she stepped away from her chair.

"... with Stefan in tow," Clive continued.

A faint prickle grazed the base of her skull. "Who else?" The question arrived on a whisper.

"Ray, with Lewis and Mike ..."

She made the drop down from the porch to the grass without taking her attention from Clive.

"... and Ian's come on his own in the third car ..."

The ground beneath her ballet pumps held springiness, as she unconsciously stepped back again.

"Guess Don really did go and make the announcement official, then," Clive said, cursing under his breath.

Brook stilled. "What announcement?"

He straightened from his spying and turned back to her, a deep sadness reflecting in his eyes.

When he didn't speak, her jaw clenched. "*What* announcement, Clive?"

His chest rose with his deep sigh. "That you're ready to become a Queen."

"No." She shook her head, disbelieving, despite Stefan's warning, despite all the visitors and interest evidencing exactly that, despite Clive's confirmation. "*No!*"

She spun and bolted for the trees.

"Shit!" Feet thudded the ground after her. "Brook!"

Brook only ran faster.

Clive and Stefan and all the other male Toms could have their height, their bulk, and their extra strength. Brook would take her speed any day. After all, that had been how she'd survived growing up around the males all those years.

The barely-there breeze would have meant a stagnant atmosphere, if not for the fresh crispness winter brought with it, and she sucked in air, as her arms pumped at her sides, blowing it back out again as her feet pounded leaves that had fallen but made no effort to depart. She paid no attention to the other occupants of the woodlands as she made sharp veers in an attempt to cut the shortest path. Little other than the heavier footfalls of Clive carried over the roar of blood rushing through her ears, anyway, and even that soon dropped, both in nearness and volume.

Weaving around the trees took little skill. With no foliage to add substance to the timber, very few obstacles reached out to snare her passage. She didn't seem to have any particular plan in mind—certainly no route mapped out. Brook simply knew she needed to escape, and she'd never feel as though she'd accomplished that while on the side of the perimeter housing all those trying to suffocate her.

In less than a minute, she could distinguish the fawn-hued bricks of the bordering wall from the knotted density of trunks, and she forced herself faster.

"Brook, don't!" Clive growled like he'd guessed her intent.

Ignoring him, she raced for a tree whose branches hugged and overhung the stonework.

Muscles contracted throughout her thighs and calves as she thrust herself upward. Fingers gripping one of the leaner branches, she hauled her body up, swinging higher than the limb. Her knees bent, body crouched, and her soles barely made contact with the bark before she sprang across and landed atop the wall.

She pivoted just as Clive slammed to a halt below her.

"What the hell are you doing, Brook?" His chest heaved as he fought to regain his breath from the sprint. "It's not safe out there for you on your own."

She jerked her chin toward her father's house. "What makes you think it is safe for me in there?"

"Dammit, Brook. If you'd just give me a chance, you know I'd protect you."

She shook her head. "I cannot *deal* with this."

"Then *Choose me*." He brought his fist to his chest. "Choose me now, and this will all go away. I'll *make* it go away."

"I can't. Please ..." Her brows pulled tight at the beseeching in his expression. "Do not make me .... I can't." She took a step back.

Clive matched her with a stride forward. "Brook, please ... *stay*."

She shook her head and dropped down the seven feet, until uneven dirt greeted her feet and a shockwave pulsed through each leg, despite the bracing of her knees.

"Goddamnit, Brook!"

She pressed her forehead to the wall, closing her eyes. "You say you're my friend, Clive."

"You know I am," he said, his voice deep.

"You say you care about me."

"You *know* I do!"

"Then, you'll cover for me, because if I do not get out of here, I will go insane."

When no argument arrived after a pregnant enough pause, she turned and walked away.

A thump hit the bricks before she'd taken more than a handful of steps, and she spun back to find Clive balancing atop the structure.

Hands fisted, his body leaned toward her as though it took effort to hold himself off. "Tell me you're coming back," he said.

She couldn't help the hesitation before she gave a reluctant nod.

"*Promise* me, Brook. Swear on it that you'll be back, or so help me, I'll jump down off this wall and drag you back inside, even if it means you'll never forgive me."

The gulp attempting to block the words leaving her throat should have shocked her, yet she couldn't bring herself to be surprised at her disinclination to return. Still, she gave another small nod. "I promise."

8

"Get a move on, you three!" Dad's gruff voice boomed up the stairs, only slightly muffled by the water hitting the shower glass.

"Before I have to come drag you down here myself," Danny said, impersonating dad.

"Before I have to come drag you down here myself," Dad said.

Dan chuckled and the sounds of teeth brushing kicked back in. Knocking off the faucet, I gave my head a sharp shake to loosen the lingering moisture from my ears, and nudged open the door to a room almost as fogged as the section I stepped from. Towels sat in their usual pile on the hamper; I grabbed one and wrapped it around my waist, and a second one to scrub over my hair.

"You almost done?" I asked Dan, who'd gone into trance mode in his brushing.

"Woh?" He twisted round, white froth covering his lips, and pointed to his ear. "I can' her ylou wi all thisss stdeam."

"Idiot." I tossed the towel at his head, reaching for another as a thud hit the bathroom door.

It swung inward to expose Josh. His gaze landed on me. "Either that's your mobile buzzing in your room, or there're sex toys you haven't told us about having a party in there without you."

"Shit." I shot forward, sending a growl at Josh when he sidestepped into my path. "Move, moron."

"You know I could've just answered it myself, instead of telling you." He wiggled his eyebrows. "Found out who your mystery caller is."

"Not if you want to live to see twenty-five," I said, shouldering him out the way as I ducked onto the landing.

Seven long strides and a right turn took me into my room. Only silence came from within. I retrieved my mobile from beneath my pillow, glancing down at the screen. Two missed calls.

Both from P.

Bollocks.

"Who is it, then?"

I turned.

Josh stood propped against my doorframe, hands tucked into the pockets of his sweatpants.

I marched across to him. "Out!" A shove against his chest sent him to the landing, and the door slammed shut on him with a kick of my foot.

Static hit my ear for a second after I pressed dial. As it rang out, I perched my rear on the end of my bed and rubbed the towel across my hair some more.

Breaths blasted into my ear. Loud. Panted. Uncontrolled. Accompanied by a quiet pattern of beats—like running feet. "Kyle." The word sounded more like a gasp.

My heart thumped inside my chest as I thrust to my feet. "What's wrong?"

"Had to ..." The cadence of the footsteps slowed, and she drew in a few long inhalations. "Had ... to get out."

"I'm coming to get you." I slid my top drawer open and yanked out the first pair of boxers my fingers folded around. "Where are you?"

"On my way to you," she said, breaths a little less erratic.

"On foot?" *Shit!* Something must have gone really wrong for her to take off like that. I dropped my waist towel on the floor and fed my feet into my boxers. "Listen, just hole up somewhere, stay put, and I'll come grab you."

"Okay ..." Her steps started up a new pattern, less aggressive than before. "There's a roadside diner on the A-forty-nine—"

"I know the one." I'd driven past it on my way to and from Brook's. "Just get there and wait. I'll be as quick as I can."

It took less than a minute once the call had ended to pull on jeans and a lumberjack shirt. With a pair of socks in my hand, I yanked open my bedroom door.

Josh still stood there—exactly where I'd shoved him to. "Going somewhere?"

"Yes." I jogged down the stairs, pausing at the bottom to sit and pull on my socks and trainers.

"Where?" The top step creaked as Josh lowered to it. "Need some backup?"

"Mind it. And no. I got this." I gripped the newel post to tug myself up, and rounded the staircase toward the kitchen.

Dad leaned against the sink, his folded arms reflecting his impatience over us not being ready. His gaze chased me as I crossed the room and grabbed my truck keys off the rack. "At least one of you's ready."

"I'm not coming," I said without turning.

"Care to run that by me again, Son?"

I glanced over my shoulder, already heading for the hallway. "I have to go out."

His footsteps followed. "I hope you mean to Nate's."

"Not today," I said, twisting the catch of the front door. Chill air snuck into the house as I exited. I hopped down the couple of steps to the driveway.

Dad's shadow merged with mine, he stuck so close. "Care to tell me where you think you're going, instead?"

"Out." I hit the remote for the pickup. The lights flashed twice as the mechanics of the locks whirred. "I have something to do."

"We're expected at Nate's in ten minutes." Although nobody really minded whether, or not, we turned up at each other's houses on time, Nate and Dad always had it stuck in their heads about it being rude to show up late when someone else was cooking a meal. "You missed dinner with them a fortnight ago. *And* a couple of weeks before that. This isn't acceptable, Kyle."

I opened my door and turned to face him. "It's not the end of the world if I don't eat with you."

"I expected you with us this week. I assured Nate I'd make sure you showed."

"Well, you shouldn't have."

He stared at me a long moment, disappointment warring with anger in his eyes. "What the hell is going on with you?"

"It's nothing."

"It's not *nothing* when you start putting it before the pack."

I opened my mouth to argue more, but figured I didn't really have much of a case. "I gotta go," I said, and climbed into the truck, the slam of my door shutting out his retaliation. I couldn't bring myself to look at him as I started the engine and drove away.

The roadside diner, ingeniously named THE ROADSIDE DINER, looked exactly how it sounded. A silver, rounded caravan-type structure resembling places typically seen in American films, set back a little from the road, with a couple of trees snuggled close, and a petrol station as companion. Beyond the bus-like windows, people occupied two thirds of the inner space, and on an outside bench that had tree trunks for legs sat Brook, face hidden behind her long curtain of dark hair.

With her hands tucked between her knees and shoulders hunched, she looked frozen—probably was with only the shirt on she wore. I brought the truck to a stop and gave a quick blast of the horn.

Brook's head snapped up, her gaze instantly locking onto mine. I waited for the inevitable smile. It didn't come. In fact, she seemed weary as she pushed up from the bench and stretched out her fingers and shoulders.

I watched her closely when she began the short trek across the grass to where I'd parked, my attention snagged on her every move. The pale denim covering her lower half hugged every inch, even more fitted than the khaki green shirt she wore gaping slightly over her breastbone, where she'd left the top buttons undone. Even the mud on her feet looked like a lucky bastard from where I sat.

Had I really almost ended it less than two days ago? I shook my head at my idiocy.

By the time Brook reached the passenger side, her expression had softened a touch, and she showed a small smile when she pulled open the door. Trouble brewed in her eyes, though, darkening them to a pale terracotta, and I knew somebody, somewhere, had pissed her off. "Hey," she said.

I inclined my chin. "'Sup?"

She shook her head and climbed up into the seat. "It's nothing." The words sounded as big a lie as when I'd spoken them to Dad before leaving. "I just needed to get out for a while."

I stared at her for a few seconds once she'd shut her door, hoping she'd change her mind and spill her worries, but she didn't. She didn't even meet my scrutiny. "Okay," I said, not pushing the matter. "Where did you want to go?"

More silence followed for a few beats. When she swung to face me, her gaze skimmed past before darting back to settle on mine. "Somewhere ..." She sighed, the action full of something akin to sadness. "Somewhere I can just be myself."

Fighting a frown, I nodded, the gesture slow and deliberate as my mind raced over the decision it made. "No problem. I know just the place."

Even as I wove us toward the exit, I couldn't help but question the sanity of my plan.

***

Brook had never been to Kyle's home, only Ethan's—and the similarities between the two properties surprised her. Each had a double fronted, gated entrance, and a sweeping driveway, which spread outward to the surrounding trees and disappeared around both sides of the house.

If not for the resemblance, Brook may not have realised their destination. "Kyle ..." She twisted in her seat, her heart thumping, head already shaking at the thought of the reception.

"No one's here," he said. "We're safe." Despite his words, his eyes held a platoon of worry, and he seemed to be bracing himself as he blew out a breath and gave a small nod. "Let's go."

He climbed from the pickup, and Brook followed suit, though she couldn't help but send a hesitant glance toward the house as her feet landed on the driveway.

"It's fine," Kyle said. "I promise."

It probably took only seconds for Kyle to work open the front door, but it seemed much longer to Brook as she tossed glances over each shoulder, expecting to be caught. She only realised entry had been permitted when a slight tug on her arm drew her into the hallway.

Even through dimness born of winter light, Brook could see the interior resembled the Holloway's house as much as the exterior did, with its pale walls and high ceiling, as well as three panelled doors leading off the space around the staircase that stood to the right.

Kyle reached around her, and the front door clicked shut at her rear, deepening the shadows further. When he drew back, his gaze landed on hers, expression loaded with questions Brook didn't know how to answer—or didn't want to.

"You okay?"

She nodded, a jerky action—one the tightening of Kyle's eyes told her he saw right through.

After a few long beats of her staring at him, mentally willing him to let it go, he jerked his chin to the right, a smile pulling at his lips. "Want the tour?"

She released a small breath, thankful for the distraction. "Sure."

The door on her left led to a generous sitting room, with walls painted a warm vanilla and chenille furniture in a rich shade of plum. As Kyle stood with his hands tucked into the pockets of his jeans, Brook imagined him stretched out on the largest sofa surrounded by his brothers, while their father watched over them in that quiet way of his she'd once observed.

"It looks warm in here," she said, mind instantly flashing to the cool whites of the lounge at home.

"It used to be," Kyle said, his tone almost matter-of-fact. "Before Mum died." He shrugged when she looked to him, already twisting back for the door. "Come on. I'll show you the rest."

The entrance opposite the sitting room swung open with a nudge of Kyle's fingers. A huge corner desk dominated the space, supported by a room-wide bookcase filled with rows of red binders.

"Dad's office." Kyle barely even stepped in as he pointed to the far wall, where maps and charts, some kind of blue prints, a whiteboard calendar and a pin-board hung in orderly haphazardness. "He's better at the paperwork side of the business than Nate, so this is pretty much the control station for the company. Exciting stuff."

Brook's lips threatened to curve at the droll quality to his voice, and she twisted to follow when Kyle backed out of the doorway, pausing as he balanced on the bottom stair.

"Not much up there." He pointed over his shoulder toward the upper landing, a shyness seeming to shroud him as he gave a small shrug. "Other than my room." His mouth twitched a little, along with his eyebrows. "Want to see?"

"Yes." Her response came from burning curiosity as much as the chance to hedge for longer. "Of course I do."

With a quiet chuckle, he began a slow backward ascent, his gaze holding Brook hostage as she trailed him, each step giving a tiny creak beneath their weight. Five doors stood along the landing, two on each side and one directly ahead. If the same as the Holloway house, Brook already knew the bathroom faced her, and the other four would lead to bedrooms.

Kyle halted between the first pair of doors, and tugged down on the handle to the one on Brook's left, inviting her in with a sweeping wave of his hand. "My pad."

She poked her head around the frame, absorbing all, from the cool grey walls to the granite coloured carpet, and bedding as black as the coat Brook donned as cat. Entering and stopping at the foot of the bed, she reached down and brushed her fingers across the dark cotton as she inhaled, long and deep, her lids lowering for an instant at the masculine musk she drank in. "It smells of you in here," she said.

"I wish it could smell of you." Heat hit her back as he came to stand right behind her. "Do you have any idea how much I've fantasised about you being in here?"

Probably as much as she had herself. She shook her head.

His breath fluttered her hair as he leaned in close, arm snaking around as he pointed to the bed. "All I have to do is close my eyes, and I picture you there."

Brook stared at the spot, easily imagining a few scenarios of her own. As her head tilted to the side, Kyle's hand slid across her waist, toying with the flesh beneath the hem of her shirt. When his face nuzzled past her hair to the pulse below her ear, her breath caught, releasing as his nostrils flared against her skin, and a low groan left his throat.

She contemplated giving in, relaxing back, allowing Kyle to support her, to pleasure in that way of his that always left her purring.

Until her earlier conversation with Clive forced its way in, resounding inside her head like the worst passion killer on earth. Her shoulders stiffened.

Kyle halted—his lips against her neck, hands across her stomach. He seemed to hover there, as though awaiting explanation.

How could Brook explain, though, that her mind had been elsewhere? Or where, even?

He pressed a single kiss to her jawline. "Hungry?"

She gave a small headshake. "Not really."

"Well, I am," he said, linking his fingers through Brook's and drawing her along with him as he crossed to the door. "I'm missing out on dinner right now, which means I need to feed myself. Keep my energy up." He paused on the landing, his eyebrow quirked up. "I'll be little use to you if I'm passed out."

Brook trailed after him as he took the first step. "Do not be so sure of that."

9

The first time I'd shown my dick to a girl, at age fourteen, had been pretty awkward. Topping that was the afternoon I lost my virginity to Louise Beckett a couple of years later, when I'd had no clue what to do with my tool in relation to a female—though, that soon changed.

Neither of those equated to the nerves that'd kicked in at the thought of finally getting Brook in my room—and then she'd gone and planked on me, making it a hundred times worse.

Brook had never seemed uncomfortable around me before—not even the first time we hooked up after she'd returned home from the kidnapping. A coffee had led to a kiss; the kiss had led to an afternoon in a hotel room. Every meeting since had ended up as heated as the first.

Whatever had been bugging her when she'd called obviously hadn't abated. Maybe she'd come to the same conclusion I had about the hopelessness of our so-called relationship.

Maybe *she* planned on ending it.

My breath stalled as that possibility smacked me. Sure, I'd been all for doing exactly that the next time I saw her—but the second I'd spotted Brook sitting outside that diner, I knew I wouldn't be going through with it any time soon.

What if she took that decision out of my hands, though?

A sideways glance toward Brook on our descent of the stairs exposed none of her intentions, and my fingers held a sudden itch to grab her by the shoulders and shake the words out of her.

I resisted, though. As much as I wanted to demand she explain her mood, I figured pushing her would get me nowhere. Since I'd picked her up, her lips had been clammed up as tight as a secret agent's.

Swallowing my concerns, I led Brook into the kitchen, swinging her around and settling her cute butt into a dining chair. "You sure you're not hungry?"

She merely shook her head.

"I won't poison you. Promise."

Her lips curved in a small smile that didn't reach her eyes, and she still only responded with a half-shrug.

Biting my tongue against words I wanted to spew, and clenching my hands against reaching for her, I spun away.

Coolness bled out when I opened the fridge door. The bizarre array of food within would never have worked together in a million years for anyone who lived for Michelin grade meals. Me, though? I didn't much care so long as the stuff was edible.

Silence hit my back like a barrier to her emotions, as I slid out plates, cans and jars, and wedged them onto a tray. I wondered if she watched me as I worked, but I forced myself not to check, to remain facing away. If nothing else, my lack of focus on her might result in her arranging her thoughts to share.

I only hoped they wouldn't leave me reeling.

Once I had as much grub as the tray could hold, I added a spoon, pasted a grin onto my face, and turned back to find only a heavy blend of misery and worry in her eyes. I wanted to drop the tray and wrap her in my arms there and then, but instead I gripped the handles tighter and brandished the offering beneath her chin. "Chocolate mousse, pickled onions, cheese, cherries, salami and ... squirty cream."

Her nose scrunched up a little. "Interesting combination."

I plonked the tray down on the table and sat in the chair beside her. "Food's food. The company, however ..."

She stared at me for a few long beats. "Ditto."

"Really?" I popped a cherry in my mouth and chewed, tossing the empty stem back onto the tray. "'Cause you don't seem too happy to be around me today." Frowning at myself the instant the words left me, I ripped off a chunk of cheese and rammed it in my mouth, like that would propose an indifference my tone hadn't offered.

"It is not you," she said, averting her eyes.

I swallowed, the cheese seeming way too big as it passed my throat. "This, um ... this the whole *it's not you, it's me* speech I sense coming on?"

"What?" Her gaze flashed to mine. "No. Nothing like that. At all."

I released a breath. Eyebrow raised, I waited for her to elaborate. When she glanced away, I wondered if she would.

Females, as a species, didn't generally baffle me. I found one I wanted, invited her to play, she usually accepted, and we parted with false promises to call. Brook, however, and my inane need to repeat-perform on every damn meeting, posed a whole alien set of rules and practices and crap to interpret—none I'd probably ever figure out.

She reached past me for the tray and plucked up the spoon, scooping out a blob of mousse and aiming it my way.

I lifted my gaze from the dessert, finding her focus on me, imploration in her eyes. "Trying to shut me up with food?"

"You said you were hungry and needed to eat."

I obediently opened my mouth, and she slid the unwavering spoon across my tongue, giving a nod of satisfaction once I'd swallowed.

Taking her cue, I picked out a fleshy cherry, squirted it with cream, and waved it at her. "It's no fun eating alone."

Her lips parted with far more compliance than I'd expected, the cream smearing the corners as they folded around the cherry.

Unable to help myself, I ducked closer and licked across the synthetic sweetness.

She stiffened beneath my touch.

Again.

Poised a hairsbreadth from her, tension knotted across my shoulders as my mind conjured reasoning it could scarcely bear to contemplate, as well as a question my throat wanted to block from leaving. "Did ... somebody hurt you?"

Her head jerked side to side, a slight tremor rippling through her body as glossiness invaded her eyes.

I blew out a slow breath, relieved yet apprehensive all at once. "Then, talk to me." Pressing my temple to hers, I lowered my lids. "'Cause ... Christ, Brook, your muteness today is driving me crazy."

Her breaths drifted across my cheek. In my periphery, her hand curled into a fist. "My father is going to make me a Queen."

I frowned—at her low tone as much as the words—unsure if I'd heard her correctly. When I drew back, her eyes held a hint of something I thought—*hoped*—I'd never see in them. *Fear*. "I don't understand."

The clock on the wall behind the table ticked alongside the expanding silence, and my pulse picked up its pace to match.

"A Queen ... is a female deemed ready to breed," Brook said, her voice small—resigned.

I stared at her for a long moment, the words echoing in my head like a distant spattering of incoherent sounds. The second they glued themselves together, I shot to my feet, the chair clattering a protest, and as I stalked away, my hands clenched and unclenched, pulling the tendons taut throughout my forearms.

A smear across the bottom corner of the window marred the clarity of the grass, as I stared out at the garden, pain pounding the inside of my chest. "He's going to mate you. That's what you're saying, isn't it?" I could barely squeeze the words out, my jaw locked so hard. "To one of your own? Like some primeval fucking pre-arrangement."

"Not exactly."

I tossed a quick glance over my shoulder, catching the despair in her eyes, and turned away again. "What does that mean?"

"The Coalition is governed by its own rules."

I growled. "And what the hell does that *mean*, Brook?"

"In the Coalition, only those on the Council are entitled to unquestioned long-term mating." Her voice sounded heavy with emotion, despite the calmness with which she spoke. "All others have to prove they have been in a monogamous relationship for it to be approved and permitted to continue as such."

Somehow, I doubted ours would meet the mark. I fully turned, bringing the high shine of her amber stare into view, the twisting of her hands in her lap, the way she chewed at her bottom lip. "Is that what you've been trying to tell me? This what all that *it's not you, it's me* shit was leading up to?"

"No."

"That you've had something more permanent—"

"No."

"—going on—"

"Give me a ch—"

"—and I've just been some experiment of curiosity on the side?" Each word rumbled from me, sending vibrations through my chest.

"No, damn you!" She shook her head, a tear leaking from each eye and balancing on her lashes. "When you are announced as a Queen, it is not to choose who you will be mated to." Her chest heaved beneath a shuddered breath. "It is to choose who will get to impregnate you first."

I blinked. "Excuse me?"

"They will make me breed with whoever is Chosen." She rubbed at her face, almost as if to hide, before her hands returned to her lap. "As soon as I have produced

81

their offspring, I will be put through the whole process again. And again. Until I am matched with a Tom who decides he wants to keep me and has enough standing to make the claim stick." She swiped at her still-damp lashes. "And I have no idea how to stop it from happening."

"Simple." My teeth ached from all the clamping. "Don't fucking play by their rules."

"I do not have that liberty." She turned away, but not before I caught the tremor of her lips. "As part of the Coalition—as a Council member's daughter—I am expected to obey."

The last few months proved she didn't always follow the rules. *Why the hell now?* I tamped down my rising fury. "Then, don't go back."

Her head whipped round to me. "Do you not see? I have nowhere else to go. Nowhere else I belong."

I wanted to yell at her, that she did fucking belong. She belonged with me, dammit. "You certainly don't belong with someone who doesn't deserve you. Someone who'll try to steal away everything that's you." I sniffed in a long breath through my nose, steadying my emotions as I studied her, usually so alive with self-assurance curled into herself. "Fuckers have already stolen enough of your fire."

"They always do. I behave like myself, they douse it. I argue, I dare speak out of line—have an *opinion*—they douse it. They always have." The skin pulled tight across her forehead, around her eyes. "You and Ethan are the first people in my life who have never tried to control me."

The aching in my chest intensified. "Because your attitude is one of the things I love about you. And your spark. Your energy. I love—" Swallowing down the near confession, I whirled back to the window, bounced my fist against the steel of the sink.

Brook didn't utter a sound as I stood there, didn't even seem to shift in her seat.

Beyond the glass, a patch of lawn glowed brighter than the rest beneath a snatch of sun. My pulse thrummed at what had almost left my lips—but I'd have meant it, if I'd said it. I'd never have meant anything more, and that should have terrified me.

Maybe it did.

I spun and marched back to her, righting my seat as I sank to its surface and faced her. "I love everything about you," I said before I could stop myself again. "And you're wrong. So wrong. You do have other options. Let me help you. I'll find you somewhere else to be. Somewhere close to here. To me. Where I can watch over you. The company has apartments," I said, my mind racing at dumb miles per hour, quashing any questions over what seemed an obvious solution. "I can locate an empty one if you just give me a couple of days—"

"You make me sound like a mistress you are too ashamed to show to your family."

"No! It wouldn't be like that!" I untangled her hands, clutched them in mine, panic I couldn't quite decipher firing the blood through my veins. "It would only be until I can tell the pack about us. Just until then."

Brook's stare never wavered from mine, a storm of emotions roiling through the rustic orbs.

I tightened my grip, tugging her forward until only a handful of inches separated me from her. "You deserve better than being treated like a—" *Whore*. I bit back the word. "Shit, you deserve better than *me*."

"Maybe I only want you," she said.

My heart booted my ribcage in approval of her words, and I bridged the gap until my lips met the corner of hers, pressed a kiss there. "Then, let me help you," I said without moving away. "Please." Another brush of my lips followed with a heady inhalation. "I need this, Brook."

Moments passed before she whispered, "Okay."

"Okay?" I twisted my head a little, bringing her eyes into view.

She nodded, a tiny movement.

Before she could change her mind, or maybe to prevent it, I threaded my fingers around the nape of her neck and covered her mouth with mine.

As I knew she would, she yielded, her lips parting. A small sigh drifting from her, she gripped my shirtfront. When she gave a pull, I complied until my chest pushed against her arched body, and wove an arm around her until her butt sat snug in my palm.

Her thighs parted when I pulled her across mine. A slight lift tucked her pelvis snug to my stomach. Heat chased her hand as it trailed up from my chest and into my hair, her tug tilting my face up as her tongue darted out and her lips took more. "

Kyle." A breathy whisper.

I growled, grasping her tighter, my hips all but screaming to be urged up. When I nipped at her bottom lip, a tremor rolled her entire length, and her lids fluttered closed before reopening to reveal golden pools so filled with desire they almost spilled over.

"Run with me," she said.

I never needed asking twice. Never.

Thrusting to my feet, my arms ensnared her even as her thighs trapped me. On my march for the back door, I nibbled along her jaw, and her head tipped back as a long, slow purr vibrated from her. Suckling on her throat to the sound of her quiet moan, I grappled for the door handle, snatching hold and yanking the door open.

Coldness attempted to shroud us as we exited, but it barely penetrated the little bubble of warmth created by the proximity of our bodies. Still lost in her scent, her taste, I swept one hand the length of her spine, tangling my fingers in the trailing strands there, and the other beneath her, squeezing her butt until she pressed tighter against me than ever.

The lawn held springiness beneath my feet, despite the winter chill hardening it, or the sunshine that had dried the moisture from its tips. Finding her earlobe, I gave a small nip, chuckling at Brook's tiny yelp.

"You play with fire too often," she said, her head dipping down, doing some seriously amazing nuzzling of her own and kicking my thrum of a growl up a notch. "When will you learn I always get my own back?"

I shivered as her breaths snaked beneath my shirt collar to warm my chest. "Hopefully, never."

In under a minute, the first shadow of the tree line coated us, and I grasped Brook's hips and swung her down to her feet.

Blinking, she turned to the right, her eyes clearing fast. "Kyle ..." She glanced to the left. "You are insane. We can't run here."

"It'll be fine."

Living on opposing sides of the forest meant we could travel between each pack house as wolf, and we took full advantage of it whenever possible. Dad and my brothers had gone to Nate's through the forest—which meant they'd also be returning home that way.

However ... "We have hours before any of the others will pass through here." I ducked in to snatch a kiss, my fingers already reaching for her shirtfront, managing to get three of her buttons undone before she stilled my hands. "Trust me," I said, unfastening her some more.

In that moment, I could think of nothing better than experiencing my own forest with Brook, instead of having to sneak around in public woodlands where we constantly had to watch our backs.

"It'll be amazing," I said.

In my mind, it'd also be worth the risk.

10

Brook's entire being rebelled at the thought of going into the pack's forest, but Kyle's calm tone and the serenity in his eyes assured her of his confidence on the matter. Without even realising it, she'd stopped fighting with his fingers as he undid her buttons, though the distraction of his lips against hers might have been a contributing factor in that.

Kyle worked the linen of her shirt until it slid along her arms and fell to the ground. As Brook reached up and tugged at the buttons of his, he grinned against her lips, his mood vastly altered from his earlier sombreness.

She'd been to blame for that, though, hadn't she? Burden eased, from having shared her problems, she'd been left tangibly more relaxed herself. She could not believe she'd considered keeping it to herself, couldn't believe she'd made him beg to be told before opening her mouth.

His tug on her jeans stud, as she finished unfastening him, brought her bare torso into contact with his, and he abandoned the task only long enough to yank off his own shirt and toss it aside. Once he'd unzipped her, loosening her waistband, he smoothed his hands around her hips, over her lower back, dipping down until the denim hung below her hips. As his fingers found her rear beneath her knickers, he pressed her against his erection, chuckling when she gave a quiet gasp.

In response, she swept her palms across muscles that had become as familiar to Brook as her own, up over his biceps, across solid shoulders, tracing the scars left behind by the vampire bites. With a handful of his tangled hair, she yanked him down and reclaimed the kiss, her thigh already rising to hook over his hip, her lids already half-closed thanks to the tease of his tongue against hers.

"Keep this up ..." He grabbed her lip between his teeth, licking it on release. "... and we'll never get round to running."

"You say that every time," she said, though she lowered her foot back to the ground. "Yet, somehow, we always do."

Wriggling from his grasp, she flicked her pumps off and hooked her thumbs beneath her waistband, taking step after step backward as she worked the jeans over her thighs.

His gaze on her, Kyle lost his own trainers and unbuttoned his jeans. He and Brook shoved downward at the same time, kicking their denim off the rest of way until they both stood in no more than their underwear.

Brook shivered as she took in her fill. Shiny-white scars decorated the expanse of muscles across his chest, as well as his left shoulder, and she traced them to his right hip, across to the trim of his stomach, following his navel hairs all the way south to the evidence of his arousal.

With a slow smile, she brought her gaze back to Kyle's as she reached behind and unhooked her bra.

"Need some help with that?" he asked.

"I have had plenty of practice."

"Yeah, well, *I* could do with the extra practice. Takes way too long to get those things off."

Brook laughed, a low throaty sound, as she dropped her bra to the ground before shimmying from her knickers. Straightening, she allowed her gaze to travel the full length of him, her eyebrow arching up at his still-donned boxers. "Maybe it is you who needs help."

Kyle looked about to agree as he took a half-step toward her, but he halted and jerked his chin toward the trees to her rear. "Go on. Go, sniff around. I'll catch you up."

Brook breathed out a laugh and ducked behind the nearest oak, her mind already calling forth her beast, inviting her in to play.

The Shift prodded its way to the surface in response, and in the time it took her to emerge from the far side of the aged trunk, her form had altered. Front paws padded down on a mulch of fallen leaves, her thick coat already working to ward off the cool air, nose already searching for alien scents.

Recoiling at the overpowering concoction of the entire pack, she gave her head a sharp shake and switched to listening out for anything untoward as she slunk a slow circle around Kyle.

Through each break in the trees, an inward glance showed him crouched, the concentration in his features, the bulge of his muscles giving away the strain his change put upon them.

She paused for a second, head tipped to the side, as a ripple washed over him, causing anomaly to what she only saw as perfection. The moment his breaths snorted white puffs into the air, his hands fisting against the hard earth, she recommenced her sentry circumference.

As shifter, Brook's body did pretty much that—shift from one form to another. No pain. No discomfort. Only a tingle of sensation, like a delicate touch to newly-anaesthetised skin, fleeing across her body in a top-to-tail wave that lasted a couple of seconds.

Kyle's change, though, took minutes.

Minutes of bones breaking, each and every one giving a significant crack amongst the twisting of his muscles, and the snapping of his tendons like twanged string—throughout which, Kyle's body writhed into deformity as though it could escape the chasing agony if only it got out of its path.

Although his head hung during most of it, nothing could hide the strained veins at his temples. Nothing could disguise the grunts or gasps that gradually descended into growled interpretations. Nor mask the stench of sweat that made a slow saturation of his flesh with each new bone broken, each sinew stretched.

Despite how much it disturbed her to see him in so much pain, she always watched. The only stage Brook consciously looked away from was the restructuring of his spine. The rapid unlocking and locking of vertebra sounded on par with a sports clacker, to someone with enhanced hearing, and as the only time Kyle's complaint escalated to a groan, she could never bring herself to witness it, for she knew it had to be worse than what she could hear.

A creak of undergrowth had Brook's head whipping to the left. Farther along a trodden path, a brush shivered, settling a moment later once a bird broke free. As its wings hummed an enticement that sang to Brook's soul, her legs braced to run in temptation to play.

Only the stillness coming from Kyle's direction and his heaved breaths kept her steady.

Sending a hiss at her missed opportunity, she wove back around and padded into her worn circle to lounge down before her wolf.

His rustic coat held a shagginess Brook adored, especially on extremely cold evenings when curled up outdoors, its density more evident over his chest and around his throat, leading to finer hairs that speckled a muzzle not yet fully formed.

He lifted his head from where it hung, his gaze meeting Brook's for a moment as his breaths panted from him. When a quiet whine accompanied the stretch of his neck, Brook dipped her face to lick at her upturned paw, saving him the degradation of being stared at through his final stage, though no aversion could block out the crunch of restructuring facial bone.

Claws outstretched, she cleaned crumbs of soil from between her pads, her eyes closing at each sweep of her tongue. Even once Kyle's grunts had diminished, signalling an end to his torture, she continued with her lapping, feigning an indifference that would no doubt test his patience if she kept it going for too long.

A quiet huff came from his direction.

Brook paused for a second, smiling to herself as she swiped across her paw once more, before she dropped it to the ground and peered off to the side as though she hadn't heard.

His second beckon arrived in the form of a growl.

Taking her time, she pushed out her forelegs as she straightened her hinds, her tail giving a flick of faux annoyance. A little to her left, the gnarled roots of an oak escaped the hard earth, and she twisted that way. Her claws unsheathed en route, and she dug them into the exposed timber, using the anchor to steady herself as she stretched once more.

A slight head tilt showed Kyle, head low, shoulders high, eyes shining with anticipation, and quite possibly impatience, directed at her.

Whiskers twitching, she sniffed at the air. As wolf, Kyle's scent intensified, and the travelling breeze seemed filled with his flavour. Drawn by the enticement, she released her scratch post and slunk right, her body dropping low to the ground before she'd even reached him.

He didn't move, though the slant of his head suggested he tracked her, and the bunch of muscles throughout his legs told her he braced for her welcome.

With her chin dipped, the tips of her ears flattened as she nudged at his side, and he held himself steady as she slid beneath him. A rumble vibrated through her skull when she passed below his chest, and along her spine as she emerged on the other side, her body already angling toward his downturned face. Still partially entwined, she licked at his jaw, an upward sweep of her tongue that ended at his ear.

He gave a chuff, his rumble increasing, and she wove herself around his front, her eyes closing as she pushed into the thick ruff of fur protecting his throat, her pads pressed hard against the ground to get herself nearer.

Still, he didn't budge him from his position. He merely stood there as she slid around and began her inspection along his right side, pausing to sniff at his shoulder, his ribcage—his groin.

He growled and stepped away.

Brook chased him and brought her paw down on his flank, an effort to pin him that only resulted in a deeper warning and a jerk away of his tail end.

She hissed his way, and received a snorted response.

After staring at her for a handful of seconds, he edged closer, butted at her side. When she didn't heed, he took off at a run, and she twisted to follow, her pace matching his within a few beats.

As Brook became swallowed whole by the forest, surrounded by spectral shadows from looming trees, all of her concerns rapidly vanished, and her troubles became inconsequential whispers lost to the back of her mind.

Somewhere beyond her subconscious, animals fled their route, breeze stirred their sanctuary, the sky above altered hue to an icy pale grey. So in tune with the wolf racing at her shoulder, his muzzle thrust forward, ears pressed back, each thump of his paws matching a quieter echo from her own, she could have been in another world. One where all that existed was she and Kyle and a sense of freedom Brook seldom experienced.

As usual, while running with Kyle, everything else ceased to matter. Alongside awareness of each and every movement Kyle made, Brook silently registered each and every one of her own. The jolt of each landing. The contraction of muscle. Each upward leap for fallen tree limbs, each swerve around trunks.

The beat of her heart pulsed through her as a viable force, louder to her than that of the wolf beside her. A wolf she'd come to consider her own.

Their unlikely pairing should have been unnatural—canine running with feline, side by side—but it didn't seem that way to her. Brook could think of no place she'd rather be.

Ears constantly listening beyond whichever clearing they occupied, nose deciphering the atmosphere, and eyes peeled to see ahead, Brook located the perfect spot before they reached it.

She veered that way, a tight turn that Kyle mirrored.

No more than twenty feet away, a sycamore leaned as though drunk, its trunk bent and gnarled just above ground level, providing an ideal angle for her plan.

Waiting until parallel to the natural ramp, she made a subtle leap to the right, paws hitting bark, and she raced along the upward slope without a hitch to her stride.

Fifteen feet up, thick limbs branched off. Brook hopped to one on the left, to another afore it, and halted on the arm. Her balance swayed as she peeked over to the forest floor below with eagerness racing through her soul.

Nothing.

She inhaled.

Kyle's scent spiralled up on the breeze, so Brook knew him to be close, yet he didn't appear.

She tilted her head, ears twitching for sound.

Whenever she had pulled her stunt before, Kyle had continued running, oblivious to her deviation, until she would bound down from above, landing atop him, and take him by surprise.

She checked again, inhaling deeply.

Still no Kyle.

The branch she favoured trembled beneath her as a groan travelled through the wood like an echo, and she spun back the way she'd come.

Kyle balanced on the arched base of the trunk, his gaze on her, his front paw raised as he made a step upward.

Sneaky.

Maybe he hadn't always been as oblivious as she'd assumed. Knowing Kyle, he'd probably played along simply to keep her content.

Brook turned and settled on her perch, more than willing to wait out the show. She had never witnessed a dog climb a tree before, but then she had never hunted with a dog before she'd met Kyle.

He wobbled a little with his step.

Resting her chin down upon her foreleg, she gave an upward flick of her tail.

Much bulkier than Brook—weightier, too—Kyle seemed to swamp the wooden walkway as he made another move forward, and the entire tree shook beneath the pressure.

Brook lifted her head, tilting it when Kyle's low growl rumbled from him, her eyes half-closing in a pretend display of boredom.

As Kyle padded forward, she uncurled to stand, her chin dipped as she studied him.

A grunt burst from him, followed by a huff and a rough utterance, and he gestured off to the right—a series of complaints followed by an order to get down.

If able, Brook would have laughed aloud at his attempt at authority while in no position to negotiate.

In a show of defiance, she coiled her muscles tight throughout her shoulders and haunches, and sprang toward the intersection of branch and trunk. Her impact shook the tree, a ricochet of vibrations that shot toward Kyle and sent him into a sideways stumble.

He caught himself before toppling, his claws scratching at bark as he attempted to regain his grip. A growl rolled from him as he swung his head up and narrowed his eyes in her direction.

Crouching, Brook gave a deep mewl and sprang off to the right in a dive for the ground, leaving Kyle scrabbling for traction once more.

Small jolts splintered into her forelegs as she landed. She tucked in her hinds for the race away. Less than a second later, teeth clamped around her neck and drove her into the dirt.

With a screech of annoyance, she kicked back a leg, though the irritation was aimed far more at herself for underestimating Kyle than at her wolf himself.

She should have known better than to turn her back when taunting.

Her attack slid between his legs, missing any kind of target, and she wiggled harder.

Giving a quiet grunt, he nudged her down again before releasing his hold.

Brook rolled over to find him standing tall, his torso shading hers as his ears and nose twitched, his entire body tense as though on full alert.

She gave a questioning mew, but he continued to stare off somewhere into the distance, head tilted, bobbing his flared nostrils into the air. He sniffed, long and deep, his body leaning toward where his nose led.

With a grunt and a flick up of crumbling soil, he dove from over her and bolted into the trees.

Left behind on the hard ground, it took Brook only a singular inhalation to detect his enthusiasm.

Rabbit.

Brook took off after him with a yowled whine to wait.

11

Changing hurt like nobody's business, and only a werewolf without an ounce of common sense would jump up and race off when they didn't have to, especially since every one of my muscles screamed like the dude from *Psycho* had taken to them with his blade.

Despite it being bullshit, the pep talk Dad had given me as a teen, pre-transition, had always stuck in my mind as clear as the day he'd spoken it: 'Remember, Son, changing to wolf is the hard part. Everything else after that is easy.'

He'd forgotten to mention that changing *back* stung just as much.

The reversal used to bug my butt. *Still does*. With the initial transformation, the promise of a hunt always made the effort worthwhile. All I had to look forward to once I'd turned back was a trek home and the knowledge it would take hours to work off the lingering high on limbs already more than spent.

That had been before I met Brook.

The cat—getting to be with *her* post change—seriously made up for *any* amount of pain.

Head hung low, I attempted to reclaim control of my body, each breath I took heaving my chest. The breeze had picked up during the afternoon, and it chilled the sweat rivulets trailing the length of each arm. Though my eyes remained shut, inhalations detected every scent, my ears every sound, and I caught both feline musk and softly padded steps making a direct journey for me.

Barely below the surface, my inner wolf warred with wanting to curl up and play and needing to kick into action and attack.

Luckily for Brook, I couldn't be bothered to move.

The tickle of hair hit my butt first, and Brook's body slid the length of my spine, her breasts pressing against my back as her arms snaked around my torso.

My dick hardened in instant approval.

"Take your time, dog." The humour in her warm tone tugged at my lips. "I can wait."

I smiled, opening my eyes. "Evidently."

Her chuckle hummed through my spine, a second before her right hand shimmered into a black paw against my chest.

Oh, hell. "Don't be pulling none of that partial shift shit—" I sucked in breath when claws pierced my flesh, let out a growl as a second set of claws scraped across my abdomen. "Marking me again, Puss?"

"Always." As her breaths snaked over my back, her claws released their hold—but not before they'd scraped a duet of tracks across my ribs.

My lids fluttered on a groan, as my hands curled into fists against the urge to drag her down beneath me and lose what little control I'd regained. "Why don't you quit making like a rucksack and get your sweet arse where I can see it, instead?"

"And give in to your belief that I am easy prey?" Her abrasive tongue scratched across my lumbar. "Never."

In the next breath, she'd vanished.

Shit. Brook in a frisky mood meant she'd make me work for our fun. Better a frisky mood, though, than the one she'd arrived in, but then a good hunt could do that for the soul.

Ignoring the lingering ache in my limbs, I pushed up to stand, the muscles through my thighs clenching and releasing with the action. A quick glance around showed only bare timber, wiry brush, and hulking shadows.

No Brook.

I knew her to be near, though. She never went far.

A barely audible crunch sounded off to the left somewhere.

Closing my eyes, I rolled out the stiffness in my shoulders, stretched out the tightness in my neck, while trying to control the twitch of my lips.

My forest.

My rules.

My domain.

I knew what every single sound signified. Knew if the tremble of brush belonged to wildlife or wind. Recognised which species trod the ground, or cracked twigs, by volume alone. Could even chase the path of the breeze by the creak of timber.

I also knew Brook well enough to recognise exactly which footfalls came from her.

A soft step sounded, almost like a whisper of unsettled dust, a little to the right, sharing Brook's intention of circling me.

A chuckle threatened to brew, but I kept it contained, sliding a palm over my stomach until I gripped my hardness below.

"Maybe I should just start without you."

A rapid pitter-patter of steps placed her at eleven o'clock.

Better view from there, Puss?

Eyes still closed, I gave a slow stroke of myself, my lips slightly parting for effect.

She took a step toward me, the tiny snap of a twig giving her position away.

I held my ground, head tipping back as I continued the show, pretending I didn't notice when two more soft footfalls sounded. Feathering my other hand across my hip and over my groin, hoping to distract, I opened my eyes to slits as my chin made a slow tilt back down.

Brook hovered on one foot, about to move nearer, hunger heating her stare she had aimed at my groin.

Before I could stop it, a low growl rumbled in my chest.

Brook's head whipped up. Her gaze locked with mine.

A smile curved my lips.

She spun away and bolted.

Darting forward, I caught her before she'd gone more than a few feet.

One arm wrapped around her waist, and I whipped round the other and grabbed her wrists, manacling her as I sandwiched her between my chest and the nearest trunk.

She twisted her face to the side and panted out a breath. "I swear you get faster and faster every time I see you."

"You just like to keep thinking you're better than me." I stretched her trapped hands up above her head, pressing into her back. "And I love to prove you wrong."

The breeze fluttered her hair up, tickling my shoulder. "I am better than you," she said. "You just happen to be faster."

I nodded, burrowing my face into the strands covering her neck and inhaling. "Yet, you still seem to think you stand a chance at getting away. Why would you bother when this …" I slipped my hand down over her stomach and cupped between her thighs, smiling when she emitted a soft moan. "… tells me that's not what you really want?" An upward tug lifted her feet from the ground, high enough to slip my erection forward until the tip united with her heat. "Is this what you want, Puss?"

Her whimper only made me harder—painfully so, when she arched into the contact, and my brewing growl escaped at the aroma of arousal firing my synapses.

"Is it?" I asked, my voice a deep grumble as I pushed through her thick, dark strands and bit down on her nape.

She gasped, curving tighter against me. "Yes."

Unwrapping my arm from around her waist and my jaws from her neck, I lowered her feet back to the ground and took a half-step back. The instant her soles hit dirt, she spun, her arms tangled above her in their still trapped state. Her hair clung to cheeks dampened by perspiration, and trailed over her shoulders all the way to her flat stomach, hiding scarring she'd accumulated while in the vampires' grasp.

As her gaze lifted to mine, the honey irises blazed a molten gold. "You already know I shall not beg."

"Yes, you would."

I swallowed any retort she might offer with a kiss.

Soft, supple ... *hot*. The lure of her lips always left me wanting more, but I kept what I knew she wanted out of reach.

Beneath her curtain of hair, sweat coated the back of her neck, where I held her to me. Her tongue darted out to mine as I tasted her, her lashes flickering. From her lips, I skimmed across her jaw, catching her earlobe between my teeth before suckling the length of her neck to the dip at her throat.

Above me, her breaths hastened.

Below, her breasts all but swelled.

Unlocking my hold on her wrists, my fingers teased along her inner arm as I moved lower. When I took her nipple with my mouth, her fingers dug into my hair, an arm clasped onto my shoulder, and my name whispered from her.

The muscles of her stomach tightened as I brushed my lips downward, the hand within my hair fisting as I dropped to my knees and licked at her navel. On my way lower, fingertips dug into my shoulder as though encouraging my route.

Her legs parted for me, and my dick throbbed at the sight of the exposed moisture. A low growl hummed within my chest as I sampled there before nibbling along the inside of her thigh, my hands gripping her in place as she gave a groan of protest and attempted to chase the caress.

"You will be sorry if you continue to tease."

My lips curved against her skin as I nibbled a slow path toward her knee.

Before I could reach it, a heavy force smacked my chest, and my body flew backward. As my butt and shoulder blades thudded against dirt, Brook's hands landed either side of my head, and her length covered mine.

"I warned you." She hissed.

My chuckle escaped. "I'm flat on my back with you on top of me. What the hell have I got to be sorry about?"

"Because, Mr Control Freak ..." Her eyebrow quirked up. "You no longer have me trapped."

I closed my eyes as her hair feathered across my skin. "Actually, Puss, you're exactly where I want you."

"Not for long." Her chest lifted from mine as she pushed away.

My eyes snapped open, and I shoved up onto my elbows, my teeth catching her lower lip and holding on. "Uhn-uhn."

She remained there, my captive, each breath brushing her heartbeat against my own. Her fingers folded against my shoulders. Her eyes burned a coppery hue. I half-expected her to flee, to offer another challenge. Instead, she gave a low moan brimming with frustration and all but yanked me in for a kiss.

Throughout my thirty-five years, I'd snogged a lot of females. Shagged more than my fair share, too. Not a one of them came close to Brook. Not one of them set my nerve endings alight, or sent tingles shooting through every damn muscle. Certainly, none of them made me want to eat them alive.

Brook's kisses alone, though, hit like a libido-jacker.

Bringing my arms around to hold her, palms sweeping across skin like silk, I accepted her lips. Her tongue. The tiny bites along my jaw, down to my throat, across my collarbone. Even the pierce of her nails as they scraped into the flesh on my shoulders.

My hands found her hips. Warm. Delicate. Each gentle gyration matching the cadence of her mouth as she worked back up to mine.

Gripping her harder, I pressed her down against me, releasing a growl at the spill of moisture across my abdomen. As my own hips urged up, seeking her arousal, a quiet gasp left her, flicking my hormones into a giant ball of need.

Flipping us over, fuelled by her feminine sound of surprise, I nestled my hips between her thighs, demanding my body hold back, even as it all but screamed to enter her.

Beneath me, her chest rose and fell, providing intermittent warmth against the gathering cool air. As her fingers made delicate, almost unsure reaches for me, and her legs slid around to embrace, all I could do for a moment was stare.

Her eyes, so damn expressive, more than I'd ever seen on another soul, with their altering hues from burnt maple to pale honey, revealed her mood and emotions. Her hair, the way it splayed out around her, like a pair of dark wings, exposed the angel within. Even her lips were as swollen and red as bracken fruit begging to be picked.

Everything about Brook screamed of a hidden wildness.

One I hoped nobody ever tamed.

Her calves tightened around my hips, and her heels dug into my butt—an unspoken demand—one that brought a smile to my lips.

"So impatient," I said.

"For you." She lifted her hips up. "Always."

When her legs drew me against her again, I finally thrust into her, my quiet snarl merging with her tiny, high-pitched gasp. I withdrew, and drove forward a second time, a third—hitting a lazy rhythm that shot sparks through both thighs, up through my groin, until a thrum announced contentment within my chest.

In time with each of my movements, Brook's gasps evolved to small panted breaths, like a creature starved of oxygen.

Had I become the air she needed to breathe as much as she had become mine?

Propped on one elbow, I touched a fingertip to her parted lips, watching as her tongue slipped out and wetted the skin.

When my palm slid over the contour of her jaw and came to rest at her neck, the hastened drum of her pulse beat at my index like a coded call of invitation, and my own lips rippled as my rumbled response departed.

Lower still, across her clavicle, my hand swept until I cupped her breast, encouraging her tautness toward my awaiting mouth. As I suckled, her left leg entwined with my right; as I nibbled, her other leg rose to encompass my waist. Both actions united our bodies with more depth while denying any harboured fantasies of escape.

As if I had any.

A whimper gasped from her, as rigidity claimed her muscles, and I glanced up in time to see the lowering of her lids, the tip back of her head, her fingernails digging into earth at the ends of her outstretched arms, as her body made a slow arch upward.

For moments, she seemed suspended there. Like a goddess poised in ecstatic repose.

Hooking an arm beneath her butt, I lifted her as I drove into her, and a mewled cry spilled from her lips.

As her body convulsed beneath, *around* me, I scooped her up, shoving back onto my knees before her orgasm even had chance to subside.

Flopping her arms over my shoulders and securing her thighs around my hips warned her to hold on, and as I grasped her hips, demanding she meet my pace, she gave me control.

With her head tipped back, eyes scrunched closed, and lips chanting out a blend of gasps and cries, the trailing ends of her hair feathered across my thighs, as the muscles there bunched and released to each of my upward thrusts.

As Brook found ground with her feet and urged against me herself, each swing of her hips matched the tug of my hands until heat swept through my body, bringing sweat to the surface.

"*Brook*." Her name teetered off into a ragged growl, my eyes locating the pounding throb at the side of her neck. The beat from within seemed to echo right through to my soul, as though seeking its partner, luring me closer, and my own heart gave a manic beat of response.

A metallic tinge—Brook's blood, a scent as intoxicating as the female herself—penetrated every layer of her flesh separating it from me.

My throat contracted. Saliva pooled.

Unable to help myself, I slipped my arms around and drew her in close, dropping my nostrils to the invitation. With darts of my tongue, I tasted the flesh there as each inhalation spun my head in a dizzying rush.

Not a sliver of air remained between Brook and Kyle, as his arms pinned her body tight against his.

Laps of his tongue treated the flesh at her pulse. Nips of his teeth. Suckles from his lips. All while, over and over, he drove his hips upward, into her, the humming of his body matching the purr within her own chest, the entire scenario one they had played out many times before.

Never, though, had she seen his guard quite so lowered. His resolve so thoroughly snapped.

Rather than be afraid of the unusual strength he so often held back, Brook found herself endeared to his undercurrent of vulnerability and only wanted him more.

Clutching harder at his shoulder, she threaded the fingers of her other hand into his hair, whispering his name against his ear. In a need to see him, she urged his face from its burrowed position, and his mouth skimmed across her flesh until it found hers. Breath evaded her for seconds beneath his bruising demands, the all-consuming way in which he kissed her, only returning as Kyle drew back.

His lips, as swollen as any male's in ecstasy, rippled from the power of the ever present snarl spilling from his throat.

No longer, though, did the pretty hazel shade of Kyle's eyes surround pupils fenced by faint specks of green. Instead, blackness attempted to claim the colour, bleeding out over the irises, veining the whites. In a captivating performance, dark wisps unfurled toward the rims before recoiling, as though testing their territory before fully committing.

Unable to look away, Brook didn't fear what it signified. She hadn't since her first time with Kyle, when her witness of it happening had been Kyle's first alert to the abnormality.

As the inkiness spread farther, poking its boundary, past experience told Brook Kyle's eyes would soon be fully black.

To Brook's knowledge, only one type of supernatural bore such a trademark.

Vampire.

Also to Brook's knowledge, Kyle had never shared his affliction with anyone but her.

With her fingertips cutting marks into his flesh, Brook rocked her hips even faster, faster still at the baring of Kyle's teeth. It took little for the slow simmer of heat to rekindle deep in her groin, and her groan arrived long and low as the first tendril began to uncoil. As though in response, the thrum within Kyle grew in volume, deep in the pit of his stomach, cutting a path straight up to his chest in time with the daggers of pleasure spiking Brook's abdomen.

When every muscle throughout Brook's body hit spasm, Kyle's body stiffened alongside her.

He sucked in a breath. His lids dropped. On the exhale, his lips funnelled, and an ear-shattering howl departed his throat.

Every downy hair of Brook's stood as the call washed through to her soul. Even with his eyes closed, his body wracking with sensual convulsions and chest heaving, Kyle's face had never been so expressive, with his cheeks puffed out, a throb pulsating at his temple, and the tension of his jaw stretching the tendons of his neck.

When he finally ceased to tremor, his arms softened around her. His face tucked in against her neck, and as his tongue left traces across her skin, the slight stinging there told Brook his teeth had cut the surface, while he lowered her back to the ground as though settling his most prized possession.

12

Well, that's a new one.

I'd howled before. Of course I had. During a hunt. As a wolf.

In human form, though? During climax?

Definitely a new one.

With my body swaying to the rhythm of my heartbeat, the after effect had left a buzz that tickled within my chest.

"Kyle." She gave gentle nudge to the side of my head, like she wanted me to lift from her throat.

Did I want to, though? Did I want to leave the sweet scent of her, even for one moment?

More so, did I want to see a second confirmation in her eyes that mine had done their crazy shit?

Again.

Her sigh bristled my hair. "Kyle, please do not hide from me."

Every muscle through my neck seemed to have softened, when I raised my head to eyes glistening a burnished gold. "They did it again, didn't they?"

I didn't know why I felt the need to ask. They'd bloody done it every damn time. Maybe in some tiny corner of my mind, I still hoped it'd quit, and I'd go back to how I was before fucked-up-edness.

Her stare met mine, no hesitation, no cautiousness, holding it before she gave a small nod.

As pathetic as it seemed, I found myself grateful for her boldness—relieved beyond freaking words that I didn't creep her out.

'Cause I sure as hell creeped myself out.

"Bad?" The fact I whispered told me more than my head would ever admit that maybe I didn't really want to know.

Her eyes flickered side-to-side. "It's clearing already."

As I pressed a kiss to her lips, I slid from within her, yet didn't feel ready to move away completely—not when hovering above Brook chased off the chill.

Besides, who wouldn't choose to stay lying chest to chest with such a beautiful view while wrapped in the most amazing legs?

"Did you ask Gabe about this yet?" she said.

Bringing the pup into the chatter diminished the moment. Especially since what she meant was, had I asked Gabe if he suffered the same problem, because he'd been hit with even more vamp juice and anti-venom than I had.

I almost said I hadn't seen him, but that would have been an outright lie, and she'd have known it. Though, really, what the heck did she expect me to say to him, anyway? *'Hey, Gabe, when you shoot your load, do your eyes turn black, by any chance? Oh, they do? Cool beans. Have a nice day, buddy.'*

Yeah, that'd work. *Not.*

"I haven't had chance," I said.

The slight narrowing of her eyes told me she didn't believe me.

"But I will," I added. "Soon."

Her brow smoothed as she breathed out a laugh. "Liar."

With a chuckle, I dipped my lips to hers again, contemplating if we had time for another session, but halted at a crack in the distance.

My head twitched to the side, as a trample chased the sound. A succession of thuds followed. Growing louder. Closer. It took less than a beat to identify the pound of paws against earth.

Crap.

I knew the exact moment Brook heard them, too, by the twist of her head to the right. "Kyle," she whispered. "What was that?"

"Our cue to lea—"

Nate crashed into our clearing and skidded to a halt. His muzzle lowered, a quiet rumble kicked up in his chest, and the hairs along his spine erected.

Almost unconsciously my arms tightened around Brook, and my body made the slow angle to cover hers a little more. Not once did I take my attention off my Alpha, the confusion in his stare, the rapid darts of his eyes like he couldn't quite believe the scene in front of him—not even when Dad erupted into the clearing, followed by Ethan, Dan, and Josh.

Every one of them stumbled in their sudden stop. Every one of them, bar Ethan, dropped into a pose that mirrored Nate's.

Double crap.

The surrounding forest seemed to silence beyond the grumbles rolling from four of the five wolves before me.

My gaze remained on Nate, as I said, "You're early."

A snarl rippled Nate's lips. The muscles bunched throughout his legs.

As he sprung in my direction, I shot to my feet, my own growl breaking free as I aimed to divert him from Brook.

The bulldozer of a wolf hit my chest, something akin to a slab of concrete smacked my back, and a tonne weight sandwiched me somewhere between the two, gushing out every ounce of my breath.

His face pushed into mine. The first drip of saliva overhung his lip.

I could have shoved him off. Hell, I could probably have taken him.

Only someone with a death wish challenged an Alpha while he had his pack at his back, though—which meant I knew shit was about to fly, the instant I spotted the black blur in my periphery.

In the next beat, Nate had vanished, Brook stood over me looking like a scary-as-heck fur-ball, with hisses flying from her mouth.

Snarls escalated from the rest of the pack before Nate'd even flipped to his feet. And as soon as he made the turn back toward Brook, with fury in his eyes, I smelled an imminent fucking disaster.

13

I rolled up into a crouch, somehow looping an arm around Brook, scooping her behind me, and placing myself between her and Nate.

In front of me, Nathan tensed, and I flung my palm up.

"Nate, wait!"

Brook hissed at my rear, and
I tightened my grip.

"Brook, quit a minute."

Body still poised to fight, Nate sent me a growl and a jerk of his head that pretty much meant get the hell out of the way.

Brook's shoulders bashed mine, bowling into me as she wriggled in my hold.

I sent Nate a rapid headshake while flexing my twisted arm around the solid mass of muscle attempting to break free, at the same time as trying to keep track of the rest of the pack.

Especially Dan. He stood a good few steps closer than I'd realised, and his body language set damn alarm bells ringing in my head.

A yowl hit my ear. Claws sliced my lumbar.

As I arched and cried out, Brook's weight disappeared, Nate jerked a step forward, and Dan left the ground in a dive.

Toward Brook.

I spun toward Dan in time to see Ethan barge him aside, a warning ripping from him.

Before I could even nod out my thanks, motion drew me back—to Nate ramming against Brook, as she flung herself at him.

With a screech of protest spewing from her, Brook skidded across the dirt flank-side with claws scrabbling a trailing trench.

I shot that way. Hit the ground somewhere between wolf and feline, as Nate circled around and sent her a snarl that any of the pack would have translated to: *stay the hell out of my way*.

All probably would have been good at that point.

If Dan hadn't darted around Ethan, and Ethan hadn't taken him down by the throat.

If Dad hadn't jolted toward to Ethan, and Josh after Dad.

If Nate hadn't let the lot of them distract him and turned to see what the fuck was going on.

Because the second they all had their attention elsewhere, Brook skirted me in a bulleted dive, her paws kicking me aside as she passed.

All within a fraction of a beat, every head whipped around toward Brook aiming for their Alpha, leaving me with no choice but to bloody tackle her down.

Either that, or leave her, which would have only resulted in all five of them on her back.

Feet ramming against dirt, I thrust myself forward, my arms slinging around Brook and giving her nowhere to go. She hit ground with a grunt, followed by a deeper one, when I landed atop her and smacked my chin off the top of her skull.

The blow loosened my arms.

She rolled in the tight space beneath me.

As she spun onto her back, her hind legs came up, and her claws across my abdomen cut like a newly-sharpened blade.

"Fuck!"

Again.

"Shit!"

Again.

"Fuck!"

Somehow, I managed to hold my position, though. Worming my arms between us, I cursed through each added stab, snatched hold of her forelegs in one hand and her hinds in the other, and only just jerked my head out of the path of her snapping jaws.

Her body squirmed as if in spasm, once again resisting my grip.

The second time her head jolted upward, her teeth grazed the tip of my ear before I could get out of the way.

A snarl hit me from the left, and I caught Dan's intention in the set of his shoulders, in his eyes. Without a second thought, my own growl rippled free.

Not at Brook, though. Not at the one slashing and biting and cutting me up.

At my own pissing brother.

"Stay the fuck back!"

Like I'd hit some sort of switch, the pack eased off. Though they still shuffled from foot to foot, though their bodies all held more tension than a bungee, they all paused like I'd brought them to a standstill, uncertain glances passing between them with low rumbles in their chests.

All while beneath me, Brook struggled like hell.

Too fast for her to intercept, I clamped my teeth around the back of her throat and nudged her head to the ground. Sadness poured through every inch of me that I'd had to even contemplate using force, and I closed my eyes as I said a silent sorry to her. Though she still wriggled, employing the full weight of my body held her steady, and the tightening of my jaw quietened her for a moment.

I chanced loosening my hold.

When she didn't react, I brought my lips to her ear, and opened my eyes to my watching pack. "Please don't fight me, Brook," I whispered. "You need to shift back ..."

The entire time I whispered reassurances, that she needn't be afraid, that I was there for her, that everything would be okay— *yeah, right!*—I kept my gaze on my brothers, on Nate, on Ethan. Yet, somehow, I couldn't bring myself to look at my dad.

Hours went by in my mind, but more accurately, less than a minute passed when I sensed the magic of Brook's shift against my flesh, the tickle of the change washing from head to toe that left me no choice but to release her limbs as the solidity of feline muscle moulded into the soft curves of femininity.

The heave of her breaths hit my cheek, sending her chest rising to greet mine. Her fingers curled around the skin at my waist, the flex of them holding a desperation I suspected she'd go to the ends of the earth to disguise.

"Okay." I pressed my lips to her temple and blew out a sigh. "It's okay."

A grumble from Nate drew me back. He snorted. Gave a sharp jerk of his head. Another of his canine orders I'd seen a few times.

With a reluctant nod, I made a slow climb to my feet, tugging Brook up with me and blanking the pain as each movement stretched the slices across my skin. "Come on. Let's go get our clothes." When I tucked her tight against my side, she didn't protest, and I ushered her in the direction of home.

Brook paced the kitchen, her hair swaying with each step and flicking aside with each spin. Her scent, merged with her lingering perspiration, wafted beneath my nose each time she passed. I'd suggested, after dressing, that she go wait in my room. Offered to take the flack on my own. She'd refused. Unsurprisingly. Though, that might have had something to do with how pissed she'd been at herself, when she realised just how badly she'd cut me up. Apparently, I'd probably 'bleed to death' if left alone for any length of time.

Leaning against the doorway to the hall, I pressed a cloth to the worst of my wounds—the only one that insisted it keep bleeding—and watched her, surprisingly calm considering the bollocking I had coming. "You sure—"

"I said, *no*." The adamant response came as she tossed a glance my way over her shoulder, before twisting back, pivoting, and re-treading the path she'd just covered. "This is my fault."

"How many times—"

"If I had not called, you would not have come." Spinning, she glanced my way and paced again. "And we would not have met today."

I opened my mouth to argue, but realised I'd not only be calling her a liar, but would have as much effect as fighting thin air. Besides, Brook didn't exactly like coddling. She had a tendency to prefer facts and truths.

She halted in her journey and turned toward the window. "Your brother is coming."

I pushed up from the doorframe and glanced through the upper pane of the back door.

Dan strode across the lawn, fists tight at his sides, gaze downcast, every muscle across his naked body pulled taut. I'd have questioned what had his goat going, but I imagined my behaviour toward him would be a big part of the answer.

Only as he reached for the door handle did he look up, and I didn't like the attitude I saw in the hardness of his eyes, or in the slight curl of his lip.

The door swung inward, and he followed through, not even bothering to close it behind himself before he rounded the table and made for the hallway. His focus stayed on me the whole time.

"Where's everyone else?" I asked, as he ducked from the room and turned away.

He vanished as he took the corner for the stairs. His passage banged each step on ascent, and I tracked his route, into his room, where he made a shedload of noise, into Josh's room, and finally into Dad's.

"You gonna answer me?" I called, as he stomped back down the stairs.

He swung around the banister wearing workout gear with a pile of sweats over his arm. "Waiting for clothes,"—he waved his chin toward Brook—"seeing as how you want to bring *guests* home without even telling any of us." His shoulder brushed mine as he pushed through the doorway into the kitchen.

I grabbed his bicep and stalled him before he could strop off again. "What were you all doing in the forest so early, anyway?"

"What?" He took his time about twisting back my way, his eyebrows raised. "You're putting the blame on us for you getting caught out?" When I glared at him, he huffed out a breath, shaking his head. "You called, Kyle. That's why we were there. That's what we do—watch each other's backs. So, you call, we come."

I frowned, until understanding dawned. That damn howl. Right on climax. *Ah, shit!*

"Yeah. We thought you were in trouble. Stupid us." The glance he sent Brook held only contempt. "Turns out you were only *inside* trouble."

"Don't you speak about her—"

He snatched his arm free of my grip, and shrugged his shoulders high as he made for the door. "Can't believe we didn't smell it sooner," he said, pausing on the threshold. "Whole damn forest stinks of cat."

My growl chased him out the door, but Brook pulled on my wrist, as I took a step forward to follow.

"Please, do not fight with your family," she said, giving another small tug. "Not over me."

"He'd no right talking to you that way. Hell, he's no right talking *about* you that way."

"He's just confused," Brook said.

"Maybe, but I'd never speak to Jem like that—or Shelley. And I never once spoke to Dan's last girlfriend like that, and she turned out to be a fucking psycho."

115

As I twisted back to her, her gaze lowered to my stomach. I'd been unable to fasten my jeans on dressing, and ended up having to leave my shirt undone. Her grip on my arm had drawn away the wadding, which meant a trickle of blood worked its way south from the broadest and longest gash, one that had only just missed dissecting my belly button.

"Your family probably think that of me, also, after my performance in the forest," she said.

I shook my head. "You're being too hard on yourself."

"I messed up." She took the red-stained muslin from me and placed it back over my oozing cut. "I did not intend to hurt you."

I tipped her chin back up until I could see her eyes. "I know."

"I cannot believe my behaviour."

"In all fairness, theirs wasn't much better." My thumb brushed along her jaw. "It's no bloody wonder you panicked."

"They can hardly be blamed. We took them by surprise," Brook said.

"That is somewhat of an understatement," Dad said, stepping into the room.

Nate came in behind him, and the other three followed like a procession of judge, jury, and executioner. None of them smiled. None of them looked amused. Only grim expressions arranged their features as they all turned and faced me.

I drew Brook in a little closer. *Here we go.*

14

Dad, Nate and Dan all stood, legs braced, arms folded. On one side of the trio, Ethan rubbed a hand around the back of his neck, utter disappointment in his eyes, and while Josh mirrored Ethan's action on their other side, he seemed a little more unsure as he glanced between us all.

I'd expected Nathan to tear into me at his earliest convenience. Instead, he aimed his glaring eyes at Brook. "I do not appreciate being attacked while on my own property."

"I apologise for that," Brook said, "but I thought you were going to hurt him."

"Take a better look, cat." Dan pointed my way. "You're the only one who sliced him up a treat."

"Leave it, Danny." I said.

"Are you kidding me?" He prodded the air with his finger. "Maybe you should take a look in the mirror, Kyle. You look like a damn extra for a crap slasher film." His attention swung back to Brook, along with his finger. "You really did a number on him, eh?"

"It was an accident," I said. "And leave Brook out of this."

"Danny," Nate said, his voice low.

"Leave her out of it?" Daniel asked like Nate hadn't even spoken. "She *is* it!"

I growled his way, even took a step forward. "What the hell's wrong with you?"

"Danny." That time the quiet warning came from both Dad and Nate.

"You're what's wrong with me!" Dan's hand quit pointing and fisted at his side, as his torso leaned toward me. "Your lying. Your sneaking around. Your bloody attitude and detachment from the pack. All for ..." Both hands fisted, he flung his arms toward Brook, though his gaze stayed on me, his mouth open for a second like he couldn't figure out what he wanted to get out before he said, "... *this*."

The growl in my chest that hadn't quite dissipated deepened as I went to storm forward and teach him some manners, but Brook swung in front of me, stalling my plan.

"Kyle, *please*."

"Danny, that's enough." Dad's hand slapped down on my brother's shoulder. "You should quit before you say something you'll regret."

"I doubt it," he said.

"Josh, how about you take Daniel upstairs to cool off, so your father and I can talk to Kyle calmly about this?" Nathan said.

Dan didn't look anywhere near ready to give it up, with his lips set in some kind of twisted snarl and arms tensed like he prepared to throw a punch, but he didn't object when Josh grabbed hold of his biceps and steered him toward the door.

He halted alongside me and Brook. "Just so you know," he said, peering down at Brook, "this is nothing personal."

"What, then, Dan?" I asked, as he shrugged free of Josh and strode from the room. "What the hell is it?"

"It's unnatural," Nathan said.

I swung back to him as his words resounded in my head.

Undoubtedly, a whole bunch of shit to do with myself felt unnatural, and had for months. The swirly eye action. A simmering temper beyond anything I'd ever been known to show, bubbling away just beneath my surface. Even the way, when I sometimes sat quietly alone, I seemed able to track the passage of blood through my veins, seemed able to close my eyes and visualise each much needed beat of my heart.

The deal with Brook, though? *Hell, no.*

For the first time, I decided my Alpha talked shit about stuff he didn't know.

Brook stared at Nathan as his word choice swam in her head. She could have described her relationship with Kyle with plenty of other words. Forbidden, exciting ... *right*, to name a few.

"It does not feel unnatural to me," she found herself saying.

"Maybe amongst your race, crossbreeding is a given or accep—" Nathan seemed to still suddenly, before he rubbed a hand across his face and gave a low groan. "Please tell me you two have, at the very least, been using precautions."

"Oh, Jesus," Kyle muttered, his jaw jutting out as he shook his head. "Seriously?"

"Yes, I'm serious," Nathan said.

Kyle's father, Connor, went back to folding his arms, but his stance more than said he wouldn't budge, either, until they had gotten an answer.

"It is unnecessary," Brook said.

Connor's head tilted as he stared her way. "Sorry, young lady, but I disagree."

"No. You misunderstand." She held up her hands, mentally squashing any inner embarrassment she might ordinarily have felt over speaking so candidly to the opposite sex. "It is unnecessary because I cannot fall pregnant outside of a Season. And I haven't had one yet, since meeting Kyle."

Nathan's eyebrows lifted. "Season?"

"Yes, Mr Holloway. I am a feline Shifter. And our females have Seasons, which happen to only occur once a year."

"Well, that's something, I suppose," Connor said.

"Maybe." Nathan nodded. "But this is still a mess."

Kyle gave a low growl in the back of his throat, and Brook caught the shift of Ethan's attention as it flickered toward her wolf.

"So, do I want to know how long this has been going on?" Nathan continued like Kyle hadn't even reacted.

"Since ..." Brook glanced at Kyle, and back to Nathan at the slight nod she received. "Since October."

Nathan's head slanted a little, his brows bunching, the pale blue of his irises lightening a shade as his gaze darted between her and Kyle. "October?"

Kyle's nod matched her own.

Nathan rubbed at his face again—harder than the last time.

Stretching a few feet to his right, Ethan flicked on the light switch, the strobe-illumination blasting out the shadows lengthening across the winter afternoon.

Brook instantly wished he hadn't, even if the fading light had only provided a fictional barrier to their spotlight.

"I guess we at least now know why you never said anything," Connor said.

"Yeah, 'cause the reception's been awesome so far," Kyle said beneath his breath.

"Well, your lack of honesty has more than contributed toward that." Nathan heaved a deep sigh. "I'm shocked at you, Kyle. And disappointed. And I need some time to think on this—"

"There's nothing to think about," Kyle said through rigid jaw.

"There is *to me!*" Nathan's stare turned even chillier, if possible, and seemed to hold a brim-full of warning as he aimed it Kyle's way. After a few seconds, he switched his attention to Brook. "I think you should go home for now—"

Kyle nodded and shifted forward, his arm already encircling Brook's back. "Good. Let's go."

"*You* are not going anywhere," Nathan said.

Kyle's head snapped up, the grinding of his teeth audible as the cold fury in his eyes gave Nathan's a run for its money. "Then, how the hell is she supposed to get there?"

"Ethan can take her."

Both Brook and Kyle twisted toward Ethan, and Ethan inclined his chin to Brook. "You okay with that?"

"Yes," she said.

"I'll get her home safely," Ethan said to Kyle, holding out his hand. "Truck keys."

"Hall," Kyle said, reaching for Brook before she could follow Ethan out. As he swung her to face him, his hand cupped her cheek, and as the other lifted, he swept her hair back from her forehead. "What I said to you earlier?" His eyes held a deep intensity as they stared into Brook, and she nodded. "I meant every word. Okay? Every word. Everything'll be all right."

She wanted to believe him. God, Brook had never wanted anything so much. She'd seen everyone's responses, though, just as vividly as Kyle had. Nathan's disapproval. Connor's disappointment. Josh's disbelief that almost balanced out Daniel's reaction, which had bordered on fury.

She'd also noted the way Ethan had stared at his friend with barely a word to say on the matter, barely a word to say *to him*.

Where did Kyle think he'd find even one ally in a household so lacking in support? Though, what had they expected? Hadn't the fallout been the very reason they'd met in secret all along? Of course it had.

Unable to dissuade the conviction she witnessed in his eyes, however, she merely gave another nod. "Okay," she said before lowering her tone. "I will call you tomorrow."

As she sent an uncertain glance toward Nathan and Connor, Kyle's sigh fluttered the hairs lingering around her face, and he ducked in closer, bringing his lips to her ear, and whispering, "Call me *tonight*." He drew back, pressed a kiss to her temple, his lids lowering as he pulled away. Nostrils flared as though committing her scent to memory, he finally released her, though his eyes remained closed.

Unsure whether, or not, to bid farewell to the two mature wolves, she opted to just leave, but she couldn't deny the dull ache that settled heavier and heavier through her with every step taking her farther from Kyle.

The shadows that had threatened to overtake the Larsen's kitchen had deepened and spread, and engulfed the cab of Kyle's pickup. For ten minutes, they had been on the road, and Ethan had not uttered a single word. Many times, Brook had glanced at him in her periphery, trying to gauge his mood, his standing on it all. If he noticed, it didn't show. He just kept facing forward, hands tight over the wheel, arms rigidly straight. He hadn't even responded with more than a grunt and shifting the truck into gear, when Brook had told him to head toward Cheshire.

The transition to evening brought with it a chill that had Brook questioning the adequacy of her shirt on the short route from house to vehicle. Thankfully, inside the truck, subtle warmth blew from the vents to chase off her shivers, adding to the background noise of passing cars and hedgerows, the *vwhum, vwhum, vhwum* of white noise buzzing around the recalls in Brook's mind of the scene they had just left.

Another a few minutes ticked by, each lamppost they passed intermittently blinding Brook. Deciding she would rather take her chances with her escort than the flashbacks happening in her head, she twisted a little in her seat.

Ethan gave no reaction.

She shuffled until she'd turned a little more.

Still, he stared toward the windscreen, though the tiny twitch at the corner of his eye told her he'd noticed her adjustment.

After a long inhale and exhale, Brook said, "I hoped maybe you, of all people, would be a little more understanding."

"Why?" he asked, focus still on the road.

Because you are you. Because I have witnessed your loyalty. Because if you do not support him, then who does he have? She settled for, "You are his best friend."

His fingers flexed straight atop the wheel before they resumed their grip, the knuckles across both hands lightening in shade. "I always have his back, and he knows it. So I'm trying my best. But this ..." He looked her way at last, but only for a split second. "... this is just ..."

"Unusual?" she asked, when he made no move to continue. "Unconventional? Take your pick. There is no shortage." She returned to her original position and peered out through the passenger window at a white-fronted property flashing past, with lantern lights lending a multi-coloured glow to its porch.

"Actually," he said after a few beats, "I was thinking more like fucked up."

She wanted to be annoyed at his bluntness, but instead a breathy laugh seeped out before she could stop it. "I think I prefer your description to the others," she said. "Yours is one I can work with."

When he chuckled, a low sound that worked its way into his shoulders and took them along for the ride, she relaxed herself, until she remembered she headed toward home.

15

Watching Brook walk from the house, knowing what she headed back *toward*, almost tore me in two. I wanted to chase after her, sling her over my shoulder, and seclude her in my bedroom with a big *screw you* to the rest of the pack. If Dad and Nate had taught me anything, though, they'd taught me that patience and rationalisation got far better results than their opposites—even if my body and mind screamed for neither.

Even once the door had closed at her rear, I stared that way, the image of her lingering, my heart thudding like a huge chasm had split the ground between us, rather than the couple of days' organisation it would take me to hopefully be able to offer her a better life. One that involved me.

Only after the grumble of the engine had dwindled away did I turn back to Dad and Nate, and the expectations dominating their opinion-jaded stares. "Okay, hit me with what you've been holding back on." I drew out a chair and plonked myself down, wincing at the stinging that zapped my abs again. "Get it off your chests."

Dad rested a hand on the table-top as he leaned over it toward me. "Do you have any idea how disappointed I am in you right now, Son?"

I nodded. "Yeah, I kinda got that. But I also get that you're expecting me to be sorry when I can't."

"And I think *you're* misunderstanding exactly what you should be sorry for," Nathan said. "Do I think you should apologise for your female of choice? The only person a male should apologise to when he makes a mistake in that department is himself. However, when your choices, or behaviour, or the effects of either, affect the pack or your family, then, yes ..." He nodded. "You owe us an apology."

I stared hard at him for seconds, trying to work out if I could justify giving in, especially when I knew damn well taking any other route than the one I'd trodden would only have resulted in the current conversation taking place earlier. Instead, my head decided to justify *itself.*

"If I'd have told you sooner, would anything have been different?" I asked. "I mean, even now, I see it in your eyes, Nate." I peered across at Dad, still hugging the table-top. "I see it in yours, too. Not quite so condemning as the others, but it's there, all the same."

"Can you blame us?" Dad asked.

Yes, my head demanded, as Nathan voiced what I didn't want to have to admit out loud:

"Anyone with a brain cell knows the biggest reason you kept her a secret is because you know it's inherently wrong."

"You don't get it, do you?" I looked between the two of them. "It doesn't feel wrong *to me.*"

"She is not one of us," Nate said. "She's not even close—"

"Was Jem one of us when Sean met her?" I lifted my palms, straightening in my seat like acting antsy would help. "How about Shelley?" I swung my hands Dad's way. "What about Mum?"

"That's different," Dad muttered.

"*Why?*"

"Because you're using humans as your examples," Nathan said. "And every supernatural race out there taps into the human pool as the surest compatible option for mating when there are none of their own. It doesn't work the same way when you're crossbreeding races. In fact, it can't work, at all. What you have at the moment is what you get. All you get. There's nowhere for that kind of relationship to go."

I didn't want to deal with his words—no matter how loudly they rang and paralleled thoughts I'd already had. No matter that my body responded with a dull ache in my chest and constricted my oesophagus. "Are you going to order me not to see her?"

"You'll be giving up the chance of a future, Kyle. A chance of siring young. Of continuing the race and your family's name. Is she really worth all of that?"

"Are you going to order me not to see her?" I asked more forcefully.

"I can't order a heart to behave to my command," Nate said.

My breath caught as I tried to interpret his words. Was he ordering me, or not? Would he stop me seeing Brook, or what?

"But it's in your best interests—both yours and Brook's—if the two of you don't see each other again," he said, before my thoughts had finished forming. "So I'm asking you, out of respect for me, your father, and out of respect for the pack, to walk away."

"And if I don't?" I asked, not wholly sure I wanted to know the answer.

"Then, yes ..." Nathan nodded. "Force me to, and I will make it an order."

A half-mile prior to reaching her parents' property, Brook made Ethan pull over, where she bid him farewell.

After jumping out, she turned back toward the open window of the truck. "Please, do not be too harsh on Kyle. He needs you right now."

At Ethan's small nod—whether one of agreement, or acknowledgement, she didn't know—Brook broke into a jog alongside the narrow verge, as the engine rumbled to a quiet hum in the opposite direction.

Brick lined one side of the quiet lane, and trees dotted both, some spilling over from her father's land, others sentinels to the property on the opposite side of the road. The cool, gentle breeze from before had evolved into a brittle wind that seemed to stab ice into her skin with each penetration of her shirt.

Ahead, a streamed glow shot across the dark tarmac, warning of a vehicle passing through her father's gates.

She halted a moment, swaying against the sudden stop while she stood poised and waiting to see the direction the vehicle took.

She wondered who it would be. Which of her self-proclaimed suitors had visited last, or which of them had shown persistence by remaining the entire day?

The Kings, maybe.

She shook her head. While Stefan ultimately got what he wanted, he rarely expelled energy on pointless endeavours, and she presumed he would not have considered staying without Brook's appearance.

When the car pulled out and turned right, its taillights glowing at her as it slid away, she released a breath. Though, identifying the vehicle as belonging to Wayne Lovell set her teeth into a grind. Yet another determined Tom to add to the ever-growing list.

Only a handful of metres separated her from where she'd left Clive, yet she didn't move for minutes. Her attention still chased the scarlet glow, her mind longing to understand how it would feel to have the freedom, like Wayne—and *all* the Toms—had, to leave anytime she liked. At the same time, she grew increasingly aware of the hour, of the falling night, of the fact she'd spent far longer with Kyle than sensible. No doubt her father would have noticed her absence. Had they scoured the woodlands for her? A procession of Toms all marching, all pretending to work as a team, while harbouring private fantasies of finding her first and hoping to win the favour of the highly-esteemed Donald Nicholls?

How she hated the life her parents had spent twenty-four years trying to convince her was right.

She turned toward the wall, her gaze skimming upward to the route she knew she needed to take, but her body seemed to be refusing to carry her. Where else had she to go, though? Kyle's words—that he would fix everything—could ring in her head as much as they wished, but Brook had seen the disdain in his family's eyes, had experienced their reception. More so, she could not quite lose the expression of utter detestation she had witnessed in Kyle's brother.

Before she so much as registered her decision, Brook had crossed the tufts of grass coating the hardened soil. "Better the devil you know," she muttered.

With a small jump, she reached high enough to hook her fingers over the brickwork, and hauled upward until her feet found the top.

Dropping into an immediate crouch, she scoured the darkness. Branches creaked. Stranded leaves whispered across the ground. When nothing other than nature shifted, she dropped over the other side, landing with a quiet thud, and leapt straight into a run toward the guesthouse.

Despite her reluctance to return, Brook found a quiet comfort in the familiarity of the woodlands. In the sounds that chased her. In the scents engulfing her. Ones whose identity she had mastered, as each and every one of them had accompanied her life. From the squirrels, to the larks, from the musky dampness of timber to ... *Clive?*

The vice snapping about her waist doubled her over and stole her breath, but she sprang backward, the momentum tumbling her to her rear. She threw out a hand, saving herself from a total smack-down, and glanced upward as Clive's hands clamped over her biceps.

"Where the hell have you been?" he asked, swinging her upward and giving a small shake as he set Brook on her feet. "Six hours, Brook! What the hell have you been doing for six fucking hours?"

She twisted free of his grip and went to duck around him. "None of your business."

His arm whipped straight out at his side, bruising her chest as she hit it, sending her back another foot. "It *is* my business when I'm the one who's spent those hours lying to everyone on your bloody behalf about where you are. I've been bored out of my brains hanging out in that guesthouse and trying to pretend you're in there with me."

"Yes, well, I am certain convincing Stefan you have the upper hand has more than made up for it for you," Brook said. "Give it to him in detail, did you?"

"You're not a conquest to me, Brook." He grabbed her cheek, his touch softening as he brought her to face him. "When are you going to see that? This is not some sort of competition. This is real. What I feel ..." He moved closer. His face lowered to hers. As his nostrils flared and he drew in a long inhale, the gold of his eyes hardened to bronze and he jerked back an inch. "You fucked somebody."

Oh, no, no, no. Bracing her palm against his chest, she went to push away, but his hand slipped around the back of her neck and held her in place.

"Who the hell have you been with, Brook?"

She tried to shake her head, tried to shove herself back from him again, but his grip tightened and stilled both actions. Even as she struggled, she tried to formulate a decent answer, though his continued inhalations told her anything she had to say would not provide the truth her scent exposed.

With little other option, she went with the only one she could think. "I am not answerable to you. Wait until my fath—"

When he rammed her close enough that her chest banged against his, she knew she was in trouble. His face dropped to the opening of her shirt, his nostrils tickling as he scent-searched the exposed flesh there, and Brook's front dropped and made way for desperation.

"Clive, please. Let me go. I can explain."

"You can?" Voice tight and barely controlled, he lifted his head, and his eyes came back into view. A distraught mistiness coated them, but beneath that, a rampant fury swirled within. "Then, explain to me why you smell ..."

Hands planted firmer, she tried to squirm from his hold. "Let—"

"... like you've had ..."

She thumped a hand against his chest. "—me—"

"... sex with ..."

"—go!"

"... a *dog*, Brook."

One massive thrust and a kick out of her foot against his shin finally got her free, and she smacked ground with her bum hard enough to clatter her teeth.

Looming over her, Clive curled his hands at his sides, his teeth all but bared as emotions roiled across his features, as though he couldn't decide which to feel more. Disgust. Hurt. Yearning. Betrayal. "Tell me it isn't true." He seemed barely able to move his lips beneath the clench of his jaw. "Tell me you have not been blowing me off ... for a fucking ... *dog*!" Each time he said the word, an echo rumbled from within him in an obvious fight to keep his feline contained. "*Tell me!*" His control waivered for a moment as he roared.

Brook shook her head. Answers refused to spill from her lips as they opened and closed.

"How could you do this to me, Brook?"

She longed to run. To bolt.

Clive dropped to a squat, his entire body leaning over where she sat splayed as though unable to move. "How could you do this to *yourself?*" His final word rolled out on an extended growl, and Brook shivered beneath the frightening iciness creeping into his eyes.

Again she tried to form words, yet failed. Her body, her mind, wanted nothing more than to hide forever and never emerge.

She knew that would never work, though. She'd be forced to come out and return to the politics that dominated her life. Just as she knew the only one within the Coalition aware of her secret stood before her, and if she hoped to keep it that way, she would have to beg Clive for his forgiveness.

"Clive, please ..."

"Please *what*, Brook?" Clive snapped after seconds of her just staring up at him.

"Please ... do not tell my father."

His fisted hands ground into the dirt on either side of her thighs. His jaw worked overtime as the heat pumping from his body radiated his inner fire. "Give me one good reason why I shouldn't."

"Because—"

A crack to Clive's rear had both of them freezing. His expression spoke a million words, all in a singular second, before he peered back over his shoulder toward the sound.

As Brook leaned to the side to see around him, her gaze landed on the last person she wanted to see.

"Sounds like you've been misbehaving, Princess." Stefan's smirk lifted a corner of his mouth, matching the upward arch of the eyebrow above it. "Wonder what Daddy will have to say about that."

Before either she or Clive could retaliate, he vanished into the darkness in a flat-out sprint.

Toward the house. Toward her father.

16

Brook's heart panic-thumped, as she stared at Stefan's vacated space. "My father is going to kill me."

Clive groaned. "Oh, Christ." He grabbed Brook's upper arm. "Get up. We need to cut him off."

She allowed him to tug her upright, his feet already moving in the right direction, his continued grip hauling her along behind.

No matter how fast they weaved through the trees, Brook could not see, nor hear Stefan anywhere ahead.

"It's too late." She panted, as she and Clive kept pace. "We're too late."

"Not yet, we're not." Clive grasped her hips and sailed with her on a leap of his own over a gnarled trunk bent and twisted with age.

She supposed anyone else would have questioned why Clive aided her. She'd seen the pain in his eyes, the disgust when he'd realised her secret, so why on earth would he wish to help? As much as she appreciated Clive for the companionship they'd shared since childhood, she knew he'd spent every one of those years longing for something she'd never give, and she had a deep suspicion his support would come with a price.

Brook could not concern herself with that right then, though. The lights of the main house glowed up ahead, softly unfocused as sweat beaded the skin around Brook's eyes and lingered on her lashes as it trailed a path south.

"Faster," Clive said, his voice a low growl, as he chucked Brook ahead of him over a dense cloister of brush.

She landed a moment before him, and a final dive threw them both onto the lawn, as the garden door of the house slammed open.

Clive collided with her rear, as she halted.

Ahead, her father's form filled the space, little more than an outline against the harsh lights of the mudroom. "*Brook*!" The masculine silhouette became visible as he stepped outside, and the illumination lent shine to his dark hair, softening his profile, as he glanced right toward the guesthouse. "Brook!"

"Tell me now we're not too late," she said.

Donald's head whipped around her way. She knew the second he'd spotted them by his rocketed walk in their direction. Hands balled and swinging with his arms at his side, his shoulders bunched like a bull prepping to charge.

The fluttering of a Shift pricked across her scalp and poked at her brain, as though begging her to take defensive form, to protect herself—hell, to flee, if she had to. She couldn't comply. She'd spent her entire life trying to stand up to her father, and no matter that she had never won an argument, pride insisted she not cower.

Resisting the urge to scramble back as he grew close enough to merge with the shadows engulfing her, she thrust to her feet, her shoulders squared, chin set high. Before she could even open her mouth to speak, Clive ducked around her, his hands up as though requesting peace.

"Don, you shouldn't listen to everything Stefan tells yo—"

The ram of Donald's shoulder knocked Clive aside. "Stay out of matters that don't concern you, boy!"

He didn't even spare Clive a glance. His focus was all for Brook, and his torso had already begun the twist, his arm to swing back, his fingers to uncurl.

Brook took a step away, lifting her palms. "Daddy, wait!"

Her head snapped back, her shoulders spun, and her hips followed. The assault sent her whirling a full three-hundred-and-sixty degrees, as sparks flashed behind her eyes, and when her legs finally tangled and gave out, she punched the ground hard enough to send a buzz through her spine and into her skull.

Even as she blinked lucidity back to her vision, the reach of her father's hand registered, and she kicked back, arms up to shield her face. "N-no! No!"

The rough handling of her wrist burned her skin, the sharp haul of her arm tore at her shoulder, and her short flight through air as Donald flicked her over his shoulder sent dizziness crashing through her head. Brook let out a hiss, her fingers automatically clutching at her father's shirt, the bone of her cheek, where she'd been struck, screaming in pain as it bumped against his back.

With an upward shove, Brook glanced back. The house stood mere metres away and grew closer with every bouncing step. Beneath her, her father hummed with a low level growl that tugged her hairs erect.

Clive kept a safe distance behind them, as his pleas of, "Don, come on," and, "Hear her out," led the way. When his urging switched to, "Don, you're being rash," her father whirled on Clive so fast, Brook saw only arced light.

His steady growl ripped open into a booming roar. "Do not presume to tell me how to deal with my own."

As Donald spun back and resumed his walk, Brook's fight instinct finally kicked in. Her knees knocked as she wriggled in an effort to get them loose, but the action only ended in her father squeezing ever tighter, until the skin of her thighs pinched even through her jeans. She gave another hiss, her elbow catching her father's ear as she tried to thrust herself over his back.

A hand grabbed hold of her offending arm and forced it downward. Fingers weaved through hers, and a hand lifted her chin until her gaze met with Clive's.

He vehemently shook his head at her. *You'll only make it worse*, he mouthed.

The gnarled branches of the woodlands seemed to be waving their windy farewell as crass illumination replaced the overcast twilit sky. The open exterior door flashed by, to the utility machines, the Belfast sink, the boot rack and coat hooks. They passed through an archway, and the small space opened up toward the washroom on Brook's left, exposing the corner shower her mother expected visiting Toms to use, so as not to have their hunt mud cross her kitchen tiles.

"Behave like a filthy whore,"—her father's gravelly mutter brimmed with hatred on their entrance to the kitchen—"expect to be treated like a filthy whore."

"No!" Snatching her hand back from Clive, she shoved at her father's shoulder.

While not spoken often in her twenty-four years, Brook had heard enough variations of her father's words to know what they meant. Whether he considered her to have behaved like and need treating as a brat, or a peasant, or any way he deemed unsuitable, the statement always— *always*—preceded Brook being tossed into cellar. Always for as many days as her father believed fit the crime.

"No, Daddy, no!" She struck out with her foot, as they neared the hallway, whipping her head up to glower at Clive as it caught against the wood plinth of the doorway.

He'd halted, midway across the kitchen, his hands fisted in his hair.

She hissed at him, at his cowardice.

So many times Clive had been present during Brook's punishment. Not once had he found it within himself to intervene too far. It did not matter to Brook that panic, sorrow, helplessness etched across his features, as her father manoeuvred her through the doorway and into the hall. What good were his emotions if he refused to use them for fuel?

Teeth gritted, she latched her fingers onto the frame, instead. "Do not let him do this, Clive!"

He gave a tiny headshake. A shuffle of his feet. Useless regret in the grooves of his frown, and the small blown out breath.

As the jangle of keys sounded out, followed by the click of a lock, the yank around of her body that snatched her free took Clive from her sight and filled it with her mother.

"Is it true?" Collette asked.

Brook clenched her jaw so hard, her teeth hurt, and the denial she couldn't give clogged in her throat.

Her mother's eyes narrowed, mouth curling into a cruel line, as she spat, "A *dog*?"

In a pathetic bid for understanding she knew she would never get, Brook lifted a hand toward the woman in front of her. "Mother, please?"

"How could you do this ... *this* ..." Her mother's rage distorted her features into even deeper ugliness, and the blow of her hand hit the same spot on Brook's cheek that her father had.

The still-lingering pain exploded until Brook's entire head swam in a dizzying swirl of agony.

"You disgust me. With your lack of respect. With your—" Fire blazed across Brook's scalp as her hair yanked taut and cranked her head along with it, telling Brook her mother hadn't quite finished.

As her father secured his arms around her legs more tightly and began moving again, her mother's voice followed.

"How could a daughter of mine become such a treacherous whore? Get her out of my sight. Get her out of my sight, Donald."

The tension on her head released, and Brook's face smacked against her father's back again.

"I cannot stand to look at her right now."

Against her better judgement, Brook strained to glance upward as her father made the descent of the cellar steps. From beyond her mother's grotesque expression of loathing, something much worse stared back.

Smugness—on the face of Stefan.

Brook's scream of frustration echoed off the walls.

Dad had ordered me to my room. I hadn't wanted to go.

Nate had ordered me to shower. I'd wanted to tell him to shove it.

My entire being hummed to rebel, my voice to scream, my legs to run, and my hands had itched to destroy.

The table that Dad always tried to keep dead centre in the kitchen, with all its intricate scratches and grooves, each one of them a memory etched into a fabric of the house—I'd wanted to smash it up.

The deviant trees that had somehow found their way into the back garden, no doubt spawned from wayward seeds carried in on the breeze—I'd wanted to hack their fucking trunks to pieces, furious with them for getting away without conformity when that option shrank from me.

My truck. The one item I could have done whatever-the-hell I wanted to without consequences, Ethan still hadn't brought back—which was just another tick to add to the list of stuff pissing me off.

To make matters worse, the more I'd twitched in every direction my destructive mind wanted me to go, both Dad and Nate had shifted and tensed, like they knew my intentions and arranged themselves into a barrier they both knew I'd never break through.

After our silent showdown following their commands, Nate had hit me with, "I think you'll find neither of those were requests."

Thanks to them, water—far hotter than necessary—scalded my wounds and reddened my skin. The glass enclosure of the shower had steamed over, cutting off the outside world and lending the illusion of a secluded and way, way too-small prison. Two steps took me to the left edge, and three recovered paces took me to the right. For a moment, I kind of knew how a pinball must feel—assuming it pumped itself up on adrenaline and pent up aggression it knew it would never get away with unleashing. My fists even curled tight. Like all it would take to break me free of the invisible bonds would be a good old pummel against the panes.

Maybe if I smacked hard enough, I could do some damage to the wall tiles, too.

Then the shower itself ... *Yeah, that'd be satisfying ...* the bath, maybe ...

I gave a groan and scraped my forehead against a line of grout, begging the sensation to drag me back to calmness.

Breathe deep. I inhaled.

They hadn't forbidden me from seeing her. *Not yet.* I exhaled.

Still time to make them see sense. My inhale burned on the way down.

Would they listen, though? The breath rushed from me.

I'll make them.

"Just the shock, that's all," I uttered.

Not like Brook's appeal hadn't been a shock to me, too, at first.

They just needed space to adjust.

A rapid shake of my head sent water spraying in all directions as I shut off the power, and an eerie quiet filled the place of pattering.

I emerged from the cubicle and snatched up a towel like it'd offended me, shook it out like it deserved my wrath, and secured it about my waist like it should bow down to my greatness in return for my disrespect.

Which probably meant I was losing my damn mind.

Coolness bled into the room and attacked the steam as I pulled open the bathroom door. The light bulb shone from its spot on the landing ceiling, but below, the hallway sent only shadows along its half of the stairs.

Two doors down on the right, my bedroom door stood ajar—just as I'd left it. I stepped out to make the short trek, but didn't make it all the way past the first set of doors, when something thudded against my right ear.

My hand shot out and saved me from bashing against the wall.

With a high-pitched whistle ringing through my ear, and a growl scratching at my throat, I made a slow clockwise pivot and peered into the room before my own.

Lounging back on his bed, legs crossed at the ankles, elbows propping him up, Dan tapped a finger to his temple and lifted it to me in salute.

My teeth ground. "Wanna try that again?"

"Chuck us the ball back, and I'll be happy to," he said, though no humour entered his tone, nor softened his features.

A glance to the floor showed a tennis ball beside Dan's dresser, just inside his room. Lifting my gaze back to my brother, I lowered to a squat and scooped it up, my palm squeezing the rubber way tighter than necessary. I stared Dan down and contemplated lobbing the ball back, preferably with a decent aim straight for his eye.

Not once did he look away, but just kept glowering at me, his usually grinning lips set in a hard line of distaste.

"I'm waiting," he said after I hadn't moved for a while.

My arm tensed. My fingers brushed across the tufted coating of the ball like they considered stealing the decision to act from me. At the same time, some dark corner of my mind *wanted* me to reciprocate, almost like a whispered urge to give it to him good.

A creak on the stairs sucked me out of my blackened thoughts, and I turned to see Dad ascending.

He stopped partway up, his eyebrow arched. "Problem?"

I wanted to yell, *Yes, there's a freaking problem! He's the problem! You're the problem! Nate and the whole blasted pack are the problem!*

Keeping my mouth shut, I slid a sideways warning glare Dan's way and covered the rest of the landing to my own room.

With the door closed behind me, I heaved a deep inhale, like oxygen had finally showed its face after evading me. Maybe I'd held my breath the entire time Dan prodded at my patience. Maybe I'd scarcely breathed for months.

Tossing my towel aside, I stalked across the room, left to right to left again. Goosebumps sprung across the surface of my flesh by the time I slumped down on the end of my bed. I didn't mind them. I sort of liked the distraction. Like it offered a reminder of my ability to feel something other than all the other shit pumping through me and tearing me up.

Only thing you're feeling is sorry for yourself.

I gave a low growl and flicked up my wrist. The almost unconscious action sent the ball I still held into the air, and I caught it on the downfall. I tossed it up a second and third time. Lifting it to my face, I studied it for a few seconds, my thumb rubbing across its texture again, before I peered beyond it at the wall. In the next breath, I hauled my arm back, thrust it forward, and sent the ball hurtling toward a spot just west of my wardrobe.

It hit with a rubbery thwack and rebounded. Fast.

I caught it with a stinging slap against my palm and threw it again. Harder.

Caught it again—the sting spreading into a dagger that spiked into my flexed wrist.

The next shot hit harder still, the one that followed no more than a blur of movement, until I'd kicked up a demented rhythm of pull back, tense, fling, brace, catch—one that made me feel like McQueen must have in *The Great Escape*.

Except, for McQueen's character, it seemed to contribute toward maintaining his sanity.

For me, it seemed to help strip it away.

17

To the beat of the swelling beneath her eye, Brook paced the space she loathed more than any other place she'd known. Stone floor, stone walls, a stone ceiling that seemed to crush down on her, and strips of matted windows no more than three inches in height. Although a light fitting hung overhead, it held no bulb. That had long since been removed.

A true feline shows no fear of the dark, her mother used to tell her as a child. *A true feline needs no light for guidance.*

Brook used to hate her mother's lectures. They always left her feeling inadequate—still did. A particular favourite had to be, *A true feline has no need for clothes. They are merely a commodity. A privilege. A* right.

She'd heard that reasoning every time she'd been ensconced in the damn cellar and made to strip down. No matter that she'd complain of the cold. No matter that she'd beg for the comfort. Her mother would always respond with, *But, Brook, you already have a coat of your own.*

Just another means with which her parents could add to the torment. It would be considered bad enough that they locked Brook away, at all. To be encaged as feline, however, in her form that craved liberty and longed to run, was nothing less than torture.

Experience told Brook she'd last only a few days before her body would want to Shift, and her mind would want to hunt, and the denial would end with her wanting to claw her way out of her own skin in search of relief that would never come.

Closing in on the corner, Brook hopped up, slapped a sole against the frozen wall, and kicked off into a spin to re-tread the path she'd just walked. Her arms hugged her chest, while her hair provided at least some shelter for her back. Despite suggestions by her parents to the contrary, keeping her hair long had been one battle she'd actually won. All it had taken were the right words revolving around it being a preference of the young males she knew, and their shallow minds had accepted the excuse with vigour.

With the grimy, inadequate windows at her rear, a sliver of filmed moonlight showed the way to the opposite corner in her diagonal walk. As the cellar never got used for anything other than punishment, no cleaning occurred down there, and mossy mould clung in a desperate ream along each wall edge and within every groove the original adherent had escaped. Worse than the damp stink emanating from that, though, was the stench spilling from the watering hole beyond the rotted door to her left.

An hour she'd been down there, and no one had visited. Even after deeds her father had deemed to be her worst, her mother would usually allow Clive down, but only after filling his head with words of wisdom he would be expected to impart. A conspiracy to teach her how to better behave. He'd never admitted it, but Brook often wondered how much of the lectures Clive actually believed, and how much of his part was played to keep her parents sweet.

An icy tendril snaked her way across the floor and wove itself around her calves. On her corner pivot, she sent a glare toward the far right window, and the tiny crack allowing the breeze entrance to freeze her further. She also sent another of her silent curses in the direction of the ceiling for her stolen clothing. Though, in spite of the prickles taunting her flesh, of the numbness that had fast spread into her feet and fingertips, Brook found herself far more furious at the loss of her mobile phone tucked into her jeans pocket. Not that they'd find any condemning evidence on there. Both Brook and Kyle made it a point to delete any contact made to each other. Brook's frustration came wholly from her inability to make the call Kyle would be expecting.

She stiffened at the scuffle of feet outside the door. Head tilted, she listened as a key made its metallic clink, and she slow-pivoted toward the steps as the lock turned.

A strip of gold from the hallway light crept across the wall with the inching open of the door. As the gap widened, a booted foot appeared, followed by a jeaned leg, and Brook eased out a gentle sigh of relief. Her father never wore denim; he considered himself above such attire. Not bothering to inhale, or wait to see which Tom the leg belonged to, Brook snapped her focus from the door and resumed her feeble attempt at staying warm.

Boots clomped downward. "Hey."

Clive. Though tension seeped from her shoulders, his refusal to help denied her complete relaxation. She turned to find him at the bottom of the steps, the waistband of his quilted jacket bunched up to allow his hands access to his jeans pockets.

Brook drew in a deep sigh. "Why are you here?" Her voice hardened as she added, "Or have you been sent on your usual errand of filling my mind with testicular nonsense?"

"I'd be lying if I said I wasn't here in part for the latter." He shrugged. "That's the only way I can ever get down here."

"Ah." She nodded, breathing in long and hard through her nose. "I see your own standing with them is still more important to you than me."

"If I didn't maintain my own standing with them, there would be no longer *be* you."

"How many times must I tell you? There was never any me to begin, where you are concerned."

He growled. "And I keep telling you that's bullshit, and if you weren't off fucking around with mongrels, you'd have figured that out for yourself."

143

She released a low growl of her own, a sound born deep in her throat, and showed him her back. Why she had expected the encounter to go any differently, she didn't know. "Be sure to shut the door on your way out."

"I'm not done yet," he said.

Her brow arched, though she didn't face him. "Really?"

"We should talk about this."

Her hands pinched her skin, as she clenched them and hugged herself tighter. "Which part do you not understand about *there is no we*."

"If you don't change your tune, you're never gonna get out of here."

She grunted.

"Besides, you owe me an explanation, at least."

Her teeth squeaked, she ground them so hard. "I owe you *nothing*."

"Dammit, Brook! You're *not* the only one hurting here!"

She spun around, more than prepared to attack with a tirade of words, but he'd removed his hands from his pocket, and rubbed them across his hair, across his face. As they dropped to his sides, his gaze focused on her, full of the pain he described.

"I'm hurting, Brook." He shook his head, a tiny movement, the lines of his eyes pulled taut. "You have no fucking idea how much. I mean, my head wants to scream at you. To ask you what the fuck I ever did to you to be treated this way. To get treated like shit on a daily basis and constantly told no, and then I find out that all this time you've been ..." He pressed at his chest. "And at the same time, even when I feel like you've shit on me bigger than you ever have before ... for some *stupid* fucking reason ... I can't stand to see you like this. I can't stand being up there"—he pointed to the ceiling—"knowing you're down here. I mean, look at you, Brook. You're fucking freezing to death." He sidestepped to the right, bringing him closer. "So, you can accuse me all you like of being down here for *them*,"—he jerked his head toward the steps—"or for my own selfish reasons. But the truth is, I needed to check you were okay." His shoulders lifted with a long inhale. "Which probably makes me the biggest idiot on earth, I guess."

Unable to look him in the eye any longer, Brook dipped her chin until her hair fell forward and obscured her face. She hated when his tenderness arrived. Hated that he dropped his guard long enough to show her his vulnerabilities, even after she'd been a bitch to him. At the same time, that was also what she loved about Clive, and the biggest reason she'd tolerated his company more than any of the other Toms over the years.

His boots scuffed the rough stone, and she peeked through her dark strands, watching him make his way back toward the exit. She thought then, she'd blown it. However much his presence could annoy her, she knew she preferred it to being alone.

When he reached the steps, he didn't mount them, but dropped his hide onto one and began tugging off his boots. As he placed them aside and tucked his laces into them, he shook his head as though he exasperated himself. Next, off came his socks, which he arranged on the step beside his thigh, before slipping his bare feet back into his leather Timberlands.

Once he'd retied his laces, he glanced her way. "Come here," he said, his voice a growly murmur as his crooked finger beckoned her closer.

Brook hesitated only a moment before shuffling across the floor. Just like she'd done whenever they'd bordered on making up over the years, she kept her head hung low, face hidden, movements unsure. Some rituals tended to be hard to break.

She stopped in front of him.

"Foot."

She dutifully lifted it, bracing a hand on his shoulder as she did so, and he slipped on one of his removed socks. Thanks to their difference in shoe size, the sock reached to just below Brook's knee, the density of the wool bringing immediate warmth. With one protected, they completed the routine for the other foot.

"Thank you," Brook whispered.

With a nod, he parted his jacket, holding it open wide. "You wanna get warm while you can?"

Ideally, Brook would have preferred the clothes off his back, but would never ask for them. The last time Clive had left her with more than his socks, it had resulted in a month-long banishment for him by her father. He would never take the risk of that happening again, not when her Season loomed so close.

Brook's second pause lasted only a beat, and she sank onto his lap, tucking her shoulder into the dip of his, curling her knees up to her chin and her heels to her bum.

"Dunno how long we have," Clive said against her hair. "Probably until that dickwad has finished kissing butt."

Brook's spine stiffened at the mention of Stefan, but Clive closed the jacket around her, his arms coming around to hold it in place, and as his body made the heat transferral almost immediately, she closed her eyes.

"So we better make the most of it."

Brook did not question his use of 'we' again. As she curved into his warmth, inhaling his familiar scent, the only other half of 'we' on her mind seemed to be nowhere within her grasp—no matter that she couldn't seem to let him go.

18

She hadn't rang. Not the night before, like I'd asked of her. Not that morning before work. As I hopped from Dad's truck, after a journey led by steely silence, she still hadn't called.

A glitch seemed to hit the site's stride, when Dan's Hi-Lux drew up alongside us. Sean paused in his hoist of some wood, his body still half-bent, his gaze lifting to me. Ethan spared barely a glance before giving a shake of his head and ducking into the cabin. Besides Gabe, who didn't even stop, only Nathan seemed still able to fully function, as he sent a nod Dad's way and set the mixer to work.

The doors opened on the Hi-Lux, and Josh and Dan hopped out.

Josh's covert peeks my way through breakfast had driven me nuts, like he had something he wanted to say but thought better of it, but even that hadn't done my skull in as much as Dan. He'd yet to quit stabbing me with his dagger glares.

I'd stayed out of his way the night before—as much for his own good, as mine—but it had seemed a wasted effort, when I'd come down for breakfast to glowers and lip curling and the discovery he'd made food for everyone bar me. My patience had shown some serious cracks in its façade by the time we'd left the house for work, so I understood Dad's insistence that we needed the two vehicles—whether we really did, or not.

Doors slammed shut on the truck, and I turned away, beginning the trek across the gravel toward the hut for my hard-hat—anything to keep our much-needed distance. I'd scarcely taken more than a few strides, though, when a thud against my shoulder sent me stumbling to the side.

I shot out a foot to catch myself, and the growl ripped from my throat before I could stop it. Whirling back around, and bringing my hand up, I snatched hold of Dan's jugular before he could back away.

His fingers stretched the skin across my forearms, his lips parting in a snarl.

"Enough!" Dad said.

Ignoring him, I yanked my brother in close to my face. "You're pushing your luck, Dan."

He tugged his head to the side, but I tightened my grip— more to prove a point than to hurt him—until he booted against my kneecap hard enough to twist my damn leg. As I fell backward, I shot out an arm, kicked out a foot to catch the stumble, and thrust myself back at the little shit.

Dad's palm smacked against my chest, knocking the breath from me. His fingers fisted in my shirt front, his other hand grabbing hold of Dan's, and the glare that whipped between the two of us killed the retaliation in my throat. "I ... said ... *enough*!" The deep reprimand rumbled from him—a tone I hadn't heard since we were kids. "Back up, the two of you."

"Fine!" I eased from his hold. "Then, tell him to stay out of my way."

"With pleasure," Dan said, cocky swagger in the step he took. He sniffed, long and hard, staring off somewhere in the distance. "I think I prefer it better when you stay out of ours, anyway."

It wasn't until I broke away and resumed my trek that I noticed I'd clenched my hands so tight every tendon along my wrists burned, and that a bitter tasting pool of saliva had puddled in my throat. Somehow, I'd held onto my temper, though.

That time.

"Kyle, I'm not done with you, yet," Dad said.

His fingers wrapped around my shoulder, and I halted, allowing him a sideways glance without turning, until he nudged me and forced me around.

"Wasn't my fault," I said before he could start in on me.

"Things would probably settle down faster if you apologised to him, though."

"No."

His eyebrow arched up. "No?"

I shrugged, a nonchalant gesture. "I don't see what I have to apologise for."

"How about choosing a female—an *outsider*—over one of your own?"

"Then, I'd be lying. Because I'd do it again in a heartbeat. So, Dad," I said, pulling my shoulder free of his hold, "you have all the relationship advice .... What does that tell you?"

Without waiting for an answer, I spun and stalked away.

The rest of the morning passed with little occurrence. Like the pack'd grown bored of the latest spectacle. Or I'd just ceased being worth conversing with. Either way, I decided to be grateful for the small reprieve—despite the fact I still hadn't heard from Brook.

It bugged my arse that I couldn't call her, but that had been an agreement we'd had from the off. The phone calls would always be made by Brook. unless she gave a pre-arranged time, a time she knew she'd get some privacy, a chance to chat without getting caught.

As I thought back over the past months, the amount of sneaking around that had been necessary for us to meet, at all, Nathan's words from the night before rang through my head—about its wrongness being the biggest reason I'd kept schtum.

Growling at myself, at *him*, I tugged my mobile from my jeans pocket for about the fifty-billionth time and stared down at the crappy swirly screensaver and lack of call alert.

Yeah, and the biggest reason I haven't heard from her, yet, is because you lot scared her off.

149

I spun toward where they all worked as my thoughts darkened, more than happy to stick all the blame on them.

Pain splashed across my jaw before I made the full turn and splintered into my temples as I freefell. My back smacked earth. My skull cracked back. Somewhere in my dulled senses, the skittering of my mobile over stones registered, and I blinked up at Ethan standing over me.

One hand fisted, the other pointed at me. "That ..." he said, "is for thinking you couldn't come talk to me about this shit."

He stalked away, his boots kicking dust at me as they stomped the hard ground.

I let my head fall back. "Fuck!"

The march of his retreat ceased beneath the churn of machinery and the scraping of tools. I forced my head up a little, watching the tense lines of his shoulders as I rubbed at the tenderness of my jaw. After a couple of seconds of inaction, he spun back around and barrelled toward me again.

He flung his hand down, holding it out. "Here."

Quitting with my self-pampering, I reached for the offering and thrust my legs straight as he hauled. "Thanks."

"Sure." Ducking a few feet to the left, he scooped up my fallen mobile, handing it over as he straightened back up. "You're going to need that for when she calls."

I breathed out a gush of air, half-scoff, half-laugh. "She hasn't called yet."

His eyebrows quirked up. "Can you blame her? Yesterday, you toss everything at everyone in pretty much one go. No warning signals. No gradual build-up. Not even a, *Hey, guys, I have something I think I need to tell you*. No, you smack everyone in the face with the blow, and invite Brook along for the show, then wonder why you end up with the aftermath of a train wreck in a blender."

When put like that ... "Maybe she's already questioning if I'm worth the hassle." I shoved my phone into my pocket and rubbed at an ache in the back of my neck—probably an echo from Ethan's hit.

"Nah." He shook his head. "Brook's a lot of things. Stupid isn't one of them. Though ..." He looked me up and down, his gaze shifting top to toe and back. "This might just alter that."

"Screw you, pal." I glanced away.

He chuckled, but it lasted only a beat before he glanced around, too, like he'd noticed watchful eyes as much as I did. "Come on ..." He started walking. "Kettle on. Drink. You make."

Resisting thumping him for the snapped order, I followed, and within no time, we both sipped from steaming mugs in the onsite hut, with the door closed to the rest of the pack.

He frowned at me over the rim of his cup, when I withdrew my mobile again and clicked to illuminate the screen.

Still no call—missed, or otherwise. No messages, either.

"Checking it every two minutes won't change a thing," he said.

I slid the device into my back pocket, my crappy reasoning suggesting I'd feel the vibration faster in there, and returned to my drink, staring at the warm brown liquid as the steam warmed my face.

"*P* ..." Ethan said after a long stretch of quiet. "... stands for Puss, right?"

I nodded, my lips twitching at the memory of when I'd named her as such.

He snorted. "Figures. Should've guessed sooner. So, if you're so desperate to hear from her, why not just call her yourself?"

"Can't," I said, resisting the itch of my fingers to hold my mobile again. "It's too tricky for her if I call. Her family's always around, and they question a lot harder than the pack—than Dad."

"Yeah, well, maybe *we* should've questioned harder."

I sent him a cool glare, and he lowered his mug a little.

"I just meant that it might not have come to this if we had."

"You say *this* like it's a frickin' disease with no cure," I said.

"There's a cure. There always is. But whatever treatment you're using right now just isn't working. Not if Dan's attitude's anything to go by."

"Dan can go suck—"

"Exactly my point."

I growled. "How am I supposed to fix something when he looks at me like I'm filth? Even I'm not laid back enough to ignore *that*."

"Kyle, you're no longer laid back, at all."

As he stared hard into me, the words he'd probably left off on purpose wisped through my head.

That I'd been that way for months. Since the fighting. Since being bitten.

In essence? Since getting fucked up.

"What about us, though?" I asked, like I needed at least one bit of my life to be still on track. "We good?"

"Dunno." He shrugged. "Up the dose a little, maybe, and we'll take it from there."

"Arse," I muttered with a twitch of my lips.

He tipped his mug at me as if in toast. "Ginger freak."

I smiled alongside him at the smashed barriers between us, but I couldn't help the ache in my gut at his description of me. Despite the fact he'd used it countless times over the years, never before had it seemed so bloody accurate.

19

Feet beneath her rear to keep her butt off the frozen floor, and hair spanning her back to keep that off the equally frigid wall, Brook scraped the last of the macaroni and cheese from the bowl her mother had allowed her.

For around the previous fourteen hours, her flesh had stood in perpetual prickles, each and every downy hair across her body erect and defensive. With each of her shivers, the spoon had clashed with ceramic, and she'd lost half of its scooped contents en route to her mouth.

As she chased the dropped pasta around the bowl, the overhead door opened, and steps too heavy to be her mother's tapped the stone. Lowering her scraps to the floor, she angled her head to better see who'd descend, though she should have recognised Clive's boots before he rounded the corner.

He held a bowl in his hands, steam pumping out vaporous puffs into the shaded space. "Hey."

"Hey," she whispered.

"Told your mum I'd come eat mine with you."

The line of Brook's mouth hardened for a moment at the idea of having to sit and watch him eat what smelled like bacon and fried potatoes in front of her, until he covered the last remaining gap and dropped into a squat.

"What she doesn't know ..." He reached for her hand and wrapped it around the bowl. "Eat."

She did, gripping it with one hand, grabbing the fork with the other, her heart thudding its gratitude as he made his way back to the steps. "I thought they had perhaps sent you down to bring me out," she said, licking at her lips.

He sank down onto the third step up and rubbed at his lowered head as his elbows settled onto his knees. "Not exactly." His gaze returned to hers and seemed filled with forbidden explanation.

Brook's hand paused midway to her mouth, a small shiver trembling the fork. "What does that mean?"

He glanced behind toward the exit, and back to Brook, giving a small shake of his head. "Nothing."

"They are planning to let me out, I presume?"

"They're planning something, all right."

Her eyes narrowed. "Clive?"

He heaved a deep sigh. "Forget it. It's nothing," he said with a little more force. "They *are* planning to let you out. Just ... not today. Now, eat." He pointed toward her forkful of greasy sustenance, still hovering beneath her chin, and turned away.

She stared hard at him for longer, before giving her attention to her food when his downturned face told her he'd no intention of saying more on the matter. The saltiness of the bacon, mingled with the sweet buttery-ness of the potatoes, slid across her tongue as she watched Clive fiddling with the laces of his boots.

"Did you bring me more socks?" she asked around a mouthful.

He lifted his head, a smile tugging at his lips. "You know me too well."

Though said in lightness, she heard the heavier implication within his words. She did know him well, a familiarity he reciprocated in spades. Hoping to shut down the conversation, she unhooked one of her legs and waved her foot at him, his sock from the night before baggy around her calf.

"Still thinking you can treat me like your slave." His voice came out a low grumble but only held a half-hearted intent, and he still tugged at his boots and did her bidding.

By the time he padded across to her, sans boots, even thicker socks than the already-donated pair in his hand, she'd chewed on and swallowed the majority of his lunch.

"Food, socks," he said, squatting before her, "soul on a platter." He worked on his socks, both of them rising as high up Brook's legs as the other pair they covered. "Anything else?"

She prodded the final couple of potato cubes and speared the evasive strips of bacon lingering in the bowl. "For how long do I have you?" Knowing it could be many hours before she'd get to eat again, she held the final mouthful on her tongue as she waited for his answer.

He shrugged. "Dunno. Why?" Suspicion moved into his eyes. "What did you want?"

She placed his empty bowl within hers and swallowed. "I was going to use you to help me get warm."

His left eyebrow made a slow journey upward. "Use me?"

She scowled. "Not like that. I meant exercise. I need to get my blood pumping."

A smile pulled at his lips as hunger heated his stare.

Brook let out a growl. "Forget it. I do not know why I thought it would be a good idea, anyway."

"Sitting down here all night has made you even crabbier than usual. I was just messing." He straightened his legs, holding out his hand. "You want to spar? Let's spar."

She hesitated for only a beat before placing her hand in his and allowing him to tug her to her feet.

"'Make it fairer ...'"

Brook crossed her arms and glared.

"Chill. I was gonna say, to make it fairer, I'll leave my boots off,"—not that he'd have been at a disadvantage, with the second pair of socks he'd obviously donned under the proffered pair—"and you can have my shirt."

"You presume I *need* you to make it fairer," Brook said.

"Who said I was making it fairer on you?"

Brook breathed out a laugh and motioned him forward. "Then, you may give me your shirt."

Stripping it off left his upper body naked. Easily as big as Kyle, Clive's biceps bunched and flexed as he pulled his shirt over Brook's head.

"Now we're both half naked," he said.

"Or half dressed," Brook said, feeding her arms into the sleeves. "Depending on how you view it."

Features sobering, a dark seriousness entering his eyes, Clive stilled before her, his fingers playing with the hem of his T—almost as though he awaited some kind of response, as though he needed to see if his nearness, his bareness affected her in some way. In truth, the only images his naked torso stirred were of Kyle.

Before her thoughts could linger too long, she ducked into a low kick, spinning until her left foot connected with Clive's Achilles.

Upper body unbalanced, his right arm wind-milled, the palm of his other hand slamming against stone. His narrowed gaze cut to her. "Like that, is it?"

With a smug smile, Brook dived to the right.

Fingers trapped her ankle before she'd landed, and her hands smacked down to save her face from the floor. A twist of her body, a snap back of her free leg, and her foot thwacked the side of Clive's head, sending him tumbling sideways onto one knee.

He gave a sharp headshake and turned to face her. "You been working out, Brook? Taking self-defence classes I don't know about?"

No, she wanted to say, *just holding my own against a wolf who's more dominant than the Toms I have spent my life playing with.* Instead, she smiled and flipped onto her feet. "Maybe you are just out of shape."

A deep growl left his throat as he lunged.

Brook threw herself to the side.

His fingertips scraped her forearm on his sail past.

She spun back, as his feet booted the wall, sending him straight into a follow up attack.

Right for her.

Her hips jerked to the side, scarcely missing his blow, but the fold off his fingers around his shirt yanked her after him, as he scraped across the stone with a heavy *thunk* of a landing.

The air whooshed from Brook as her chest crushed to his. Her teeth jarred as her forehead butted his jaw with enough of a jolt to throb through the facial bruising her parents had given her, and pain pummelled her kneecaps on their collision with the floor.

Blanking it all, she thrust up her torso before he could recover, and mashing a hand against his cheek, she shoved his face to the side until he bussed concrete.

His snarl blasted hot breath against her palm.

A smile breaking loose, Brook leapt backward. As her soles slapped down, her fingertips pressed to the floor, fronting her crouch and adding stability.

Other than the draw up of a knee, his leg swaying side-to-side, Clive didn't move.

Eyes narrowed, senses alert, Brook waited.

He groaned. His hand lifted to his face, falling across his eyes, his brows, his other hand flopping out at his side.

Brook frowned. "Clive?"

When he didn't so much as twitch, Brook edged closer, her body still low, her eyes alert and searching for a ruse. Within a foot of him, the only alarms ringing in her head were for Clive's wellbeing.

She shuffled to his side. "Clive?"

What if he'd hit his head going down? And she'd sent him to say *hi* to the floor.

She folded her fingers around his wrist and eased it from his eyes. "Clive?" That time, the prompt left as a panicked hiss.

A low rumble responded, and Brook should have recognised it for what it was long before it erupted from his mouth as laughter. Long before his eyes snapped open. Certainly long before his hand twisted so he grabbed *her* wrist instead and jerked her in, before his bent leg surged him up, and he flipped around to land on his feet.

Though she twirled away, her foot slipped on the stone as she made the pivot, and his grasp of her ensured she didn't get very far. A sharp tug on her captive arm spun her back around, and the propulsion of his lunge sent them both toward the wall until her rear smacked hard enough to vibrate her skull and bring glitter to her vision.

Her breath left her on a grunted cry.

"Shit."

She blinked.

"Brook?"

Blinking again brought his concerned features into focus, close enough she could see the tiny sequins of sweat glistening upon his skin.

He released her wrist, bringing his hand up and sweeping her hair from her own dampened face. "You okay?"

Despite her still wavering eyesight, she thumped her fist against his sternum.

His *Oooph!* blasted her face.

With a wriggle of her body, she followed up with an elbow to the gut.

His grunt spittled her ear.

Another few inches of squirming, and a boot back of her leg connected her foot with his shin, sending him skidding away a half-dozen inches.

"Shit!" His fingers scrabbled for her hips, but she writhed around in another half-turn, her other elbow stabbing into his ribs. "Fuck!"

On her continued whirlwind, she brought her hand up, ball first, aiming for a straight uppercut to his nose.

Clive snatched her approaching wrist before contact and pinned her forearm against his clavicle as his knee wedged between her thighs and prevented her making the full turn.

Brook jerked back but got nowhere.

She tried to kick up, but Clive slammed her back down.

With each of her tugs, her grunted attempts for freedom, Clive's smile grew wider across his face.

"Warmer now?" he asked.

Her frustration growled out of her, and she swung her other fist up.

Clive caught even that, drawing it round behind her, tucking it close to her bum, until her arms stretched in both directions and insisted she couldn't move.

"You've definitely been training," he said.

"Let me loose, and I will gladly show you just how much." She urged the false bravado through gritted teeth.

Beneath the pale mop of hair slickened to his brow, his warm amber eyes burned, and his smile relit. "What?" He loosened the grip of her wrist he held behind her back. "Like this?" He glanced toward the hand he'd let slip to his chest. "How about this one?" His fingers sprang open as he turned back to her. "Your move."

The only part of her he still trapped was her left leg, where he'd hooked his foot behind her ankle, and she knew he would never let her free as unhindered as he suggested.

She contemplated Shifting, even allowed the first tingles to dance over her nerve endings, the first spattering of silken hair to sprout from the flesh at her temples.

Clive's smile diminished a little. "Didn't have you down as a cheater."

"I prefer cougar," she said, pulling back on the Shift.

Clive's laugh burst from him, short and sharp. "Brook, you ain't old enough to be no cougar."

"And you," she said, her smile sickly sweet, "are not good enough to win."

Slamming her palms against his chest, she pushed away while pivoting on the leg Clive had caught with his, her elbow aiming for his kidneys.

She hadn't counted on Clive chasing her move, though, and the two of them ended up in a warped dance, of spinning bodies, flailing arms attempting to block, legs cutting or axing, which created a tangling of limbs that should not have come as a surprise.

Her arms pinioned by Clive's meant she had no way of breaking her fall, and Brook's yelp sounded out as the room tipped off kilter.

Before impact, one arm crushed her to his chest and his other shot out, cushioning the drop, though the second she landed, Clive squashed her beneath his weight and forced the air from her lungs.

Breaths heaving, Clive stared down at her, and Brook stiffened at the unwelcome glint in his eyes.

She may have been cornered by Clive before. He'd certainly shown her his intent on more than one occasion. However, none of those instances had ever occurred while Brook lay so vulnerable with no means of escape.

She silently cursed her stupidity at not ending it before his demeanour had altered too far. She should have known better. Should not have let her defences drop so low.

With her hands wedged between them, she pushed against his chest. Hard.

It did little to budge him.

His gaze flitted to her mouth. To her eyes.

She wanted to scream at him to get off, cuss him for his presumptions, but his face lowered toward hers, and her entire body froze. Including her vocal chords.

He paused a hairsbreadth from her lips. His nostrils flared. The flutter of his lashes as his lids closed swept alongside her nose with the tilt of his face.

Finally relocating her muscles, she turned her own to the side.

Undeterred by the action, he merely switched route, his nose trailing along her jaw, his inhalations long and deep. He hesitated at her ear, each of his breaths loud, each of them moist, and his nose ceased to tickle as it urged itself closer—until all Brook could think of was Kyle, and how that spot was all his, and it seemed wrong, so wrong, that Clive invade it with such careless ease.

Yet, as Brook closed her eyes, becoming flooded by images of Kyle's constant claims to her, the demands his mouth made, the way in which her mere scent evidently affected him—in that same moment, it also seemed so right.

Lips brushing the flesh at her pulse. An arm tightening its hold around her. A warm palm pressing between her shoulder blades. Even the vibrations hitting her chest from the one lowering closer.

A tongue scratched in place of the lips, and a soft sigh left her.

Kyle.

A scrape of teeth followed, and her fingers flexed, their tips digging into the fleshy weight holding her down.

Kyle.

The solidity of an arousal gave a gentle nudge to her pelvis, and she responded with a soft, uncensored whimper, matched by the deeper pitch of a quiet growl.

Kyle.

As the caress worked a sensual path along her jawline, Brook's face twisted back in search of more, into the stirrings of arousal pumping into the air like a misted aphrodisiac to any willing participant—into a scent so far from Kyle's, it snapped her back to reality like a splash of ice water thrown in her face.

She froze.

Not Kyle.

It hadn't been him, at all.

How could she have been so damned foolish? How could she have been so close to disloyalty of the worst possible kind?

Because you're desperate, that is why, a harsh voice spoke through her mind. Desperate. Cold. Just about as lonely as she'd ever felt.

Above her, Clive paused, his cheek still against hers, the rapidity of his breaths apparent in the shallow action of his chest. "Is it the dog?" he asked.

Brook didn't answer. What could she say? *He is* all *I think about? All I* want *to think about?* Instead, she mustered a truth in place of the one screaming the loudest in her head. "If I had to Choose, I would have Chosen you."

"Brook ..." He sighed, a long, heated breath that coated her skin. "What world are you living in? You did—*do*—have to Choose." He lifted his head until she could see his eyes, where she found hope and determination tainted by a heavy sadness. "And as far as I can tell, I'm the only one here right now."

"Maybe *I* do not want to be here—no matter who is on offer."

He frowned. "And maybe those vampires really messed that head of yours up."

It was so typical of him to find an outside source to blame—to refuse to acknowledge the flaws in their lives. "You would prefer that explanation, wouldn't you?"

His fingers reached up, his gaze tracking them as he tucked a stray hair back from her face. "I'm trying my best to help you here, Brook. Why won't you just let me?"

Help her how? By taking advantage of her while weak? Attempting seduction? "Seems to me you are trying your best to help *yourself*," she said, pushing against him.

"You're wrong," he said, his unmoving form as solid as a wall made of granite. "You're so wrong, it's not even funny."

"None of this is funny," she said through gritted teeth. "Do I look as though I am enjoying myself?"

His gaze flashed back to hers, a swirl of gold patterning the irises. "You did. A moment ago."

She growled and shoved up again, yet scarcely shifted his bulk more than an inch before he settled back down. "Move!"

"Why do you have to bloody fight me all the time? Why can't you see I'm trying to help dig you out of the fucking hole you've tripped yourself into?"

"With no ulterior motive, whatsoever, I am sure." Another low growl forced out with her second attempt at freedom.

"Okay, then, yes!" he said, the admission stalling her for a moment. "Yes, I have an ulterior motive. Yes, I have wanted you for more years than I can remember and would go to the ends of the earth for you to want me in return. Happy now?"

"Ecstatic," she snapped, as he continued over her with, "But this is not just for me."

"No?" she asked, a sneer in her tone.

Hurt filled his eyes as he shook his head. "For God's sake, Brook, when have I ever made this heavy a demand of you? Do I really push you *this* far? Make you feel as fucking trapped as your eyes tell me you feel?"

He stared down at her, his breaths mingling with hers as she fought the denial she knew she had to give. "Not you. Them."

"Then, shit, Brook, let me help you. Let me help you escape. Let me help you before I can't." His voice lowered as he ducked back in closer until his lips almost touched hers. "Before it's too late."

He poised there, as though waiting permission to bridge the final gap, and while Brook registered his concluding words in an obscure corner of her mind, that singular magical word he'd uttered—one her soul responded to without permission—beat out a far louder tune like a siren of promise.

Escape. Escape. Escape.

No matter his means of escape would be a far throw from those Brook had in mind. No matter his *idea* of escape would in no way match her own.

All Brook could concentrate on was the thought, the mere *notion* of getting out of her current situation, because she knew she had no chance of doing so alone.

Her gaze met Clive's. "Help me," she whispered.

20

The instant Brook had uttered the words, the intensity in Clive's eyes consumed her. His fingers brushed across the bruising on her cheekbone and along her throat, before he hooked them over the neck of the shirt she wore and gave a gentle tug. "Where?"

She knew he meant to physically Mark her. A branding of claim-ship. Of submission on her part. One that would ensure her immunity from the other Toms—at least for a little while.

Yet, she hesitated, her mind flashing to Kyle at the idea of his territory being compromised.

Is it, though? Could she still even be considered his?

His family would argue otherwise. Her own family already had. Did the unobtainable idea of Kyle even continue to exist?

Either way, she could not remain a puppet of the Coalition, hidden away as she awaited her role in their games.

For freedom, she reminded herself. The only kind she had left to her.

Ignoring the sharp pain stabbing her chest at the realisation of what she'd lost, she turned her head to the right and exposed her neck.

Her pulse kicked up a storm as Clive dipped down to the skin there, as his rough stretch of fabric tightened the shirt across her nape.

Her chest made a shuddering journey upward as the beginnings of a growl slow-spilled from his throat.

A lap of his tongue scratched, followed by another and another and more, each layer of roughness stronger than the last until discomfort made the U-turn onto the path of numbness. Though, as Clive's head drew back, Brook still braced herself.

In her periphery, his lips rippled with the deepening of his growl, and her lids slammed shut, when he lunged for the bite that would brand Brook as his.

Another growl rumbled through the air, louder than Clive's and wild with fury.

As Clive's weight vanished from over her, Brook's eyes snapped open, only to find Stefan grabbing Clive around the throat and hauling him from the floor.

Rammed against the wall, a grunt erupted from Clive, but it took only a second for his hands to fist in Stefan's shirt, for him to shove back, for the two of them to smack against the next wall.

Oh, God. Brook kicked back, shuffling out of the way of the tussle until her rear hit stone.

Clive might have outweighed Stefan for bulk, but no one in the Coalition could deny Stefan's ability to fight, and the Tom looked mad enough to cause a lot of damage with his elbow jammed against Clive's throat, his features scarcely flinching from the sharp jab Clive sent to his ribs.

"Stop!" Brook shouted, taking a step forward.

A roar spilled from Stefan, and the hard outward thrust of his arms sent Clive tumbling to the left and onto one knee. Feet buoyant in his barely contained anger, Stefan pointed down at him. "You sneaky bastard." He swiped his forearm beneath his nose, from where blood trickled. "Jumping the fucking line with sweet talk."

Clive pushed to his feet, his fists clenched and body poised for more, but Stefan swung toward Brook.

"That all it takes?" he asked her. "A few whispered promises? Hell, I can make promises. Promises are just fucking words."

"Don't listen to him, Brook," Clive said, his muscles coiling tight. "It wasn't like that."

"Did the *dog* make you promises, too?" Stefan took a step Brook's way, his lips spreading into a smile that sent a chill right through her. "What promises do you want to hear from me, Prin—"

Clive bashed into Stefan's side, his arms snapping around the Tom as he lifted and dropped him to the floor. Following him down, Clive drew his arm back and drove his fist into the other Tom's face.

Crimson flecks sprayed upward from Stefan's nose, yet Clive still pulled back again and smashed back down. His blood-spattered forearm yanked back a third time, and a screeched yowl broke from Stefan, his fingers scrabbling for a hold on the attacking Tom, his head twisting to the side as though in attempt to escape.

Brook bolted forward. "Clive, stop!" She tugged on his arm. "Stop!"

Stefan surged upward, Clive shot backward, and as the duo went tumbling across the floor again, Brook flew back and bounced on her butt.

"What the *hell* is going on?" Donald's demand preceded his appearance at the bottom of the stairs. He came to a standstill, his eyes flicking from the scrapping Toms to Brook and back again, before he marched across the room. Grabbing the back of Stefan's shirt with one hand, and Clive's jaw with the other, he tore the two apart with a, "That's enough!"

Chests heaving, Clive and Stefan glared at each other, fists curled tight, feet fidgeting as though still itching for the fight.

"Upstairs—now! And don't you dare disrespect my home with more of your stupid bickering!"

Two lots of, "Sorry, Don," were ground out before both Stefan and Clive turned for the stairs, Clive pausing at the bottom to allow Stefan past as though he held all the respect for him in the world.

Wiping his palms across each other, Donald's focus swung toward Brook, and his brows lowered. "Clive, you're missing some clothing."

Though his shoulders stiffened, Clive didn't argue, but spun back and hopped down from the step he'd climbed. A bagful of apologies seemed to glow from his eyes, as he crossed the space to Brook and held out his hand until she tugged off his shirt and gave it to him.

Her jaw ached with the effort of containing her retorts, though her anger was all for her father rather than the one Tom who'd seemed to genuinely want to help.

Donald cleared his throat, and Clive hesitated in his walk away, his head tilting when Donald pointed.

Toward Brook's feet.

Her huff refused to be controlled as she lifted one after the other and yanked Clive's socks off, her grunt helping to express her opinion when she pounded them toward the floor.

Scooping them up, Clive sent her another of his rueful glances, and after grabbing up his boots, he made a slow climb from the cellar.

Alone with her father, an uncomfortable quiet seemed to seep from the walls, like a palpable evil tainting the air.

Donald simply stood there, his hands resting lightly on his hips. The amber of his eyes darkened to rusty brown, belying his almost casual stance.

"I am disappointed in you," he said.

"I did not do anything," she said through gritted teeth.

"I would say you never do. But that would be a lie. Wouldn't it, Brook?"

He didn't await an answer, just turned and walked away. His leather-soled shoes scraped each step. His slam of the door resonated down to her like a mockery of what her life had become.

Leaving Brook alone.

Naked.

Back to square one.

"So much for escape," she uttered, before she began to pace.

21

The tennis ball had become my best friend. Actually, the tennis ball pretty much seemed to be my only friend. Its coarse surface rubbed against my thumb-pad beneath the small circles I made, as I stared out my bedroom window at the driveway—where my truck still didn't sit, and hadn't since Ethan had taken it the night before.

A creak on the landing had my ears twitching, and an inhalation identified Dad.

"Dinner'll be ready in fifteen," he said.

I presumed he referred to the chowder I could smell, one Beth had made for us and sent over in a casserole pot—something she tended to do most days.

I nodded without turning.

"I expect you to eat with us, whether you want to, or not," he added.

I stretched out my neck, brushing harder at my ball. "When can I have my truck back?"

"Probably when Nate decides you can," Dad said.

My right eye twitched a little, as my gaze flickered across to the duo of pickups doing nothing down below. "I could just take your truck." My tone came out way more petulant than intended. Might as well have added, *and there's nothing you could do about it.*

"You're right. You could." Dad's sigh drifted across, and a few beats passed before he said, "So ... you want to fight me for the keys, then? Should I go and get my sweats on?"

I finally turned.

He stood just inside the doorframe, a small wooden chest in his hands. He held it out. "I thought you could use these more than me."

Slipping my tennis ball into my pocket, I rounded the end of the bed and took it from him. The clasp flicked up with ease, like the box had been opened way too many times, and the wood had bare patches in the varnish, like it'd been stroked too many times. Lifting the lid exposed a couple of squishy testicle-looking *things*. Completely out of shape. Well and truly pummelled.

My life felt as though it was breaking apart, and my dad had decided stress balls would help?

"Don't knock it 'til you've tried it," he said, like he'd read the direction of my thoughts. "Those beauties helped keep the house intact on many an occasion after we lost your mother."

I lifted my gaze to his.

He merely smiled. "See you downstairs."

The tennis ball had some competition. All through dinner, I'd kept the stress balls in my pocket, one hand tucked in there, crushing the life out of them, while I used the other to scoop up fishy soup. I was pretty sure they saved Dan's skin, the couple of times he pissed me off, too.

The first had been when he bumped the table with his hip, sending my meal sloshing over the side of my bowl as a result. The second had been when he'd 'stretched out his legs' and mine had just so happened to be in his way.

Little squirt had been lucky I didn't send his kisser into his own soup. I'd wanted to. Instead, I'd withdrawn my new best friends and hidden them below the table while I treated them like enemies.

Oddly enough, nobody had invited me to stick around after dinner, and I'd rushed back to my room at the first opportunity I got, where I discovered the stress balls had limited skills and the tennis ball once more won the popularity contest.

Mastering the art of bouncing rubber off the ceiling to the wall to the dresser to me, while lying on my back on the bed with my mobile resting on my chest, took immense skill—yet, somehow, I achieved it. I was a ball bouncing genius and had never even realised. Not even Josh appearing in my doorway and just standing there wrecked my flow.

Five minutes passed, more triple rebounds, more catches. Flex, throw, brace, catch—Josh hadn't moved, hadn't said a word.

"You know," I said, tossing the ball again, "if I was in the circus,"—triple bounce, catch—"it'd cost you a lot of money"— throw—"to stand and stare at me like that." The ball smacked against my upraised palm, and I chucked it again.

"Don't you think you're a little old for her, anyway?" he said.

I twisted toward him, batting the ball aside before it could bash my temple. "You for real?"

He shrugged.

"The entire pack's ragging on at me about the whole cross-species issue, and you want to complain about an eleven-year gap? Give me a break, here, bro."

"Forget it," he mumbled, turning away. "Was just trying to start a conversation, is all."

Had I seriously become that tough to talk to? I sat up before he could vanish around the corner. "Josh?"

He stopped, his mouth set in a line of attitude as he glanced my way.

I waved him back. "Come on in."

His lips curved a little as he pivoted and made a lazy traipse into my room, his bare feet sweeping the carpet strands on his way to my chair.

"Your mission," I said, quoting *Mission Impossible* as he sat, "if you choose to accept it ..." I waited until I had his attention. "Is to help keep me sane."

He blew out a breath, shaking his head like I'd asked for the impossible, indeed, before he chuckled and snatched the fallen ball from the floor. "Then, we're gonna need this," he said, and flung it my way.

I caught it with a hollow slap, arced it back.

"All those scratches you kept appearing with make sense now," he said, catching the ball before his smile widened. "Guess this makes you well and truly pussy-whipped, huh?"

22

The sun blazed down in that blinding way it had, over the equipment of the construction site the next day, but I could have been smack in the middle of a hurricane and I wouldn't have cared.

Neither did I care that the rest of the pack had stripped down to just T-shirts, and even those had sweat drenching the backs, as they dug and carried, and mixed, and built— while I just paced around as though clueless about what to do.

Forty-two hours since Brook walked out of my house, and I still hadn't heard from her. My hands shook every time I checked my phone, like an addict in withdrawal, and I knew if I left it much longer, I'd crack.

Or crack *up*.

It took all of five minutes before I couldn't take any more.

A quick check of the others assured me of their preoccupation, and I strode from my position near the chain-link and snuck into the hut.

From the outside, the walls appeared insubstantial, but the second I closed the door, all site noise reduced to a muffled din. I sank into the office chair, the suspension squeaking beneath my weight, and cupped my phone in my lap, like hiding behind the desk would make the task easier.

Illuminating the screen taunted me with its blankness. I blew out a breath at the lack of alerts—one filled with irritation as much as resignation. Did I need to give her more space? More time? Or maybe the space she'd already had was too much?

Should I have ignored the deal and just called her, anyway?

Before I could change my mind, I pressed the green button, scrolled straight to P, and slid my thumb across the screen to dial.

Momentary silence greeted my ear when I lifted my phone up, before the click of connection was followed by a nasal-sounding recorded female stating she couldn't connect my call.

"Shit!"

I flicked it off and glared at the moody coloured walls like they were what separated me from seeing her. My hand tightened into a fist around the phone, the other opening and clenching against my knee. I should've brought those damn stress balls to work, too.

At the same time, my heels hammered the floor, like they itched to run over to Cheshire to find out for sure that her incommunicado meant what I suspected.

I probably would have done exactly that—if I had my truck, or the keys to every other pack vehicle hadn't done a David Copperfield.

"Shit, shit, *shit*."

When the cabin door squawked open, who knew how long later, I still hadn't moved from the swivel chair. I lifted my head from the spot it had adopted in my hands, to Jem's entrance.

Behind her came Poppy, trusty sidekick and all-round best friend.

One glance at me, and Jem halted. "Kyle?"

Poppy's too-wise eyes peeked around Jem's shoulder, her mass of red curls framing them. "How you doing, sweetie?"

"Hey, Poppy, I'm ..." I trailed off with a frown, unsure how to finish—certainly unable to mutter my accustomed 'good'. "You?"

She smiled, but it held more sympathy than pleasure. "I'm doing okay."

"Poppy, can you give me a minute?" Jem asked.

"Sure, hon." After one more smile that her eyes didn't share, Poppy about-turned and left the two of us alone.

Without speaking, Jem padded around to my side of the desk, hiked her bum up on it, and leaned down to wheel my chair in close. Tipping up my chin with one finger, she stared into my eyes. "You're worrying me, Kyle."

If one of my pack brothers had collared me like that, I'd have shrugged them off and knocked them out of my path. *Damn Jem for being female.* All I could manage in response was, "Sorry." Last of the witty comebacks.

"That the best you've got?" She sighed, releasing me of her hold as she straightened a little. "As annoying as you and Ethan can be in your double act sometimes, I miss your mojo. When's it coming back?"

"Kind of hard to keep hold of it when the entire pack's pissed off at you." Could I have sounded any more sorry for myself?

"They're not really mad at you. They're not," she said, when my narrowed gaze cut back to her. "It's just that they don't get it. That, and they have no idea what to do about it."

I frowned. "I'm not asking them to do anything. Except leave us be." My head cocked a little. "And maybe *try* to accept it."

She gave a small smile as she tugged at a curled lock of my hair. "That's pretty much the part they're struggling with."

"And you?" I asked, trying to keep the desperation for just one vote of support out of my voice.

She shrugged. "I'm not bothered by it all, if that's what you want to know."

Unable to stop myself pushing it that little bit farther, I asked, "You like Brook?"

"I liked what I saw when she stayed at Nate's those few days." She meant the days following the vampire saga, when Brook had insisted on sticking around long enough to make sure I'd survived my ordeal okay before heading home. "That's enough for me, for now, so long as she doesn't turn out to be a psycho."

"So, why can't the others think like that?"

With a sigh, she swung her legs to the side and slid off the desktop. "You forget I have different roots than you guys," she said, heading for the coffee corner. After flicking the kettle on, she swung back and faced me, sweeping a couple of loose strands of her hair off her face. "I come from a society where change is acceptable. Where relationships that were once upon a time banned—due to race, or religion, or social standing, or whatever—are now acceptable and even considered the norm. But you lot live in the dark ages, with your preconceptions and gender inequality crap, and seriously? It's about time you caught up with the times. If the world around you can change, then maybe it's time to accept it can change for you, too."

I swallowed down on the lump working its way into my throat. "Want to tell this to Nate?"

"Already did. Last night."

"And?"

"He'll come around." Translation: It hadn't gone so well. "You've just got to give him time."

Yeah, right. "What chance is there of that, when everyone else agrees with him?"

"You're wrong. Not everyone thinks he's right." The smile she gave seemed to hold a heap of knowledge. "But the others know it's too early to start batting for your team." She turned away, filling mugs with coffee. "Have a little patience, my friend."

Yeah, like I had a whole lot of that.

Two days. Almost forty-eight hours of shivering, of twitching in her own skin, of plotting the impossible, of interminable pacing.

Only Brook's father had visited the cellar in that time, and even he had ventured only as far as the lowest step, from where he deposited her meals and sent her glowers of disapproval, before tip-tapping his way back up to the warmth and light.

Brook had seen nobody else, or heard them—not even her mother.

Until Stefan arrived.

The instant the steps hit stone, Brook knew someone other than her father had come. The slow, almost taunting descent he made should have warned her of who approached before his jeans appeared, his too-tight sweater, and his cocky grin that she automatically wanted to erase off his smug face.

He halted at the bottom, head slanted as his gaze skimmed down her body and back up to her eyes. "Princess."

She desperately wanted to adjust her hair for cover, to fold her arms across her chest, but refused to show that his scrutiny, his visit even, unnerved her as only Stefan could. "What are you doing here, Stefan?"

"Had a word with Daddy for you." A couple of sauntering steps brought him closer, and Brook had to deny her feet their urge to back up. "Told him, so long as you're fed all the while, he has nothing to barter with for your compliance."

Brook's eyes narrowed as she absorbed the underlying message in his words. "Bastard," she muttered, before she added, "Compliance for what?"

His smile broadened. "You'll see." He darted forward a few yards, and Brook's foot snapped behind into position as she braced herself, fists clenched and ready. Barking out a laugh, he halted. "As edgy as always, I see. You need to loosen up a bit, Princess. I'm just playing with you."

Still, Brook didn't relax her pose. She couldn't afford to. Not around Stefan. "Where is Clive?" she asked, knowing the question would irk him.

On cue, his jaw flexed. He visibly relaxed it. "Got kicked out last night. Moron brought it on himself with yesterday's stunt."

"If that is the case, why are you here?"

"What can I say?" He shrugged. "My dad has more power than yours. Clive's doesn't."

"And yet everyone still wonders why I hate politics," she said.

"Tough, because politics is a game you're gonna be made to play." He jerked forward again, snapping out his hand for her and sending Brook into a backward jolt that banged her against the wall. "And guess who's running for captain of your team?"

Brook's *pffft* arrived loud. "You could not even captain a bag of marshmallows."

He gave a growl as his palm smacked against the stone above her shoulder, and he leaned in close. "You should think yourself lucky Daddy can still match you, with your dirty little secret threatening to leak." His words arrived low, almost spat like venom. "You realise everyone'll be pissed if they know the truth, don't you? They all think they're vying for a pretty little virgin with a cherry to pop." The vicious glint in his eyes made way for an equally malicious smile. "Personally, I think the dog did me a favour."

Pulse stuttering beneath his nearness, Brook held her breath, as well as her tongue when she wanted to ask what he meant. She suspected she did not want to know.

"He probably has you well-seasoned. Bet he's taught you a few tricks, too." His free hand came up, fingers smoothing over her bruises before nudging her hair aside, as he stared down at her body. "And now you're going to be performing them for me."

Her temper fired at his presumptuous words, and she slapped his hand aside. "Pathetic!" Her palms smacked against his chest hard enough to knock him back a couple of steps. "You spout off as though you are the most eligible Tom in the Coalition, yet when have you ever been Chosen by a female, Stefan?" She twisted around him and stormed off toward the far corner of the room. "Your sad little dreams are all you have to keep you company."

"You're the pathetic one, you spoilt brat," he said, striding after her. "Too blinded by your own self-worth to see what's going on. What do you think the old guys are discussing up there?" He came to a stop, as Brook whirled on him, her fists clenched. "Everyone has a price, Princess. And you can bet your life yours won't even be that high."

Before she could conjure a response, Stefan spun away.

His feet stomped up the stairs, and the cellar door slammed.

Both sounds vanished beneath his disturbing parting shot as it left Brook's mind humming.

23

After spending the night tossing and turning, waking to no alerts and Brook's phone still switched off, and being ordered by Nate to quit moping about and pull my weight, my mood Wednesday morning could've had trolls seeking out their bridges to quiver beneath.

Probably the reason why I slopped on cement, and the bricks I wedged into place resembled vandalised tombstones, which was definitely why Ethan kicked me aside and confiscated my trowel.

"Move your useless hide, if you're going to trash the job," he'd said, ordering me off to sulk in private.

I'd done exactly that, and behind the cabin would've been a good pacing place—plenty of unobserved strides in which to mentally torture myself—if Sean hadn't rounded the corner.

He veered my way, no doubt to speak his two penneth on the current happenings.

I'd begun to feel a little like I'd entered an alternate reality, one where I hosted a freakishly long funeral wake, and everyone in attendance would very slowly, one by one, all sidle over to pay their respects—except maybe I was the one who'd died.

Sean didn't stop when he reached me, but slapped my shoulder on his way past. "Supplies run. Let's go."

Apparently, I'd reached the ultimate low, where pretty much everyone I worked with realised just how unproductive I'd become to have around. The knowledge didn't stop me spinning to follow, though.

We took Nate's Ford pickup, windows slightly cracked, Radio Two drolling up the atmosphere with some Irish guy spouting syrupy waffle, but even in there, I couldn't stay still.

My forehead pressed against the window glass, watching the world no one seemed to want me to explore, while below, my toes fidgeted in my boots. My hands twitched in my lap, too, thumbs flicking across the pads of each finger like they'd taken on their own task of counting off each additional second I didn't hear from Brook.

Sean reached over and knocked the stereo down until only an incoherent hum remained. He settled back in his seat. Looked my way. Back to the road. To me again.

Each of his movements, I caught in my periphery.

My thumbs danced faster.

"It's tough being separated from your mate, eh?" he finally said.

My thumbs stilled. "She's not—"

"Don't even go there. Been there, done it, remember? Went through it when I first met Jem." He braked for a red light, shifted down the gears, glanced my way. "Finding what my soul knew it'd been searching for, then having it ripped away, hurt like nothing else on earth. I see it in your eyes, Kyle—the same pain I felt back then." He turned back to the road, one hand braced on the wheel. "If Dad could hear me, he'd probably go nuts, but if you want my advice?"

Frowning, and not one hundred percent sure I'd like what he had to say, I nodded.

He sniffed in, a long deep breath, like he had to prepare himself, releasing it just as slowly. "Ignore him."

My eyebrows winged up.

He slipped the stick into gear and pulled away as the lights switched to green. "Ignore the damn lot of them." His head bobbed as though to reinforce his opinion. "Because only *you* know if she's worth fighting for, or not. And if she is?" His attention flashed to me and back to the road, but I caught the determination in his dark eyes.

Maybe I did want to hear his thoughts, after all.

"You'd better damn well find a way to do so," he said. "Otherwise, it'll slowly kill you from the inside out." His head nodded again. "Sure, you might be breathing. Might think you're fooling everyone else into believing you're still functioning. But really? It'll rip you apart in here." He pressed a hand to his chest. "And in here ..." With the same hand, he tapped his head. "You'll have so much buzzing going on—if you don't already—it'll be enough to send you on the downward slope to insanity. Then, before you can even realise it's happened, you'll have ceased to *live*."

My frown deepened throughout his speech, as each infliction he identified resonated within me, where the early symptoms had already begun to blossom. "Is that how bad it was for you?" I asked.

A long pause was chased by his, "Almost."

I shifted in my seat, my hands progressing to curling and uncurling as I returned to staring out the window.

Females strolled the pavement, either guiding pushchairs or leading trolleys, or darting around slower ones like they had urgent tasks to complete. Amongst them, elderly folk walked with oversized shopping bags, and the occasional couple held hands.

Turning back to Sean, I rubbed my palms along my thighs to stop them flexing. "What if I don't know how to get what I want?"

"Anyone can obtain the unobtainable. You've just got to want it enough." Slowing the truck down, he swung into the builders' yard. "And I think you do, Kyle. So, you'll figure it out." After sliding us into a parking spot, he switched off the engine and opened his door.

"Sean?"

He hopped out and turned, leaning against the frame.

"How did you ..."

He glanced off, his expression intense as though he saw something there I didn't. "I took the first opportunity I had," he said, looking back, "and I marched in there and snatched her from under the bastard's nose."

Biggest problem with Sean's method? I had way more than one bastard blocking the way to Brook.

Heaving a sigh, I climbed from the truck.

Pallets of bricks lined the exterior fences of the yard. Garden stones in every shape and colour. Ornaments, too, from bird troughs and tables, to naked kids with a water feature sticking out in place of a dick. The high squeal of the bench saw could be heard over in the wood storage somewhere to the back of the yard.

We passed heaped piles of sand, cement, gravel, both in stacked bags and loose, and rounded the display of fish ponds on our way to the service hut.

Inside, a gas heater pumped mediocre warmth out to anyone who got within an inch of its grill, while making enough noise to drown out a tractor. Rows of racks of screws, nails, raw plugs, and other paraphernalia to give builder-geeks a wet dream, went from wall-to-wall.

I bypassed those, leaving Sean to order the supplies, and headed straight for the drills and Hilti guns.

Picking up the latter, I tested its weight out in my palm, wondering just how long a nail it could hold. How much damage it could do if shot at a Tom's skull.

Thinking of Toms had my musing returning to Brook.

It bugged my arse to epic proportions that she still hadn't rang.

It equally bugged my arse that her phone remained switched off.

Maybe her phone was always switched off, though. Not like I could claim any different, with our agreement for her to initiate our calls, but after the weekend conversation, the promises I'd made to her, it didn't make sense. Did she think I'd no longer uphold those vows because of the pack's discovery of us? If anything, I'd only become more determined since Sunday night, though how could I bring anything to fruition when I was the only party playing along? Didn't she realise the timescale we had to work with? How long had she said until her birthday and Season? *Less than two weeks ...*

Sean peeked around the aisle toward where I stood. "Ready?"

I stuck the Hilti gun back and fell into step beside him. "What if Brook can't afford for me to wait for an opportunity?"

He frowned. "She in some kind of trouble?"

I knew Jem had been—technically. She might only have been human at the time, and within a human existence, but the ill treatment from her shithead of a husband had definitely been incentive enough for Sean to act.

Was Brook in trouble, though—or would she be, once her timer had ticked down? Or had she simply had enough? Of me.

"Honestly?" I pulled open the truck's passenger door, but hesitated over declaring absolutes and settled for, "I don't know." Climbing into my seat, I added, "But something's not sitting right in my gut."

Sean slid in beside me. His hand paused over the keys he inserted into the ignition, and his eyes held alien-probe intensity as he stared my way. "You ready to tell someone what's going on inside that head of yours, yet?"

My initial reaction was to scoff and shake my head, until common sense put in a rare appearance and reminded me Sean might just be the only pack brother who'd *get* how I felt. "You prepared to listen—to only listen?" I asked. "Without blabbing to everyone else." He could take that how he wanted, though his interpretation would probably be spot on, and he'd know I meant Nate and Dad.

As he started the engine, he sent me a nod. "Talk."

I told Sean everything. Exactly how it all began. How I felt. As well as all that Brook had shared with me on Sunday. Once I'd finished, he'd made me promise not to race off and do anything stupid. And if I could hold it together for a half-day, in return, he'd sort something out.

He'd asked me to trust him.

I did. With my life.

Trusting him with Brook's seemed a little harder, however, and by dinnertime, I wanted to dig out my own eyes for distraction.

Which meant that, once again, I sat at the kitchen table with my feet tapping, my right hand loving up the balls in my pocket, and my left almost crushing the mobile's shape while I held it to my lips so I'd feel even the slightest vibration if she called.

Over at the cooker, Dad squatted in front of the oven, mitts on his hands as he checked on the meat pie. The gravy smelled like it'd had ale added to it, and my stomach gave a small gurgle of approval.

Sounds of the TV drifted in from the living room, where Josh loafed over the entire sofa last I checked, watching a dodgy old rerun of *Scooby Doo*.

Unfortunately, Dan had chosen the same place as me to sit out the wait for his meal.

Across the other side of the table, he bent over a sketchpad, pencil in hand. He'd used to draw a lot as a kid, and Mum had always encouraged it. Said it made a change for one of us to be doing something non-aggressive. His supplies hadn't seen light so much since she died, and his pastime had dwindled away to an occasional one—usually saved for when he had something on his mind.

The pencil slid across the page, creating a build-up of what just looked like random lines to me, but probably meant a whole lot more to Danny.

Again, like something might have changed, I drew my phone away from my chin long enough to click the screen and confirm what I already knew. No calls.

"Will you quit staring at that thing?" Dan asked, his gaze leaving his artwork as his hand snapped toward me across the table. "You're embarrassing yourself."

I snatched my mobile away, my other hand pumping against the balls in my pocket.

"Should've bought you some tissues for Christmas," he said as he settled back into his seat. "Or some notepaper so you could write off to Dear Deidre and asked her to help sort out your life—and no, you're not having any of mine." He drew a few more lines, while I did my best to keep the brewing rumble in my chest under wraps and jigged my damn feet like I needed to pee. "She's a cat, for crap's sake—and you're acting like an idiot over her."

"Danny, that's enough," Dad said, pouring potatoes into a colander over the sink. "And mind your language at the table."

"Well, he is," Dan said.

"I have not had one peaceful meal this week," Dad said. "Do you really want to push me to lock you two in the cellar every dinnertime?" He began mashing the potatoes like he had some aggression to work off himself. "Don't think I won't."

Sending Dan a final warning glance with eyes that seemed to burn even my sockets, I shuffled back into position, my fist jacking off my balls, lips kissing the phone, and closed my lids on the bothersome shit across the table.

For some reason—probably because of Dad's warning—dinner passed as the quietest meal all week. The pie held enough gravy and steak to leave a hungered man groaning, the mash melted on my tongue Dad had added so much butter, and along with the carrots, they all filled a spot I realised I'd been neglecting. Even Dan seemed contented enough to keep his trap shut for a while.

As I scooped up the remnants of mash and gravy from my plate, a low rumble carried in from the driveway—one I recognised as Ethan's truck. I lifted my head, catching Dad's gaze on me.

"Expecting someone?" he asked.

I shook my head, hoping my features stayed as impassive as I tried to make them, and peered back over my shoulder toward the heavy footsteps approaching the front door.

A few seconds later, it swung open to reveal Ethan.

I frowned, wondering if Sean had anything to do with his appearance. I knew he'd said to let him sort something out, but he hadn't once mentioned his intentions.

Ethan headed our way, but didn't enter the kitchen, just leaned against the doorframe and jerked his chin up in greeting. "Hey."

"Everything all right?" Dad asked.

He nodded. "Just thought I'd pop by and see if Kyle wanted to get out for a while." His gaze swung to me. "Thought he could use the break."

"And us," Dad said beneath his breath.

"Sounds good." Ignoring Dad's dig, I pushed back from the table, hoping the stare I sent Ethan's way held enough of a question about his true reason for showing up, but if it did, he didn't indicate. After depositing my plate and cutlery in the sink, I headed into the hallway for my boots and my shirt.

"Ready?" Ethan asked, once I'd finished kitting myself up.

I nodded, and we ducked outside into an evening rife with roiling grey clouds and the initial spatters of rain.

Ethan tossed the truck keys to me. "You drive."

"Good of you," I said, rounding the pickup to the driver's door.

"Not really. Apparently, you're the only one who knows exactly where we're going."

We both climbed into the truck, settled into our seats, and I twisted to Ethan as I inserted the keys. "And where's that?"

"Brook's. Because my brother's as big a fool as you when it comes to females, and he seems to think it's a good idea. Now drive."

"Says the guy who thinks he can save the universe," I said, swinging us toward the gates.

"And pull over around fifty yards down the road on the left," he said.

"Because?" I asked, checking for traffic rolling in from the right before making the turn onto the lane.

"Because, why have only one fool on a mission, when we can have two?"

I frowned at him.

"Dad thinks I've headed out with Sean for some guy time. Connor thinks I've headed out with you for some guy time. What they don't know won't hurt them."

"And if we get caught out?" I asked, like it'd make the slightest bit of difference to us going.

"Make sure we don't. Because if you and Sean get me into any trouble, or captured, maimed, or tortured, Kyle ... I'm going to hurt you like never before."

I shouldn't really have found his threat amusing because I had little doubt he meant every word, but I still grinned. Spotting Sean a little way up ahead, hugging the grass verge, I drove a little faster with the first soar of hope I'd had in days.

24

By the time I parked in the same spot I had for my last visit to Brook's, rain sloshed against the windscreen like we sat under a waterfall, and wind beat about the sides of the truck, making it sway left to right.

I switched off the engine. "This is it."

Sean's head appeared between the front seats, and his squinted eyes matched Ethan's, as they both stared toward the property. "Is there even a house beyond those walls?" he asked.

"Two," I said. "If you count the guesthouse."

He gave a low whistle, as Ethan asked, "Do we even have anything resembling a plan yet?"

No. Though, I kept that to myself. Even Sean had admitted he didn't have much of an idea when we'd discussed it on the drive over.

"I mean, we can't march up to the front door and ask to speak to Brook, because her dad acted like a jerkwad around us last time we met," Ethan said. "We have no idea which window on the main house leads to Brook's room, because you've never been that far. All we know is the way to the guesthouse, correct?"

I gave a half-nod, half-shrug.

"Then, let's head that way, and figure it out from there."

On my step from the truck, rain pelted my head and shoulders, as the gale forced my hair from my forehead and sent my shirt billowing sideways. Without bothering to speak, because I knew Sean and Ethan would follow, anyway, I spun for the wall and hopped up onto the top, pausing only for a few fast inhalations before dropping down to the other side.

A trio of quiet thuds sounded out on our landing. Standing in the shade of the wall, my pack brothers either side of me, I peered through the dark trees, around their limbs frantically waving a pattern, searching for movement.

Nothing. Unsurprisingly. The cats had no reason to suspect an unexpected visit, and no one in their right mind would've been out for an evening stroll—the rain had won its battle against the wind, and my hair already clung to my forehead in a heavy clump.

Again, I ducked low into a crouched jog toward the guesthouse, my shoulders leading the way into the right and left weaves. Beneath trees bare of foliage, intermittent drips continued to soak my upper body, while mud flicked up to speckle my jeans.

Nearly soundless at my rear, the steps of the others followed my route, and I paused for a couple of beats, when the outline of the guesthouse loomed through the downpour. No internal lights shone out amongst the white panelling, but I still checked the clearness of the route, before racing toward the tree edge and the last of our coverage.

As soon as I'd left the trees, I broke into a sprint for the back porch of the building, the gale blasting me from the left, whipping my hair across my eyes. A leap onto the raised decking put me back in shadow, and I spun to face outward as Ethan and Sean joined me.

Quiet remained beneath the rage of weather, more stillness beneath the dance of nature.

So far, so good.

"Way in?" Ethan asked beside me.

Around four feet to my left, and up, the balcony to the master suite overhung the rear decking—the only balcony to the property. I pointed that way and, following my own direction, took a singular stride and made an upward leap. My fingers grasped the railing, and I hauled myself over the rest of the way, slapping down a little louder than I'd have liked against the wooden boards.

I leaned over the ledge, beckoned to the other two, and turned for the potted topiary tree in the far corner. The last time I'd snuck in, Brook had told me about the key they always kept hidden, for Toms to gain entry in time of need whenever no one was home, and that had been my way in, too.

As I dropped into a crouch, the rain found its way below the collar of my shirt, as if saturating my lower back wasn't bad enough. Light scuffles hit the deck at my rear, and I held my breath as I scraped through the soil supporting the plant, until my fingertips grazed metal.

Drawing the key out, I twisted and held it up, grinning at Ethan's raised eyebrow.

It took less than a minute to unsecure the door and get all three of us past the heavy drapes protecting the exit and into the master bedroom. Blinking a couple of times to adjust my vision, I scanned the tightly-made bed, the fitted wardrobes, the unused lamps on their bedside stands. A quick inhalation revealed little, and certainly not Brook. Not that I'd expected it to. Brook had told me she preferred the smaller, less-touched suite to the one used by guests.

"Well?" Sean asked, stepping around me. "What now?"

"Doesn't appear to be anyone here," Ethan said. "Can we see the main property from one of the windows?"

"Should be able to from the front. It's only a little ways from the driveway and the garages, so ..."

"Let's go, then." Ethan made for the door. "Keep moving."

I followed behind, with Sean at my shoulder, the thick carpet beneath my boots setting a slight spring to my steps.

Departing the room took us to the landing. The bathroom door stood ajar in the adjacent wall to the right, second bedroom on the left, and beyond that, the room I'd shared for a few hours with Brook.

The door that'd lead to the windows we needed stood opposite, but I couldn't stop my eyes flickering toward the room at the end, nor my nostrils flaring in their perpetual hope of catching a whiff of the cat, before yanking down the handle and leading the way.

Smaller in size than the master, with furniture of the Formica variety, the bedroom we entered had the less-than-alluring view of a mini car park, just as I'd hoped.

I'd taken only a few strides, when a rattle carried up from below, and I froze, glancing toward the two brothers, both poised on the spot, both with their heads tilted.

A crunch followed.

"Someone's coming in," Sean whispered, at the same time that I identified the sound as turning keys.

Ethan tugged on my arm. "Back out."

"No." I gripped his wrist. Brook often used the guesthouse for alone time—she'd told me that herself. "Wait and see."

All three of us stiffened, as light footsteps tapped downstairs and a door clicked closed. The steps travelled across what sounded like a hardwood floor, toward the west side of the guesthouse. Toward the staircase.

"Nudge the door to," I whispered, as a faint blush of light inched along the outside landing.

Sean reached out and pushed the door swinging over the carpet with a low swish, leaving a sliver of a gap we all huddled to the right of.

"I meant what I said," Ethan began, as footsteps ascended the stairs and a brighter light bled through the slit in the door. "Get me in any kind of trouble, and I'm kicking your arse. Both of you."

My lips twitched as I elbowed him over a little and leaned in closer.

The nearing footsteps didn't hold enough weight to be anything more than a small female. I tried inhaling, but with no breeze to help any scent along to us, very little other than all the combined essences I'd already detected got sucked in.

A partial shadow blocked some of our light as the footsteps halted.

"Flipping heck." Definitely a female's voice, though not the one I'd have preferred to hear. "She could've said someone had mucked all the bloody carpets up here."

Ethan's drawn brows and tightened lips held a heap of meaning without him even having to say a word. My own internal groan put in an appearance, because I had about as much certainty as he probably did that the mess she complained about had been made by us. All she'd need to do was take a peek into the master suite to see where it came from—a glance to her left to see where it led.

A scuffle carried through—like she'd taken an uncertain step.

A click, followed by even more illumination, and the female's shadow shifted in and out of the narrow slice of light across the carpet where we stood.

"You've got to be kiddi—"

Quiet ensued beyond our breaths and hers.

The tiniest of tiptoes began edging our way, along with a rapid heartbeat that seemed to increase in tempo.

Crap.

I took a step back. Not surprisingly, so did Ethan and Sean. Despite there obviously only being a female on the other side of our barrier, we all three adopted a defensive stance, all three curled our hands into fists.

"I got this," I muttered as low as I could.

A faint rumble came from Ethan. "Like hell."

"You need me to step in, children?" Sean asked at my right.

The door brushed forward, catching the carpet strands, as more light bled through and surrounded the human shadow. It nudged forward another inch, and another, its slow sweep toward us portraying the intruder's caution.

A sudden thud smacked the other side, and the door shot wide open.

A young female, no more than early-twenties, stood silhouetted in the doorframe, blonde hair framing her shadowed face, a slight chubbiness filling out her clothing.

She squinted into the far corner of the room for a beat, before her shoulders stiffened, and her head snapped around—toward us.

As her eyes widened, and her lips parted, I bolted forward. My hand pressed over her mouth as her squeak erupted. My other arm slipped around her to prevent her taking a step back.

I brought my face level with hers and inhaled—damp human. "Shh," I said. "I'm not going to hurt you, okay? I swear."

Though her eyes made frantic left-to-right darts and her mouth offered tiny panting gasps against my palm, the tiniest jerk of her head told me she'd listened.

"Brook ..."

Her gaze flashed to the side—toward the main house.

"Do you know where she is?"

I loosened my hand just enough for her to draw breath.

"She's at the house," she whispered, the words gasped out, panicked.

"Is she okay?"

Her chest heaved, up-down-up-down, each of her breaths short and shallow, and she seemed to study me, almost as though she had something to say but couldn't quite figure out if she should share it *with me*.

With no time for unnecessary shit, I gave her the slightest of shakes. "Tell me. Is she okay?"

"She—" The female's head twisted to the right at the opening and slamming of a door downstairs.

"Elise!" another female voice snapped.

The woman I held jerked in my grasp, the beginnings of a muffled shout bursting from her lips, before I smothered them again and held her tighter.

"Elise! Where are you?"

"Time to leave," Ethan said.

I gave a tiny nod. "Answer her," I whispered to the woman, lifting my hand.

She stared at me, the fear in her eyes matching that which pumped out in her scent, but a moment later, she cleared her throat. "I'm up here, Mrs Nicholls. Tidying the master suite, as you said."

I stuck my hand back in place and gave a nod of approval.

"Yes, well, I have changed my mind about the towels," the female called out, footsteps click-clacking across the floorboards downstairs. "They need to be suited to the Chosen ..."

As the steps grew closer to the staircase, Sean grasped my upper arm. "Wrap it up. We're leaving."

"... and I seem to recall the Kings have a preference for gold." The approaching female's voice heightened in volume as it crept up the stairway instead of sifting through the floor.

"Now," Ethan said.

I ducked my face even closer to the woman. "If you think anything of Brook—anything—you'll keep schtum about this."

At the hint of a nod, I released my grip on her, swinging her back onto the landing with a nudge toward the stairs, and slunk off in the other direction into the master bedroom.

"Good idea, Mrs Nicholls," the woman said, as I tugged on the balcony door and squeezed through with Sean and Ethan on my heels.

Without pausing to lock back up, I hopped up onto the railing and sprang over the other side with enough boost to reach grass and soften the blow. My knees bent to accommodate the ping through my lower tendons as I landed. On straightening, I caught the mirroring of Sean and Ethan's positions, and I glanced left and right through the rain as it attacked once more, gluing my hair to my forehead and clouding my eyes.

"Clear," Ethan said, and we made a run toward the trees.

More rapid in our sprint, less cautious in our observations, the return trip to the truck seemed to take fewer minutes than the one we'd made upon our arrival. After vaulting the wall, climbing into the pickup, and slamming the doors on the worsening weather, I closed my eyes and calmed my breathing.

"What now?" I asked, lids still lowered, head back.

"Well, now we've been here, you can tick it off your list of immediate avenues, and you can go home and get some rest while we figure out the next one," Sean said.

"Yeah, figure out more stupid ideas." Opening my eyes, I reached forward to stick the keys in the ignition.

"Tonight wasn't a stupid idea," Sean said.

"How'd you work that out?" I asked, twisting the keys until the engine rumbled to life. "We learned nothing."

"Muppet," Ethan said, shaking his head.

I turned to face him.

"Okay, so, yes, I agree that tonight was a stupid idea," Ethan said, glancing from Sean to me. "But we learned plenty. One,"—he held up a finger—"Brook is here somewhere ..."

Yeah, she was there somewhere and still hadn't called. What did that tell me?

"Two," Ethan continued, "they have a lot of Toms stay over in that guest house because the place stinks ..."

"That is not enlightenment to me, pal," I said.

"And three," he said, like I hadn't interrupted, "they're planning something important."

Sean nodded. "Agreed. We just need to figure out what that is. So, we'll go home. And we'll sleep on it."

"Sure," I said, "sleep on it."

Yeah, right.

25

Eighty, ninety hours had passed since the beginning of Brook's banishment to the cellar. Or there abouts, at least. She had begun to lose track, and knew only that another day arrived by the first lightening of the sky, and the fresh chill early winter mornings brought with them, although thankfully, the rain that had slashed the grounds the entire night offered an element of insulation against that.

For the past two days, her skin had itched to stretch, to allow fur to surface. Her bones, her muscles ached to Shift. Fighting it off had become a matter of pride, and she did so at each impulse until her effort-filled breaths yowled past her lips. She had no desire to be as feline for any visitors—no desire to permit them to witness her weakness.

Especially her parents.

Since Stefan's unwanted trip to the cellar two sunsets before, nobody had descended the stone steps bar her father. On each of his trips, he had deposited her meal at the bottom, before locking her back in, and each of the meals had been heartier and bigger than the last.

While her body revelled in the sustenance, her mind couldn't help but question their motives, especially considering Stefan's mocking. Her parents had never shown mercy before in their discipline.

Arms hugging her up-drawn knees, chin resting atop, she flexed and un-flexed her fingers, studying the way her flesh rippled over the knuckles. The light coating of black fur that kept dusting her forearms, until with teeth gritted and lips pursed tight, she willed it away, and skin reappeared. Aside from throwing energy into remaining in control, she had little else to focus on, anyway—each time her concentration slipped, her mind refused to grasp a singular thread of thought, and each cranial image she conjured seemed to a send a lightning flash to the back of her eyes, like an old film reel playing on a sheet. She'd, hours before, learned that channelling her emotions to the moment kept her marginally saner than pondering that which remained out of her grasp.

The lock chinking in the cellar door above sent a twitch through her muscles.

Other than a brief pause, during which her gaze flickered toward the staircase and back, Brook's attention remained on her limbs.

A footstep hit the upper landing—a high-pitched tap much lighter, yet much more demanding in attention than her father's footwear.

Brook's ears perked up as the same tone bounced down to her from each stone step, but she had no need to glance over to see who descended. She would recognise the abrupt beat of her mother's shoes anywhere. Lord knew, she had heard them enough times.

The approach ceased, and a single, sharp command of, "Up," took its slot.

Brook didn't move, her refusal to react acting as an indifference that would drive her mother wild, and had many times. Each of those occasions had led to punishment, but she did not fear her mother's strikes as much as she did her father's.

"Do not play games with me this morning, Brook!" Heels scratched at the floor as her mother came closer.

Still, Brook held her position, watching only through her hair from the corner of her eye.

"I do not have time, nor the patience, for any more of your tantrums." Her mother marched the rest of the way toward Brook, and her fingers wrapped around Brook's upper arm, a singular yank hauling Brook to her feet. "It is about time you learned your place."

Brook's hands curled into fists against the urge to fight her way out of there. "How have you stood it for so many years, Mother?" She lifted her face to the woman who'd relentlessly tried and failed to mould Brook into a replica of herself, bracing for the blow as she added, "Living a lie?"

A flash of fury crossed Collette's features before she whirled away, snatching Brook along with her as she strode for the steps. "Gratitude!" she snapped out as she went. "You have never shown any. Nor respect. Well, you will wish you had shown the former." She dragged Brook toward the upper landing. "And you will learn to show the latter."

In Brook's opinion, her parents had given her little to be thankful for, beyond a fancy roof over her head and all the material things she could wish for, and that respect was something to be earned—but one glimpse of the open cellar door above, and the brightly lit hallway beyond that, had her lips clamping shut over vocalising as such.

Her eyes craved darkness as soon as she emerged from murky gloom to natural light, which seemed to blast into the wide glass-fronted hallway, despite the fine drizzle that remained as an echo of the night's rain.

A squinted scan of the space showed her father propped against the doorframe of his study, the steely way in which he observed her appearance daring her to defy. From farther down the hallway, sounds clattered out from the kitchen and dining room, from where the scents of roasting chicken wafted, sending Brook's stomach into a gurgling mess.

Following behind her mother, Brook passed the lounge, and her eyes narrowed further at the floral displays decorating the table-tops, the chairs that had been added from the living area of the guesthouse.

What is going—

"Do not dally, Brook!"

A yank on her arm took Brook around the newel post, and she had little choice but to mirror her mother's ascent of the stairs, her father's warning gaze catching on hers again before she climbed out of his range. Once on the landing, her mother led Brook into her doily-filled bedroom, where she towed her directly across to the far doorway and the en suite that lay beyond.

"Do you remember how to shower?" her mother asked, pushing her inside. "Or do I need to ensure your hygiene myself?"

Brook shook her arm free and twisted back. "What is the occasion?"

"You lost the right to ask questions, the moment you betrayed your race."

The door closed in Brook's face.

My entire body jolted as I woke, like some bastard had crept up on me while I slept and zapped me with a few thousand volts. My heart hammered inside my chest, along with the tail-end of a growl, and it took a few side-to-side eye darts for me to get my bearings. To recognise the ceiling and walls of my room and the scent of my bedding draped across me.

Detangling the sheets, I flicked my legs over the side of the bed and stumbled to the mirror, bracing a hand against the wall beside it as I leaned in close.

From within my eye sockets, solid black glossiness shone back at me.

Shit.

Staring harder at my reflection, I willed the darkness to disperse from my eyes, for the whites and hazels to return. Just as I had every other time it'd happened.

Whenever I woke with a heavy craving clawing at the back of my throat, one I didn't even want to think about, I never knew what had preceded it, what images my mind had worked through to get me to that point. I didn't for the latest incident, either, but my dick hanging unusually limp below my hips told me the experience hadn't been good.

With a little deep breathing, the heaving of my chest lessened, and the first splinter of white poked its way into my left eye. I allowed my gaze to lower—to all the jagged scars caused by the bastard who'd bitten my life-as-I'd-loved-it away, the remains of shredded skin that served as a reminder every damn day. At least the crazy eye shit only occurred every once in a while.

I'd managed to keep whatever it was happening to me from everyone but Brook, and I needed to keep it that way. Because how could I want anyone else to see something I didn't even want to see myself?

"Come on," I whispered to the mirror. "Clear."

At a knock on my door, I jumped.

"Kyle?" The handle squeaked down.

I spun away and snatched up a shirt from my corner chair, tugging it over my head as the door brushed over carpet.

"You're up," Dad said.

I nodded without turning, head hung low to conceal what I didn't want him to know.

"Ready in an hour."

"I'll be ready," I said, my voice a little edgy.

A few beats passed, and I knew he still stood there, from the weight of his damn scrutiny pressing down on my shoulders. Just when I thought he'd never leave, he said, "Make time for breakfast," and my door clicked shut.

Grabbing up boxers, and hopping into them, I made my way back to the mirror and peeked around the frame.

Discounting the tendrils of white prodding inward, blackness remained, like a shattered ink-screen, a bleeding battle for dominance.

A battle I hoped my dad never had to witness—if only because I knew it would kill him to see.

Just like it slowly killed me on the inside.

Brook's first thought had been to escape.

She was alone. No longer in the cellar. A window only a third shorter than herself beckoned from the opposite wall.

It would have been the perfect route, via the pear tree that stood close enough to reach with a small well-aimed leap. After all, Brook had left the house undetected that way before—why not do so again?

Except, the window had been locked when she tried to open it, the handle unmoveable, and breaking the glass would have only brought her father running.

Forehead pressed to the frosted pane, Brook thought through her options, realising all too fast how few she had.

"You are trying my patience, Brook," her mother's voice snapped through the door. "Get. In. The shower."

With little other choice, Brook complied.

Work combats tucked into boots, flannel shirt hanging open over a work-stained T, I studied my eyes for a final time as I pressed my mobile to my ear.

As expected, it went straight to voicemail, and that irritating woman who gave me the option of leaving a message. Just as I had the previous night when I tried, I listened to the recording in its entirety before hanging up with a tightness in my chest.

We'd established Brook's whereabouts, but that by no means made me feel better about the whole situation. While I had to admit the possibility that she just didn't want to know anymore, the scenario refused to sit well in my gut. The idea that she'd make that decision and not bother to let me know? I didn't buy it. She wouldn't take the coward's way out—not Brook.

However, if my musings proved right, what did that say about her constant inaccessibility?

For some reason, the other option only made me feel worse.

***

Brook emerged from the bathroom, wet hair hanging low down her back and soaking through the towel she had wrapped about her body, and paused on finding Elise laying out clothes on her bed.

The woman had been working for the Nicholls since she left senior school with no qualifications, thanks to tending to her mother's final cancerous needs. Somehow, she had managed to retain her kindness, and her natural efficiency—as well as her discreetness—ensuring she rarely warranted Brook's mother's reprimands.

Elise glanced up from her task and smiled Brook's way, yet her smile held more sadness than warmth. "Missed you," she said.

Brook's own lips curved in response.

Straightening, Elise glanced from Brook to the open door of the bedroom and marched that way. "Best be closing this door, if you're to get ready," she said, her voice slightly raised. As soon as the door shut, Elise dug into her pocket and crossed to Brook, holding out a small folded piece of paper. "Message for you," she whispered, taking Brook's hand and wrapping her fingers around the square. "And there were three gentlemen looking for you last night at the guesthouse."

Brook frowned. "Who?"

Elise shook her head. "No idea. Never seen them before."

Brook's heart thrummed within her chest. "Strangers?"

"Yes. And one seemed mighty concerned about you, too."

The thrum within her chest heightened in volume, and Brook placed a hand there as though she could stem the sound, scarcely daring to but asking anyway, "What did he look like?"

"Tall. Big. *Strong*." Her quiet words tumbled from her lips. "Rusty hair."

Kyle. He had come. Why had she even thought he wouldn't? "Do my parents know of this?" Brook asked.

Elise glanced toward the door, the headshake letting Brook release her sigh of relief.

However, if Kyle's appearance had nothing to do with the morning's strangeness, Brook still had no idea what was going on.

26

FORGIVE ME.
CLIVE.

Brook frowned at the square of paper in her hands as Elise pulled out a chair at the dresser. Given the woman's shared news, Brook had half-expected the note to be from Kyle.

Why would Clive slip her a message? *And forgive him for what?*

"Sit," Elise said, tapping the white, wooden seat. "Before your mother comes back," she added in a whisper.

Brook did as commanded, slipping the scrunched paper into a drawer of the dresser, as she sank onto the springy cushion. "Maybe you could enlighten me as to what, exactly, is happening?"

Elise met Brook's gaze in the mirror and her mouth opened as if to speak, but the woman jumped when the bedroom door whooshed open.

Collette paused in the frame, eyes narrowed. "How is she coming along?" Even her tone dripped with suspicion.

"Just fine, Mrs Nicholls." Elise swept the brush through Brook's wet hair. "We'll have her ready in no time."

"Make sure you do. The guests will be arriving within the hour."

"Guests?" Brook asked, swivelling in her seat. "For what?"

Her mother glowered in Brook's direction like she found the sight of her offensive. "I will be back up shortly to oversee everything."

Without another word, she spun away and enclosed them in the room once more.

***

Thirty minutes passed, with Brook blasted by a hair dryer, and her hair stretched by a straightening iron, before Elise wound it into a chignon so tight at the rear of her head, it tautened the skin either side of her eyes. During that time, Brook alternated between trying to pry details from the woman and mentally plotting her escape.

If she knew nothing else, she was at least certain she did not want to be a part of whatever her parents had planned.

"Will you not at least tell me who the guests will be?" Brook asked Elise, as she stared at her own reflection. The impeccability of her appearance did little to assuage the sense of dread, which had increased from a light veil of silk to a heavy cloak of iron in burden.

Elise's expression held only a stifled desperation, which made Brook even more leery. "I told you, I don't know who's coming."

"To what?" Brook asked for the tenth time.

Elise held Brook's mirrored gaze for a few long moments, and Brook thought she might have actually broken through, but Elise released a heavy sigh with a headshake. "Your mother wants some makeup on you."

Brook's eyes flicked downward—toward her own reflected face. Toward the mustard-hued mark across her left cheekbone, the only evidence of the abuse she'd suffered at her parents' hands. "Yes, I would imagine she does," she said.

More than aware of where her inner anger should be aimed, and knowing her refusal to obey would result in admonishment for Elise, Brook slid around on her seat to face the woman. What else had she to do? Although she could hear her mother's shoes clicking constantly downstairs, and her occasional snapped out orders, she didn't doubt for a second that any exterior exits from her room had been left guarded. Most likely, her father had a few of his pathetic minions positioned about the property, too, to ensure Brook's security. After all, she had lived within the Coalition for the past twenty-four years and understood just how seriously an act of disloyalty could be treated, had witnessed just how far they would go when a line had been crossed. Brook had not merely crossed a line. She had faked her passport and jumped the border into a forbidden land.

So far, she had gotten off lightly, and she knew it.

Elise swept a cosmetic brush across Brook's forehead, and Brook closed her eyes as it travelled lower around her temple.

If a Tom had behaved with such disregard for the race, he would not have emerged from the cellar so soon. In fact, the last one had been nigh on unrecognisable after his three weeks of punishment under Rufus King's command.

So, why, exactly, had Brook gotten off so lightly?

And why all the pampering?

Again, the entire situation refused to settle in her mind.

"That should do it," Elise said with a final feathering over Brook's damaged skin.

"Mother would disagree," Brook said, opening her eyes.

The woman shrugged a shoulder, her lips curving at one corner.

As she slid her tools back into their pouches, Brook twisted for a glance in the mirror, but stalled at the rumble of vehicles outside on the drive.

Her gaze caught on Elise's frown when she thrust to her feet and crossed to the window. Even that was covered in ridiculous lace, and Brook knocked the netting aside as four cars rolled across the gravel.

All of them Coalition cars. All of them containing Toms.

She wouldn't have ...

Footsteps creaked upon the landing outside her bedroom, before the door swung open, and Brook spun around to her Mother's appraising gaze.

"I will take it from here. Thank you, Elise," Collette said. "You may take the rest of the day off."

A sudden and irrational—or maybe rational—panic clawed along Brook's throat, even more so at the apology shining out from Elise as she gathered herself and walked from the room.

The door snapping closed left Brook alone with her mother.

Brook's hands curled at her sides, the muscles in her legs tensing as though for flight.

"Be sensible about this." Collette headed for the wardrobe and unhooked the dress hanging there, her dismissive air confirming Brook's suspicions of her being guarded. "It is supposed to be a day of celebration. I shall not have you ruining it with unnecessary melodramatics."

"Tell me you haven't," Brook said.

"You should be thankful." Her mother carried the dress over and stood before Brook. "You deserve the chance to gain a strong Tom, who will stand for no nonsense. One with the potential to mould you, with a firm hand, into the Queen you should aspire to be. And your father and I have ensured this."

"I do not want to be moulded into someone else's interpretation of who I should be, Mother." Brook's voice arrived on a low hiss, barely making it past her gritted teeth.

Collette's hand snapped out and grabbed Brook's chin. "Such ingratitude." She released Brook's face and unhooked the towel from her body, tossing it aside and leaving Brook standing naked. "You should be proud you have so many suitors ..."

So many? The air within the room seemed to thin as Brook's breaths hastened, and still a corner of her mind hoped she had viewed it all wrong.

"... grateful," her mother continued. "Phoebe Dawson only had ten Toms show up to her Seasonal Party ..."

My God, she would, and she has.

Her parents intended to make her Choose.

27

In a dress deemed suitable by her mother, Brook emerged from her bedroom with her pulse racing and breaths clogging somewhere in the back of her throat.

Carpet strands tickled her bare feet. Her mother had scoffed at Brook's mention of shoes.

You'll not be walking out of here of your own accord, Brook.

However, it had been the, *You'll have no need for underwear*, retort that had truly rocketed Brook's panic into a frenzy.

Despite that, Brook had not disputed her Mother's clothing of her in an outfit more apt for an early-day hussy, with its straps too loose to stay on her shoulders and buttons that barely concealed her breasts. Neither had she protested her mother's ushering onto the landing, following the almost-compliment of, 'Why, Brook, I have never seen you look so tame'.

After all, Brook knew how to survive—she'd had plenty of practice.

An entire lifetime spent in an organisation dominated by males meant she'd had Tom after Tom to hold her own against.

When caged by the vampires the autumn before, she had done what had been needed to survive. She may have relinquished control to her body while there, but it had not once let her down when she had needed to fight.

During those weeks, Brook had learned to defend herself well, in whichever way required, no matter the casualties, while she awaited some kind of end to the living hell. She had presumed that end would arrive once the Coalition tracked her down. Instead, it had arrived with a couple of werewolves. The least selfish souls she had ever encountered in her life.

It would be an insult to their efforts if she gave in, if she did not fight once more. Even if she hadn't owed it to herself, she owed it to them—to Kyle.

For that reason, Brook had spent the previous twenty minutes appearing as the compliant daughter, as her mother listed instructions and her expectations of Brooke, making it perfectly clear that disobedience would not result in a second chance—all while formulating a plan.

Carrying out that plan would involve playing the sick games of the Coalition, and so she forced her feet to carry her toward the staircase, toward her fate.

"For goodness sake, Brook. You are already late to your own party." Her mother's shove against her back sent her forward a stride. "Do not keep your guests waiting any longer."

From somewhere below, deep chatter travelled upward, the excited babble of anticipation and the low chuckles of camaraderie amongst it all.

Drawing in a long breath, Brook closed her eyes and sent a silent apology—to the one owed it, though he'd never hear. Her exhale arrived just as heavy, as her lids lifted, and she turned the corner to the staircase.

The first Tom came into view as soon as she'd taken her first step.

Dressed in a tie-less shirt tucked into black pressed trousers, and with a half-full long-stemmed glass in hand, Ray snapped his gaze to Brook's like he'd purposefully opted to stand there for first glance at the prize. As one of the slightly more mature Toms of the Coalition, rumour had it that he had ceased looking for child bearers and intended to Mate.

While Ray may not have been as high in standing as some of the Toms, Brook knew her father would have ensured only Toms he considered powerful enough would be able to attend—another reason politics and the manipulation they brought made Brook sick, because, once again, a narrowed choice stripped away free will.

Ignoring Ray's grin, and the way the voices seem to slowly dwindle, as though everyone downstairs had become suddenly aware of her approach, she stepped down again, bringing the next Tom into view—followed by another step, another Tom. Once she'd reached the bottom, all conversation ceased to be, and Brook finally understood the depth of the waters into which her parents had thrown her.

No wonder her mother thought the other Queens' parties to be small. Eight Toms stood in the hallway alone, and the three Toms leaning against the doorframes to the lounge and dining room told her that both of those spaces held Toms, too.

The air her throat seemed so insistent on holding in caught again until only the tiniest and quietest of pants could squeeze through, as Brook's gaze travelled across each of her so-called matches, landing finally on her father.

He stood exactly where he had before, in the doorway to his study, crystal tumbler in hand, as though he, too, found the occasion reason to celebrate. The harsh glint in his eyes sent her plenty of warning, quite the contrast to the expression of the young Tom in pride of place at his side.

Stefan bloody King.

Part smug, part excitement, part deviousness, Stefan looked as though he already believed he had his cat in the bag.

Over my dead body.

A hand brushed her shoulder, and she shuddered, gritting her teeth against the urge to shrug it off and knock the presumptuous Tom aside. Once again, she wanted to kick and claw and scratch a way out from her life, but she knew that would be a step backward, and forward was the direction she needed to go.

Only one Tom could get Brook out of her predicament, and she had yet to spot him. Even the scents that made it to her senses did not expose his attendance, not with so many through which to wade.

Please be here.

Facing ahead, she stepped forward a few paces, passing another two Toms.

"You look real pretty today, Brook."

She glanced up to her left, into the eyes of Wayne Lovell. While not a bad looking male, with his chestnut mane that fell to his shoulders, Wayne had already sired three young, and clearly had no plans to settle for one female when he could have them all. Brook ducked her face again, a coy action, and one she knew her parents would approve of, as she whispered, "Thank you," and continued on her way.

Passing one more Tom sporting a leering grin, Brook reached the first doorway. She peered around the corner, eyes scanning the contents of the lounge in a single sweep.

Roland King stood in the far corner, chest puffed out, arms blocky at his sides as though she might be impressed by his bulky strength—though, in all fairness, the male pretty much only had his body to offer, as his mind was filled with poison, and his actions led by spite. She could not believe Stefan's audacity in tagging Brook as spoiled, when he and his brother came as prime examples.

She allowed her gaze to linger on Roland's primeval attempts a little too long, but when it resulted in him taking a hesitant shuffle forward, she broke away and spun back to the hall. She had no business in a place that didn't hold what she sought.

From one King to another, heading toward the dining room, Stefan came into her direct line of sight. Rather than the gentle approach she'd seen so far from the others, he stood with his arms crossed over his chest, head cocked to the side, lips twisted into a half-smile of self-assurance.

She paused in her passage when Lewis Carmichael poked his head around the corner, his frown stretching into a grin, the moment his gaze landed on her.

He jerked his chin up. "Brook."

Circumstances aside, a smile visited her face. "Lewis."

That Tom had always been the joker amongst the younger Coalition members, the daredevil who never backed away from a bet and often ended up flat on his rear in such an entertaining manner that each of his escapades had gained an audience.

To his left, a scowl marred Stefan's features—her father's, too, though only for a second before his mask of impartiality slipped back into place.

"You look good in a dress," Lewis said, like he hadn't even noticed the tightness to Stefan's shoulders, or the glitch to Donald's facade. "Should wear one more often."

"And you look good with clothes on," Brook said, because Lewis's antics often led to him racing around in the nude. No doubt, he'd been invited for his father's wealth and ever-growing business more than for his own personal appeal.

The comeback earned a few chuckles along the row of males in the hallway, and Brook used the momentary distraction to slide past Stefan, and squeeze around Lewis and the other Toms crowding the doorway through which she needed to pass.

She turned her back on her father's disapproval and Stefan's low growl once in the dining room, but still itched beneath their heavy scrutiny as she skimmed her gaze over the Toms. With the way they all lined the walls, and with the table missing from the centre, they could have been at a traditional ball awaiting pairing to dance.

In the right corner sat Mike, farther across Ian, while Brad Campbell dominated the far corner in his upright stance, his hands tucked deep into the pockets of dark grey trousers below a shirt and tie that matched them for shade. His unsure smile filled with vulnerability and hope, and those startling aqua eyes of his peering up at her from his slightly downturned face made him stand out from the tougher and more certain attitudes of those around him.

All except for the Tom on his right.

Tucked into the nook of the room, hunched over in a chair with elbows propped on knees and his forehead resting in his hands, his fingers raked into white blond hair Brook would recognise anywhere.

Clive.

The tension coiling Brook's muscles eased off a little as she headed that way, one slow step at a time, overly aware of every watching set of eyes in the room. As she neared, Brad's face lifted, and he glanced to the left and right, straightening his posture. He rubbed a palm across his buzz cut, an act of male self-preening she saw all too often, before setting his shoulders back and allowing anticipation to enter his eyes.

Pity he had never stood a chance from the start.

When she came to a stop before Clive, Brad peered down toward him, a flash of confusion across his face like he'd never considered the Tom a contender—which just about showed how much attention he paid. Brook doubted any other Tom at the Choosing Ceremony would be surprised by which male she had approached.

Including Stefan, or her father.

Clive didn't look up, didn't stir from his position. Had he his eyes closed? His senses, too? Or had she truly pushed him too far and earned herself his disinterest?

A few shuffles to her rear told her of the others' attention. A few whispers travelled in a stream, probably making their way along the hallway to those out of viewable range.

Resisting the urge to tug at her dress, to hide behind the wrap of her arms, she pushed pride aside and asked, "Clive?"

His face made a slow tilt up toward her, but held only immense grief—not at all what she'd expected. Rubbing a hand across his brow, he gave a small headshake, the weighted downturn of his mouth seeming to carry a hoard of emotions.

She dropped to her knees before him, uncaring if the others might see it as begging. "I ... don't understand."

His gaze jerked back to hers, a soft glossiness heightening the gold. "I'm sorry, Brook." A hoarse thickness roughened his voice. "I can't."

28

Since leaving school, I'd worked for the family business, a job I'd always been content with, relaxed in the knowledge it kept me close to the pack.

That morning, for the first time, the mere sight of the construction project twisted an ugly knot in my stomach, one full of resentment at having to be there instead of finding answers to the questions driving me nuts.

Over an hour before, I'd arrived in Dad's pickup, jumped out with a scowl, and marched straight for the cabin. The scowl had yet to leave my face, and my body had still to do anything useful.

When Nathan had summoned me over to keep his bricks stacked, he'd gotten mad after the fourth time of reaching for his supply and finding it lacking—resulting in me being sent to find someone else to assist and Gabe taking my place.

Even Dad had puffed out an exasperated breath, when I'd tripped over the beginnings of his wall and knocked his blocks askew, and he'd told me to help Josh.

Finally, my lack of paying attention had ended with cement all over the ground, when I forgot to secure the mixer in position. At which point, Nate blew a gasket and ordered me to grab coffees.

The fact he'd told me to find a coffee shop for them showed just how much he wanted me out of his way— either that, or he didn't consider me capable of using a spoon. He even sent Ethan along. Probably in case I got lost.

Within metres of leaving, I'd pretty much set the tone with my mutterings about Brook.

"You don't know that she's not okay," Ethan said for the second time.

"I also don't know that she *is* okay."

"Look, I know I said otherwise, but ..."

I sent him a glare, digging my hands deeper into my pockets—one mashing the balls I'd remembered to bring, the other attempting to bend my mobile into shapes it wasn't meant to go.

"But," he said, glancing my way before turning back to the path ahead, "maybe you might need to consider the possibility that—"

My hands squeezed harder, my teeth gritted behind my lips.

"—she doesn't want to know anymore."

I growled. "Like you could believe that in this situation."

"You forget," he said. "I did."

"You think it counts, when she eventually came around?"

"Then, maybe that's all you need to do, too." He shrugged. "Give her space."

The swing of my body held a whole heap of attitude as I rounded a corner, but I slammed to a halt when a car buzzed to a stop at the junction and sent a small wave of gutter rainwater my way. I glowered in the direction of the elderly driver, but fingers gripped my arm and dragged my feet into motion.

"Don't even think about it," Ethan said.

"What sort of idiot gets that close to the kerb?" I shook my leg out, somehow still managing to keep moving. "I'm frickin' soaked."

"Any other day, you wouldn't have given a shit."

"Any other day, I wouldn't have had the week I've had."

I'm sorry, Brook. I can't.

Clive's words.

Ones Brook didn't understand.

For years, Clive had followed Brook around. For years, he had let his desires be known.

Brook had depended on his participation in her plan. How could he let her down when she finally needed him so badly?

"What did I do?" she asked, more than aware of their audience, yet uncaring.

Jaw tensed, he gave a low groan as his face ducked away. "Nothing, Brook."

"Then, why—"

He blew out a breath. His gaze lifted, but rather than meet her, it snapped higher, toward a spot somewhere behind her, and a harsh chill lightened his eyes.

Glancing back over her shoulder, Brook let out a muttered curse.

Stefan stood just within the dining room doorway with his hands fisted at his sides. His attention fired heat in her and Clive's direction, while all the other Toms in the room seemed to be trying to look anywhere but at Stefan.

She spun back to Clive. "What did he do?" she asked.

His growl arrived as no more than a low grumble. "Nothing."

Brook pushed up onto her knees, taking her face closer to Clive's. "Do not give me that." Her words came out whispered, rushed. "He has said something to you."

Clive continued to stare across the room, his teeth grinding hard. "Leave it, Brook."

"Since when have you answered to Stefan King?" She took his face in her palms and forced him around to her, yet still, he seemed unable to remove his gaze from the other Tom. "I am asking you to take me out of here, and you would let him stand in your way?"

His eyes flickered toward her at last, though a frown pulled the skin tight at his temples.

"Don't you *dare*!"

Without even turning, Brook knew the warning come from Stefan, just as she knew she had little time before one of her parents would intervene.

"No fight. No argument." Hooking a finger over her dress strap, she slipped it aside, tilting her head and exposing her neck. "Take me from here now, and I shall willingly come."

Clive's swallow arrived loud. The intensity in his eyes glowed to a powerful draw.

"*Clive!*" The second warning came alongside a rumbling growl.

"Please," she murmured. "You are the only one I trust."

His gaze dropped to her flesh, longing, hunger, desperation, all roiling across his features, and as footsteps began their way across the carpet, Clive's lips rippled, and he released a snarl.

"*No!*" Stefan shouted, as Clive's teeth sank into Brook's skin.

Her entire body jerked beneath the assault, and her cry belted up from her throat. Before she even had a chance to recoil from the sharp pain, hands slipped beneath her rear, and Clive lifted her as he stood, his arms engulfing her body and pressing her to his.

Crimson marred his lips when he released his maws from the dip in her neck. "Get out of my way."

Though Brook knew Clive aimed his demand elsewhere, he stared at her, and she dared not look away. To do so would be considered disrespectful, and her role in the plans she had made would likely not be over for many hours.

A few long beats passed. No movement came from behind her.

Only the quiet hum of anger buzzed in the room.

Brook wondered if they would ever get out of there, at all.

"Stefan." The call came from the hallway—from her father. "You know the rules. She has made her Choice. Let them go."

When rushed footsteps stamped away, a smile twitched at the corners of Clive's lips, and he marched from the room with Brook in his arms.

Out past the whispers and heaved breaths.

Out into the first fresh air Brook had tasted in days.

Arms braced against the counter of the coffee shop, I watched the barista fella pour milk into a silver jug and stick it under a nozzle on the machine. "I'm going back."

"You've got to be kidding me," Ethan muttered.

"Tonight." I twisted and, meeting his dark gaze, nodded. "I need to know."

"I think you should wait."

"What if I can't?"

"What if you have no choice?" When I released a low growl, he straightened from his propped position on the counter and turned to me. "Listen, I get that you're antsy."

I could've argued that he didn't 'get it', but knew it'd just make me a git—because he *would* get it. So I kept my mouth shut and let him get the lecture off his chest.

"I get that you feel like shit over it all. But she obviously needs space. If this week tells you nothing else, it should tell you that. Besides, it worked for me. With Shelley. Doesn't that tell you it's worth sitting back to wait and see?"

"My gut's calling the shots here, though." I shook my head. "And it's seriously fucking unhappy with the situation." I glanced up as two large takeout cups clopped down in front of me.

"That's just your head messing with you," Ethan said, as the server twisted back and began making the other six drinks for our order. "You think I didn't wake up panicking every damn morning that something bad was going to happen to Shelley and Gabe if I wasn't there to take care of them?" He tapped his temple. "Amazing how much females and shit can screw with our minds."

219

I still didn't buy it. Hell, my stomach churned and curdled like it attempted to projectile-reject his rationalising.

He must have seen something in my expression, because he blew out a breath and rubbed hard at his face. "Okay." He gave a small nod. "I'll cut you a deal."

Ethan's deals usually ended up with me agreeing to whatever he had in mind, so I knew how much I clung to the hope of support when I told him, "Go on."

"Tomorrow is Friday. That's one day 'til the weekend. You and I both know we can't keep heading off and making up stories each end about where we are and who we're with. Dad and Connor talk. And they're far from dumb, so they'll figure us out, and then you'll be back to square one, except they'll be crabbier and full of a whole lot of suspicions." He paused as two more coffees appeared with the first ones. With a little privacy again, he continued, "So, last out until the weekend. Drag your arse through work like your head isn't off visiting the la-la land it's been stuck in, and convince Dad you're getting back on track. Which will give Brook that tiny bit more time she might need. Then, if you still haven't heard ..." He shrugged like he didn't expect that to happen, but I didn't miss the tightening of his eyes. "Hell, I'll come with you myself to find out what's going on, as many times as it takes to get to the bottom of it."

"And if—"

"Probably should've mentioned," he cut in, his lips curving into a smile I knew all too bloody well. "The deal is non-negotiable."

Across the gravel driveway and up the wooden steps of the front porch, Brook remained in Clive's arms. Even once he'd unlocked the door and let them into the living area, she didn't struggle to be put down. She still had many hours of her charade ahead, and she could not risk tipping him off before she had figured out the rest of her plan—despite his pledge of only wanting to help. At least the air of the guesthouse held a fresh cleanliness the main house lacked. Over there had seemed tainted. Soiled.

After booting the door closed at his rear, Clive strode toward the open-plan kitchen and rounded the counter. Her bottom met with the chill countertop, when he set her down and un-tucked his chin from the spot it had claimed at the crook of her neck. Without glancing at her, he marched back toward the front door, keys in his outstretched hand, and locked and double-locked them in.

On his return to Brook, he stood gazing into her for a few beats, a hand propped either side of her thighs, before backing away and leaning against the opposite counter.

At his sides, his fingers flickered and flexed, but his eyes, the slight curve to his lips held a hint of astonishment, as though he couldn't quite believe the situation—him, alone with Brook, for the strict purpose of mating.

Neither could Brook.

"Here we are," he finally said.

Trying not to fidget when her nerves put in a new appearance, Brook said, "We almost weren't."

The suggestion of a smile vanished as he turned away, his hands curling into fists.

"What happened in there?" She inclined her chin toward the house, allowing forced irritation to quell the butterflies taking up residency in her stomach. "How could you humiliate me like that?"

He spun back. "You think I wanted to?"

"How would I know?"

A growl rolled from him, and he thrust forward so fast, Brook scarcely registered the movement until he stood right before her. "Don't act like you don't know me, or my feelings, Brook. I'm worth more than that."

She wanted to lean back, as his face pushed close to hers, as his fists planted either side of her thighs once more, but didn't. "So, tell me," she said. "Why?"

His jaw worked—like he wanted to speak but anger hindered the action.

"Did Stefan say something to you?" She had already asked once, and although she'd received no satisfactory reply, she wanted one.

Clive heaved a sigh, but tension crept into the set of his shoulders, even more so than before. "We don't all have daddies in high places, Brook."

Brook frowned. "My father has never treated you as though he considers you below him." He had his faults, but he had never done that.

"Maybe not, but Rufus likes his power." Rufus King—Stefan and Roland's father—a pompous Tom who insisted on a farmhouse disguised as a mansion and a hoard of feet-kissers to pander to his equally pompous whims. "And you know as well as I do, Brook, the next in line after him for prosperity and respect is Don. Apparently, he intended to have you mated to at least one of his sons, whatever it took."

A low growl eased past Brook's clenched teeth. "You know this? For fact? Or is it more rumours made for entertainment purposes?" Because every organisation, no matter how sturdy it considered itself, found intrigue in the news of others, uncaring whether they were truth or lies.

"Don took me aside last night. Told me he knew how much today meant to me, but he needed me to step away." Clive's teeth ground beneath the tightening of his eyes, and Brook sat up straighter as what he had just said settled within her chest like a fist of iron. "He all but promised I'd get my chance," Clive continued. "Just not this time."

"The note," Brook said, her own eyes narrowing. "Your apology. I presumed, after today, that was what it was for. But there was more to it."

Clive's gaze darted away.

"You knew." Brook nodded, certainty spreading through her and fuelling her with its heat. "You knew about today. And you never once said a word."

He lifted his hands, raking his fingers through his hair.

"Why did you not say something? A warning would have been appreciated." Her pitch escalated with each tempered word. "How could you leave me to walk into something like that, Clive?"

"I couldn't, okay?" He dropped his hands with a groan. "It's not like I didn't try to help—to warn you, for God's sake. I even tried to stop this from happening, at all, dammit." Which somewhat explained his behaviour in the cellar the other day. "But I couldn't tell you why. If I had, I'd have lost my right to attend today. I'd have lost my shot. Sorry, Brook, but I couldn't take that chance."

"What did it matter?" she asked. "You were not allowed to show yourself as a contender, anyway. In fact, why even bother to come?"

"Because I hoped." His chest heaved as he banged a fist against it. "I hoped, in here, you'd still Choose me on your own. Because that, they couldn't dispute." The gold of his gaze shone as it re-met Brook's. "And you did. You're here. Exactly as I hoped."

29

Clive reached out and placed a palm to Brook's cheek. A moment later, his face neared, and the twitch of his searching nostrils tickled her cheek as he pressed his lips to the corner of hers. "Do you have any idea how long I've wanted this?" he asked, a deep groan rumbling from him, before his arms snatched her up from the work-surface.

A cold draught swept around her thighs, the few strands loosened from her pleat tickled her face, and Brook's entire body stiffened, the instant her mind registered the movement. The flight across the living space. The first creak of the stairs.

Within her chest, her heart raged liked a trapped beast, screaming for the escape Brook craved.

Where had her window gone? That sliver of breathing space?

The chance with which to finish formulating her plan?

Where, even, was the chance to *accept*?

Although she understood fully the situation in which she had placed herself, she'd never completely believed she might actually have to go through with the act until the very end. As though her mind had convinced her the inevitable wouldn't really happen, that she would walk away, she would be saved the degradation of forcing herself to respond to a male she didn't want—Clive would be saved from more lies on top of all the other hurt she knew she'd cause him.

It was too late, though. Too late for her. Too late for him.

Too late for Kyle?

The hollowed echo of the stairs exchanged places with the deep thud of the landing. Without even realising, Brook's fingers clutched at Clive's shirt.

In response, he tightened his hold and strode faster.

The landing corridor and the doors either side narrowed within her view as she stared over his shoulder, and the reality of their destination grasped at her until fear filled her throat and her chest heaved against his.

"*Clive.*" His name escaped as a strangled utterance, scarcely more a whisper—one that did nothing to halt his journey.

The door to the master bedroom slammed open behind her. Pale walls vanished either side of her tunnel vision, and warm butterscotch took their place.

From the speed at which he had carried them, she expected to be tossed to the bed, her scrap of fabric torn from her, his attire discarded in his haste for release.

Instead, he settled her upon the springy mattress with a tender-filled care, then headed across the room, closing the door with a quiet click.

The blazing intensity of his eyes, when he swung back, had Brook's body begging for flight.

She cared little that she had known Clive all her life. That she did not fear him. Nor that she trusted he would never harm her. Her body refused to acknowledge any of that, and her lungs refused to expel air with the slow prowl he made her way.

His knee nudged onto the mattress beside her calf, the depression dipping her body toward his arm, as he placed a fist down, and the clattering of her heart all but banged out her panic. She rolled slightly to the other side, when his right knee slid onto the surface, and as he leaned forward, reaching down with his other hand, his body inched closer—his face, lips, those eyes that sang out his needs.

Brook dug her fingers into the caramel comforter to restrain herself from bolting, though she could do little about the stumbling of her pulse, the rise and fall of her chest, or the rigidity of her body. When his breaths skated around the downy hairs of her face, she slammed her eyes closed, as though she could defend herself with blindness alone.

The instant his lips touched hers, however, the panic forced her voice box into action, enough for her to whisper, "Stop," as she placed a hand to his chest she hadn't meant to raise.

He halted. "Brook?" His voice arrived deep, gravelly.

She lifted her lids to a world of confusion and hurt clouding the otherwise burning orange of his eyes. "I ..." Her mouth hung there for a moment. What could she say? "... need a moment," she managed. *Please.*"

Clive stared down at her, his eyes seeming to search hers so deeply, she feared he could see through to the secrets darkening her request. After a few beats, he hadn't moved, to the point she believed herself busted, unveiled, but he gave a small nod and brushed his lips across hers.

"Okay," he said, backing off a little.

Shuffling from beneath his body, she slid to the edge of the bed, ordering herself to walk calmly when her feet wanted to race for the door in the corner of the room the moment they hit the plush carpet.

She reached out for the handle as soon as it came within reach.

"Just don't be long," Clive said from behind her.

She paused long enough to nod, attempting with her entire being to portray a surety she by no means felt on the inside, and ducked into the bathroom.

With the door closed at her rear, she flipped the bolt across and leaned back against the heavy panelling, heaving out her breath as though it had been stored for an eternity.

One breath became two. A third followed. "Okay, *think!*" she hissed at herself as she pushed away into a pace of the room.

While only an en suite, the floor tiles held enough square footage for a good few strides in each direction. To her right, a vanity sink sat beneath a generous wall cabinet, flashing her image into her periphery with each pass.

At the toilet, she spun, placing her reflection to her left as the glass-fronted shower cubicle, six feet wide and set into an alcove, took its spot on her right.

Back at the door, she pressed one hand against the panel and gripped the knob with the other, but hesitated in exposing herself.

Shuffling drifted through from the bedroom. "You okay in there, Brook?"

She shot back from the door like she'd been zapped. Hand clasped over her chest, she sucked in a deep breath, released it on a slow exhale, and managed to say, "Of course." Her gaze flickered to the side, to the shower, and she darted out a hand and twisted the valve, sending water spattering against the glass enclosure. "I am just freshening up," she said, hoping to buy herself some composure time.

A quiet thud tapped the other side of the door, too high for his hand. His head? "I'll be waiting," he said, before the sweep of feet travelled away from her hiding spot.

She balled her hands and pushed them against her temples, as though she could somehow knead and massage her thoughts into order. "What am I doing?" she asked herself. Her hands trembled when she lowered them to her face, and as she tracked them, she caught sight of her reflection again in the mirror above the sink.

Eyes wide. Mouth open. A grotesque mask of fear. Something she'd never expected to see within herself.

She twisted closer to the glass and forced her jaw closed. Frowned until her eyes narrowed.

Neither action worked. Neither quelled the bubble gradually expanding within her chest.

Get a hold of yourself, she mentally ordered.

She turned away from the image bothering her and sniffed in, long, slow, until hear hurt, before twisting back.

Her image hadn't changed. Even the palest yellow to which her eyes had faded remained

Brook Nicholls. Do not *panic.*

She shook her hands out, stretched her neck with a side-to-side slant of her head, and rolled her shoulders.

Pull yourself together. You can do *this.*

Grasping hold of the vanity edge, she reconnected with her unchanged gaze.

Could she, though? Could she truly do what the job would entail?

Giving an internal groan, she pushed away from the unit, and without even acknowledging an answer, resumed her pacing.

It had been a good question, though. *Could* she do it?

She knew the real answer. She just did not want to admit it.

Brook didn't lose. Didn't admit defeat. She fought to the end, if only so she could hold her head high and walk amongst her own kind with pride.

Did she even want to walk amongst her own kind any more, though?

More than that, *what* about going through with *it*, exactly, would even allow her to walk proud?

She stalled in front of the mirror again, her gaze catching herself, the emanated guilt, the burden of it all reflecting back at her as the answer to all her questions pushed its way to the forefront. *No.* She shook her head at herself as if to emphasise. *Nothing.*

With that realisation came the enlightenment that she was going to need another way out. As if her subconscious lived one step ahead, her fingers gripped the handle to the cabinet, eyes instantly seeking something—*anything*—that could relieve her of what she hoped to avoid.

So little sat upon the shelves within. Shampoo. Conditioner. Shower gel. Shaving implements. No more than the average guest would require for a short stay.

No pills. Not even any blasted painkillers. Absolutely nothing Brook could work with.

Though, really, had she truly expected to discover sedatives in plain sight within the main suite?

She stalled a moment at that thought. She knew—she *knew*, dammit—that her father insisted on some kind of sedative being present within the guesthouse. Although its main purpose tended to be for injuries and the like, she knew he had an underhanded reasoning, for Toms he did not wholly trust.

As fast as that recall dawned on her, so, too, did the position of the drug.

In the first aid box. In the kitchen. Downstairs.

Brook released a low groan, her hands covering her face and tugging at the skin as she rubbed.

Clive had shown patience so far, but even he would question a venture downstairs. Or, maybe she just had to appear to be playing their game.

Stepping away from the mirror, Brook all but tore her pathetic dress from her body, and the temperature of the water scorched her when she hopped into the shower.

She ignored it, twisting to soak her shoulders and, more importantly, her hair.

On emergence, she reached for one of the guest bathrobes off the hook in the corner and shrugged into it. With a towel from the rail, she dabbed at her soaked strands and unlocked the door.

Clive jolted from his slouched position on the bed, as she stepped into the bedroom. "Better?"

She nodded. "Bathroom is free." Despite her nerves, authority commanded her voice, making his cleansing an order rather than suggestion. She veered toward the landing door, when he all but bounced from the bed. "I shall fix us some drinks for when you come out."

If he wondered over her course, his, "Good idea," didn't reflect as such.

Thankful for that, Brook sailed from the room with the most carefree attitude she could muster, picking up speed and losing her front the instant she rounded the corner to descend the stairs.

Agility tended to be on the side of felines, which meant the leap to the bottom once she'd crossed the halfway spot, ended with a near-silent landing—as did her race across the living space and into the kitchen, where she dropped to her knees and yanked open the cupboard beneath the sink.

The white wooden chest sat exactly where she hoped it would, and she reached in for it, flipping the lid up as she set it on the floor. Each item had been compartmentalised. Dressings. Bandages. Needle and thread. Ointments. Even slings.

"Come on," she whispered, hooking a finger under the small handle of the top storage. Lifting it up revealed everything else— pins, tweezers, and meds. Including the extra-strength sleeping pills she had seen administered a few times too many.

Sending up a prayer of thanks, Brook slipped the packet out, settled everything back into place, and closed the box back inside the cupboard before climbing to her feet and heading for the wine rack.

From whites at the bottom, to rosés, reds and sparkling, the shelves always held a decent selection for a fairly compact space, and Brook immediately reached for the Merlot, knowing its dark tones would help disguise the drug.

She set two of the largest flutes on the counter, poured in wine almost to the rims, and began popping the pills from their packet—never had Brook been more grateful that her father preferred capsule-enclosed powders for the exact purpose she wanted them for. According to the box, one of the extra-strength sedatives would help an average human sleep within a couple of hours. Brook did not have a couple of hours. To top that, Clive was no average human—so Brook used all ten of the blister pack, stirring the wine around the glass with her finger until every visible speck of the powder dissolved.

From overhead, a dull thud told her Clive had exited the shower stall, and she quickly tossed the packing in the bin, poking it down to the bottom of the bag and folding the plastic around it to disguise her actions.

With the tainted drink in her right hand, and the clean one in her left, as well as the rest of the bottle tucked beneath her arm, she headed back for the bedroom with a million mantras and silent pleas whistling through her head.

30

Brook had rather hoped to find Clive as encased as herself in the second guest bathrobe. Instead, he lay sprawled against the pillows with a towel barely big enough for the job covering his hips—leaving her with no doubt as to what he planned for them next.

He pushed up onto an elbow as she entered the room, the almost shy smile she had seen earlier putting in a reappearance, as though he still couldn't quite believe the situation.

The mere expression lanced through Brook, but she couldn't allow herself to be deviated by emotions. If she didn't escape the Coalition before day's end, she suspected she would end up trapped for life.

Brook held out Clive's tainted drink as she settled cross-legged onto the mattress. "Red."

"No shit," he said, grinning when Brook gave the glared response she knew he'd expect, and he tipped his glass toward hers until they clinked. "Thanks."

Taking a sip of her drink, Brook slid the half-empty bottle down to the floor and gazed toward the window. Even some of the rooms in the guesthouse had been dressed in the ridiculous frills her mother had a fondness for, but the waning light of day managed to filter in, as though attempting to coat the bed in a dreary spotlight.

Which summed up Brook's life to a T. Nothing about it had ever been particularly bright.

At least, not until she met Kyle.

"You okay?" Clive asked, snapping her back.

She went to nod, but shrugged before completing the action. "This just feels ... somewhat awkward. Does it not to you?"

"Awkward how?" he asked, pouring a wholesome dose of his drink into his mouth.

Brook tried not to stare too hard at the path of the drugged wine as she answered, "The entire"—she gestured with her hand and glass—"pushing together business."

Clive's brows drew together. "Is that what all the stalling's been about?"

"I have not stalled," she said.

"Liar."

Her lips curved slightly, but only for a fraction of a beat. "I just .... It ..." She released an extended breath. The longer she could keep him talking, the better. "I have known you my entire life, Clive. As a Coalition brother. As ... as a friend."

"Your best friend?" His accompanying smile seemed unsure.

What did that even mean? What comparison did she have to help set Clive aside from the others? Although, had she truly ever had real friends, when even those had been handpicked? She knew for certain that she trusted Clive more than anyone else she had been forced to grow up with. He knew far more of her secrets than anyone else. "Okay, yes," she said, nodding. "As a best friend."

His lips curved higher as he took another drink. "It's not unheard of for best friends to become more, Brook."

"But ... you are like a brother to me."

"And the benefit of best friends taking that additional step," he continued, as though she hadn't spoken, "is that they already know each other's bad habits."

"I do *not* have bad habits," she said, taking advantage of his comment to twist the serious tone to banter.

"No?" Clive's eyebrows arched. "You snore in your sleep."

"Do not be ridiculous," she said, though her lips twitched.

"And don't think I can't remember the amount of times you wet the bed when you were little," he said, the beginnings of a chuckle rumbling within his throat.

233

"Oh, no." She gave a slow headshake. "You did *not* just bring that up."

"Not to mention your space hogging," he said, downing the rest of his wine and setting his glass on his bedside table behind him.

Her eyebrows shot up. "Excuse me?"

"For someone who doesn't take up much standing room, you seem to take up plenty whenever you sleep."

"I think not, thank you very much."

"Do, too, but ..." He took Brook's drink from her hand and placed it behind him beside his own empty vessel. As he turned back, he hooked an arm over Brook's hip and tugged her down onto her back before she understood his intentions. "Brook, you can take up as much room as you like, so long as I'm the one laying next to you."

Brook's heart pounded as the gold of his irises simmered, even more so when he propped back up on one arm and tucked her in closer until his arm circled her ribcage and his chest half-covered hers. If Kyle had drawn her to him that way, her fingers would have itched to trace the lines of his jaw, his lips.

With Clive, her hands only seemed capable of forming fists.

His gaze cut to her right hand, and he wrapped his around it, unfolding her fingers. "Talk to me, Brook."

"It just ..." She sighed deep, her chest rising with the effort. "Does it not make you uncomfortable? It does me."

"What does?"

"The fact we are only here because of the Coalition."

His head shook, a small motion. "Not me." He stared at her before he blinked hard and a frown appeared. "Are you?"

Yes, her mind answered, while her lips formed the less incriminating response of, "Their part in it all taints everything about this. Takes away from what should be a natural choice."

"Only if you let it." He yawned, but shook his head as if to expel it faster.

"There is no letting it. It is there, anyway," she said, trying not to let it show just how hard she scrutinized his weary placement of his chin on her shoulder. "The Coalition and their damned demands hang over everything, with its manufactured relationships and—"

"It's okay, Brook. You're scared. Scared of what might be. Of taking the next step. I get it. It's natural."

"I am not scared." A lie—though, a more apt description would have been terrified. "Are you?" she surprised herself by asking.

"I'm not scared of what might be. I'm only scared of screwing up." He shrugged, the gesture joined by a second yawn that stretched his lips wide. "But I have you for a guaranteed couple of weeks—at least until your Season kicks in. So, for now, will *you* at least pretend this whole setup doesn't repel you, and hold me like you mean it for a little while? All I'm asking is that you try." He laid his head down on her chest, his arm sliding back around to encase her in his bear hold. "Baby steps, Brook. You can take those, right?"

"Right," she whispered, regret already shrouding her mind and her soul, even as his breathing began to slow.

"Thanks," he murmured.

Though she suspected he would be retracting the word the moment he awoke, she still asked, "For what?"

"For giving me a chance."

Brook swallowed hard, lifting her gaze to the white ceiling when prickles danced at the corners of her eyes. As she lay there, the warmth of his breaths seeping through her robe, the odd twitch of his fingers tugging at her side, the first tear spilled over and trailed across the side of her head.

She reached up the hand Clive didn't hold and swiped the tear away before it could reach her ear, parting her lips and releasing a heavy sigh.

How could doing what was right for herself hurt so much?

She could predict exactly the amount of pain Clive would be in, when he woke to find her gone. Though, as much as she wanted that to be reason enough to stay, she knew he could never make her feel the way Kyle did. Just as she knew any relationship built for her within the Coalition was doomed to an epic failure, anyway, simply because she opposed their ways so verdantly.

Closing her eyes until every inch of flesh around them pulled tight, she chased away her misgivings and told herself she'd be taking the right path. After all, Kyle had given a vow to help her—had he not?

Would that still stand after their days apart?

If he'd been honest in his words over the past months, she had no doubt he would still aid her.

If he hadn't ... it didn't change anything because she still wanted out.

Gritting her teeth, as though to prove her own determination, she grasped Clive's shoulder with one hand, brought the other up to cup his head, and rolled them both to the right until his back met with the mattress and their roles reversed.

She hovered there, studying the slight ripple to his lips, the way his eyeballs appeared to be twitching side-to-side behind his lids. When he didn't speak, didn't move, or protest her removal of him, she slid to the edge of the bed and onto the floor.

Brook had no desire to ever again wear the dress provided by her mother. Luckily, the four bedrooms of the guesthouse each had general supplies in their wardrobes, as, oftentimes, a Tom would arrive with only his silken coat to keep him warm. Also, because of the amount of hours Brook, herself, had spent there, a slow steady stream of her own items had trickled across, and often got left behind.

Her soles squished into the landing carpet as Brook made her way to her preferred bedroom—the one nearest the stairs. When she pushed open the door, she drew in a deep inhalation, hoping that at least a little of Kyle's scent might remain to help solidify her cause, but only artificial chemicals greeted her, the undertones supposed to be redolent of lavender but missing by miles.

While not exactly flattering, the black workout clothes Brook pulled from the wardrobe would offer far more warmth and practicality than the discarded cotton dress—no shoes, though, much to her regret. It took mere seconds to exchange her robe for the fleece-lined clothing, and she headed from the room and bound down the stairs.

In the living space, she crossed to the wall dresser and slid open the top drawer, taking out the notepad and pen she already knew would be in there. After ripping out a sheet, she slipped the rest of the pad back in place, but hesitated when she pressed the ballpoint to the piece she'd taken—only for a moment, though, before resolve set in.

Now I need for you to forgive me.

—Brook

With the note in hand, she turned back for the stairs, no longer leery of the noise levels as she took two at a time in her ascent.

Clive still hadn't moved when she rounded the doorway into the master suite. If anything, his chest rose higher with each inhalation beneath his right hand resting on there, and his breaths had evolved to soft but gritty snores.

After balancing the note against the wine glasses, ensuring he'd spot it upon rousing, Brook trotted across and into the bathroom, the flutter of her pulse slowing slightly upon spotting the pile of clothing left in there by Clive.

It took a little pocket rummaging to find not only enough notes in Clive's wallet to cover a taxi fare to '*anywhere else will do*', but also his mobile phone.

Ignoring the heavy guilt that seemed to be yanking at any part of her heart it could get a grasp of, she about-turned, sparing a final glance and a whispered apology to the sleeping Tom, and padded across the bedroom to the balcony doors.

While the elevated route would require her to jump, it would also raise less suspicion should she be seen leaving the building, and so Brook slipped outside into the crispness of midday winter with little concern for observers. She only truly tensed upon overhanging the railing, from where she scoured the trees and property as far as she could see in each direction.

Voices drifted over from the direction of the house, which meant if she took her usual path through the woodlands, she could remain undetected.

After a backward glance to ascertain she had secured the doors closed behind her, she hopped over the railing and landed on the wooden decking. She instantly folded into an elegant crouch, the entire drop made with little more sound than the flutter of butterfly wings.

Still, no more sound reached her ear than the murmur of masculine tones from where she'd detected them before, and she leaped into a sprint toward the trees.

Freedom always tended to taste sweeter after a bout of confinement—in Brook's experience, anyway. Despite being a few minutes from the border, her shoulders still dared to relax a little with each inhalation of the woodsy aromas surrounding her. Greenery, though absent upon the timber, still showed its presence in the mulched staleness collected around trunks. Wisps of still-pulsating meat pumped to her on the ever-chilling breeze alongside the quiet scurries of the residents. To an unknowing observer, she would most likely appear the outsider—a dark streak blurring the barky landscape in her gazelle-like weaving—but the woodlands were the only part of her father's property Brook truly felt at home.

Less than sixty yards to go, Brook brought up Clive's mobile, her mind conjuring a number she had memorised many weeks before, and her fingers tapping it in just as fast, but with the stone wall waving its welcome ahead, the first prickles of unease tugged at the hairs across her nape. Without breaking stride, Brook spun and switched to running backward, scanning the trees left, right, behind.

Nothing.

Still, she sensed something—she just didn't know what.

Shaking it off—she'd be gone soon, anyway—she fumbled her thumb over the 'call' button, twisted back around, and urged herself forth faster.

The jerk of her body to the left gave the first indication of her error.

The second arrived when pain exploded throughout her skull.

Before she could even swing toward her attacker, her body plummeted, her mind refused to work. She scarcely heard the thud of her collision with the ground before blackness surged in to consume her.

31

Jesus Christ.

Why the hell had I agreed to Ethan's deal?

One day down, and I literally wanted to bust out from my skin, claw out my own brain, and take down a tree, or two.

Who knew how I'd go another day, pretending I was all *healed*. Everything was A-Okay. Smiling when, really, I only wanted to scream at them for not *getting* my issue, or being more bloody compassionate toward it. All of it made worse each time I itched beneath their appraisals and nodded encouragement, any time they caught my eye.

Keeping up my game until finish time had almost tipped me over into the bottom-most pits of insanity.

At least I had distractions at home. Mostly balls, but distractions all the same.

With a flick of my wrist, the bright green orb streaked through the evening shadows toward the house, rebounding before its signature rubbery echo reached me, and finishing with a smack against my palm.

The contact stung, but I didn't care. The harder I threw it, the greater the pain. The best redirection without a prescription for all the other kinds of crap thudding out their bongo messages within me.

Thanks to the winter daylight hours and the darkness already claiming dominance, no reflections obscured my view of the lit kitchen through the window beside where I bounced the ball.

Inside, Dad leaned against the doorjamb to the hallway, doing his usual pretence of casual chatting while, really, he supervised Josh's preparation of dinner.

I didn't blame Dad for the overseeing. I loved Josh silly, but cooking and he didn't often get along. Good job the meal Beth provided meant he only had stuffing to prepare.

In truth, it would've been safer for Josh to skip his weekly turn—Dad made us all take one—but he hated being babied. Probably because we'd all done it since Mum died, and he said it only amplified her absence. Quitting something so natural to us, though, didn't always come easy.

I paused in my ball tossing. "Be sure to take the peel off the onions this time, Josh," I said through the glass pane.

He glanced up. "You're funny," he said, twisting away from Dad and flicking his middle finger up at me. "Should take a job on the stage. Hey, who knows? Maybe you'd do better at that than the sucky effort you've been putting in at the site lately."

If Danny had said that to me, after the week we'd had, my blood would've probably boiled and steam erupted out my ears. With it coming from Josh, accompanied by his goofy expression and tongue hanging out his mouth, my first genuine laugh of the day burst from me, breaking into my dark mood—though only for a split second before I plummeted again and the laugh died an impressive death.

With a heavy blown out sigh, I twisted away and chucked the ball again.

On about the seventh rebound, my mobile buzzed in my pocket—almost in synch with Dad's ringing inside the house. I drew mine out, stared down at Ethan's name across the screen. Harbouring the bubble of hope, that he had better plans for me than my current ones, I answered. "Change your mind?"

"Not exactly."

I almost asked 'What?', but he cut back in with, "Muhammad has no need to go to the mountain when the mountain comes to him."

My breaths stalled at his words. "Brook—Brook's there?"

"Uh ... no. But that's definitely a bunch of Toms I spy gathering outside our gates, if their scents are anything to go by—like some kind of fucking lynch mob ..."

What the ... My feet began moving toward the forest like they had a mind of their own, nearly stumbling in their haste.

"Including Brook's dad. You done something you didn't share with me to piss them off, by any chance?"

"I'm on my way," I said, cutting him off and thrusting into a sprint, as the back door of the house opened at my rear.

Dad's voice boomed out for me to wait.

I couldn't wait.

I needed to know what the hell the Toms wanted.

On a normal day, I'd have paused to change under the cover of the trees, knowing I could have run faster as wolf over the five-mile distance. I hadn't had any normal days in a while, though, and the browns and reds of barks whipped past, as my legs and arms pumped me forth and my bare feet smacked dirt and bracken. With all the questions I had swirling round in my head, I scarcely noticed them, or the speed I travelled, or the shouts to 'wait up' growing more distant the deeper I went.

By the time I erupted from the trees and ducked under the arches into Nate's garden, way faster than I'd ever made it on foot before, I'd convinced myself the Coalition had arrived to warn me away from Brook, and the rumble in my chest, the shading I sensed already beginning to coat my eyes, seemed to be preparing for the big *fuck off* I had planned. The fact the evening breeze kicked up a swirl didn't help either, because I smelled the damn Toms from the off.

Feet pounding grass, I didn't stop running until I smacked into the near corner of the conservatory. My shoulder burned with my grasp of the doorframe to haul my butt round.

In the kitchen, I slammed to a halt, just preventing collision with Beth, as she rounded the table toward the hallway with Lia's blankie and favourite rattle in her hands.

One glance up at me, and she stopped dead as her eyes connected with mine, her frown confirming what I'd already suspected, but I didn't care.

I only had one goal in my mind.

Put those fucking Toms in their place.

With a mumbled, "Not now, Beth," at the parting of her lips, I squeezed past her and strode toward the glass-fronted entrance to the house.

Nathan and Sean butted shoulders in the darkened passage, staring outward, and Nate turned, as my feet slapped the cool tile of the floor.

He opened his mouth, but frowned—exactly as Beth had.

Ignoring him, I peered round his shoulder and through the glass, pretending I hadn't seen Sean's double-take and unfolding of his arms when he glanced my way, too.

Outside, Ethan stood shoulder-to-shoulder with Gabe, in front of what looked like a shitload of Toms blocking the entrance to the driveway, and the rumble in my chest bubbled out as a low snarl.

"Beth, go back upstairs and don't come down until I call you," Nathan said before turning to me. "Kyle, I don't think you should go out there."

"Should and am." I reached around him and snapped the door open before he could stop me, ducking between the two of them.

A quick jog down the porch steps took me to the block-paved drive, and the instant I began marching toward the intruders, their attentions left Ethan and Gabe and latched onto me.

Though my appearance earned me a standing ovation of sneers and curled lips, not one of them said a fucking word. Just stared. The lot of them. Like the bunch of pussies they were.

Weaving around Ethan and Gabe, and pushing my way past three of the Toms, I didn't stop walking until I stood peering down at Brook's dad, my lips half-curving into a

243

smile I doubted the rest of my face joined in on. "I presume you're looking for me."

Disgust, distrust, temper, surprise, probably caused by my eyes—a good few choice emotions flickered within his features, before he asked, "Where is my daughter?"

I caught myself before I took a step back, though I doubted I kept the shock from my face. "Funny," I said, my hands flexing and un-flexing. "I was planning to ask you the same thing."

His amber eyes narrowed. "Do not play games with me."

"Nothing concerning Brook is a game to me." I glanced around at the sea of copper-hued irises, all slightly glowing in the darkening eve, and a twitch set in just below my left eye when I caught a waft of familiar spice and musk. "Now, where is she?"

"Enough of this." The Tom to the right of Brook's dad took a step forward, his chestnut hair shaking atop the tension rolling through him. "Let's just go in there and get her ourselves."

"Not yet, Stefan," Brook's dad said, placing a hand on the younger Tom's chest. "Diplomacy states we must first give him the chance to surrender what does not belong to him."

"Screw diplomacy," the young one said, on cue with my huffed out laugh, aimed more at their blindness than methods. "I want her back."

My attention snapped toward the Tom, my growl all but clawing at my throat, even more so when a stronger dose of the scent I'd caught earlier hit a little harder.

"I will ask one more time," Brook's father said. "My daughter. Go and tell her to come down."

"Man, you are all so meowing up the wrong tree." My head made a slow tilt his way as my temper vied to be set free, my vision darkening even as an alarming acuteness set in. "Take a sniff, puss. I don't even smell of her. In fact ..." I ignored his growled response to step to the side and chase the familiar scent that kept calling to me. "The only one here ..." Every Tom seemed to square their shoulders as I began nudging my way past their rigid forms and forcing them aside. "... who smells ..." My nose twitched with every step. "... of Brook is ..." I paused in front of a golden-eyed male, who met my stare with a defiant one of his own, his almost white curls tickling at his forehead with the breeze. That same breeze blasted me with a wholesome dose of Brook's scent—mingled with his. "You."

With a snarl, I grabbed hold of his throat and tossed him down against the blocks of the driveway, not even stopping to consider just how many freaking allies he had. His arms flailed outward but his rear still dragged across the bricks a few feet before he stopped.

Blanking the crescendo of girlie hisses sending spittle flying my way, I bolted toward the dropped Tom with the intention of stripping him of flesh and hair and every ounce of scent he had no fucking right to. When arms flicked under my armpits from behind and hands slapped hold of my shoulders, I charged forward harder.

The clamping hold tightened, swinging my feet from the floor. "Kyle, it's me!"

Ethan's low grumble hit my ear, but I tried to shrug him off.

I had a mission to fulfil.

"What the hell are you trying to do? Start a war."

Though my gaze remained riveted to the intruding cat, my feet ceased to move, my chest heaving beneath Ethan's stronghold. "I never started this. They did."

"Matter of opinion," he said, his arms loosening a little. "But trying to finish it isn't going to solve anything."

Though it stung, I had to admit Ethan may have been be right, because I'd stand no chance of winning Brook's family over by kicking up shit.

Hell, who was I kidding? I'd had no chance of that from the start.

Still, I turned my back on the blond Tom, as he booted away and up onto his feet, and focused on my pack buddy, as his hands gripped my shoulders, instead of all the intruders behind him—at least, until Brook's dad's right-hand kitty almost bashed me over as he rounded us where we stood.

"Screw this," he said. "I'm going in for her."

Whirling like a Tasmanian devil on speed, I lost Ethan's shackles, snatched up the cat by the collar, and on the full turn back round, one hand slung him like a limp Guy Fawkes against his fellow pussies, while the other rammed Ethan from my path.

The Tom's hisses spat from him, his arms flew out, and on his fall, his flesh receded as black glossiness stole surface. He hit the ground at a roll, his high-pitched wail airing his frustration, as his feline limbs fought against the restriction of his already tearing clothing.

A snarl ripped from my throat on my dive toward him, but my entire body stumbled to the right as a sharp blast of pain exploded through my skull, and as my head whipped around to be fronted with a second smack to my jaw, whatever tatters of a tether that might have been doing at least some kind of job of holding me together snapped and flayed like an out of control bungee.

My fist bulleted to the side. I paid no attention to whoever might have been standing there, just revelled in a sick sense of pleasure when pain lanced my arm on contact.

Pivoting, my other arm thrust out, and another crack vibrated along the limb, dancing the message to my ears that someone's nose had broken.

Another twist. Another punch. Another fucking crack.

I whirled again, but a vice of bloody steel wrapped itself about my midriff and halted my attack. It took me a half-beat to realise the trapper had my arms pinned, too.

They knocked me forward a step.

I slammed my foot down afore me and tried to thrust back again, but the barrier held and shoved me forward a step more.

That same titanium grip had my shoulders before I could blink. When it flicked me round, I threw myself into the motion, facing the assaulter with a snarl upchucking from my mouth.

It only took the flash of pale blond hair for my fist to swing again.

Mid-lunge, an arm smacked it aside, sending me off balance.

All the deferment succeeded in doing was adding fuel to my already erupted temper.

I swung again.

The Tom ducked.

Except, it didn't smell like a Tom. Nothing smelled right.

Nothing looked right either, as I spotted familiar-yet-unfamiliar eyes glaring out at me from beneath pale curls.

My falter allowed them to get a hit in—one hard enough to shake my entire skull—and the accompanying muttered, "Fucking quit already," sounded a whole lot like Gabe.

Dropping back a pace, I blinked hard, but ended up with a too-strong palm cupping the nape of my neck in a non-too-gentle grasp, and another holding my jaw in a way that would seriously bloody hurt if I dared moved.

"They. Are. Not. Worth it." His words came out slow, measured, far deeper than I'd ever heard Gabe speak, and I took a moment to focus on his face.

On his eyes.

Ones that had black circumferences so bold in design, the bright blue trapped within seemed almost incongruous—more so with the sharp splinters stabbing outward and inward from each ring with a ferocity that made Gabe's eyes appear broken.

Every muscle in my face seemed to harbour a nervous tic as the notion of what I witnessed settled through me.

For some reason, concentrating on those tiny spasms helped me clutch at a gradual awareness of everything else.

Of the rumbling like a distant thunder tickling the inner-side of my chest, while it heaved—up-down-up-down—like it couldn't get enough air, or never would again but simply refused to give up trying.

Of the rush of blood through arties, the throbbing of pulse points—not just mine, but in those stupid enough to still be standing close.

Of the way quiet settled over the entire driveway like a suffocating cloak, as though all sound had been stolen, leaving only stillness that belied my previous outburst.

Even the Toms seemed to stand rigid. Unmoving. Beyond Gabe's shoulders. As though awaiting the slightest twitch from me—an excuse to jump back in and finish what I'd started.

Somewhere to the right, I sensed the pack. Their scrutiny. Their presence. Their awareness of me, just as I knew of them—an instinct that accompanied me always, but more so during a hunt.

I didn't dare glance that way. If I feared little else, I feared what I might see in their faces if I had the courage to find out.

"Filthy mutt!"

My head whipped left at the insult—toward the chestnut-haired Tom with the high self-esteem. Blood lined his chin, a path trailing downward from a globule overhanging his lip. When he swiped a backhand against it and leaned my way, my entire body tensed for retaliation, pushing against Gabe's tightening hold.

With his hands fisted so tight his arms seemed to strain against the tendons, the Tom bounced back on his heels. "Nothing but a fucking freak!" He spat as he jerked forward and flobbed a spray of bloody phlegm—toward me.

Before the speckles had even hit my face, the snarl tore from me, whatever control Gabe had conjured from my depths vanishing even faster than the last time, as I threw myself toward the Tom. I scarcely made it more than an inch, though, my neck twisting in agony beneath Gabe's hold, my body slamming into his braced body as he sidestepped.

I pulled back, rammed forward again.

Back again. Another dive jolted every bone in my body.

Over his shoulder, the Tom's lips curled and twisted around words the static buzzing through my ears didn't let me hear, the jeering expression of the other intruders adding to it and stoking my fury further—like petrol splashed over already high-licking flames.

Through each collision, the pup just stood his ground, his hands refusing to let me go—a formidable, unmovable barrier I wanted to tear down but didn't seem to have the juice for, no matter how hard I raged.

Somewhere around that, shouts arrived from the direction of the pack, Gabe's quiet voice mumbled in my face about how I needed to stop before I forced him to do something he'd regret—more noise, more static, more fucking distractions driving me wild.

Until my head exploded in agony.

Followed by a ripple of hurt across my shoulder blades.

I knew when a juggernaut crashed on top of me, and I blinked up, gasping for air, at sky surrounding Gabe's golden halo … the pup had thumped me one again. Not just a regular thump, but an incapacitating blow of epic proportions.

Chest heaving as hard as mine, he stared down at me through blue and black kaleidoscoping eyes that somehow managed to portray the same regret the clenching of his jaw enhanced.

My reflexes had me gripping his shirt, already bracing to toss him away and finish my job, but my gaze flickered to the right, where Brook's dad entered my periphery and pointed my way.

"How could something like *you* ever believe you would be good enough for my daughter?" Venom dirtied every word further. "You're nothing but a rabid animal with no control."

"That's *enough!*"

Nate's roars had a tendency to make everyone shut up and take notice, and it had pretty much that effect then.

Even I paused in my struggle with Gabe to glance across at him, as he strode forward toward the head Tom, impressed, despite my situation, by Dad standing just as strong at his side.

Shoulders hunched high beneath the tension roiling through him, barely contained fury humming within his chest, Nate pointed toward Brook's dad. "Get off my property. Before I remove you myself. And take your feral pets with you."

Mr Nicholls glowered at Nate, his entire body poised tight enough to spring, as if he considered the fight worth it, while the rest of the Toms either matched his stance, or sent unsure glances to their leader like they needed instruction even to breathe. After too many long seconds, he said, "This is not over," and made the slow pivot away.

Only once the Tom had stepped beyond the gates did Nate peer down toward where I still lay pinned, hitting me with a full frontal of just how pissed he really was. "Gabriel, get him inside."

32

In the kitchen, I snatched away from Gabe's stronghold with more force and aggression than intended—though the walk of shame past Dad and my brothers, and the disappointment in their eyes, had ensured my attitude hadn't simmered down much.

After stalking across the kitchen to the corner, I spun back toward Ethan, the only one of the pack to have followed us in. As backup, Nate had said. Like I was an outsider who needed an escort.

Staring my way, with an expression I couldn't decipher, Ethan propped himself against the oak-fronted counters to my right, folding his arms across his chest and half-blocking any access to the conservatory.

Hands still fisted, Gabe stood sentry beside the exit to the hallway.

Brilliant. They'd taken to boxing me in—which only added to my way-too-dark mood, as I levelled my stare on my best friend. "Thanks for the help out there."

The walk inside, the shock that had been mingled with the disappointment in my family's eyes, had allowed enough time for realisation to sink in. That, other than Gabe's intervention and Ethan's attempts to block my arse, none of the pack had stepped in to actually *help*.

"I was just following orders. Gabe, too, before you rag on him." Ethan's eyes flickered in an obvious scrutiny of mine. "Anyway, thanks for the *trust*."

Tou-fucking-ché.

Outside, the quiet squeal of the gates preceded the familiar clank of the lock, and seconds later, feet hit the hallway tiles. Nate appeared through the doorway first, trailed by my dad and brothers, who sent uncertain glances toward me. In all honesty, I didn't search much deeper than that for their opinions. I could only deal with so much in one go.

As soon as Nathan had taken a stand behind his usual seat at the head of the table, he turned to me, arms folded across his chest—just as Ethan had done. "Care to tell me where she is?"

I frowned as confusion nudged my temper aside. "What?"

Taking a step forward, he uncrossed his arms and pointed at me—a small gesture, but with massive impact when coming from Nate. "I am giving you one chance, Kyle, to tell me where she is."

"I already said. I don't know. Do you seriously believe I'm hiding her?" I glanced from him to Dad, then round at the others.

Every one of them stared my way like they waited for answers. Not one of them looked convinced. Which only seemed to re-poke my still simmering flames back up from their embers.

"Come *on*. I haven't seen Brook since she walked out with Ethan on Sunday. What the bloody hell do you think the last week has been about?" I turned back to Nate. "Do you really think I'm that good of an actor?"

"Who knows?" The skin beside his eyes tightened. "Lately, I don't feel as though I know you, at all. And it's not like you're incapable of keeping secrets, is it? You managed to keep all this"—his hand waved toward my eyes—"from me—from your dad—with no problem."

My teeth ground as the fire threatened to blow back up into an inferno, to the point my brain boiled with the heat travelling a rapid journey through my veins. "I had no choice."

"You had every damn choice!" Nate said, his voice hard, despite its volume scarcely rising. "You just, evidently, didn't trust me enough."

That word again—trust. Except I did trust him. "I trust you with my *life*."

252

"You did not trust me with *this*!" He thrust a finger toward the floor.

"What about Gabe?" I swung an arm out toward the pup, feeling like a total shit for deflecting by snatching him into the argument, but unable to stop the words leaving my throat. "I don't hear you ragging on at him about his eyes."

"That's because I've known about Gabe's problems for the past two months." Nate's level stare sent icy waves running through me, almost as much as his words did. "Because *he* trusted me enough to come to me."

"And you didn't think *I* should know something like that?" My other arm flew out until I held them both at my sides, but I jolted when Nathan's fist pounded down against the wood of the table with a loud crack of a bang.

"He came to me in confidence! That's what I'm here for." He tapped a finger to his chest. "And then it's *my* decision if I warrant it as needing to be shared with everyone else. And even then, I only share what others have shared with me, *if* I think it will benefit the rest of you to know. Or *if* I think it places the rest of you in danger. Or *if* the issue is affecting everyone else. I didn't believe Gabe fell into any of those categories."

"Unlike me, you mean?" I asked, taking a step back as the hurt of that zinged through me.

"Yes." Nate nodded. "Very much unlike you."

"That is not fucking fair."

"You want to talk about fair?" Nathan's fists landed on the table as he leaned forward. "How about how your lack of trust has resulted in total disregard for the pack? Is that fair? How about how that very disregard has now brought trouble to *my* doorstep. To my *home*." His finger prodded against the oak beneath it. "Both Shelley and Mia are upstairs with Beth and Jem. All of them having to hide because of you. My granddaughter is having to be hidden up there, too, because of *you*. We cannot risk bringing these kinds of trouble here anymore, Kyle. Not when there are females and a child to protect."

253

"What's Brook, if she's not a female who needs protecting, Nate? What about her?"

"Brook is not the pack's problem."

Hands gripping the lip of the table, like that could anchor me against the tidal wave of fury attempting to drown any sense of rationality I might have left, I found myself mirroring Nate's pose. "She's *my* problem."

"Let it go, Kyle."

"How can I, when I know she's in danger? How can I when I know what those ..." My arm thrust out with the point of my finger. "... fucking animals do with their females? They use them for breeding. *Just* for breeding. What kind of race does that? Makes them mate with one bloody male after another until they've fulfilled what the males decide is enough. Or until one of the males wants to fight to keep them. Hell, the females don't even get a choice over *that*." I shoved away from table. "And you want me to leave her there?"

"In case you hadn't noticed," Nate said, his voice still infuriatingly calm, "they don't have her, either, Kyle."

"Then, *where the hell is she*? Why am I the only one who gives a flying fuck about this?"

With my lips clamped tight over the roar of rage begging to be released, I spun away, my fist forming before I could stop it, my arm thrusting without order—the entire action only registering when agony smashed through my knuckles and reverberated up my forearm. For good measure, I disconnected my hand from the dent I'd made in the fridge door and slammed my knee against the victim instead, and finished by pressing my head against the cool metal way harder than could be considered healthy.

"Urgh. Seriously?"

I stilled at Jem's voice and twisted around with my chest going crazy beneath my laboured and gravelly breaths.

She stood in the doorway to the hall, a scowl of irritation wrinkling her forehead. "What's the bloody deal with all you ..." She waved her hands round at us. I expected a lecture on males and their tempers, but instead, she said, "Why does sex always have to be the flipping motivation for everything?"

"It isn't," Ethan said. "It's the simple case of survival of the fittest."

"Same damn thing," she said.

"And don't stick us in the same box as them, Jem." I took a step forward and swung an arm toward the front of the house, toward the driveway they'd not long stood upon. "We're *nothing* like them."

"Finally," Dan muttered. "Acknowledgement for the fucked-upness of your situation."

I spun toward him, a growl ripping from me, but didn't even make the full turn or first stride before a flash of blond body-slammed me. Nor did I get to take my next breath as pain bulleted through my shoulder blades, crackled through my brain, and enough weight to cause constriction piled atop me.

I blinked a few times, gradually focusing on green eyes staring back at me amidst hair the colour of dried corn, and beside that, crowns of auburn and dark brown.

Sean and Dad climbed off me first, leaving only Josh, though Dad hesitated a beat and gave a headshake that spoke volumes. Josh pushed up to a crouch, but didn't move from over me, and I frowned at the brightness coating his eyes.

"Please stop, okay?" he asked. "Because you're scaring the shit out of me, Kyle."

The green of his irises shone with a heavy beseeching, blocking my warpath, crashing through barriers I didn't realise I'd erected as something tightened in my chest. I reached up, and his shoulders stiffened like his trust wavered, agonising me with the realisation of just how far I'd gone, but he didn't flinch away when I gripped the nape of his neck. Rolling up to sit, I drew him to me, tucking his chin against my shoulder as I had when he'd been a kid.

He didn't pull away, but mumbled, "I want my brother back," and my other arm reached around, clutching him in the kind of hug I hadn't given him for years.

"I'm sorry," I told him, as every little detail of the past hour tornadoed through me, capturing my scattered thoughts and hauling them around and around, before flinging them free to hit me full force with just how much I'd alienated myself from the pack.

From my family.

"I'm sorry," I whispered again.

In my periphery, an arm slipped around Jem toward Lia's changing stuff I hadn't noticed in her hands, followed by a shoulder hidden by a curtain of long dark hair.

Hair that looked exactly like Brook's.

My heart that'd just begun to steady rammed me from the inside out, and I kicked up to my feet, bashing my shoulder blade off the nearest unit in my haste—sending Josh scrambling back like he'd been zapped.

I probably should've dealt with the confusion his face showed, but my attention only seemed interested in the dark-haired female—until she flicked her head, sending the long strands over her shoulder, and I realised my error.

Not Brook. Not Brook, at all. Though, where that thought had come from, I didn't know. Had I truly believed she might have been in the house the whole time, that the pack could be cruel enough to keep up with that deep a pretence?

As if my attention on his mate unnerved him, Gabe straightened from the wall, making an almost imperceptible shift to the right, but Jem merely smiled at Mia. "Tell Beth I'll be up in a sec with Lia's food," she said, pointing out the cries I hadn't even heard coming from upstairs.

As the young female padded off down the hallway, her hair trailing behind her in a way Brook's had all too often, I scraped my fingers into my own hair, letting the tightness to my scalp ground me, and I took a few disjointed steps toward the back door.

"I can't stay in here," I said at Dad's questioning gaze loaded with worry. "I ... I'm going for a run. I need to get out. I need to ..." Fingers still clinging onto my hair, arms tucked tight against cheeks, I strode past the pack, past all their opinionated stares, and bust out into the conservatory.

Fresh evening air enveloped me in the garden, and I gulped it down, huge lungfuls, like if I could only get enough then my body would cease to feel starved. Dampness had claimed the lawn beneath my feet, and the coolness seeping into my soles warred with the temperatures still buzzing through my body, as thought after thought went into a battling gambol through my mind, to the point I had no idea which to focus on.

Instinct said Brook—screw the rest—so Book took precedence, but the distraught gleam of Dad's eyes, right before I marched out, elbowed that thought aside before tackling Josh, Dan, Nate—my reaction to Mia—which brought me right back to Brook.

"Hey, wait up."

Ethan. Should've known he'd follow, but I couldn't handle company right about then. Not after my episodes. Besides, his face, when he'd called me out in the kitchen, still sat strong. Often, with Ethan, a lesser expression meant a lot more going on beneath the surface.

Ignoring the increased speed of his feet squelching the grass, I upped my own pace.

I'd managed to duck beneath the arches before he grabbed my arm. "I said, wait up. I'm coming with you."

I rounded on him far faster than intended.

He backed off a step, palms up. "Hey, whatever you need, buddy. You want to run, let's run. You need something to pound on,"—he opened his arms wide—"take your best shot. But I'm not going to let you do it alone. There's been enough of that already."

My growl rolled out before I could stop it. "Nate send you after me?"

The step away he'd taken vanished as he retraced it, the first hint of a threat in his body language. "I'd have come, anyway, and you know it."

"Well, you shouldn't have. I'm fine on my own."

"Yeah?" He jerked up his chin. "How's that been working out for you so far?"

Jaw tight, I stared off to the right, inhaling hard through my nostrils and finding the promise of rain moistening the air. "You don't get it," I said, my voice low, before looking back. "None of you get it."

"Fuck you, Kyle. You haven't given us a chance to." As he slapped the back of his hand against my shoulder, my growl re-brewed.

"I gave you a chance. I told you today, I thought something might be up. But you"—I prodded him—"made me fucking wait. You"—I shoved my face close to his—"wanted me to wait 'til tomorrow. Well, guess what? Your idea sucked. Because if I hadn't listened to you, then I might have stopped Brook from going who the hell knows where."

"Again, Kyle, fuck *you*!" he said, pushing back against me until we practically butted chests. "If you'd have spoken to us—to *me*, even—before it had gotten to this point of being out of control, then maybe today would have gone differently. Hell, maybe Sunday would've gone differently. And then I'd have stood at your side in there"—he jerked a thumb over his shoulder toward the house—"through both of these shit-fests you've caused, instead of wondering where the hell my friend's gone, and what the fuck I did to make you believe you couldn't trust me."

Air heavy with tension, we stood chest to chest, both of us glaring, both with muscles coiled tight enough to snap. I snapped first, twisting away and stomping off into the shadows of the forest. "Screw this shit. I'm going for my run."

A hard slam against my shoulder blade sent me stumbling forward a foot. "And, like I already said, I'm coming with you." He pushed around me, taking the lead, and lengthened his strides until they outmatched mine. "Whether you like it, or not."

33

The entire side of Brook's face and head hurt, like a pulsating life-form had attached itself to her and took prompts from her heartbeat. She chanced opening her eyes, but even that hurt, each dull thump at her temple strong enough to be visible beyond her right one, which seemed to be opposed to achieving much more than a slit.

For minutes—maybe hours—she lay there, trying to recall what on earth she had done to herself. Until the texture of the ceiling focused through the darkness, exposing the lack of whorls etched into the textured coating, and it suddenly dawned on her that she didn't lay in her own room.

She bolted upright, hissing and pressing a hand to her head as the action sent pain searing through it. Refocusing took immense effort, too, and as she peered through the dull space, unrecognisable to her, recollections flashed through her mind.

Of her week in the cellar. Her humiliating Seasonal Party. The time spent in the guesthouse with Clive.

Her eyes flitted to the side, the movement creating an ache in the depths of their sockets, and her sights settled on a door to her left, and to the right, on a window that allowed no light in, despite lack of drapes.

Where ...

Not in the guesthouse. Certainly not there. Did that mean Clive had brought her elsewhere?

But ... why?

More to the point, why couldn't she remember?

She swung her legs over the bed's edge until her feet found the floor, her teeth clenched in a constant wince against the pressure building in her head from each slightest manoeuvre.

A tightly woven, rough cord carpet scratched her soles as she pushed to a stand. She'd scarcely gotten upright when nausea swelled in her stomach, doubling her over as a retch tore up her throat. No vomit arrived with it, and body swaying, she clutched at the itchy blanket on the bed, swallowing down the urge for a repeat performance as she reclaimed her balance. Only once certain she had it under control did she straighten and make slow, wobbly steps toward the door.

A second appraisal showed what her first had missed—the lack of light stretched beyond her immediate surroundings, as no glow bled around the gaps in the doorframe. She wiggled the knob, but it didn't twist, just rattled—which meant someone had locked her in.

A harder tug on the handle did little to change that, and her pulse sped up at what her predicament could mean. Why on earth would Clive do that to her?

Exactly, she thought, *why would he?*

She lifted a fist and pounded against the solid wood of the door, ignoring the answering throb through her skull. "Clive?" Another thump, another, louder yell. "Clive!"

When no sound responded, not even a creak, she dropped her hand, closing her eyes for a moment as she steadied her breaths again, and leaned an ear against the panel.

Absolutely, definitely, nothing moved beyond her space.

"Time for a little light," she mumbled, sweeping her palms across the wall on either side of the doorframe and auto flipping down the switch when her fingers skimmed over it.

Nothing.

She flicked the switch up the other way. Still nothing. Though, Brook had no idea if that meant lack of power, or merely lack of source in her holding room.

Spinning fast enough to induce dizziness, she marched quicker than her brain truly considered wise, around the three-quarter bed she could study from her new angle, and stood at the window on the far side of the room.

As with most standard UPVc windows, the latch had a button to depress with an inset keyhole. Hoping the lock hadn't been utilised, Brook pushed in the button with her thumb and tried to twist, gushing out a huge sigh when the handle slid upward with a quiet click.

Even with the window open, the darkness beyond didn't alter.

Concern kicking back in, she shoved out a hand, growling a little when her fingertips smacked something solid. She pushed her hand out again, swallowing at a dull thud on contact, and again when a heavy knock echoed back beneath a rap of her knuckles.

Wood. Someone had boarded the window over. Taking a step back, she shook her head, her murmured, "No," joining in with her denial.

"No!" she said again, louder, stamping forward again and slamming both palms against the panel, grunting out her frustration when it didn't budge, didn't even shake.

Hands fisting at her sides, she whirled back to face the room, all but glowering around at anything and everything. "I am going to kill him," she said, her hands clenching tighter.

"Clive!" Her shout seemed to reverberate forever, but rather than hinder more effort, it only served to fuel her growing temper. She raised her right foot and stomped it against the floor, uncaring of the jarring affect it had on her worsening headache. "Clive!" The second time, she jumped up with both feet, slamming back down hard enough to send a tremor racing across the flooring and make the bedframe hum. "Clive!" That shout arrived louder than even the others—growly and drawn out until it scratched at her throat.

When she still gained no response, she went back to smacking against the wood of the window. Maybe enough hits would help vibrate it loose.

However, when her palms began to smart, and her arms to burn, and the sweat trickling over whatever had happened to her right temple seemed to enhance the ever-growing agony there, she knew she fought an unwinnable battle and snapped back to the room, stumbling as she spotted a second door in the wall to the right of the bed's headboard.

In less than fifteen graceful strides, she reached the exit, grasping the knob and twisting at the same time. The door flung wide with her yank, and as she righted herself, she squinted into an area even smaller and darker than her current one.

The glass panels came into focus first, identifying a corner cubicle. Followed by the unmistakable porcelain of a toilet bowl and tiny hand-basin.

Nothing more than a bathroom.

Needing to double check, she felt the walls for a light-switch and flailed around for a cord on finding the wall bare, tugging downward when her fingers folded around a thin string.

The click sounded loud, but no light arrived, and even a second check showed not even the hint of a window, which put Brook in no better a position than she had been to begin.

Stuck in a room, set in where or what she didn't know, and with no clue as to how, who, or why.

Growling out her frustrations toward the ceiling, she paced back to the bed, where she settled cross-legged onto the mattress, with her glower aimed at the door, and hoped, for the sake of her captor, that someone came and let her out before her mood could plummet much further.

34

Ethan hadn't been kidding when he'd endeavoured to show his support. Even once he'd stuck on my hide throughout our run, he'd chased me back home, hanging out in whatever room I happened to be in, finally flopping onto my bed and refusing to budge.

For the entire night.

On top of that, every time I'd checked my phone—despite my gut seeming to know ahead of me the zilch activity I'd find there—Ethan had tried snatching it away and telling me to quit torturing myself.

At one point, he'd said, "You wanna go stake out the cats, see what they're playing at?"

To which I'd said no, because I already knew in my heart that I had every intention of hunting Brook down, no matter how many Toms I had to go through to find her. Just as I knew acting on that impulse would land me in the biggest pile of shit with Nathan to date. I respected Ethan too much to drag him that deep into my mess. I'd rather him be pissed at me for exclusion, than because his access to time with Shelley had gained hitches.

So, when my mobile vibrated for the first time in days, I found myself wholly thankful that he hadn't insisted on shadowing me into the bathroom for my morning shower.

Nearly falling out of the stall, I grabbed a towel and dried my hands en route to snatching the phone up, rubbing the same towel over my soaking hair as I stared down at a number I'd never seen before.

Regardless, I clicked the connect button and placed the phone to my ear, desperation forcing out my hopeful, "Brook?"

Static answered for a few beats, then, "This the dog?" a male voice asked.

Like a switch had been hit, the hackles rose along my nape beneath the tingle of spontaneous hate. Removing the phone from my ear for a moment, I strode across to the door, forehead pressed against it as I listened for eavesdroppers.

Satisfied, I headed back across to the window. "If I'm the dog, you must be the cat," I said into the phone. *But which one?*

More static filled the gap of quiet. I wondered at one point if he'd hung up.

"I want to talk to you." His voice sounded strangled, as if the admittance had taken a lot of effort.

"I'm not interested," I said.

"I think you are."

"Actually, I heard enough of your bullshit last night."

A quiet growl travelled the line. "You know what? Forget it. Should've known this'd be a waste of my time. Just go back to sniffing butts, or whatever the hell it is you do. I'll find Brook on my own."

"Talk," I said, before he could hang up.

"Got your attention, did I, dog?"

I gritted my teeth. "Just fucking talk."

"Not here. Not now. Somewhere private."

My scoff arrived as a snorted growl. Like I'd fall for that trick.

"Choose the fucking place, if you're that scared," he said.

First instinct had me braced to snarl out a massive *Screw You!*, but I knew that'd only bring Ethan, or Dad, or somebody running, so I swallowed it down. "If this is some kind of pussy ambush, I'm going to fucking kill you."

"It isn't. And *you* better come alone, too."

"If I come alone, it won't be because you told me to. It'll be because there's no doubt in my mind that, no matter the size of your posse, I can take each and every one of you out without even breaking a sweat." Another growl hit my ear, but I ignored it. "There's a B-road that runs alongside the east side of our forest." Better to meet on home turf, and play that choice he'd given me to my advantage. "Park up by the bridge over the river, and follow the current south for around a hundred yards until you come to a clearing. You have thirty minutes, or you lose."

Disconnecting the call, I stood staring toward the door, battling the temptation to call in Ethan as backup—if only because the damage control could be minimalised that way, on the off chance the Tom didn't stay true to his word and come alone.

As fast as the notion arrived, though, I quashed it. I'd already decided to leave Ethan out of my crap. All I had to do was shake him off and make a run for it—even if he would slaughter me when I showed my face again.

I just hoped, with time, he'd thank me for the consideration.

While leaving the shower running and leaping from the bathroom window might have been the easier and fastest option, running off on my mission with zero attire hadn't exactly appealed. That meant I had the task of heading to my bedroom and tugging on some clothes, and grabbing my boots from the hallway, slipping those on—all without looking like I had an agenda.

On reaching the hallway, my break arrived. My family, as well as Ethan, all seemed to have huddled in the kitchen, from where low mumbles drifted—probably mumbles about me—so after successfully slipping across the hallway to the living room unseen, I'd unlatched the window in there, swung my legs over and out, and hopped to rain-soaked and freezing freedom.

At the end of the driveway, a seven-foot-high brick wall fronted the property, as well as along both sides of the house, halting where the rear garden met forest. Beyond the wall at the front, a B-road ran, and on the other side of that, the forest continued for another couple of miles. We tended to stick to the forest within the border of the roads—less chance of the local bigger-than-regular wolves being spotted by motorists that way—so taking a low-ducked sprint to my left, I'd flung myself up and over the wall, landing with a thump on the other side amongst the trees.

From there, instinct and knowledge of my home had guided me to where I needed to go—until I got close and my nose picked up a singular alien stench. Every one of my nasal hairs twitched against the rankness, until I knew exactly where to find him. And not where I'd told him to be, though at least he had come alone.

The Tom's scent led me to a tree—a huge F-off tree. One big enough to conceal his ugly rear. I rounded the trunk and found him squatted on his haunches, back to the bark. His fisted hands, resting over his thighs, contrasted with the complacent air he seemed to be aiming for. The mop of blond hair blowing in the wind got my attention the strongest, though.

Growling, I snatched my hand out, caught him around the throat before his kick-off could get him out of reach, and slammed him against the tree. "You smelled of her yesterday. Why?"

He didn't bother to fight me, as if he'd been expecting the greeting, but merely glared at me with eyes of bright amber. "Because I was the last one to be with her."

My snarl erupted before I could curb it, and I whipped my arm to the side, sending the Tom flying, until he smacked against a solid oak with a grunt and a curse.

Not even giving him a chance to find his footing, I leapt his way and grabbed him again. "Why?" I said, digging my fingers into his throat, ignoring the scratch of his nails against them and the attempted twist away of his body.

"Because she Chose me."

That time, I didn't bother with the flinging but hauled him up and ran at the next tree, only stopping when collision gave me no other choice, and I would have head-butted the arsehole if I hadn't braked. Beneath the rain of wet twigs, I pushed my face into his. "She would *never* have chosen you. If you fucking touched her. If you laid one finger on her—"

"I didn't." His hands tugged at my forearms, but he'd had too many dopey pills if he thought I'd let go. "It didn't get that far."

"Then, how about you tell me how far it did get. All of it. And any time I think you're lying, you lose a whisker."

He booted a foot against the trunk at his rear, his thrust forward actually knocking me away by about an inch.

I shoved him back again. "Tell me," I said, the two words grating past my throat and between the ripple of lips I scarcely maintained control over.

His struggle stopped, though his chest heaved. Maybe he realised we'd get somewhere faster if he just answered the damn question. "She blew me off. Okay?" His jaw clenched beneath the cool glint of his eyes. "And then she drugged me."

I stared hard at him, seeking the lie, the truth, the slightest flinch that would suggest either. "You better start talking," I said once satisfied. I figured, as he might be the best lead I had, I may as well listen to the Tom. For that moment, anyway—unless he turned out to be more useless than he looked.

"I would've done already, if you'd given me a chance," he said.

I let him get his footing and released him, but didn't lower my own guard, and it took all of around ten minutes for the Tom to fill me in on the previous day's events. One after the other, starting with the Choosing Ceremony, to her Choosing him, each addition sending my teeth into a grinding frenzy, my muscles coiling tight enough to spasm, and an unsettling thunder clapping around within my chest.

Wisely, he skimmed over whatever the hell happened in the guesthouse, taking his recount right up until he'd conked out.

The rest of it turned out to be nothing but assumptions.

She'd nicked his phone, which had pissed him off. *Good.* From there, nobody knew. Nobody'd seen her. Nobody'd talked to her. Though, she'd evidently intended to call me, as the digits she'd pressed in had remained on the screen when they found his phone abandoned near the boundary to Brook's home—explaining how the Tom'd got my number, as well as what had led them to me.

Cue their appearance the night before.

"Screwed up with your assumptions there, didn't you?" I said.

"You'd have been our first path to follow, anyway. We all know she's been whoring arou—"

I shot forward and snuck around his back faster than my heart could pound its next beat, my arms sliding around and grasping his head. "You won't finish that sentence if you want to live." I gave enough of a tug to show him my intent, blanking his grunt and fumbling fingers trying to pry himself loose.

"You won't kill me. You need me."

"Nah." I shook my head. "With or without you, I'll get Brook back. *You're* here because you need *me*."

He growled, releasing a gasped breath at the small yank I gave his head to shut him up. "I must have been insane to think you'd listen."

"Maybe *you* all should have listened to Brook a little harder," I said next to his ear. "And then she wouldn't be missing to begin."

"I should've expected you'd send the blame elsewhere."

"Excuse me, but you're the one who turned up here. And I'm guessing that's because you don't trust your own kind."

"I'm here because Brook, for some dumb reason, trusted *you*. Nothing more. Though why, I dunno. She shouldn't even be fooling around outside of the Coalition. She knew that. She deserves better, dammit. She deserves—

"What? You?"

His head nodded once—a tiny jerk stalled by my grasp. "Maybe."

My laugh burst out but sounded more scoffing than amused. "Yeah, well, maybe if you lot hadn't suffocated her, she wouldn't have looked elsewhere for companionship."

"Don't pretend to know us, dog. You know nothing about the Coalition. You'll never understand us."

"I know she felt trapped. She was constantly being told what to do, when to do it, who to do it with. And not just by her poor excuse of a father. By all of you. Every last one of you fighting for a piece of her. Bickering like a bunch of spoilt brats over a toy you all fucking wanted to play with. Please ..." I gripped his head tighter, and he stumbled a little. "... feel free to tell me if I've got it wrong."

"Screw. You. Coming here was a stupid idea. I should've known a dog—"

"You're mistaken if you think I need you to get her back, cat."

"Yeah?" He gave another jerk of a nod I cut off. "Well, then, good luck with the addresses."

My entire body stilled at that, and I smiled on the inside at the stupid Tom playing the best hand he had. "You're also mistaken if you think I'll let you walk away from here before I've taken your sorry hide to the cellar and beaten every last Coalition address out of you."

He chuckled, though my forearm beneath his throat made it sound strangled. "You don't scare me."

I shoved him forward, waiting for him to find his footing. When he spun to me, one hand massaging his neck, I said, "Then, we'll call that one mistake number three. So, now you have two choices. You can either tell me what you thought coming here today would achieve for

270

you. Or I can just beat what I need out of you and go on my merry way."

Loathing—lots of loathing—shone from his eyes. "What the hell did Brook see in a dick like you?"

"I ask myself that question every damn day. Now, for Christ's sake, talk, because you're beginning to bore me."

Hands hooked behind his head, his shoulders tense despite the relaxed pose, he seemed to be debating whether to plough forth with his initial intentions, or just make a run for it. When his gaze steadied on me, I knew which way he'd swing. "My truck's parked out on the road, like you said to. So, how about we walk and talk? Save wasting any *more* time." He started to twist away, but the sidelong glance he sent more than shouted who he held responsible for that.

I made no move to follow. "And who's waiting at your truck?"

He paused as he went to walk off. "I told you I was alone. I have no reason to lie, dog."

"Bullshit. You have every reason to lie." I strode forward, bumping his shoulder with mine to get going. "But you hadn't better be. Otherwise, that'll be mistake number four. And you, cat, have already had two more chances than you deserve."

The Tom's 4x4 Volvo hugged the curves nicely along the A-road toward Shropshire. He'd convinced me to climb aboard upon confirmation of his solo status, with a statement of, 'I'm going to get Brook back. And I can't do it alone.' Though, curbing the urge to bash his head in at the implication that he wanted her back for *himself* had taken some effort.

"So, let me get this straight," I said, cranking down the window a little to dilute his odour. "You think someone in the Coalition has Brook. Correct?"

He nodded but didn't turn. He hadn't looked my way since I'd climbed in his ride. Instead, he peered ahead toward the windscreen, where the wipers intermittently swished back and forth. Beyond those, heavy rain splatters bounced off the dulled grey tarmac of the road.

Body twisted slightly in my seat, I studied the cat's profile. Bulky. Tall—taller than me. Both irrelevant statistics, in my opinion—just like his name. He'd told me it was Clive. I'd told him I didn't care. My own opinion aside, he'd stalked into wolf territory alone, to confront someone who'd made it quite clear he wanted the beat the shit out of him during their initial meeting, and despite his lack of retaliation, I didn't believe for one second he needed me because he was afraid.

"And you need my help, why?"

"Because I'm chasing up a lead. One that involves a member of the Coalition."

"And?"

"And if I go to the other Toms and throw out an accusation that involves one of our own, when they all have you as their hot ticket, I'll be tossed out with the trash and nowhere close to where I need to be." He glanced my way for the first time. "You think I grabbed you because of your magnetic pull? Trust me, this is nothing more than a tactical move."

"You want me to trust you? *You* don't even trust you." Of course, I could've told him that, as long as I suspected he could lead me to Brook, I'd follow him to the ends of the earth and then some. Only a moron would give him that advantage over themselves, though.

"I'm different," he said. When I sniffed in reply, his jaw tightened, and his hands flexed over the wheel. "Look, if I walk in there on my own today, without backup, I'm toast. *That's* why I called you."

My eyes narrowed. "You know who has her."

He shook his head. "Not *know*. It's a leap. That's all."

"Based on what?"

"Based on how much Stefan has always wanted Brook, and the fact he'd do anything to get that. And the fact he's been missing since last night. But he apparently bragged to some of the Toms under his dad's watch about his weekend of fun he's got planned." His teeth ground. "The Tom's a dick with an attitude problem, and an ego the size of Russia—you probably remember from last night ..." He glanced my way, and my eyebrow arched. "He had the most to say for himself," he continued, "as usual. So, anyway, if he's bragging, you can bet your life it's something big he's got going on."

Ignoring the ache in my wrists from the tightness of my fists, I asked, "Again, why do you need me? He too much for you, cat?"

"Alone, no," he said, not even rising to the dig. "But his brother's with him. Stefan alone is a dirty player—take-able, but dirty. Combine him with Roland, and anyone who goes against them won't come out the other side looking pretty."

"Nice," I muttered. "You're enlisting me—without pay—to be your bodyguard."

His lips twitched. "I prefer guard dog."

"Keep up the sweet talk, and you'll be damaged before you get there."

The longer Brook sat on the bed, the further her post-concussed mind had cleared. With that clarity had come better understanding of the events leading up to her incarceration. She recalled everything that had occurred in the guesthouse. Including the unconscious state in which she had left Clive. To begin, she had considered he may have been the better performer and outwitted her in her attempts to outwit him. That notion had fast been eliminated, though. Clive had spent his entire life wearing his emotions and feelings like a skin he couldn't shed. She did not believe he had developed the acting skills to fool her. Besides, she had watched him drink the affected wine, so she knew in her gut that the condition she had presumed him to be in was a true one.

After that, she remembered only racing through the woodlands to freedom—except she didn't make it.

So, when the hum of an engine buzzed from beyond her space, and a door finally opened and closed somewhere in the building, she had no idea who, or what, to expect.

Suddenly, Clive having stolen her seemed like the happy option.

35

After twenty minutes of driving, the Tom pulled onto a slip-road and parked up.

I stared out the passenger window. Fields. Fields. More fields. On both sides of the road. "What is this place?"

"For now?" he asked, opening his door. "The toilet."

"So, this isn't where we're headed, then, I'm guessing."

"Nope." He hopped out and spun, peering back inside. "That'd be the King's cabin."

I didn't like the sound of that. "You know, I've seen *Cabin in the Woods*. Tell me this one's different."

He chuckled. "A lot of the Coalition Toms like to have relations on the side, with human females. So, a lot of them have extra properties, far from their homes, so those kinds of indiscretions occur away from watchful eyes."

"You're nothing but a bunch of hypocrites," I said, frowning. "You all attack Brook for her choices, when the Toms are all doing exactly the same."

His amusement took a fast hike. "You're not human, dog. It's *not* the same."

"But it's the same principles. Whether you want them to be, or not."

"Keep telling yourself that," he muttered, slamming the door and striding off.

I tracked his rounding of the Volvo and down the dip to a low hedgerow. As he unzipped his pants and turned his back on me, the inevitable happened—in the form of my mobile buzzing through the pocket of my jeans.

I thought about ignoring it—for a millisecond—before I wriggled it out to get whatever over with. 'Ethan' shone from the screen, and I let out a low groan. Nate, I could've handled. Maybe. He'd have likely just given me a bollocking and ordered me home. Ethan, though, would have been raging from the moment he'd figured out I'd gone, for a set of reasons all his own and all one hundred percent my fault.

Sucking in a little gusto, I clicked connect. "Hey."

"Where. The fuck. *Are* you?" A quiet aggression deepened his tone.

"Out," I said.

His growl told me he didn't like that answer, and his low spoken, "Where?" told me he hadn't spilled to the others. Yet.

I stayed mute. Beyond my window, the Tom shook his tool and zipped up, rolling out one of his shoulders before making the turn for the incline.

A heaved breath travelled the line. "Okay. If you get back here, now, I'll forget you pulled this shit on me." Ethan's measured words reflected his barely-there control. "Get back here within the next twenty minutes, and I won't even tell Dad."

So, Nate *had* sicced him on me to keep me in tow, which only added a greater burden to my conscience. I sighed, the exhale long and weighted by the refusal I had to give. "Sorry, Ethan, but I can't."

"Care to tell me why?" he asked.

"No."

"You gonna tell me what you're getting yourself into?"

"No."

The quiet hush that followed spoke volumes. I pictured the crush of his hand against his mobile. The lock of his jaw. That familiar flash of anger in his eyes— downtrodden by the wash of hurt he'd be feeling. Hurt caused by me.

"Look, I'll fill you in later," I said, as the Tom stared at me through the driver's window. "In the meantime, you do what you got to do. And I'll do the same." I went to hang up, but paused at Ethan's, "Kyle!" rumbling through the phone. I lifted it back to my ear.

"I am so fucking mad at you right now it's not even funny, but ..." His sniffed inhalation hit my ear. "If you need me ..."

I eyed the Tom, as he slid back into his seat behind the wheel. "Sure."

"*Promise* me," Ethan said, his tone heavy with plea, maybe even a little desperation.

"Promise," I said, shutting off the power, as well as the call.

"Trouble?" the Tom asked.

"Always," I said.

A little over thirty minutes later, the Tom cut off the main road onto what looked like a dirt track running between clusters of trees. He only followed that for a quarter mile before he inched off to the right and weaved us between trunks until deep enough that we could scarcely see road nor track from our position.

I peered out through the windscreen into a woodland as stretched as that at the Nicholls' property. The Tom seemed to like his remote spots for stopping, I gave him that—except, unlike with the fields, the trees provided him with plenty of coverage for sneaky fuckery.

"You got friends hiding out here and waiting to beat me with sticks?" I asked.

"Get over yourself, dog. You're not that special. Now, are you coming, or cowering?" He hopped out, slamming the door shut and leaving me no choice but to join him.

The second I did, wafts of cats—plural—drifted across with the wind, sending my hackles rising higher. "Just so we're clear. I don't cower. Not from anyone. And something else you should remember." I met him at the bonnet and prodded a finger to his chest. "I'm not here for you. I'm here for Brook. Which means I will drop you like a slam-dunk, if you so much as dip me in anything even resembling your shit. Understood?"

He knocked my hand aside and started walking. "How about we clear this up all the way to the cabin?" he asked over his shoulder. "Give them ample warning we're on our way."

Eyes narrowed, I clamped my lips together and closed the gap he'd gained until I strode alongside him, but I still stayed on alert for hidden surprises.

"What?" He glanced to me. "You got nothing to say to that?"

"You're the one who suggested we should be quiet. And yet you're the one still talking."

Luckily for him, he kept his mouth shut, and the quiet in which we trekked the rest of the way could've almost been considered amicable—if not for the reason we'd gone there to begin. Or the fact he was a cat—one I didn't like very much.

Above us, the rain that had fallen most of the day continued to hit the higher branches, playing a beat on the leaves of the few evergreens we passed. The defiant drops that skirted the obstacles dotted the ground, darkening the few patches of dirt not already muddied. It took around five minutes of trying to enjoy natural flavours tainted by Tom before a single storey home appeared up ahead.

We trekked toward it, slinking lower as we neared the treeline, and settled into our crouches behind a gathering of prickling brush, peeking through like a couple of pervy peepers.

Closer, the property looked like some kind of ranch-style bungalow. A little like the guesthouse at Brook's family's place, I guessed, except for lacking the second storey. Wide picture windows. Shaded decking that appeared to stretch the entire perimeter. Rocking chairs and swings.

My eyes flickered, taking in every detail, as my ears strained for sound.

"Nothing," the Tom muttered beside me.

"So, let's go closer, then."

He nodded. "Aim for the right of the windows and duck. And hiss if you smell anything."

"I'm a wolf," I said. "Hisses are not part of my vocabulary."

Half-squatted, we both surged forward, shoulder-to-shoulder in our aim for the same spot.

With each step, muffled grunts and cries reached me, growing louder and setting my nerves on edge, until my fists curled ready to pound—to the point I began veering off in the direction of the racket.

A hand grabbed my shoulder and tugged me on track. "Softly, softly," the Tom whispered, but the tightness in his jaw told me he didn't feel much better than I did about the sounds.

With a hop up onto the decking, we spun and aligned our rears with the wooden-boarded exterior of the house. From there, we dropped and shuffled our way beneath the first window.

I held up three fingers and ticked them down one at a time—three, two, one.

We both peeked over the sill. No Brook, though I did spot a Tom, and what I saw *him* doing on the other side of the glass sent my eyebrow arching up before I dipped low again.

"Did I just see right?" Clive asked.

I spun and leaned against the building. "Unfortunately, but I guess that explains the crescendo."

"Man." He twisted and joined me. "Never had Roland down as being into dicks."

I frowned. "What're you talking about? Those are two chicks in there with him."

"In case you didn't notice, one of those chicks *came* with a dick."

My mind disobediently flashed onto what I'd witnessed—some freaky kind of doggy-style threesome that would probably be burned into my retinas for all eternity. "Strap on," I said, adding when the Tom's face screwed up, "Chick in the middle was wearing a strap on."

He still looked like he didn't get it. Or maybe he just didn't want to.

A few shuffles to our right took us to the next window, from where a round of deep groans drifted.

"Do we really wanna see?" Clive asked.

I sent him a low growl. "Do we really have a choice?"

On his, "Go," we popped up just long enough to spy into the room.

The shithead of a cat from the evening before lay sprawled and spread-eagled on a king-sized bed. The naked females in there with him performed tongue acrobats—on him *and* each other—probably the cause of the giant smile on the male's face.

Back beneath the window, Clive glanced my way with a frown. "I thought that kinda shit only happened in Thailand."

"Or on the pay-per-view channels," I said, already moving for the next window. "And I'm pretty sure the females on those are British."

It took around five minutes to check through the rest of the windows. Every room stood unoccupied, bar the two gangbang venues.

With his reddened face, curled bottom lip, and shoulders jerking as he clenched his fists and stomped soil, Clive looked frustrated and pissed enough for the two of us. "Shit!" Hidden around the side of the property farthest from the noise, he booted the muddied ground for a second time. "She's not even in there."

"You don't know that." I stared toward the wooden structure, my mind and mood on constant overdrive. "Could have her locked up somewhere else. In the cellar, even. Making her listen to this shit."

He shook his head. "No cellar. Not on this place."

My teeth ground a little. "Another room, then. Only one way to find out, I guess. Stay here." I marched away, but made it only about two strides before he grabbed my arm, and I whirled back with a growl.

"Wait up. What're you thinking of doing? We already checked all through the windows. She's not there."

"And I already told you, she could be somewhere else."

"And you're gonna find that out, how?"

"I'm going to go in there." I pointed to the building. "And I'm going to beat it out of that arrogant cat." I peeled the Tom's fingers from my bicep. "In the meantime, you can wait out here."

His growl chased me, as I turned for the front entrance again. "So you can run in there like the knight in shining armour and claim all the glory?"

I halted and peered back to him. "No." *Not entirely.* Maybe I didn't want the Tom anywhere near Brook, if she happened to be in there. Maybe I still didn't trust that Brook would choose me after our week apart. My stronger reasoning held more depth than that, though. "You only had a hunch that Brook's with these eejits. The fact we didn't see her means there's a chance she isn't. While I fully intend to be one-hundred percent certain of that before walking away, what if someone else does have her? Or ... what if she's just hiding from everyone?" *What if that includes me?* I shrugged that thought off. "If that's the case, how are you going to find out about anything going down in the Coalition, if you get yourself kicked out?" Which is exactly what he'd told me would come of opening his mouth about his assumptions. "Right now, they"—I jerked a thumb toward the house—"don't know you're out here. So, let's keep it that way."

Without waiting to see if he agreed, I spun for the property's front, and strode off.

Brook stared toward the door of her room. She estimated around fifteen long minutes had crawled by since someone had entered the building. To begin, she wondered if her imagination had conjured the arrival, but when muffled voices suggested the switching on of a television, she knew she hadn't.

Hearing strained, she had tracked footsteps, what sounded like cupboards opening and closing, the definite clink of cutlery against ceramic. By the time those footsteps headed in her direction, her entire body sat coiled tight, muscles aching with tension, and her nerves felt about as frayed as they ever had. More so, when the floorboards creaked right outside her door, and a key slid into the lock with a metallic clunk.

36

The Toms' confidence in themselves extended to their security—or lack of it. I'd expected to have to boot the door off its hinges, but the something that told me to try the handle first got top marks. That meant I found myself standing in the entranceway to the miniaturised Playboy mansion with no hitches to the grunts and exaggerated wailing.

Taking advantage of that, I strode past an open living space on my right, and followed the sounds down a narrow corridor. Around a corner to the right, the walkway stretched alongside three doorways, two of which stood open. I headed that way, marching past the room of the first shebang without even being spotted, straight into the bedroom holding the Tom I sought.

He didn't notice me, either—not with his head thrown back and his eyes screwed tight, his muscles all tensed in preparation for shooting his load.

Ignoring the rotten stink of him, and the *human* females I didn't have a beef with, I strode over to the bed and snatched the Tom up by the throat.

His eyes flew open, his screeched, *"What the—"* cut short by the orgasmic convulsions twitching his body.

Ripping him from his moment of ecstasy, I yanked him from beneath the entourage, sending them tumbling out of the way, and dragged him from the room with hisses flying and legs flailing to the backing song of female screams.

His fingers grabbed at the wrist of my hand holding him. "Fuckin' mutt!" His ankles bashed against the corridor walls, as I hauled him along. "You're dead meat!"

I didn't bother responding, nor glancing in the first room, but the deep, "Stefan?" told me I'd finally been spotted by his brother, followed by the even deeper, "*Shit!*"

Teeth gritted, as the Tom twisted and writhed, I tightened my grip and flung his body around the corner, the upward shove of my arm leaving him to dangle in front of me.

"Move, bitch!" came from behind me before feet thudded on the floor.

Lengthening my strides to a jog, I burst from the cabin and threw the Tom out ahead of me. Whirling back, I ploughed a fist into the nose of the Tom at my rear, and without waiting to check that the snap back of his head meant he'd gone down, I spun and chased the sailing cat outside as he plummeted hard.

He hit with a screech against soggy ground that would've been dusty when dry, and rolled backward to land with a slap in the mud.

His body braced to spring, but my feet thumping either side of his hips trapped him as I grabbed his jaw.

Ramming his head back, I held him there. "Where is she?"

His legs kicked out as he thumped at my bicep. "Fuck you, dog. Go find a lamppost to piss up instead of digging holes in my lawn."

"I swear to God, if you don't start talking, I am going to smash you into unrecognisability."

"That's not even a word, moron."

With a growl, I slammed my fist into his cheekbone, the resounding crunch almost as loud as the crimson that splashed up to speckle my hand, despite my pulling the punch at the last second.

A cry grunted from him, and he quit grappling at me and covered his head.

"Where is she?"

"Fuck off!"

I drew my arm back for the second inning, but halted at the roar to my right, snapping round in time to see the brother coming at me with an axe swinging over his fricking shoulder.

Muscles tensing, I braced to bolt, until a flash of blond charged into the Tom's side, and his feet flicked up from the floor. The axe spiralled down and spliced muddied soil, as Clive dive-bombed the dick-wad against a mound of pebbled dirt.

"Should've fucking known it." The Tom beneath me writhed hard, his elbows banging against the ground and spattering him in mud. His fingers yanked on the flaps of my open shirt, while he aimed his bloodied face toward Clive. "Dirty, treacherous bastard." His lips curled. His knees bounced against my butt. "You are *finished*, Clive!"

Fingertips digging into the Tom's jaw, I pulled his head up and shoved it back down.

His gaze shot back to me, mouth wide in a hiss of impressive proportions. "You don't even get it, do you, you stupid mutt?"

The fist I'd drawn back to shut him up hovered by my chest.

"Brook never wanted you. You were nothing but a bit of entertainment on the side. An itch she wanted to scratch. A curiosity." A glower burned his eyes to a dark cinnamon as he twisted and spat a dribble of blood from his lips. "I'll bet nobody's even taken the precious princess. She's just fucking hiding from *you*!"

My snarl ripped from my throat as he dared voice a worry I'd already had, and tightening my hand around his throat, I hauled his hide from the dirt, bulleted forward, and slammed him into the nearest trunk.

His skull crashed back, the evidence of pain exploding across his features, and as his eyes began a slow roll back and the limpness of his body set in, I grabbed his head, my lips rippling like crazy as my arms tensed.

"Dog, *no*!"

I hesitated at Clive's shout, but the thunder in my chest didn't quieten.

"Step away! Fucking step away now, before you start a war you won't walk away from."

My head made a slow turn his way, toward where he stood paused in whatever scrap he'd got going on with the brother, the pair of them staring back, their gazes flickering everywhere but on my eyes. Two Adams apples shifted up and down, the sound of swallowing as clear to me as the movement, as well as the galloping thumps of their hearts.

Clive held his palms up. "He's not worth it," he said, his quiet voice a little scratchy, and he shook his head as though to strengthen his case.

Rain had plastered my shirt to my shoulders and mingled with sweat to glue my hair across my forehead, and the skin beside my eyes tightened above the clench of my jaw as I let his words sink in. The truth in them. I only wanted Brook back. Just needing that had brought enough problems for the pack. Killing one of the Toms would come with even greater consequences.

Thankful rationality hadn't taken a hike alongside my almost lost control, I didn't look back at the Tom in my hands as I unflexed my hold, nor as I stepped back and he dropped to the ground.

"We're done here," I told Clive.

Wiping my hands on the thighs of my jeans, I strode away while I still could, past the half-covered females pinned against the windows with eyes moon-wide, and around the corner, leaving behind the shouts of 'Stefan' from the moron's brother.

My strides had lengthened to a jog by the time I re-entered the surrounding woodland, and it didn't take long for the beat of Clive's feet to match my own. Although neither of us spoke on our weave through the trees, I caught the tilts of his head in my periphery, and the sideways glances.

If he didn't quit, he'd find *him*self on the dodgy end of my mood.

On seeing Clive's silver ride ahead, our pace lessened to long strides, slowing the closer we got.

"Good going," I said, needing somewhere else to direct my reducing temper. "Exposing yourself was a nice touch."

He glared at me, bronze fire all but spitting from his eyes. "Seriously? You're smacking on *me* right now?"

"I mean, your interpretation of discretion, and all, went really well, don't you think?" I continued, ignoring his jab.

"I saved your fucking hide back there." He swung an arm out as he pointed. "If I hadn't, you'd be digging an axe out of your skull, courtesy of Roland."

Sniffing hard, I peered away. "I'd have handled it."

He scoffed. "You'd also now have a price on your head, if not for me stopping your lunatic ego. What the hell were you thinking?"

"Of killing him." I looked back. "I thought that much was clear."

"Yeah, well, for someone who likes quoting mistakes at others, yours nearly took the frigging biscuit."

I growled as he turned away, annoyed more than anything over him being right. Hard enough wading through the Coalition one Tom at a time, without having to do so with an army of them chasing tail and out for my blood.

Whirling, I paced away from him, putting a little distance between us as I forced my anger to simmer down enough for me to climb in the Volvo without wanting to wring the cat's neck. Shoulders high, I hooked my hands together at my nape, stretching out my muscles as I took a few slow breaths. In. Out. In.

On my spin back, I found the Tom messing about with a mobile phone in his hand and headed toward him. "So ..." I bounced a fist off the bumper on my way to the passenger door. "... what now?"

"Now, I'm handling it. *Again.*" He jerked his head toward the car, and as he tugged open his door and climbed in, I followed suit and joined him. "Lewis," he said into his mobile. "Just wondering if you've noticed anyone not about since last night."

"I'd say you," a deep voice returned. "But I doubt you're ignoring the fact Brook's missing."

"You'd be right."

A pause followed. "Stef and Roland haven't been seen since we got back from the dog's."

"Anyone besides them?" Clive asked, omitting the fact we'd just seen them.

"Dunno," the voice said after a short pause. "You onto something?"

"Not at the moment." The Tom rubbed at his jaw. "Listen, can you do me a favour and give me a call if you notice anyone else being absent?"

"Sure. No worries."

After thanking him, the Tom hung up his phone.

"Waiting on phone calls means waiting full stop," I said.

"You have any wise ideas of where else to look in the meantime, then?" the Tom asked.

"Hell, yes. How about every damn sneaky property the Coalition Toms are responsible for?"

He shook his head. "I don't think anyone below the top caste Toms know of every property. Besides, if I storm 'round and accuse every Tom—with *you* in tow—I predict less than a half-day before the tables get turned, and I end up the one being hunted."

That had already crossed my mind when I'd been on the verge of snuffing Stefan.

"If that happens," he added, "I won't be able to help *anyone* from where they'll stick me."

Muscles coiled tight, nose twitching for even a hint of who to expect, Brook stared toward the door as the handle lowered, and the door swung inward.

She frowned at the head dusted in dark hair that had been cropped close to the skull, the furrows deepening when the Tom lifted his face to reveal the almost bashful smile below eyes the shade of the Mediterranean.

Brad. Her lips formed the word, but her mind refused to orate it as she tensed, ready to pounce. He bounced back a little into defensive stance, close enough to the door to vanish before she could even contemplate reaching him.

He held his palms out. "You should rethink your actions, Brook. I've been generous, so far, letting you loose in here."

Her eyes narrowed as a prickle itched at her nape, and for a moment she considered inviting it to spread farther.

"I'm more than happy to bring restraints into the game," he said, an undercurrent of warning to his tone.

"I am surprised you did not do so already." Though her glower remained on him, Brook settled back onto the bed slightly, but slid one foot up to rest against the mattress should she need to move fast at any point. "Or perhaps you prefer to merely beat a female into submission."

His gaze flickered over her face, where the bruising still throbbed. "I didn't enjoy hitting you. It was a means to an end."

"What end, Brad?"

"My plans." The smile that had slipped returned. "The bigger picture I intend to achieve."

"And that would be what, exactly?"

"Come on, Brook. You're smarter than you act. You can figure it out."

Yes, she could—*had*—figured it out, but to verbalise it would enforce the thoughts she wished she hadn't had.

"Me ... you ..." he said, as if trying to prompt her, even waving a hand back and forth like he wanted her to pick up and join in. "... a kitten ..."

Brook merely stared at him for a few beats. Her body, her mind, seemed incapable of any more, as the confirmation of what she feared rushed at her with the power to immobilise. "What is *wrong* with you?" she asked. "Are you truly so inept at securing a female that you have to *kidnap* one?"

He scowled, the expression curling his lip and enhancing his eyebrows. "Is that really all you think this is about?"

"Isn't it?"

"No."

Brook didn't speak, her face probably broadcasting the repulsion she had begun to feel on the inside.

He fisted his hands in front of himself and let out a growl. "I'm so tired of being treated like some kind of freak."

And you think this *is going to help your cause?* she wanted to ask, but instead asked, "By whom?"

"By you." He stepped forward, and Brook's body tensed. "Your *staring*. Just because I look different to you."

He paced across the room, his movements stilted. Brook tore her focus from the door he had left open and tracked him to the window and back, where he twisted and pointed her way, nothing but malicious intent in his chilled gaze.

"By the time I'm finished, you will be *begging* me to take you. Again and again. Because no one else will." The sudden switch in his demeanour set even more alarm bells ringing inside Brook's head until they all seemed to be competing for which could possibly be considered the worst part of her situation.

"And you *will* look at me with respect," he continued. "As will the rest of the Coalition, when they understand *I* am the one whose offspring you're carrying." He tapped his finger against his own chest. "That *I* am the one who tamed you. And the mighty Don Nicholls will have no choice but to make my standing higher when I father his grandchild."

A lump the size of a watermelon stoppered Brook's throat as she recognised the element of truth to his statement. Her father wouldn't care by whom, or how,

Brook had fallen pregnant, just that she had, and that someone had finally stepped forth to claim her. The Tom's 'taming' he spoke of would only contribute to earning her father's respect, but Brad Campbell would tame *or* take Brook only over her dead body. "You are sick," she said.

"Just quietly ambitious," he said with a smile, his words telling Brook he'd had planned it all along.

How long had he been 'quietly' planning his moves? Tricking everyone with his pleasant complacency?

Had he ever truly convinced, Brook, though? She had always known something to be off about the male, she had just never been able to pinpoint what—until then, as greedy insanity gleamed in his eyes.

"Anyway," he said, his smile widening, "I have some good news."

"I believe you and I may have differing opinions as to what classifies as good," Brook said, nausea already swirling in her stomach.

He breathed out a laugh. "Yeah, well, it's good news *to me*. Because, I found something out recently." Tucking his hands into his pockets, he actually swayed his hips a little, his eyebrows jigging up and down as his persona once more made a rapid switch.

"Want to ask me what it is?" he asked when she didn't respond.

"Not particularly."

"Apparently, the effects of a Season aren't limited to only the period of the Season," he said as if she hadn't spoken, shaking his head. "Nope. Turns out, the fertility kicks in up to a week before the Season actually starts. So, we"—he waved a hand back and forth—"get to wrap this up sooner. Like I said, good news."

"For you, perhaps," Brook said drily.

"But I'm not completely out of touch." That smug smile of his reappeared as he wagged a finger. "I know how you females like the romancing, and whatnot. I've even been practicing on humans. So tomorrow, you can take a shower and put on your new gear ..."

Brook frowned, until a scrap of something satiny appeared in his hand, and she tracked its passage as it floated toward her with a fling of his arm.

"Because you and me have a date in the morning."

"In the morning?" She had more time than that until the week leading to her Season.

"Well, I did think about starting tonight. Heck knows, I'm good and ready." He chuckled as he peered down toward his groin, holding his hands out at the same time as though showcasing his goods. When he glanced back up, a cool mirth chilled his eyes to a glacial aqua. "But I have standards, Brook. I like my females *clean*. So, be ready for me." He strode from the room.

Brook stared after him even once the door had slammed shut, the lock had clicked back into place, and the brush of his footsteps told her he'd left her alone.

She *had* to get out.

The Tom had dropped me back where we'd started, with the promise to be in touch by noon the next day, if he hadn't heard anything sooner. The thought alone of pausing the search for that long had my hands twitching and my strides jerky, and I still had to face Dad and Ethan.

For a handful of beats, as I stood on the forest boundary, staring across the back garden of home, I considered chickening out, just finding somewhere else to hole up for the hours-long wait. I had my mobile, so what else did I need? I couldn't do it, though. Not to Dad. Not to Ethan. If honest, I also couldn't be that inconsiderate to the pack— not if I didn't want them sending out a search party and hunting me down. I knew the first place they'd look would be Brook's address, and the Toms would only see that as retaliation. I probably didn't have much time before that would happen, either. Although I hadn't had the bottle to switch my mobile back on, I could predict the amount of messages I'd find on there, which meant I really had no choice but to haul my arse inside.

Didn't mean planting one foot in front of the other came easy. My feet may as well have had blocks of iron strapped to them, because they seemed to weigh almost as much as my heart.

After a check through the windows didn't reveal anyone inside the kitchen, I paused at the back door, fingers folded around the handle, bracing myself for the bollocking of a lifetime. Heck knew what they'd make of the mess. Because my stench alone would alert them to the fact I'd been fighting. My hair and clothes had dried on the journey home, but both held the paled staleness of sweat, and had dried stiff. Not to mention the blood still staining my forearm.

Knowing it would be pointless putting it off, I heaved in a breath, snapped down the handle, and stepped into the house.

The sounds of life hit my ears as I closed the door at my rear—footsteps, mumbling, TV on a low-volume—for about a nanosecond. They all cut off as though severed in one slice.

I stood poised, the dining table separating me from anyone entering, and as I drew in a long inhalation and weaved around the richness of whatever sat in the oven, I detected Dad first, somewhere close. Followed by Josh. Ethan.

Nathan, too. *Shit.*

I might have had ample warning prior to the barrage of footsteps coming my way, but that in no way prepared me for the onslaught of emotions in the four faces, as they all burst into the room. From Dad's panic, to Josh's fear, to Ethan's utter disappointment—all the way up, as though escalating along the row, to the cold fury blasting from Nate's eyes.

Instead of the bashing, the yelling, the rough-handling I'd expected, I received only silence. Silence, and scrutinisation that weighed more than every burden my shoulders already carried combined.

Myself, I wanted to scream, *for God's sake, somebody say something!* but when Nate's gaze finally met mine again, I had to fight the urge to step back, to give myself distance—scrap that, I wanted to run a frigging mile.

"Are you hurt?" he asked in that quiet voice of his.

It felt like every millimetre of my facial skin stretched tight, I tensed so hard as I gave a small headshake.

I probably should've explained. Should've told them how I came to be covered in blood. Explained that none of it was mine. Since leaving the Tom's cabin, though, the epic failure of the day had been plummeting in a direct descent straight for my head, but in slow motion as though to drag the torture out longer, and I had about a half-breath left in me before I crashed and burned from emotional exhaustion. I pretty much only managed, "She wasn't there," in a gravelly mumble that scratched at my throat.

In my periphery, Dad stepped forward, and before I could turn, his arms slapped around me. I didn't fight his tug of my body into his tight embrace. Nor did I fight the offer of support in the strength of his arms—support my own mind and body had no will to provide. I merely clung onto the one solidity in my life like just maintaining the contact would keep me grounded long enough to hold my head above surface. I was done with treading water. I couldn't do it anymore.

When I finally pulled back, I sniffed hard at gathered snot and gave Dad a small nod, barely able to accept the sympathy emanating from his eyes. "I need to be on my own a little while."

"Not yet," Nate said, snapping me back to the others in the room. "You need food." He nodded to Dad before waving me to the table, and when I dragged out a chair and flumped into it, too weary to even argue, he took the spot opposite.

To his left, Ethan took prime glaring position leaning against the wall, Josh propped himself against the doorframe on Nate's other side, and over to the left of the kitchen, the oven door creaked open, and something crock-sounding scraped across the bars inside. Only Dan hadn't come in. Not that I'd expected him to. He'd probably spent the day at Nate's filling his belly, or loafing on his bed with his sketchpad to rest it off— though, had I really expected a welcome home from him when he'd barely had a decent word to say to me of late?

"Okay," Nate said, as the rich and spicy wafts of lasagne drifted from Dad's corner. "While I'm not—*can't* condone your behaviour," he went on, "or your lack of respect, or your sheer disregard for anyone's feelings but your own, you have my attention."

I frowned. That hadn't been what I'd expected him to say. Sure, he'd hit me softly, but I'd presumed that to be tactics to get my guard lowered before the verbal pounding pierced where intended.

"Because I believe you," Nate said. "I believe your feelings for the cat."

"Brook," I said. "Her name's Brook."

Nate's sombre expression didn't show even a glitch. "But I can't let you keep running off like some chaotic avenger ..."

A plate slid beneath my nose. I didn't bother to glance down but caught the tomato-y sweetness of the sauce as scents spiralled upward.

"... because not only are you likely to get yourself hurt—or worse: *killed* ..."

A mug of something warm, steamy, and alcoholic joined the plate, before Dad handed me a fork. "Eat," he said.

"... but you are definitely going to bring more trouble down on the pack," Nate said. "And, as I've already made very clear, that is unacceptable. An unacceptable *risk*. Not just to the females, but to all of us ..."

Dad nudged at my hand, and I scooped up a blob of meat-coated pasta and aimed it where it had to go, still barely paying attention to anything but the intensity of Nate's words, awaiting the grand finale of his speech and wondering what was taking him so long to get there.

"... because we don't know, we don't *understand*, these cats ..."

"You need to drink, too," Dad said, taking the seat beside me and nudging my arm.

"... which means, as an enemy," Nate went on, "we don't know what we're up against."

Another forkful of lasagne followed the first one, and I chased it with a swig of the potent liquid when it felt like they'd both gotten stuck on their way down.

"Which is dangerous," Nate said, "when they know exactly where we're located, and have most probably already checked the land and property for weak points, because that's exactly what I would have done in their situation."

The third blob of food went down a little easier, though I scarcely tasted it over the second hit of drink and the burning flavour of that.

"You should be made aware that, at this point, I'm considering whether, or not, I need to move Jem and Beth and Lia out of the house for a little while. Because I'm beginning to question their safety during this fiasco you've caused ..."

I'd wondered how long it would take for the blame to fly. I still winced at his words, though, even glanced to Ethan like I owed him an apology for it, but fast changed my mind at the tightness in his expression.

"Enforced by the fact that I have noticed vehicles slowing by our gates today, at least twice." Nathan's eyebrows twitched. "Which means we are currently being watched."

"They still think I have Brook," I managed around another mouthful, though my tongue felt thick against the movement, and the words slurred together.

"Evidently," Nate said, like I'd asked instead of stated. "As you can see, everything you have done so far, with regards to your ... feelings for Brook, has put the pack under greater exposure and brought the danger levels a little higher."

I took another gollop of my drink, and the cup banged against the table as I lowered it, the noise like an end-echo of a bomb-blast in my head.

"So, I want your word," Nate said.

I rubbed at my eyes, at the sudden grittiness in them, blinking against an invasion of fogginess, trying to get Nate back into focus as he fuzzed around the edges.

"No more racing off."

I snapped my gaze to the right again, to Ethan, tipping my chair with the movement and finding him just as blurry as his dad.

"No more conspiring behind our backs."

I glanced down toward the table, but couldn't tell what remained on my plate with it all waving about in a psychedelic dance.

"No more behaving like a one-man show."

I shoved my plate away, the cutlery *thunk*ing off the table with a dull thud, before clattering off the floor tiles at a higher pitch, though even those sounds seemed distant and hollow. Like my heart, as it began to dawn what the heck they'd done.

"You have one more chance, Kyle. From now on, you *will* talk to us."

I forced my eyes upward, but skimming them through marshland mankified by turds and acidic sand would've been easier, and relocating Nathan's form took immense effort. "Oo drud me?"

"You didn't really leave us much choice," Nate said.

As my forehead bumped the table-top, my "Fuck!" only just about squeezed out.

37

Music swam through my skull like a police siren on crack. Even wrapping my head in my arms didn't dull it, nor did burrowing beneath my pillow. The bloody racket just kept on and on and on and—*shit!*

Diving from the bed earned me a tangling in the sheets, a thump to my head from the bedside stand, and possibly a bruise to my butt where I hit the floor.

A quick glance around the room and a tilt of my head determined the Kings of Leon tune hadn't come from within my walls. "Crap!" I kicked at the covers binding my ankles, and made a jump for the door, fighting off fuzziness in my vision, dizziness in my brain, and dragging limbs that didn't particularly want to play.

I paused as I rounded my doorframe onto the landing, where I tracked the tune to the right before stumbling down the stairs on my descent.

Rounding the newel post at the bottom, I headed for the kitchen, and crashed into the room to find my family sitting at the table around breakfast plates—and my mobile in Dad's hand.

I probably should have begged him for it. At least shown a little politeness. Instead, I completely ignored the stares, the curiosity-filled concern in Dad's eyes like he sat poised and waiting to see what I'd do, and I dove across the table and snatched my mobile straight from his hand.

"Talk to me!" I said as soon as I'd hit connect.

"'Bout time," the Tom said down the line. "I have another lead."

Blanking Dad's scowl, I backed off from the table. Josh's gaze followed me, but Dan hadn't even glanced my way once since I'd come down.

I massaged my forehead like I could erase the dullness going on in there. "Solid?" I asked the Tom. I didn't think

I could stand the idea of another epicly-false lead. Though, I doubted I could stomach the thought of sitting around doing nothing all day, either.

"About as solid as we're going to get. You in?"

Dad's chair scraped the tiles as he stood. Dan's, too, except his clunked against the floor a couple times as he slid it aside with his foot before stomping from the room without even a hint of acknowledgement for me.

Meeting Dad's gaze head-on, I said, "Do you even need to ask?" into the phone. "Where, when and who?"

"I'll explain the who when you get here."

"You're not coming for me?"

"Uh, yeah, there's a problem with that."

Dad's narrowed eyes told me he listened in, as I asked, "What kind of problem?"

"As in the Coalition kind. Don's still convinced you have Brook."

I'd figured that much out myself. "Even after yesterday?"

"Yeah, thanks to Stefan's false reports of what went down," Clive said. "Either way, you've been rewarded with Toms watching the pack property. And if you leave, they're gonna tail you."

"Newsflash. I don't live at Nate's property. So I'm not where they—"

"They know," Clive cut in. "They have Toms on *both* of the pack properties. And every one of them is just waiting for you to make a wrong move."

"Shit." Stifling a yawn, I tried to wake my brain up faster, grinding through the problem like every cog in there had gone rusty overnight. As an inkling of a solution began peeking through the fog, I nodded, catching Dad's intense stare, and Josh's frown as my head bobbed even harder. "What vehicles are they in?"

"What ... *what*?"

"The Toms—what cars are they driving?"

"I dunno. I'm not there. But probably something big enough to be comfortable for their stakeout. Wh—" He paused a breath before asking, "You have a car fast enough to outrun them?" No mockery in his tone—only a serious question.

"No." I peered through the window, out across the garden, toward the forest and beyond in my mind. "But I know someone who does."

"Good, then meet me in the lay-by just after Hotspot Cafe on the main A-road running south into Warwick. I'm already on my way, and I'll meet you there."

Confirming I would and ending the call, I peeked up at Dad, tucking my mobile into my pocket. He stared back. I doubted he'd looked away once since I'd erupted into the room on a whirlwind, like the psycho on a mission they probably viewed me as.

I stepped toward the back door, but he mirrored my move.

"I have to go," I said, my tone deepened by the conviction that I'd do pretty much anything necessary to get my rear out of the house.

Dad shook his head. "Not alone, you don't."

My chest rose high with my sigh, a long, weary inhalation. "Okay," I said with a nod, and stood long enough to witness the tension ease from Dad's shoulders.

I felt like a major shithead when I bolted for the door.

Dad's chasing feet and shouts to 'Wait up' faded after a couple of minutes of racing through the forest, but their absence made far too much room for the rapid and freezing wind of the early morning to swirl my thoughts. Of Brook. The potential of finding her. The hour of the day—just after eight, according to my phone—and how long she'd sat waiting for us to get another bite—*while I'd slept*. That led to the dodgy memory of being opposite Nate at the table the day before—which explained the crappiness of my head that even the cool patchouli freshness of our sanctuary couldn't clear.

The arches to the Holloway property stretched across the treeline ahead, and I surged toward them, bulleting across the patch of barren land between, and beneath the bricks into Nate's garden.

My bare soles mashed the damp grass, but the nearer I got to the house, the more my hopes of cornering Sean undetected diminished when I spotted pretty much everyone in the kitchen.

It didn't deter me, though. One way, or another, I would get out of there, and I didn't particularly care how.

Gripping the handle, I pushed down and opened the door to the conservatory. Nate already peered my way through the glass of the French doors. Beside him, Ethan stared back at me, too.

Sucking in a deep breath, I stepped into the kitchen.

"'Morning," Nate said.

"Nate." My gaze skimmed left, landing on Ethan, at the dark worry warring with determination in his eyes, and I nodded a greeting before turning away.

On my side of the table, Jem sat looking my way, a soft flannelette sheet draped over her shoulder. Sucking slurped from beneath the covering, and tiny toes peeked from the edge on the ends of fidgeting legs. Jem offered up a small smile that warmed her already warm eyes. "Hey."

"Hey," I said, leaning in to drop a kiss on her head, and pausing to nod to Beth on straightening. "Beth."

"Want some breakfast?" she asked.

"I ... don't really have time," I said, continuing around the table until I stood before Sean, where he sipped on his coffee propped against the doorway into the hall.

His eyebrow twitched upward. "Everything okay?"

I banked any ideas of a gentle approach and held out my hand. "I need to borrow the Porsche."

Chair feet scratched at the floor as Nate rose in my periphery. "What's going on?"

I didn't remove my gaze from Sean. "Please."

"Are you going to answer me?" Nate asked.

The feet pummelling paving hit my ears prior to the conservatory door swinging open, and my shoulders tensed the second Dad swung into the room.

"I thought I told you to wait," Dad said behind me.

"I didn't fancy being drugged again," I said without turning.

"Do *you* know what's going on?" Nate asked—probably to Dad.

I didn't see his response, didn't want to lose Sean's attention. "The Tom I was with yesterday has another lead," I told him, but my body jolted when a bang bounced off the table.

"Tell *me!*" Nate roared.

I twisted and found Nate glaring my way, his fist against the table-top. "There are Toms out there." I nodded toward the front of the house. "Watching for slipups. From me." I looked back to Sean. "Please, Sean, I need something fast enough to lose them." I didn't care what position the request put him in, my expectation for him to support me over his own father, his Alpha—I only cared that his agreeing might take me closer to Brook.

I almost growled out my relief when Sean stepped toward the rack holding the keys, cut short by Nate's quiet order of, "Wait."

The entire room seemed to still. Sean's gaze flickered between me and his Dad.

I swallowed as I turned to Nate, but the lump in my throat didn't want to go down. "Don't—" I shook my head. "Don't do this."

Beside him, Dad stared from me to his best friend, a screaming desperation widening his eyes.

"Talk to me," Nate said.

"I can either walk out of here with your permission," I said, ignoring the portrayed authority in his tone we'd all learned to obey. "Or I will walk out of here without it."

The skin beside his eyes tightened, highlighting the creases that had begun to form there.

"Because, make no mistake, Nate," I rushed on, "you forbid me to go, and I *will* leave. I'll walk."

Ethan leaned back in his chair, that same determination still in his eyes when he glanced from me to Nate. "Let him go, Dad. I'll even go with him."

Nate's attention never left my face, and the cool chill of his eyes would've unnerved me if I hadn't already been way beyond that. "You would choose Brook over the pack?" he asked, his voice quiet.

My teeth ground beneath the working of my jaw, as I matched Nate with an unflinching passion of my own.

Dad's hand gripped the back of a dining chair in my periphery. "Nate?" he asked, a plea deepening his voice.

"Nathan?" The quiet murmur from Beth came from behind me, but Nate's glance and minute nod in that direction told me he'd heard.

He looked back to me. "Answer the question, Kyle. You would choose the cat over your own family?"

I answered him with a jerk of my chin, neither of us looking away, even at another, "*Nate*?" from Dad.

Moments passed, my heart seeming to count off every second, before a deep sigh heaved Nate's chest high, and he rubbed hard at his face. "Okay," he finally said, settling his hands on his hips. "You can go."

My sigh breezed past my lips until he butted back in with, "But ... you *will* do this my way."

Nate's 'way' had actually been pretty genius and had gotten us well on track toward Warwickshire with not a Tom in sight.

After ringing Josh to come team up with Ethan as escorts, he'd sent Sean out for the Porsche, stuck Dad in the passenger seat with his head lowered and only the hair colour I'd inherited on show, and used them as decoy for me and my pack brothers to leave unhindered in the pickup. The Toms had bitten right away—apparently, Sean had led them on a merry ride all the way to Derby, before he and Dad headed back home.

It took around seventy minutes of Ethan driving, with Josh leaning forward on the rear bench and tapping his knee, me twitching about in the passenger seat and alternating between rapping my mobile against my lips and peering out the window, for a hut called The Hotspot Cafe to show up.

"That must be the one the Tom meant," I said, sitting up straighter. "So, we need the next lay-by."

"I see it," Ethan said, flicking the indicator down.

Metres-high bushes filled the grassy patch that separated layby from road, so I didn't spot the Tom's Volvo until we'd ducked a little behind those. The bulky four-by-four faced our way, and Ethan's Ford crunched over loose stones and chippings as he slowed us to a stop six feet in front of him.

"Looks ecstatic to see us," Ethan said.

Arms resting atop the steering wheel, Clive stared through his screen, the left and right flick of his eyes telling us he'd spotted my company, and the scrunch of his brow exposing his thoughts on the matter.

"Can you blame him?" I asked. "Imagine if the tables were turned."

"Moot point." Ethan twisted the keys, and the hum of the engine quietened. "Because you wouldn't ever have to fucking investigate one of us, now, would you?"

I didn't bother to respond, because the Tom had my attention as he pushed back from his steering wheel. I half-expected him to skid away and razz off just so he wouldn't have to deal with us, but when his door shot open like he'd booted it with his foot, I opened my own and climbed out to join him.

He didn't approach, but rounded his door and leaned his arms against the bonnet, his head ducked down as his feet scuffed at the ground. I strode across to meet him, the trainers I'd nabbed from Ethan crunching the stones beneath them.

"You know," he said, as I reached him, "that whole come alone deal I stated yesterday was meant to extend to *any* time we met."

"Then, maybe you should have been more specific in your wording." I spun and hopped my butt up onto his bonnet.

His head shot up, and any warmth I'd earned from him before had well and truly left the building. "Do not shit on my jeans and tell me it's chocolate, dog."

My lips twitched. "I think you'll find that should be piss, shoes and rain."

"I don't care," he said. "Why are they here?"

I heaved in a sigh and released it. "Long story. One that ends in the truth that it would've taken me twice as long to get out here without them—presuming I could've gotten out, at all."

He shook his head and peered away to the left. "I don't like this."

"You don't have to."

He twisted back. "Give me one good reason why I shouldn't just spin out of here and do this alone."

"Because we'd just chase you down," I said, clenching my fists against the urge to grab him and shake him into my way of thinking. "Provided, of course, you even got as far as getting back in your truck. And then I'd have to resort to that whole beating information out of you thing, and I really bloody hate regression in a relationship."

"Fuck you." Words with intent, yet only delivered in a half-hearted mutter.

The rear door on the Ford swung open, and Josh bounced out. "Yo!" He nudged his door to and turned to us. "You two having a picnic over there, or something?"

"Who's the comedian?" Clive asked.

"My brother. Guy behind the wheel is my best friend." I nodded toward the pickup, meeting Ethan's watchful gaze. "If they say they have my back, they mean it. And if you play for my team today, that means they have your back, too. So ..." I turned back to the Tom. "... we doing this? Because my nerves are frazzled. My brain is pounding. And Brook is going through who the hell knows what while we sit here pissing about."

His face dipped to the ground again. I hated that I couldn't read his thoughts. He glanced across at my pack brothers and back to me with a small nod. "Okay. Get in. Before I realise the insanity of this and come to my damn senses."

38

Advantages of being in cat form: Better fighting abilities, better vision within the gloominess of her room, better reflexes, and less chance of what had been promised to come actually occurring. In theory, anyway.

Brook had spent what seemed like an age trying to conjure a decent idea for a weapon. She had even considered attempting to unscrew the fittings from the bed in the hope of them having a sharp point. After mentally scolding herself with the reminder that she already had more than adequate self-protection at the tips of her fingers, she had spent the night upon the rough, cord carpet with her own coat for warmth and her senses on full alert.

She had no idea of the time she sat there. Lack of indication from the outside world left her blind to information she normally took for granted. Which meant she had to assume morning had arrived when the first noises from beyond her room filled the building.

She listened as water ran to the background tune of a humming boiler, and footsteps padded about the place—on stairs, too, though whether up or down, she couldn't quite determine. A couple of creaks followed. A few thuds and clanks. None of the sounds lasted long enough for Brook's liking, and far too soon, those footsteps set the stairs creaking again, the warning signal stretching through the floorboards outside her door.

Muscles that had sat dormant for what seemed like hours wound tight through her hind legs and her shoulders as she braced to leap, and her gaze fixed on the door she knew he'd step through.

At the clunk of the key, she un-sheaved her claws into the shallow threads of the carpet.

The handle twisted down. The first sliver of light bled through.

Brook shoved off in a dive for the doorway. She saw only a glimpse of Brad's face and his widened eyes before the door slammed shut again—leaving her to bash against the wooden panel.

With a hiss, she hit the floor, flipping over onto all fours, and circled back around to her original position. Ears twitching, she returned to staring at the door, watching, waiting—because Brad's low chuckle and his lack of retreating steps told her he hadn't left.

Shuffles carried through the door, and her ears perked higher.

"You know the good thing about mating, Brook?" Brad asked, his voice only slightly muffled by the barrier.

A brushing sound followed a thud against the wood.

"No matter what form we take, it still fucking works."

The door bashed open.

Brook kicked off, but scarcely moved more than a foot before the door banged closed, as a naked Brad bulleted toward the far corner of the room. After a second collision with wood, she slunk around and faced a panther both taller and bulkier than herself stalking a diagonal path toward her right and boxing her in.

The blackness of his coat seemed to emphasise the cool shade of his eyes even further than usual, and Brook latched onto those, hoping for the slightest nuance in his expression that could give ample warning as to his next move.

She missed the readying of his muscles before he sprung straight for her.

Knowing she couldn't possibly greet his attack, she spun away, realising her error the moment teeth clamped around the back of her neck.

Her teeth clattered together as her chin jammed against the carpet, the roughness beneath it scratching at her skin even through her coat.

Her growl arrived long and deep, escalating into a high-pitched yowl when his weight settled over her and panic showed up.

She tried to ram herself upward with her forelegs. To buck up her back and shake him off. To kick out with her hinds and roll herself from beneath him.

No matter her efforts, she scarcely affected the press of him against her rear, as his haunches aligned against her own.

In her mind, she screamed *Noooooooooooo!*, the escalation of her pulse whirring its siren through her ears, as her throat verbalised her opposition in the form of a feline wail.

Her claws dug through the carpet pile, but that only resulted in scratching up wool.

She thrashed her head against his hold, but that only brought further slams of her jaw against the floor.

When the first prod hit her point of entry, her subconscious took its own control of the situation, forcing a Shift and sending prickles raging the length of her body at the speed of a plutonic shockwave.

With the added range of movement for her limbs, Brook rammed an elbow up and behind—once, twice, each contact vibrating through her forearm.

Twisting until on her side, she brought up a knee and kicked down with her foot, knowing she missed her target when her heel slid over fur.

Brad growled and clamped his teeth tighter.

She cried out, but booted downward again, and again—ignoring his warnings, the scratch of his claws against her thighs, the tremors his growls sent through to her bones—all while ramming her elbow back, back, back, until he offered enough leeway for her to heave down against the carpet and roll him from her.

She gave another kick back toward his hind legs when he still refused to let go, but the second his hold slackened, she shot from beneath him and clambered over the bed. She collapsed as she stumbled off the other side, but regained her footing fast and spun around and thrust herself upright.

Shifted back also, Brad stood, his thumb rubbing across his pointer and middle fingertips. "This is going to be more fun than I expected," he said, though his expression didn't match the words as his gaze flickered to the floor and back to Brook.

Brook wanted to see what he'd glanced at but didn't dare take her attention from him. "You have a warped sense of what one should value as fun."

"You had your chance to make it fun for yourself." His gaze remained on Brook as he bent and scooped something from the floor—her discarded sweatpants—before straightening again.

"And you blew it." He darted forward.

With little else at hand, Brook grabbed the metal rim of the bedframe and flipped it up. Tucking in her shoulder, she drove it forward toward Brad, ignoring the bite of the springs as the bed hit a blockage.

Her feet slipped backward an inch—then another, and it dawned on her that Brad was pushing back from the other side.

She jammed a leg behind herself, trying to dig her heel into the carpet but failing thanks to the lack of pile.

Teeth gritted, a long growl of determination spilling from her throat, she urged forth again, but her slight frame held no competition for Brad, and she continued slipping.

As her heel met the skirting board, the bed nudged harder at her, knocking her butt back until flush with the wall.

Brad's bristly crown peeked over the mattress, and Brook snuck down before he could see her, dropping to all fours. Twisting her limbs and torso, she began the

311

awkward wriggle from beneath the bed Brad still held, praying he didn't look down.

"You're going to end up hurting yourself, if you're not careful, Brook," Brad said, his chin hooked over the upper lip of her mattress.

Her shoulders shimmied free of the bed—her torso, too. She had to roll onto her side before she could get the sole of her foot flat to the wall and push herself out the rest of the way over carpet that burned every ounce of bare flesh it scraped.

Twisting onto her front, she tucked her right knee up to her chest beneath her and dragged her left leg behind her—just as Brad glanced down.

The mattress bounced against her toes as he dropped it, and Brook bolted forward—toward the door—barely missing being smothered by the bed as it flopped to the floor.

A hard pound between her shoulder blades sent her flailing forward—the crack of her cheekbone against the wall stalling her stumble.

Another force thumped her back—against her lower spine— and Brad grabbed her wrists, wrenching Brook's arms behind her.

She cried out, her body arching into the demand made by what she presumed to be Brad's knee holding her pinned. Her breaths came fast, spittle leaving with each exhale and dampening her cheek.

A zip of a sound buzzed through her ears. She tried to strain her neck enough to see its source, but even the slightest adjustment sent agony rocketing through her shoulders. What she did manage to glimpse—the cord of her sweatpants hanging from between Brad's teeth— didn't help her escalating panic any.

"Couldn't just give it a chance, could you?" The gravelly words panted from him as he pressed even harder against her spine until she whimpered. "Still trying to convince yourself you're better than me."

Something wove around her wrists—binding them together—-tighter and tighter, cutting into her skin, and she finally found her vocal chords enough to release a, "*No!*"

The lowering of her wrists to her butt and the removal of whatever trapped her should have offered some relief, but Brad's hot breath beside her ear nulled any chance of that. "Try your dirty Shifting tricks now, Brook," he murmured.

She knew as well as he did that she couldn't, not with her arms behind her—absolutely no way would her Shift obey when to do so would result in dislocated limbs. Regardless, her mind yelled at her to do something, even to plead if she had to, but Brook clamped her lips against doing so, refusing to give him the satisfaction of seeing her beg.

When his knee nudged hers apart, some primal instinct forced her brain into action, and she lifted her foot and rammed it down over the bridge of his—hard.

His grunt blasted against her ear, but the coolness against her rear told her he'd let go, so she spun, that same leg swinging. Straight for his groin.

At the collision of shinbone with testicles, Brad's screech bounced through the room, and as his knees failed to support him, he fell to the floor with a thud.

After sending a second kick, that one to his ribcage, Brook backed away, her chest heaving, blinking back tears she hadn't realised she'd shed.

When her fingertips grazed the door handle, she fumbled until she'd grasped it, the simple act of drawing it down more difficult than it needed to be with her arms stuck behind her. The handle snapped back up twice before she finally yanked it the entire way. The moment she had, she hauled the door open, slipped outside, and found herself on an upper landing.

Two other doors led off the small area—to the left and straight ahead.

To the right, a staircase led downward.

Brook went that way.

39

"Brad Campbell?" I asked the Tom, as he sped down the winding road with Ethan and Josh on our rear.

"Yep. I've had someone listening out for me, and apparently, Brad didn't show for work at seven this morning. A little more poking, and it turns out, no one's actually seen, or spoken, to Brad since yesterday afternoon—when he ducked out of work early. And now ..." He glanced across to me. "... my source can't get hold of him. He's tried, but ringing his mobile gets a bounce-back."

"Sounds a little like the brothers' deal, in my opinion. How do we know this won't just be another dead end?"

"We don't. But it's the best I have. And better than we could ask for after yesterday's fiasco. Lewis has stuck his neck on the line feeding me this, and especially for passing me the Campbell privacy address because the Coalition has orders to detain me if I showed up, thanks to Stefan's accusations."

"You sure you can trust this source?"

"I guess we'll soon find out," he said, knocking up his indicator and swinging the wheel to the right, "because we're just about there."

I peered back through the rear screen to make sure Ethan followed the turn, nodding when his slight head incline questioned the move.

Not dissimilar to the other Toms' place, trees hugged a side road. Only, the one we drove over had been tarmacked, making the journey a little less bumpy than the day before.

"You all purposefully hunt down properties in the middle of nowhere to conduct your sordid affairs?" I asked the Tom.

"Well, it gives us the chance to hunt, too. It's expected—especially if we have guests over from other Coalition corners. We're supposed to be able to, at least, offer them that."

Rather than tackle the woodland, as he had at the King address, Clive drifted to a stop on the edge of the narrow track, tucking the Volvo beneath the overhanging branches of the adjoining trees.

"We walk from here," he said, quietening the engine and opening his door.

As I did the same and hopped from the vehicle, the doors of the pickup Ethan had parked snug behind us opened and closed.

"This it?" Ethan asked.

"A little ways in that direction." Clive pointed west. "We scout first. Decide where to enter after. Just like we did yesterday," he said, nodding at me, before waving Ethan and Josh forward. "Okay, you two lead the way."

Ethan's smile held that special quality he reserved just for outsiders he wasn't sure he liked. "Scared to have us at your back, Tom?"

"Not scared," Clive said. "Just untrusting. There's a difference."

"You keep telling yourself that." Ethan's eyes chilled above that smile of his, and I gripped his shoulder, pulling him back a little.

"Play nice, Ethan. He's on our side."

"Guess we'll soon see about that."

Shaking my head, I stalked off ahead of them all, sending a glance to Josh over my shoulder. "Come, if you're coming. We've wasted enough time."

It took two seconds, and their footsteps hit dirt.

"*Brook*! Get back here."

At Brad's shout, Brook almost toppled over the apex of the stairs.

"You're gonna regret this!" Brad's scuffles warned Brook he'd already climbed to his feet.

With her shoulder pressed to the right wall for balance, Brook raced down the stairs, the inability to swing her arms skewing her coordination somewhat and ensuring her soles banged each step harder than necessary.

The bottom opened out into a square hallway with an exit straight ahead, and Brook landed there, as Brad's footsteps hit the landing above her. Slamming against the white uPVC door, Brook spun and pushed onto her toes, her fingers curling in search of the brass-coloured handle, her breath spurting past her lips as Brad descended the stairs in her direction.

"Good luck with that," he said, at the same time that Brook's tug down didn't work, telling her the door was locked.

Trying not to let the escalating booms of her heart debilitate her, she glanced through an open door on her right—some kind of living room. Through a door on her left stood what looked like the kitchen, and kitchens often led to rear exits.

Brad reached halfway down the stairs. "Don't even think about it."

Brook threw herself to the side and kicked the kitchen door closed behind her.

Our trekking took us to the front of the property first, which we studied from behind a rugged hedgerow fashioned by nature rather than man. Totally different to the other Toms' place, the property looked like any house on any estate in any city in the country, except it stood alone amidst an acre of timber.

And the Peugeot left beside the porch assured us that someone was inside.

"Cat doesn't have much taste in wheels," Josh uttered beside me.

"Oddly enough, he doesn't have much taste in threads, either," Clive said before nodding to the right. "Let's check 'round the back."

The large kitchen sported pine cupboards along every spare space of wall, a six-seat dining table in the centre, and a room-wide patio window partially obscured by shuttered, floor-length vertical blinds.

Brook had taken only two steps, when the door crashed open at her rear, bouncing off the unit it hit, and the slap of Brad's feet hit the lino.

Without so much as glance behind, she threw herself forward, her teeth gritted in determination and her mind aching beneath her mental plea that the doors be unlocked.

Brad chuckled, a dark sound full of promises she didn't want to contemplate—the intent it held present in the depths of his eyes when she whirled around and flicked the blinds aside.

She cursed the stupid binding for restricting her movements as she flipped at the slider-lock. Her mental curses escalated to a tumbling incoherency of, 'Shit, shit, shit', when Brad's grin loomed close enough to send her pulse into a stutter.

"Where're you gonna run to now?"

She thrust a knee outward, a primal growl grating past her throat, but his hand swung even faster, and the slap of his palm against her cheek sent sparks flashing behind her eyes, a sting shooting upward into her skull, and her body spinning into a spiral that smashed her other cheek into a glass pane.

She caught only an impression of daylight and grass before his hand tore at the hair above her nape, and she only managed a whimpered protest as he dragged her backward.

***

318

We'd headed farther into the overgrown brush to get a better view of the property's rear after rounding it had showed only a manicured lawn.

As I paused, my gaze skimmed across a concrete shed in the far corner, the clear window exposing only garden tools within.

At a glacial *thunk* from the back of the house, I snapped left—just in time to see a mash of flesh against the pane and the trails of long dark hair.

The same person shot backward and vanished in a half-breath.

Brook. I darted forward.

"Holy shit, did you see that?" Josh asked.

My strides took me halfway across the lawn, picking up speed with each additional one. By the time my feet landed on the wooden decking outside the patio doors, and my fingers folded around the frame of a cast iron patio chair, my pace had reached a run.

With a roar, I swung the deadweight in a direct line toward the window, and flung myself after it, shoulder first, through the spraying shards as glass shattered around me.

The drop of the chair took most of the blinds down, and I trampled over fallen slats, freezing for a split-second at a Tom bent over a table in the centre of the room.

My focus zoomed in on the female pinned beneath him, my heart tripped big time, and the roar blasted from me full force as I threw myself forward.

Smacking aside his hands, I dug my fingers into the Tom's throat and yanked him away from my female.

I drew my fist back and rammed it forward into the Tom's nose.

It took only that singular strike, the satisfying crunch of bone beneath my knuckles, for rationality to flee. Like some crazy-shit endorphins had shot their load into my brain, I swung again—again and again—faster than my eyes could keep up with, faster than my hearing could tell me the results of my hits, barely registering the shock of pain lancing each forearm with each strike, or the phlegm collecting in my throat as growls bubbled out from deep within my chest.

Somewhere in the back of my mind, glass cracking registered, footsteps crowded into the room, and scents joined the only one important to me, yet still, I kept on. Punch after Punch. Snarl after snarl. Grunt after fucking grunt.

Above all of those, the Tom's yowls and snarls assured me I'd hit my mark every time, and his outline faded into a blurred mass of flesh and hair marred by crimson, the scent of blood joining in with those already present.

Still, I couldn't seem to halt my arms from flinging back and forth and under and up, until the pain shooting into my hands and up my arms from each impact ceased to exist, and only a vibrating numbness took residency there.

The numbness might have spread to every inch of my soul.

Eyes wide, Brook watched Kyle's attack, her heart pounding a relentless rhythm against her sternum as she tried to accept that he'd truly arrived. The methodology of his movements held beauty, and the ferocity of his actions, the savage snarls erupting from his throat entranced her, so she held only a little awareness of others entering the room.

At least, not until arms circled her waist from behind. "Brook, come on."

She stiffened when Clive's voice hit her ear, shaking her head as she twisted away from the grip, realising she'd failed when her feet left the floor.

"No," she said, as his arms carried her backward, away from Kyle. "*No!*" she said again, kicking out with her foot. "Goddammit, put me down!"

"We've gotta get you outa—"

"For goodness, Clive, *put me down*!" She stretched her toes toward the floor, squirming again. "And bloody untie me."

"Better do as she says." The familiar voice came from her right.

She turned to see Ethan and Kyle's youngest brother beside him. They stood with their intense gazes aimed at Kyle, the tension coiling their bodies tight, the fisted hands at their sides revealing how much effort it took for them to stay put. Or maybe, judging by the nervous energy emanating from them, they merely feared moving closer.

She didn't care enough to evaluate that further, when the cool vinyl greeted her soles and the tug of the bindings at her wrists assured her of Clive's compliance, despite the quiet growl of discontent at her rear telling her his true opinion on the matter.

The second her arms sprang free, she leapt forward, heedless of the sharpness biting at her feet, or the burn of flesh caused by the narrow cord Clive had removed. All she cared about was reaching Kyle—about reaching him in whatever way necessary to draw him back from that dark place his grunts and continuous punches told her he'd descended to, as well as the tarry shine of his eyes.

Flinging herself against his back, she wrapped her arms around his middle, her eyes closing as she buried her face into his shirt and inhaled his scent—one she'd missed since she last saw him.

His step back knocked her off balance. The clutch of his fingers over her wrists held an anger and feral roughness. For a moment, she expected him to spin, to toss her aside, maybe even to attack her for interrupting what his inner wolf would no doubt have seen as his kill. Instead, he took another staggering step away from the mess that remained of Brad, and though growls still spilled from him and his breaths were still ragged, his body held a stillness that seemed incongruous after his frenzied behaviour.

His arms lifted, and his body twisted, his face leading the way around to her. Head low, his nostrils flared wide as those dark glossy eyes locked onto her gaze. He ducked closer, shoulders tucked back and blood-spattered forearms corded beneath prominent tendons, and his cheek brushed hers as his loud inhalation seemed to travel the entire length of her spine.

Nose burrowed into the curve of her neck, he tugged at his clothing, dragging his shirt over his shoulders before bringing it around behind Brook and draping it across hers.

Maybe he felt the need to hide her from the others in the room, or believed she needed the warmth. Or perhaps he merely wanted to mask Brad's scent she knew would be upon her with something rife with his own.

Brook didn't care why—even less so when his arms encircled her and her feet left the floor, as he drew her close against his body and strode from the house with soft assurances whispering past his lips.

40

The vicious storm roiling about within Kyle's chest had simmered to a distant thunder, and as the control he had lost decided to put in a reappearance, the black of his eyes began dispersing, allowing the first splices of white to poke through.

Brook sat within Kyle's hold upon a brick wall he'd carried her to at the foot of the garden. His hands swept over her as though seeking out her wellbeing, while she traced, with her fingertips, the purplish slashes beneath each of his eyes—a sign he hadn't slept much more than herself over the past week.

"Did he—" Kyle's tenor sounded strangled by his swallow. "Did he—because if he did, I swear to God I'm going back in there to kill him."

Brook's mind flashed to the mess of a male Kyle had left behind on the kitchen floor—a male barely recognisable beneath the pulp and bloody gore. "I do not believe going back in there would be required. Besides," she quickly added, when his biceps twitched to a rigid tautness beneath her palm, "he—he did not." She dared not add how close a miss it had actually been, no matter how vivid the memory of Brad's hands digging into her, his hot panted breaths, the invasion of his body between her thighs.

The relief seemed to seep from Kyle's every pore as his fingers combed into the hair at the back of her head, and he held her to him as his temple pressed to hers, his lips brushing across her cheek.

Brook's lids lowered, and for a moment she gently swayed there to the rustles of nature and the tiny circles the pads of his fingers made against the small of her back through the flannel shirt he'd thrown over her.

At a throat clearing, she opened her eyes and found Clive a few metres away. As Kyle made a slow twist toward him, Clive dug his hands into his pockets, his attentions flitting toward her wolf. "Mind if I have a moment with Brook?"

Only the slight wince of his left eye portrayed Clive's nerves, though Brook had to commend his bravery in approaching Kyle, given the spectacle they had all witnessed.

"It will be okay," Brook whispered against Kyle's ear.

"You sure?"

Though she nodded, letting go brought a flash of fear across Kyle's features—a sentiment Brook would have agreed with if it had been anyone other than Clive. As he reached Clive, Kyle murmured something to him, too low for Brook to hear, and strode off toward the glass-splashed patio.

Whatever it had been, Clive hadn't responded with anything more than a raised eyebrow before he stepped forward to Brook.

"Hey," he said, his tone as quiet as the breeze dancing around the trees.

Brook toyed with the hem of Kyle's flannel shirt, the buttons he'd secured warding off the winter chill, and the scalloped tail protecting her from the scrape of the brickwork beneath her bottom. "Hey," she murmured back.

He nodded, like her return greeting warranted a response. After peering over his shoulder toward the house, where Kyle paced restlessly along the lawn edge and sent intermittent glances her way, Clive closed the remaining gap.

His hands gripped the wall either side of Brook's thighs as his head dipped before her. Without looking up, he said, "If I ask you to come back with me, will you?"

"Never," she said, with no hesitancy in her honest answer.

His bowed head bobbed like he'd already expected as such. "We could vanish," he said. "Go anywhere you want us to go. We could be anyone you want us to be." When he glanced back up, hope shone from his eyes.

"Clive ..." Brook sighed. "I do not want you to be anyone but yourself. That is the Coalition talking."

His jaw worked, as though he wanted to say something to that. Instead, he inhaled hard and asked, "Where will you go?"

Her gaze flickered from his to the left.

No longer pacing, Kyle stood facing them, his every muscle coiled tight as if it took great restraint to hold himself back.

Her Kyle. She hoped. Just as she hoped the offer he'd made the week before, of somewhere to live, hadn't expired.

"You're in love with him." Pain laced through Clive's voice beneath the matter of fact tone.

She turned back, her heart aching at the longing, the hurt she found in his eyes. "Yes," she said.

His next few breaths blasted from him, despite the clear effort he made to contain them. "I think I even believe you," he said with difficult acceptance. "Hell, I believe *him*." His head dipped again for a moment. "It's still fucked up, though."

"Perhaps that is what I am."

He peeked up, lips twitching. "Yeah, well ... it's not like you didn't have a little help to get there along the way."

Brook breathed out a laugh that lasted only a moment. "What will *you* do?" She toyed with a strand of his hair.

"Who knows?" He shrugged. "Probably free to do whatever the hell I want now. Doubt Don's gonna have me back, after this, especially if I don't take you in."

"Clive, I am so sorry."

He shook his head. "Don't. Coming after you—with him—is the first choice I ever made without kowtowing to rules and fucking expectations. Don't belittle that, or it'll all have been for shit."

The first hint of tears pricked at Brook's eyes.

"Just ... do me a favour, okay?"

"Try me," she said.

"If you ever need me. If you're in trouble—any kind of trouble. If you need help—hell, if you just need someone to talk to ... call me. Can you at least promise me that?"

Throat thick, she nodded. "I promise."

"And promise me you'll stay in touch?"

"Always," she said.

His arms wrapped around her middle, his crown bumped her collarbone, and as Brook slid her own arms around his shoulders, he drew her from the wall and pulled her close, his hold tightening as he tucked his face against her neck.

"I love you, Brook," he said, but the words were spoken so low, she wondered if he even intended her to hear.

"Easy," Ethan said, gripping my shoulder.

I ignored him, my attention locked on the cat hugging the crap out of Brook, his face too close for my liking— hell, his whole fucking body too close for my liking. Watching them made me too edgy. In fact, if he didn't put her down, I'd probably storm over there and introduce him to my fist. My fingers even flickered with the urge.

"Hey." Ethan's tug on my shoulder rocked me a little, but I still refused to budge. "How 'bout you come inside, and we'll get this place cleaned up?" I could already hear Josh's footsteps moving about inside the house. "You, too," Ethan added.

"No," I said, shrugging him off.

"Kyle, she's not going anywhere."

She could—I knew all too well she still could. I hated that she held him just as tightly as he did her, hated that the pain in her eyes told me she was hurting. Hated that with her feet off the ground, the Tom could make a run for it, and she'd not be able to do a damn thing about it other than slap him around. I might have trusted the Tom to lead me to her, but I had no misconceptions he'd done so unselfishly, which meant I didn't trust him not to try taking off with her.

"I'm telling you, Kyle. She's not going anywhere. Not without you. God knows, the cat tried," Ethan said.

My head tilted. "Meaning?"

Sighing, Ethan stepped back into my periphery, ensuring I had no choice but to see him even in my refusal to turn. "He tried to get her out of there, Kyle. And she would not go. Just insisted on him bloody untying her so she could get to you—which she did the second he let go of her. And I've got to say, the female deserves some serious kudos for that." He poked a thumb over his shoulder toward where the two of them still stood. "Because you were one badass mofo in there. A seriously scary badass mofo. Remind me never to fall on your bad side."

"Don't fall on my bad side," I said, my shoulders relaxing slightly, when the Tom resettled Brook on the brick wall and began a slow and reserved walk toward us.

He stopped a couple of feet away, the warning in his eyes not something I wanted to see, given my mood. "She seems to believe you're gonna take care of her." The gravelly deepness of his voice gave it the same tone as his expression.

My eyes narrowed. "I am."

"Then, don't fuck it up. Because I'm not scared of you, dog," he said, squaring his shoulders as he took a half-step closer with his fists clenched. "And if you so much as breathe funny around her, I will make you sorry you even had that breath to take. Do you understand what I'm saying to you?"

I sensed the adjustment to Ethan's stance on my left— probably readying himself in case I floored the Tom—but he didn't need to worry. Not when Clive's words assured me he hadn't any intentions of trying to take Brook.

"Despite the convoluted attempt at a threat, yeah," I said, "I hear you."

"Good." He nodded, striding around me and onto the decking. "Now, you think you can get your butts off Coalition property before anyone else finds you here?"

"You don't want a hand cleaning up?" Ethan asked.

He paused, peering back over his shoulder. "I just think it's easier all round this way."

Ethan glanced at me, and I offered him a shrug before turning back to the Tom. "You know ..." I wanted to make a million offers, to tell him, if ever he needed anything ... but it sounded kind of hypocritical even to my ears, seeing as I planned on taking away the one thing he probably wanted the most, so I settled for, "You're all right. For a cat."

Lips twitching, he kicked aside a nugget of glass. "Screw you, dog," he said and crunched his way inside.

41

Ethan's check-in phone call on the drive back told me to expect everyone's presence when I reached home, yet, for some reason, I still felt unprepared to face them—even more so when Brook's hand on my arm stalled my climb from the pickup where we sat in the driveway.

"Go on without me," I said to Josh and Ethan, as they went to open their doors. "I'll be right behind you."

Ethan peered back at me, eyes narrowed for a moment. "Okay, but I wouldn't be long if I were you. And, just so you know, I'm taking these with me." The truck keys dangled from his finger.

Waiting until they'd both climbed out and closed their doors, I twisted in my seat, my brows drawn in question as I studied the worry lining Brook's face. "What's up?"

"I thought ..." She drew in a deep breath, her chest sinking with her exhale. "I assumed we would go somewhere ... else. Your family did not exactly invite me to stay the last time I arrived."

"Yeah, well ..." I wound a strand of her hair around my finger. "This is my home. And, as long as you'll have me, it's now your home, too. So, the pack will just have to learn to deal with that."

She sighed, gazing away toward the windscreen, toward the house. "Kyle ..."

Cupping her cheek, I urged her back to me. "It'll be okay. I promise."

I opened my door and climbed out, reaching back in and lifting Brook down. Hands still on her hips, I pressed a kiss to the creases marking her brow, staring over her head toward the house and what awaited us. "Quit stressing, okay?" I asked, hoping she couldn't read the tension spreading through my own body. Taking her hand, I led her around to the back door.

Conversation sifted through as we passed the window, but the moment I tugged down the handle of the door and stepped into the kitchen, the chatter halted, each and every one of them in the room turning and staring at me and Brook.

Nathan sat at the head of the table, beefy arms crossed over his chest, the heavy scrutiny pumping from him masking any true opinions he might have had on the situation. Behind him, in the corner, Sean stood resting against the wooden dresser, Lia curled into his neck and making sucking noises even in her sleep. His half-smile and small headshake told me little about his thoughts. To his right, Jem and Beth sat side by side. Beth placed a hand on Nathan's arm, while the fingertips of Jem's right hand made a slow tap atop the table.

I turned toward Dad, leaning against the counters on my left, his arms as tightly folded as Nate's. No Dan, just like the day before.

Ignoring his absence, I offered Ethan and Josh a nod, both slouched in chairs at the opposite end of the table, and went around to stand behind them. Perhaps I thought they provided a decent barrier for the opposition I expected to receive.

Tightening my fingers around Brook's, I turned so I could see all of them, but primarily Nate on one side, Dad the other, and heaved in a deep breath as I steeled myself. "Brook's going to be staying with me," I told them. "Does anyone have a problem with that?"

The attention that had chased me around the room shot toward Brook, and her fingers twitched against mine. I didn't need to join them to know what they all saw, because every single one of those marks across Brook's face had been welded into my mind and would probably remain there forever. Besides, I feared, if I turned, I'd see terror shining from Brook, or a yearning to flee, and I didn't want to find out how either of those might affect me.

After way too much time, and equally too many erratic booms of my pulse, a bunch of sighs and the creak of chairs beneath fidgeting butts preceded headshakes, and my lips funnelled around my blown out breath.

The dipping of Beth and Jem's heads did little to hide the almost-conspiratorial smiles they had going on.

Beth's chair scraped back, and she slipped from her seat. "You must be hungry. I'll fix you some dinner."

"They probably should shower first," Jem said, sending me a discreet wink. "I can smell Kyle from here."

"Yeah, me, too." Sean shifted Lia to his other shoulder, smoothing a hand over her back when she let out a tiny grumble. "You shower *at all* any time this week, Kyle?"

"I, um ..." I tried to mask my smile by sniffing at myself but probably failed.

Knowing Jem and Sean, the hint probably held a lot more meaning than either of them voiced.

Pausing only to let Beth know we wouldn't be too long, I drew Brook in front of me and ushered her into the hallway.

"I'll have dinner warmed for when you're finished," Beth called after us.

We passed the open living room door and rounded the newel post. Brook's hands folded over my forearms, as I wrapped them around her and herded her ahead of me up the stairs, but a niggling itch had me twisting to peer back over my shoulder, into the hall.

Dan stood in the pale light that sifted through the glass of the front door behind him, his position shading his expression. The high set of his shoulders and the flexing of his fingers added to the tension his entire presence provided, and his glower flickered from Brook to me.

For a second, I considered approaching him, asking him what the hell was his problem, maybe shaking some sense and manners into him.

I didn't, though. Dan would have to suck it up and get over himself. Brook had dealt with enough violence and discord, without having to get it from my family.

Turning away from his glower, away from the shit I didn't want to deal with, I gave my attention back to my female. "You okay?" I asked against her ear.

"Can you ask me that again if I am still here in a week's time?" she asked, equally as quiet.

My laugh spilled out on my sigh as a little of the dread over her feelings left and helped loosen my limbs. "Sure," I said.

Though winter afternoons didn't often lend a lot of light to the house interior, the generous window and the pale walls of the bathroom allowed brightness of their own. Releasing my hold on Brook, I headed straight for the shower cubicle and knocked on the dial, sticking a hand inside to gauge the water temperature before turning back to her.

Over by the window, she peered outward, her hair seeming to hold lustre even in its dank state, as she placed her fingertips to the glass. I went to stand behind her, smiling when she leaned into me as I did the same to her.

"Beautiful view," she said.

My lips parted as I went to reply, wanting to spill something along the lines of 'Not as beautiful as the one right before me', but realising the crappy corniness of the words, I shut my mouth and reached around to unbutton the shirt she wore. "Ready for that shower?" I asked.

As she nodded, I slipped the soft flannel from her shoulders and placed a kiss to the flesh it unveiled, my nostrils sweeping along to the crook of her neck. Creating enough of a gap to drop the shirt to the floor, I tried to steer her toward the cubicle, but she turned, her hips twisting beneath my palms, and grabbed the hem of my mucky T-shirt. As I backed her up to the open shower door, my eyebrow arched in question, and she answered by dragging the fabric over my head.

Taking her hips, I lifted her over the tiny step and into the glass enclosure, but she pushed forward again, one hand cupping the back of my neck as she drew me in and kissed me while her other worked the studs of my jeans.

"Come with me," she whispered against my lips.

Shoving down on the denim like something possessed, I stepped in after her, kicking my trainers and jeans off one foot at a time, uncaring that they got soaked in the process. Because all I could focus on was the fact that Brook wanted me in there with her and my entire being wanted to bloody well obey.

My mouth covered hers as I nudged the door closed behind me. My tongue stroked across hers as we moved in a dance of touching—of needing to touch—until the tiled wall at Brook's rear blocked us going any farther.

Drawing back, I absorbed the warmth I'd missed seeing in her eyes, and my jaw clenched at the yellowed bruising surrounding the swollen right one that I hadn't so far allowed myself to study too deeply. I planted a soft kiss to the spot, and my gaze instantly dropped to the darker bloom across her cheekbone, where I set a second kiss then a third to the rawness stretching along the left side of her face.

I knew there'd be more—on other parts of her body— more that I didn't wholly believe I wanted to see but knew I needed to, and with the softest of brushes, I skimmed my lips along her jawline, locating the blossoming of another bruise as I trailed the curve of her neck.

My entire body stiffened when my lips encountered the closed and healing raggedness of torn flesh at the dip of her shoulder.

"Did *he* do this?"

Her headshake jerked her chin against me.

"Will you tell me who?" I wanted to fucking flay whoever it was.

"Yes," she said, "just ... not now."

I gritted my teeth against the urge to say more, to push her to explain, to make demands, and the spattering water boomed against the silence that extended between us for moments, until Brook cleared her throat.

"So, your family seemed to have changed their minds ... about us."

I nodded and lifted my gaze, trying to accept the switch of subject—some things could wait, I guessed. "I think they finally realised I'm insanely in love with you," I said.

A smile curved her lips at the corners, and she lifted a hand and placed her fingers against my chest, as if she could check the sincerity of my words by the beat of my heart. "I ..." Her throat bobbed as she swallowed, and she gave a tiny nod, her expression sobering as she said, "Thank you."

Anyone else would probably have been bugged by the evident struggle to reciprocate. I didn't need the verbal confirmation, though, not with the high shine of her eyes sending their hue to a rich molten gold and doing a decent job of exposing to me everything I needed to know.

Her chasing, "I missed you, too," only strengthened what she left unsaid.

My breath shuddered from me as, in return, I tried to conjure the right words, a way to convey just how much being parted from her had driven me to a level of crazy I hoped I never had to experience again, but her frown caught me short.

"Do you believe me?" she asked.

A brief smile broke free as I nodded. "Your eyes tell a thousand stories."

"Mine are not the only ones." She touched a fingertip to my lid.

Breaking the contact, I glanced away, latching my attention onto the crystal drops creating rivers along the tiles.

"Please don't hide." Her hand against my cheek steered me back to her. "They are beautiful to me."

"Yeah, but ..." I sighed. "I'm not so sure how much of that still stretches to what's within me."

"How can you say that? You're still the most good person I know. Still the most unselfish."

"I'm not so sure Nate would agree with you on that one—at least, not where you're concerned."

"That is forgivable from where I'm standing," she said with a small smile. "And the rest ..." She traced another finger beneath my eyes. "The rest can be figured out with time." Pushing up onto her toes brought her lips back to mine, and her hand against my chest rubbed a small circle. "Your heart is pounding."

"I have a feeling that might take a while to settle down. At least until I wake in the morning and find you still here. Talking of which, you know I plan to make that a regular deal, right?"

"Okay," she said.

"Okay?"

She nodded.

I squinted my eyes, like the altered perspective would help me see her thoughts more clearly. "You sure?"

On her second nod, quiet laughter breathed from her, laughter I stole as I sealed her mouth with my own.

"Good," I murmured against her lips.

I'd kind of hoped the others would have gotten bored of waiting for us by the time we left the bathroom. However, after fighting my unwillingness to leave the warmth of the water, or Brook's body, I opened the bathroom door, and we stepped out to the welcoming richness of lamb roast, and the familiar grumbling chatter of the pack down below.

In my bedroom, grey sweats and a jade-green long-sleeved T had been laid out at the foot of my bed. Though I recognised them as Jem's, their careful positioning told me she didn't mind loaning them to Brook. The two of us dressed in near-silence, Brook's expression holding a reappeared concern I thought our time in the shower had shed.

After tugging on my second sock, I reached for her hand. "Will you quit worrying?" I smoothed a fingertip across the lines etching her brow like I could iron them away. "You're here. They get that. And everything's going to be okay."

When she responded with a sigh and a smile, I led her from the room and down the stairs.

The same dullness of the bathroom had laid claim to the hallway as we rounded the lower banister. Mutterings and clanks coming from that direction told me everyone had still to leave the kitchen, and we headed that way, stepping into the only illuminated room in the house.

The second we did, Beth began her usual clucking, her arm scooping around Brook's waist and drawing her away. My shoulders stiffened beneath the threat of someone stealing her from me, but I soon relaxed, as the older female herded her across to the cooker to choose her veggies, and turned to the others in the room.

Dan remained absent, but everyone else was present.

Still in the same spot, Josh sat between Ethan and Sean, twisting away from something he showed them on his mobile—probably some deranged game—and glancing back to me with a grin before turning back to it.

Dad had taken Beth's vacated seat beside Nathan, and he stared my way, while Nate's gaze tracked Brook across the room. I greeted Dad's nod with one of my own, and as I glanced to his left, a smile tugged on my lips.

Between him and Sean, Jem held Lia out before her, making ridiculous gooey faces at her and squeaky noises that wobbled her lips. "Uncle Kyle and Auntie Brook smell sooooo much better now," she squealed like she'd had a few too many hits of helium. "Don't they?" She rubbed her lips across one of Lia's cheeks, piping up with another, "Don't they?" as she gave the same treatment to the second cheek.

My laugh snorted out of me, joined by a chuckle from Sean.

"She's gonna grow up thinking everyone talks like a banshee with its toe trapped," he said.

"And by the time you lot have finished with her, she'll be talking like a banshee who curses a lot," Jem said, adding, "Won't you?" in a squawk.

As Brook turned from the cooker, I twisted her way, still grinning at the insaneness of Jem since she'd had Lia. Plate in hand, as she stared across at the table, she seemed unsure once more—uncomfortable at having to face everyone else in the room. As she glanced to me, a chair scraped across the tiles, and we both followed the sound.

"There's room," Nate said, gesturing Brook over to the chair beside him. "We're going to need to buy more chairs," he said, his gaze bouncing toward me before finding his wife, "if this family of ours is going to keep expanding."

"Here," Beth said, folding my hands around a plate. "Eat."

Nodding my thanks, I rounded the table behind Brook. After depositing my food in the spot beside hers, I helped push her chair in. "See?" I said at her ear as I slid my own butt down next to her. "Everything's fine."

The room quieted as we settled into our seats, even more so when Brook's gaze met mine, the threat of tears there breaking my heart; they probably would've done if I thought they'd been caused by sadness. Her lips parted a little, a sigh breezing from her, like she wanted to say something but didn't know how to put it into words, or just didn't know how to express her feelings.

"It's okay," I said. "They get it."

"So, Brook," Josh said from the table's end, breaking the stifling air of expectations. When we glanced his way, he had his usual stupid grin on his face, and I just knew

337

something idiotic would come out of his mouth. "You any good at brick laying? Because, you know, he"—he jerked a thumb in my direction—"has been pretty crap at it lately."

Beside me, Brook breathed out a laugh, as I shot him a, "Shut it, Josh," and finally, thankfully, normalcy put in an appearance at last.

ACKNOWLEDGEMENTS

Man, these things always terrify me in case I forget someone. Seriously hoping I don't, here goes:

First up—as always—Mr B and the kidlets. My kids are the most understanding kids in the world. They've learned to fend for themselves. Heck, they've learned to fend for me. They also understand how much I need to do this whole writing malarkey, earning my utmost gratitude, as does Mr B.

But my man is about more than that. Because Mr B is my rock that keeps me grounded, even when times are tough. There were a lot of instances when I truly believed I would throw in the writing towel during writing Unnatural—where I *wanted* to throw in that blasted towel. Not because the writing was bad, or I wasn't feeling the story, but due to the emotional circumstances affecting my personal life. Mr B is the reason I reached a state of mind where I was able to put my head back in the game. So, if you're a Holloway Pack fan, and you've enjoyed reading Unnatural, thank the dude. He helped make sure it 'happened'.

He wasn't my only motivator, though. Nope. It was that old-age thing called encouragement. Whether from my betas: Carla Huxley, Julie Reece, Terri Rochenski, Aimee Laine, Elaine Hart, Jennifer Turner, Wendy Seagondollar, Lola Verroen (OXOXOXO) asking for my next instalment for 'the boys'; or from you, my readers, making the most amazing noise about what I have to say about these peeps who live inside my head—every single word of positivity ALWAYS spurs me to write more. Because I no longer do this only for myself. Now, I do it for you guys, too.

I'd also like to spare a moment of gratitude for the book bloggers–from the regulars who repeatedly support my blog tours to the new faces who sign up and support an author they've never heard of before. Not to mention the likes of Maghon at Happy Tails and Tales, Ambur at

Burning Impossibly Bright, Taneesha at A Diary of a Book Addict, Sandra at JeanzBookReadNReview, Danielle at Known to Read, plus many others (there are too many to name), who have all fallen in love with the Holloway Pack and constantly write reviews for my books that make my heart soar. All of you—you all seriously rock my socks!

And to you, the reader. For picking me up. For taking a chance. For allowing me some of your time which is, undoubtedly, precious. Without readers, there would be no authors, right?

So, I guess, long-story-short, what I'm trying to say is: A big fat cheers to you all.

ABOUT J.A. BELFIELD

Best known for her Holloway Pack stories and The Therapist, J.A. Belfield lives in Solihull, England, with her husband, two children, a spoiled dog and a cat who likes to vomit in unfortunate places. She writes paranormal romance, with a second love for urban fantasy. And now she writes erotic romance, too. Because she can. ;)

In 2016, Instinct [now part of Beginnings] earned J.A. Belfield International Bestseller status when it featured in the Paranormal Attractions anthology. J.A. Belfield now hopes to claim that same status solo.

To stay updated on everything J.A. Belfield, join her on Facebook in the Belfield's MotherBookers group.

TITLES BY J.A. BELFIELD

HOLLOWAY PACK

BEGINNINGS
CALLED
LURED
CAGED
UNNATURAL
CORNERED
HEREDITARY
ENTICED

EROTIC ROMANCE

THE THERAPIST

PARANORMAL ROMANCE

HER MANE ESCORT